DUDLEY PUBLIC LIBRARIES

The loan of this book may be renewed if not required by other readers, by contacting the library from which it was borrowed.

Greek Playboys

Greek Playboys: A Deal in Passion

DANI COLLINS

ANNIE WEST

MAYA BLAKE

MIX
Paper from
responsible sources
FSC
www.fsc.org   FSC C007454

This book is produced from independently certified FSC™ paper
to ensure responsible forest management.

For more information visit www.harpercollins.co.uk/green

Printed and Bound in Spain using 100% Renewable electricity at
CPI Black Print, Barcelona.

MILLS & BOON

First Published in Great Britain 2022
By Mills & Boon, an imprint of HarperCollins*Publishers,* Ltd
1 London Bridge Street, London, SE1 9GF

www.harpercollins.co.uk

HarperCollins*Publishers*
1st Floor, Watermarque Building,
Ringsend Road, Dublin 4, Ireland

GREEK PLAYBOYS: A DEAL IN PASSION © 2022 Harlequin Enterprises ULC.

Xenakis's Convenient Bride © 2017 Dani Collins
Wedding Night Reunion in Greece © 2019 Annie West
A Diamond Deal with the Greek © 2016 Maya Blake

ISBN: 978-0-263-30470-1

XENAKIS'S CONVENIENT BRIDE

DANI COLLINS

The premise of an undercover billionaire was exciting all by itself, but when I found out I would be working with Rachael Thomas and Jennifer Hayward I was doubly thrilled. They are not just talented authors but wonderful people, and a joy to work with, so I dedicate this book to them with much affection and appreciation for their input.

I would be remiss, however, if I didn't include my husband. While we were brainstorming this story he helped me come up with the heroine's back story – specifically how cruelly Calli's father betrays her. As we bounced ideas back and forth, and the stakes went up, our voices grew louder and louder, causing our (grown) daughter to come into my office and ask with trepidation, 'Are you guys fighting?' To be fair, I usually insist on complete silence while I work, so she had a right to be confused.

PROLOGUE

STAVROS XENAKIS THREW his twenty-thousand-euro chips into the pot, less satisfied than he usually was postchallenge, but it had nothing to do with his fellow players or his lackluster hand.

His longtime friend Sebastien Atkinson had arranged his usual *après*-adrenaline festivities. It had wound down to the four of them, as it often did. Many turned out for these extreme sports events, but only Antonio Di Marcello and Alejandro Salazar had the same deep pockets Stavros and Sebastien did. Or the stones to bet at this level simply to stretch out a mellow evening.

Stavros wasn't the snob his grandfather was, but he didn't consider many his equal. These men were it and he enjoyed their company for that reason. Tonight was no exception. They were still high on today's exercise of cheating death, sipping 1946 Macallan while trading good-natured insults.

So why was he twitching with edginess?

He mentally reviewed today's paraski that had had him carving a steep line down a ski slope to a cliff's edge before rocketing into thin air, lifted by his chute for a thousand feet, guiding his path above a ridge, then hitting the lower slope for another run of hard turns before taking to the air again.

It had been as physically demanding as any challenge that had come before and was probably their most daredevil yet. Throughout most of it, he'd been completely in the moment—his version of meditating.

He had expected today to erase the frustration that had been dogging him, but it hadn't. He might have set it aside for a few hours, but this niggling irritation was back to grate at him.

Sebastien eyed him across the table, no doubt trying to determine if he was bluffing.

"How's your wife?" Stavros asked, more as a deflection, but also trying to divine how Sebastien could be *happily* married.

"Better company than you. Why are you so surly tonight?"

Was it obvious? He grimaced. "I haven't won yet." He was among friends so he admitted the rest. "And my grandfather is threatening to disinherit me if I don't marry soon. I'd tell him to go to hell, but…"

"Your mother," Alejandro said.

"Exactly." They all knew his situation. He played ball with his grandfather for the sake of his mother and sisters. He couldn't walk away from his own inheritance when it would cost them theirs.

But "settle down?" His grandfather had been trying to fit Stavros into a box from the time he was twelve. Lately it had become a push toward picket fences. Demands he produce an heir and a spare.

Stavros couldn't buy into any of that so, yet again, he was in a power struggle with the old man. He usually got around being whipped down a particular path, but he hadn't yet found his alternate route. It chewed and chewed at him, especially when his grandfather was holding control of the family's pharmaceutical conglomerate hostage.

Stavros might be a hell-raiser, but his rogue personality had produced some of the biggest gains for Dýnami. He was more than ready to steer the ship. A wife and children were cargo he didn't need, but his grandfather seemed to think it would prove he was "mature" and "responsible."

Where his grandfather got the idea he wasn't either of those things, Stavros couldn't say. He upped his ante to a full hundred thousand, despite the fact his hand had not improved. He promptly lost it.

They played a little longer, then Sebastien asked, "Do you ever get the feeling we spend too much of our lives counting our money and chasing superficial thrills at the expense of something more meaningful?"

"You called it," Antonio said to Alejandro, tossing over a handful of chips. "Four drinks and he's philosophizing."

Sebastien gave Stavros a look of disgust as he also pushed some chips toward Alejandro's pile.

"I said three." Stavros shrugged without apology. "My losing streak continues."

"I'm serious." Sebastien was the only self-made billionaire among them, raised by a single mother on the dole in a country where bloodlines and titles were still more valuable than a bank balance. His few extra years of age and experience gave him the right to act as mentor. He wasn't afraid to offer his opinion and he was seldom wrong. They all listened when he spoke, but he did get flowery when he was in his cups. "At our level, it's numbers on a page. Points on a scoreboard. What does it contribute to our lives? Money doesn't buy happiness."

"It buys some nice substitutes." Antonio smirked.

Sebastien's mouth twisted. "Like your cars?" he mused, then flicked his glance to Alejandro. "Your private island? You don't even use that boat you're so proud of," he said, moving on to Stavros. "We buy expensive toys and play dangerous games, but does it enrich our lives? Feed our souls?"

"What are you suggesting?" Alejandro drawled, discarding a card and motioning for it to be replaced. "We go live with the Buddhists in the mountains? Learn the meaning of life? Renounce our worldly possessions to find inner clarity?"

Sebastien made a scoffing noise. "You three couldn't go two weeks without your wealth and family names to support you. Your gilded existence makes you blind to reality."

"Could you?" Stavros challenged, throwing away three cards. "Try telling us you would go back to when you were broke, before you made your fortune. Hungry isn't happy. That's why you're such a rich bastard now."

"As it happens, I've been thinking of donating half my fortune to charity, to start a global search-and-rescue fund. Not everyone has friends who will dig him out of an avalanche with their bare hands." Sebastien smiled, but the rest of them didn't.

Last year, Sebastien had nearly died during one of their challenges. Stavros still woke from nightmares of reliving those dark minutes. He'd wound up with frostbite burns on his fingers, but he'd been frantic to save Sebastien, unable to watch a man die again. A man whose life he valued. He felt sick recollecting it and took a sip of his whiskey to sear away the nausea.

"Are you serious?" Alejandro charged. "That's, what? Five billion?"

"You can't take it with you." Sebastien's shrug was nonchalant. "Monika is on board with it, but I'm still debating. I'll tell you what." He leaned forward, mouth curling into the wicked grin he always wore when he proposed cliff diving or some other outrageous act. "You three go two weeks without your credit cards and I'll do it."

"Starting when? We all have responsibilities," Alejandro reminded.

After a considering pause, Sebastien canted his head. "Fair enough. Clear the decks at home. But be prepared for word from me—and two weeks in the real world."

"You're really going to wager half your fortune on a cakewalk of a challenge?" Alejandro said.

"If you'll put up your island. Your favorite toys?" He took in all three men. "I say where and when."

They all snorted with confidence.

"Easy," Stavros said, already anticipating the break from his grandfather's badgering. "Count me in."

CHAPTER ONE

Four and a half months later...

SHE FLOATED IN the pool on a giant ivory-colored clam-shell, the pattern on her one-piece bathing suit a stark contrast of pink and green geometry against her golden, supple limbs. Her black hair spilled away from her face, a few tendrils drifting in the water. She wore sunglasses and red toe polish.

She was fast asleep.

As Stavros took in the way her suit painted her breasts and cut high over her hips, then smoothed over her mound to dip into the fork of her thighs, he stirred with desire. A detailed fantasy played out in his mind of diving in and coming up next to her, rolling her into his arms like an ancient god stealing a nymph and having her on that wicker sofa in the shade, behind the curtain of water on the far side of the pool.

The only sound in the high-walled courtyard was the patter of the thin waterfall. It poured off the edge of the ivy-entwined trellis that formed a roof over the lounge area and bar. The raining noise muffled his exhale as he set down the box containing power tools, a sledgehammer, trowels and adhesive compounds.

He stood and drank in another eyeful.

Perhaps being cast as a pool boy wasn't so bad after all.

Last night, he'd stood in a tiny, stuffy, *not* air-conditioned bachelor apartment cursing Sebastien with sincere vehemence.

His two-week challenge had started and his new "home" was a walk-up over a coffee-roasting operation. The smell was appalling. He couldn't decide which was worse: window open or closed. He had left it open while he compared his inventory of supplies with Antonio's photo from two weeks ago.

At least he'd had a heads-up from his friend as to what this challenge entailed. Given Antonio had been sent to Milan, Stavros had suspected he would be sent to Greece, and here he was.

Which had given Stavros a moment of pause. He didn't care if he lost the boat, and even Sebastien's grand gesture was one he could make himself if it came right down to it. He had stepped off so many cliffs and platforms and airplanes at twenty-thousand feet, he shouldn't have hesitated to step off a ferry onto the island of his birth.

But he had.

Which made him feel like a coward.

He had forced himself to disembark and walk to his flat where he had discovered that, like Antonio, he had been provided a prehistoric cell phone and a stack of cash—two hundred euros. Lunch money. But where Antonio had been given a set of coveralls, Stavros had been given board shorts.

They were supposed to go two weeks without their wealth and reputation, but apparently his dignity had to be checked at the door, as well. At least his costume wasn't one of those banana hammocks so popular on European beaches. The uniform was tacky as hell regardless, pairing yellow-and-white-striped shorts with a yellow T-shirt.

Squinting one eye at the logo, Stavros had read the Greek letters as easily as he read English, and was offended in both languages. Zante Pool Care. Sebastien had told him to book vacation time, ensure his responsibilities were covered, then had sent him to work as a *pool boy*.

His phone was loaded with exactly three contacts: Sebastien, Antonio and Alejandro. He had texted Antonio a photo of his supplies along with the message, Is this for real?

If it turns out anything like mine, you're in for more surprises than that.

Antonio had discovered a son. How much more astonishing could it get?

If Stavros had a child living here, it would be a miracle. He'd left when he was twelve and had only kissed a girl at that point. Once he moved to America, high-risk behavior had become his norm. His virginity had been lost at fourteen to a senior at the private school he'd attended. She had favored black eyeliner and dark red lipstick—and young men with a keen interest in learning how to please a woman. Scrappers were her favorite and he'd been one of those, too.

A year later, he'd been making conquests of his grandfather's secretary and the nanny looking after his youngest sister. He wasn't proud of that, but he wasn't as regretful as he probably should be. Sex had been one of the few things to make him happy in those days.

Sex with that woman right there would certainly take the sting out of today's situation. The next *fourteen* days, in fact.

Another rush of misgiving went through him. This challenge was not a simple two weeks of pretending to be an everyman. Sebastien had left him a note.

You may remember our conversation last year, when you came to visit me as I was recovering from the avalanche. You opened that excellent bottle of fifty-year-old Scotch whiskey in my honor. I thank you again for that.

At the time you told me how losing your father had given you the strength to dig through the snow to save my life. Do you remember also telling me how much you resented your grandfather for taking you to New York and forcing you to answer to your American name? I suspect you were really saying that you didn't feel you deserved to be his heir.

Sebastien had chided Stavros for not appreciating his family and heritage, since Sebastien hadn't had those advantages. In his note, he continued:

I grant you your wish. For the next two weeks Steve Michaels, with all his riches and influence, does not exist. You are Stavros Xenakis and work for Zante Pool Care. Report at 6:00 a.m. tomorrow, three blocks down the road.

Antonio lasted two weeks without blowing his cover, so I have committed the first third of my five billion to the search-and-rescue foundation. Do the same, Stavros. It could save a life. And use this time to make peace with your past.

—Sebastien

Stavros had stayed up later than he should have, some of it jet lag, but mostly conjuring ways to get out of this challenge. Besides, he couldn't sleep in that hot room, tossing and turning on the hard single bed. Old-fashioned honor had him accepting his lot and falling asleep.

Then, even earlier than he needed to rise, the sun had struck directly into his eyes. Large trucks with squeaky brakes had pulled in beneath the open window.

Disgusted, Stavros had eaten a bowl of dry cereal with the canned milk he'd been provided. He'd bought a coffee from a shop as he walked to "work."

His boss, Ionnes, had given him a clipboard that held a map, a handful of drawings and a work order. He had dangled a set of keys and pointed at a truck full of supplies and equipment, telling him to be sure to unload it since he wouldn't have the vehicle tomorrow.

Stavros might have booked a flight home at that point, but he had left his credit cards in New York, as instructed. He'd been completing Sebastien's challenges since his first year of university. None had killed him yet.

Nevertheless, as he'd followed the map, he had recognized the dip and roll of the road through the hills, eighteen years of changes notwithstanding. His heart had grown heavier with each mile, his lungs tighter.

Perhaps he wasn't defying his own death with this challenge, but the loss of his father was even more difficult to confront.

He had sat in the driveway a full five minutes, pushing back dark memories by focusing on the changes in the home they'd occupied until their lives had overturned with the flip of a boat on the sea.

The villa was well tended, but modest by his current standards. It had been his mother's dream home when she married. She was a local girl from the fishing village on the bottom of the island. She had insisted her husband use this as his base. It had been a place where he could enjoy downtime. *Quality* time, with his children. She had called him a workaholic who was losing his roots, spending too much time in America, allowing the expanding interests of the family corporation to dominate his life.

The villa hadn't been new. It had needed repairs and his father had enlisted Stavros to set fresh paving stones at the front entrance while his mother and sisters had potted the bougainvillea that now bloomed in masses of pink against the white walls.

The memories were so sharp and painful as Stavros sat there, he wanted to jam the truck in Reverse and get away from all of it.

But where would he go? Back to the blaming, shaming glint in his grandfather's hard stare? Back to the understudy role he hated, but played because his father wasn't there to be the star?

Cursing Sebastien afresh, Stavros glanced over his work order. He wasn't cleaning the pool, but repairing the cracked tiles around it. Déjà vu with paving stones. The mistress of the house would direct him.

He blew out a disgusted breath. After two decades of bearing up under his grandfather's dictates, and now facing a demand that he marry, he was at the end of his rope with being told what to do.

No one answered the doorbell so he let himself in through the gate at the side and went down the stairs into a white-walled courtyard that opened on one side to the view of the sea. His arrival didn't stir Venus from her slumber.

Damn, but his tension wanted an outlet. He let his gaze cruise over her stellar figure once more. If she was a wife, she was the trophy kind, but she wasn't wearing a ring.

The *mistress* of the place, his employer had said. He would just bet she was a mistress. How disappointing to have such a beauty reserved by his boss's client.

In another life, Stavros wouldn't have let that stop him from going after her.

This *was* another life, he recalled with a kick of his youthful recklessness.

Crouching, he scooped up a handful of water and flicked it at her.

The spatter of something against Calli's face startled her awake—in the pool, where she reflexively tried to sit up and immediately unbalanced. She tumbled sideways, sunglasses sliding off her nose, arms outstretched but catching at nothing. She plunged under the cold water into the blur of blue. Oh, that was a shock!

Ophelia.

Calli caught her bearings and pumped her arms to burst through the surface, sputtering, "You are so *grounded*. Go to your room."

But that wasn't Ophelia straightening to such a lofty height at the side of the pool. It was a conquering warrior, tall and forbidding, backlit by the sun so Calli's eyes watered as she tried to focus on him. His yellow T-shirt and shorts did nothing to detract from his powerful, intimidating form. In fact, his clothes clung like golden armor hammered across the contours of his shoulders and chest, accentuating the tan on his muscular biceps.

She couldn't see his eyes, but felt the weight of his gaze. It pushed her back and drew her forward at the same time, making her forget to breathe, making her hot despite being submerged to her shoulders and treading water.

Heat radiated through her, that dangerous heat that she had learned to ignore out of self-preservation. This time it wouldn't quash, which caused a knot of foreboding in her belly. He mesmerized her, holding her suspended as though in amber, snared into a moment of sexual fascination that seemed destined to last eternally.

He folded his arms, imperious, but his voice held a rasp of humor. "Lead the way."

To his room, he meant. It wasn't so much an invitation as an order.

She had the impression of a dark brow cocked with silent laughter, which made her feel vulnerable. Not threatened, not physically, but imperiled at a deep level, where her ego resided. Where her fractured heart was tucked high on a shelf so no one could knock it to the floor again.

Her chest prickled with anxiety and she wiped her eyes, trying hard to see him properly, trying to figure out who he was and why he had such an instant, undeniable effect on her. His T-shirt sported the pool man's logo, but she'd never seen him before.

"I didn't hear you come in."

"Obviously. Up late?"

"Yes." It struck her very belatedly that it couldn't have been Ophelia to wake her. Calli had fallen asleep in the pool because she'd arrived home in the wee hours after leaving Ophelia at her maternal grandparents' home in Athens. She had driven half the night, then dozed in the car as she waited for the ferry.

Takis wasn't here. No one was except her and this barbarian of a man.

"I was traveling." She skimmed toward the stairs at the shallow end. "I knew workers were coming and didn't want to miss speaking to you by falling asleep inside. Where is Ionnes?"

"He gave me my assignment and told me I have two weeks."

"Yes, there's a party scheduled." The roll of alarm

wouldn't leave her belly. It trebled when his shadow fell across her as she climbed the steps. He had plucked her filmy wrap from the chair and held it out for her like a gentleman.

He was *no* gentleman. She didn't know what he was, but had the distinct feeling he was *somebody*. Not a normal plebeian like her.

She took the wrap and struggled to push her wet arms into the loose sleeves. Why was she shaking? Oh, Ophelia had misguided taste! Why wasn't this wrap opaque? It was a birthday present and Calli had thought it delightfully feminine when she had opened it, but with the simple hook-and-eye closure over her navel, it was more provocation than cover, hanging open down her cleavage and parting in a slit over the tops of her thighs.

He noticed. He studied her from chin to toe polish, unabashed in the way he let his gaze move down and up, tightening her hair follicles inch by inch.

It wasn't the first time she'd been eyed up, but the locals knew she wasn't interested. Or considered her off-limits, at least. With tourists, she pretended she didn't speak English if she wanted to reject an advance.

Either way, it was always easy to brush men off, but not today. She *felt* his gaze. She told herself it was the water trickling off her, but that had never turned her inside out this way.

Once again she was accosted by defenselessness. Why? She'd been inoculated against men who used their looks to devastate.

Nevertheless, that's what he was. Devastatingly handsome. Standing on the same level with him didn't make him any less intimidating. He was big and powerful and now that she could properly see his face, she caught her breath in reaction. He wore a day's shadow of stubble and finger-combed hair, but those hollow cheeks and ebony brows were pure perfection. It wasn't the sculpted beauty of his face that arrested her, though. It was the fierce pride and unapologetic masculinity he projected.

It was the undisguised desire that flared in his black-coffee eyes as their gazes locked. The arrogant assumption he could *have*.

Because he knew she was reacting to him? Knowledge made his eyelids heavy while smug anticipation deepened the corners of his mouth.

She couldn't tear her eyes from his wide mouth, his lips brutally sensual, his jaw determined.

As he spoke, his voice lowered an octave to something that promised, yet warned. "Tell me what you want. I'm at your service."

Her body stung with a renewed flood of heat, countering the chill of her damp suit. *Please let him think the cold hardened my nipples.* But it was him. She knew it and he knew it and it scared her.

She scrambled back a step, trying to escape his aggressively sexual aura, and nearly stumbled into the pool.

He caught her by the arms, saving her from falling onto the steps under the water. It was chivalrous, but paralyzing, leaving her shaken. What was *wrong* with her?

She tried to lift her chin and look down her nose at him. "Let me go."

The amused heat in his brown eyes cooled to mahogany. "If that's what you want." He waited a beat, then lifted his hands away and straightened to his full height. "Watch your step."

He wasn't cautioning her about a slippery pool deck.

Her stomach wobbled and her heart pounded so hard she wanted to press her hand against her chest to calm it.

She clenched her fist instead, swallowing to ease the dryness in her mouth.

"Your accent is strange." She narrowed in on that as a way to hold him at a distance. Something about his voice caused a prickle of apprehension in her. "Where are you from?"

His expression blanked into what must be a winning poker face. Which had to mean he was lying when he said, "I was born here."

"In Greece or on this island?" She knew most of the locals by sight, if not by name. "I don't recognize you. What's your name?"

A flash of something came and went in his gaze. Annoyance? "Stavros. I've lived abroad since I was twelve. I'm back for a working vacation."

She might have latched on to his lack of a surname if she hadn't just realized what colored his fluid Greek.

"You're *American.*" On *vacation.*

Her blood stuttered to a halt in her veins, sending ice penetrating to her bones. No. Never again. No and no. She didn't care how good-looking he was. *No.*

As if he heard the indictment in her tone, he threw his head back, expression offended. "I'm *Greek.*"

She knew her prejudice was exactly that. It wasn't even a real prejudice. She quite enjoyed chatting with rotund, married American tourists or any American woman. She wanted to *go* to America. New York, to be precise.

No, the only people she truly held in contempt were straight men who thought they could treat the local women like amusement-park rides. It didn't matter where they came from. Been there, done that, and her wounds were still open to prove it.

But the man who had left her with nothing, not even

her reputation, happened to be American, so that was the crime she accused this one of committing.

"You're here to fix the pool," she reminded with a sharpness honed by life's hardest knocks. "You only have two weeks. Better get to it."

CHAPTER TWO

DAY THREE AND Stavros was sore. He worked out regularly, but not like this. After ten hours of physically breaking tiles with a sledgehammer and wheelbarrowing them *up* a flight of stairs, he had exchanged a few texts with Antonio. His friend's conglomerate built some of the world's tallest buildings.

Can I use a jackhammer?

He had included a photo.

I wouldn't. Could damage the integrity of the pool.

Stavros didn't have the cash to rent one anyway. If he rented anything, it would be a car. He had had to catch a lift with the coffee truck this morning and walk the rest of the way. What the hell did Sebastien think he would learn from this exercise?

Hell, it wasn't exercise. It was back-breaking labor. Which was allowing him to work out pent-up frustrations, but not the one eating a hole through him.

He wanted that woman. "Calli," she had informed him stiffly when he had asked for her name. She had pointed out the tiles that had been cracked by the roots of a tree.

Since those tiles and that tree had to come out, they were redoing the entire surface surrounding the pool. *He* was.

She had disappeared into the house and had been a teasing peripheral presence ever since, flitting behind the screened door, playing music now and again, occasionally talking on the phone and cooking things that sent aromas out to further sharpen an appetite made ravenous by hard work.

He'd eaten well the first night, then did the math and realized he would have to make his own sandwiches the rest of his time here. It made the scent of garlic and oregano, lamb and peppers all the more maddening.

Who was she cooking for? It was ten o'clock in the morning and no one else was here, not even the man who kept her tucked away on the Aegean like a holiday cottage. A married man, presumably.

Stavros couldn't quit thinking about that. Or the way she'd looked as she had risen like a goddess from the water. The physical attraction in that moment had been beyond his experience. He'd been compelled to move closer, had physically ached to touch her. His body still hummed with want and he had this nagging need to get back to that moment and pursue her.

But she had wished him dead on the spot. For being American.

It had been a slap in the face, not least because he had been working through mixed feelings over his identity for most of his life, ever since his father's father had yanked him from this paradisiacal island to the concrete one of Manhattan.

He'd always been too Greek for his grandfather's tastes and not Greek enough for his own. Having Calli draw attention to that stung.

Which left him even more determined to get back to

that moment when she had revealed she desired him—*him*. Woman for man, all other considerations forgotten, most especially the man who kept her.

He hadn't experienced impotent rage like this since his early days of moving to New York, when he'd been forced to live a life he didn't want, yet defend it on the schoolyard. And he'd never before experienced such a singular need to prove something to a woman. Force her to acknowledge the spark between them.

He wanted to catch her by the arms, pull her in and kiss her until she succumbed to this fierce thing between them, *show* her—

He was too deep in thought, throwing too much weight behind the hammer. A chunk of broken tile flew up and grazed his shin, completely painless for a moment as it scored a lancing line into his flesh.

Then the burn arrived in a white-hot streak. He swore.

Calli heard several nasty curses in a biting tone. It meant trouble in any language.

She had spent the last few days trying to ignore Stavros, which was impossible, but she couldn't ignore *that*. She instinctively clicked off the burner and moved to glance through the screen-covered door to the courtyard.

He was bare-chested, wrapping his lower leg with his T-shirt. Blood stained through the bright yellow.

She ran for the first-aid kit, then hurried out to him. "What happened?"

It was obvious what had happened. He wore sturdy work boots and had showed up in jeans this morning, but it was already hot, even in the partially shaded courtyard and with the cooling curtain running beside the outdoor lounge. He had stripped down to his shorts an hour ago—

yes, she had noticed—and now a jagged piece of tile had cut his leg.

"Let me see."

She started to open the kit, but as he unwrapped the shirt, she knew this was beyond her rudimentary skills. Good thing she wasn't squeamish.

"That needs stitches."

"Butterfly bandages will do."

"No, that's deep. It needs to be properly cleaned and dressed. Are your shots up-to-date?"

He gave her a pithy look. "I have regular physicals, and yes, I'm one hundred percent healthy."

She had a feeling he wasn't talking about tetanus, but refused to be sidetracked. For the last six years she'd been dealing with an overbearing boss and keeping his spoiled daughter out of trouble. She had learned to dig in her heels when circumstances required.

"Do you know where the clinic is? It's not a proper hospital and only open during the day. You're best to go now or you'll be paying the call-in fee for after hours. Or trying to find a boat to the mainland for treatment there."

She tried to ignore the twist and flex of his naked torso and the scent of his body as he reached to take a roll of gauze from the kit. "I don't have a vehicle."

"Shall I call your employer?"

"No one likes a tattletale." He efficiently rewrapped the T-shirt and used the gauze to secure it, then used barbed clips to fasten the tails.

"No one likes stained tiles." She nodded at the red working its way through the layers of gauze. "I meant should I ask him to come take you to the clinic. I noticed you don't have the truck today."

"He'll say I have a job to finish. Which I do."

That was a barb at her, but he had been attacking his

task doggedly, seeming determined to complete on time. Yes, she had peered out at him regularly, and his relentless work ethic dented her perception of him as a useless philanderer, intriguing her.

"Shall I drive you?"

"Look." He pinched the bridge of his nose, swore under his breath. "I don't have insurance. And I can't afford to pay for treatment. Okay?" He begrudged admitting it, she could tell. It wasn't so much a blow to his pride, though. He was impatient. Exasperated.

She was surprised. Not that he resented admitting he was short on resources, but that he was down on his luck at all. He didn't possess even a shred of humility and oozed a type of confidence she only saw in men with fountains of money, like Takis. Who *was* this man? What had happened to knock him off his keel?

"You think Ionnes will fire you if you make a work-injury claim? He's not like that. But I'll have them send the bill here. We can lump it in with the costs of the repair. My boss won't mind." Since she would pay it out of her own pocket.

She'd been at rock bottom once and Takis had saved her. She looked for chances to pay it forward. "I have to pick up a few groceries anyway."

That was another white lie and she wasn't sure why she tacked it on. Maybe to spare his pride because she knew what it was like to face losing self-esteem along with everything else.

Or because she wanted to spend time with this man, now her view of him was out of focus. She studied his stern visage only to have his attention narrow on her, like a predatory bird spotting an unsuspecting hare.

Why on earth had she thought he needed anything from her, least of all benevolence? That innate fierceness in his expression took him from handsome to all powerful. He was magnificent. She was spellbound, exactly as a bird's prey might be. Frozen in fascinated horror as she stared into her own demise.

"Your boss?" Sexual tension swooped in on the wings of a speculative look to perch between them, impossible to ignore.

Her scalp prickled and her breasts felt constrained by her bra. Who was she kidding? The sexual awareness had only dissipated because she'd been hiding in the house for three days. Had she realized he had made the same assumption about her as everyone else did she might have let the fallacy continue, since it offered a type of protection.

She wanted to be annoyed. Furious. Hurt.

She was scared. Her heart battered the inside of her rib cage like a fist against a wall. She needed protection because that youthful indiscretion that had put all the wrong thoughts into all the smallest minds was still alive in her. She had buried it deep behind the rarely used dishes, but he'd found it. He was reaching into her, bringing it to the light, blowing away the dust and asking, *What's this?*

With her stomach in knots and her blood moving like warm honey, she pretended ignorance. Indignation.

"Takis Karalis." She clumsily shoved the gauze and scissors back into the first-aid kit. "The owner of this villa. I'm his housekeeper. Why? What did you think?"

His gaze flicked over her, reassessing. It should have insulted her, but it caused a bright heat to glow inside her. She *wanted* him to discover that hidden part of her. Play with it. Polish it and make it shine.

In that moment, she wanted to be his type, able to be casual about intimacy and physical delights. There was such promise in his eyes. Such pleasures untold.

But that way lay heartache of the most shattering kind. She knew it far too well. She had to remember that.

"You're not the first to think I'm his mistress." She hadn't bothered fighting the perception because her reputation had been in ruins the day Takis offered her this job. What was one more snide remark behind her back?

She needed to hold this man off, though, or she might self-destruct all over again.

"That's really sexist, you know, to assume that sleeping with the owner is the only reason I would be living here. Or to think I couldn't own this house. Not when it sounds as though I'm a lot closer to affording it than you are."

He didn't move, but his silence blasted her, warning her to mind herself.

A power struggle with this man was deeply foolish. In fact, trying to keep him at a distance might be a lost cause.

That thought was so disturbing, she could only blurt, "I'll meet you at the car."

She charged—retreated—into the house where she quickly scraped the moussaka filling she'd just finished browning into a bowl. She set it in the fridge before collecting her keys and purse, hands shaking.

Outside, her car was blocked by the pallet of new tiles he had unloaded a few days ago, along with the bin of broken ones.

Damn. No way could she risk staining the convertible. She glanced at his makeshift bandage. That must be painful, but he was stoic about it.

"We'll have to take the scooter." She moved to the stall and reached for her helmet, offering him Ophelia's. They were both pink, matching the Vespa.

"It's too small," he dismissed with a dry glance.

"I'm sure you're right. Your big head would never fit."

Shut up, Calli. She set aside the helmet and paused before buckling on her own. "Do you want to go by yourself?"

"I don't know where the clinic is, do I? I might bleed out before I find it. No, by all means, take me."

He was being sarcastic, but his voice hit a velvety note with that last couple of words, causing a clench of heat in her. Her mind filled with imaginings she didn't even want to acknowledge. *Take me.* She maneuvered the scooter out of its spot with a practiced wangle, started it and balanced it between her legs.

He took up twice the space Ophelia did and wasn't shy about setting his hands on her hips. He guided her back-side into a snug fit between his thighs.

She tried to stiffen and hold herself forward, but that only arched her tailbone into his groin. There was no es-caping the surrounding heat off his bare, damp chest or rock-hard thighs shoved up against the outsides of hers. She wore shorts and a T-back sports cami. It was a lot of skin grazing skin. He let his hands fall to the tops of her legs, fingertips digging lightly into the crease at her hips.

She stopped breathing, held by an electrical current that stimulated all her pleasure points.

His growing beard of stubble scraped her bare shoul-der and his breath heated the sensitive skin where her neck met her collarbone. "Shouldn't you be speeding off to save my life?"

"I'm seriously debating whether it's worth saving."

He hitched forward, jamming her buttocks even tighter into the notch of his spread legs.

She took off in a small act of desperation, glad for the muffle of the helmet and the buzz of the motor so she didn't hear his laugh, even though she felt it.

Honestly.

She sensed him turning his head this way and that as

she took the shortcut over the top of the island, through the area with the very best views, between the extravagant mansions that dominated the peak of the hill. Then, as they came down the other side and the road wound toward the coast, the horizon appeared as a stark line between two shades of blue. They descended to where the land fell away in a steep cliff.

On the mountainside above them, stone fences kept sheep in their fields and hopefully off the roads. She kept her speed down just in case. The scent of blossoms in the lemon groves filled the morning air and she couldn't help relax as the cool breeze stroked over her skin.

His thumbs moved on her and she grew tense in a different way. Tingles of anticipation raced up her rib cage, longing for his touch to rise and soothe, cup her aching breasts and draw her back into him more fully.

How did she even know what that would feel like enough to want it? Her sexuality had been flash frozen before it had had time to properly bloom. She didn't want to want a man's touch. It was self-destructive madness.

Descending the hairpin turns rocked her against him, driving her mad. She had come this way because it was quicker, but she usually avoided this route into the port town. It wasn't the once-daily ferry traffic and swarm of fresh tourists that bothered her. This part of the island actually had the best beaches and the better shopping. Ophelia begged to come here and there were a handful of really great restaurants.

Unfortunately, this route took her directly past a *kafenion* where local men sat and watched the world go by. Her father was often among them and she braced herself as they approached, refusing to look, keeping her nose pointed forward as she passed.

Not that he would acknowledge her, especially with a

man behind her. He would ignore her completely, exactly as she would ignore him. She just preferred not to set herself up for that blaze of layered pain.

They hit the melee of the village streets and she was glad they had the scooter. It allowed her to zigzag around traffic snarls and down narrow alleys, coming in the back way to the clinic where she parked next to staff cars.

"Who is Ophelia?" he asked as they dismounted.

"How—?" She followed his nod at the helmet she'd hung off the handlebars. "I forgot that was there." She rubbed the small, faded words she'd written across the back of her helmet shortly after Takis had bought the scooter. *Ophelia, stop that.*

Calli was only nine years older than the girl and didn't have any siblings. In a lot of ways, Ophelia felt like a little sister to her. In others, Calli's feelings went much deeper, more maternal. She adored the girl and was going to miss her terribly, even though Ophelia could be a complete brat at times.

"She's Takis's daughter. I look after her. Takis travels a lot, but she just turned fourteen and has convinced him to send her to boarding school. She's with her grandparents, shopping for everything she'll need. She outgrew this island long ago."

Takis hadn't wanted to see it. Losing his wife had jaded him. He wanted to keep his daughter sheltered as long as possible. Unfortunately, that had meant the girl had chafed and acted out—for Calli, thanks very much.

He was finally allowing the girl to spread her wings, though, which loosened the complex grip of gratitude and genuine love that had kept Calli here, raising a child who needed her while yearning to find her own.

"So you're a nanny." He said it like he didn't believe it.

"Hmm? Oh. Yes. Nanny, housekeeper, party planner.

Whatever Takis needs me to be." She started toward the clinic. "Barring what you suggested earlier."

"Good." He moved quicker than her, catching at the door to hold it for her, filling her vision with his contoured chest lightly sprinkled with fine black hair, his skin burnished bronze, his nipples dark brown. "I'm glad you're single."

"I intend to stay that way." Her voice husked despite her attempt to sound haughty.

"Even better."

A pained fist clenched behind her breastbone. *Vacation. Playboy.* She flipped her hair as she passed him. "I should have given you one of Takis's old shirts. I'll buy you something from the shop across the road. After I make arrangements to pay your bill."

Stavros walked outside, pocketing a course of precautionary antibiotics, rolling his eyes at the primitive concoction he'd been given. He might have pointed out the far more effective class that had recently passed approval if he hadn't already been skating so close to revealing his identity.

As he had wrapped his injury, he had realized he couldn't use the global health insurance that covered Steve Michaels, heir to a multinational pharmaceutical corporation. Using his Greek surname for the admission form had been another gamble. The nurse, a woman approaching retirement, had eyed him, saying she had attended school with a local woman who had married a Stavros Xenakis. Any relation?

He had ducked raking over the past. It promised to be a lot worse than this dull ache in his shin. Besides, Antonio had managed to get through two weeks without blowing his cover. Stavros's ego refused to fail where his friend had succeeded.

He spotted Calli standing in the shade near the Vespa. As he approached, her gaze took an admiring sweep over his still-naked torso, betraying that her disdain for him was an act even as she shook out a T-shirt and offered it to him with an expression on her face like an offended matron's.

The shirt was imprinted with a subtle design of the Greek flag in stripes of white against the blue of the shirt, which was something he might have chosen for himself if he wore T-shirts with logos.

"I expected 'Greece' is the word."

"I almost got the one that said 'Made on Mount Olympus,' but, you know, why state the obvious?"

"Careful, Calli. That sounds like you find me attractive." He shrugged on the shirt, telling himself it was his competitive nature that made him provoke her. Pursue her. She was a *nanny*, for God's sake. One who was snobbishly turning down the pool boy. That made her an amusing distraction, not someone worth obsessing about.

"Keep telling yourself that." She turned to reach for her helmet.

"*You* are telling me." He caught her arm, waiting for her gaze to flash up to his. "Every time you look at me." He demonstrated by taking her other arm and gently pressing her elbows back, giving her plenty of opportunity to recoil, but she didn't, not even when her breasts nudged his chest.

She caught her breath and set tense fingers on the sides of his rib cage, even notched her chin in a signal of defiance, but she didn't tell him to stop. A fine quiver made her lashes tremble. Her pulse fluttered in her throat and she searched his gaze for his intention, but she wasn't afraid. She was excited.

She was daring him.

This was why he was obsessing. A primitive, powerful hunger rose in him, answering the siren song she was singing.

"I know the signs of desire in a woman." He looked down at where her nipples were hard beneath the soft cups of her bra. He wanted to bite at them through the fabric. "They're painted all over you. Just as I'm sure you felt me hard against your ass the entire ride down here. We react to each other. Why fight it?"

He was hard again, steely and aching as he watched her lips part. His ears buzzed, awaiting her words, but she only let panting breaths whisper between them.

The compulsion to plunder her mouth nearly undid him, but he tasted the side of her neck first, liking the tiny cry of surprise that escaped her as he ran his hot tongue over salty skin that smelled of coconut and lavender. He delicately sucked, then nibbled his way up her neck. She melted with each incremental bite of his lips against her skin.

By the time he got to her mouth, she was making a delicious noise of helplessness, leaning her body into his, breasts pressing in soft cushions against his chest. Her lips were as plump and responsive as any he'd ever tasted. More. He was starving. Rapacious. She'd been driving him crazy, invading his dreams every night and now, finally, she was his.

Releasing her arms, he let one hand trail down to cup her ass and draw her soft belly into the ache pulsing between his thighs. His other hand went into her hair, tugging to pull her head back so he could feast on her throat again, loving the way it made her knees weaken so she twined her arms around his neck and hung helplessly against him, mons pushed against his straining erection.

He wanted to back her into the shade and take her against the wall of the clinic, but he could hear a car crunching on the gravel as it entered the lot behind them.

He forced himself to lift his head and waited for her heavy eyelids to blink open, for her honey-gold eyes to focus.

"Did you want to make another remark about my finances now, to put me in my place?" He kept his tone light, but he never let anyone get away with insulting him. Screw Sebastien's challenge. He was still a man and he wasn't a weak one.

She paled beneath her golden tan and pushed out of his arms, gaze dropping with shame. "This was a punishment? Well, didn't you teach me."

The scrape of bitterness in her tone dug like talons into his gut. She covered her glossy black hair with the helmet, avoiding his gaze, but he could see her thick lashes moving in rapid blinks.

He was used to sophisticated women who made the most of their attraction and offered themselves without ceremony. Lately, since his grandfather's wish that he marry had become known, there had been an even bigger frenzy of pretty piranhas circling and luring, promising any carnal act he requested if he would only put a ring on a finger.

This one stood before him with her bare, fraught expression and mouth still pouted by their kiss, wearing an unassuming wardrobe over a body that looked fit from sporty exercise, rather than sculpted by starving herself and bankrolling a plastic surgeon. When she had kissed him back, it hadn't been the toying provocation of a woman trying to lead a man by his organ. She'd been hot and wanton, completely swept away—as he had almost been.

He put his hand on her flat stomach, urging her to pause and look at him. "I kissed you because I wanted to."

"You kissed me because you thought you were entitled to." She snapped the buckle under her chin. "I knew what kind of man you were the day we met." She grasped his finger, disdainfully peeling his hand away from her abdomen and discarding it. "I forgot once, but I won't make that mistake again."

"American?" The contempt curling her lips went into him like a blade, even sharper than the first time. "Not Greek enough for you?"

"A tomcat. Here for a good time, not a long time."

Calli caught sight of a car, *not* her mother's, but close enough to make her take the opposite direction out of town, not wanting to pass her father's end again.

Besides, she found the southern end of the island more peaceful. Fishermen launched their small boats and grape growers eked out a living from the dry, rocky land. It was very desolate, but also very Greek. It was home.

She loved this island. She had stayed after her father threw her out for many reasons, money being the big one, at least at first. She hadn't had the means to get off the island, let alone to New York, and hadn't wanted to be exiled from her home along with losing everything else.

She hadn't wanted to leave until she could go to America, but no matter how she tried, those goalposts kept moving. Takis had even tried to help her, but that had fallen apart. Meanwhile, he gave her a better job than anyone with her limited skill set could expect. The longer she stayed, the deeper her ties to him and Ophelia grew, rooting her here even more.

Staying had been a statement of defiance, too, as much as a lack of choice. Her father thought she had shamed him? So be it. She had stayed and lived in what appeared to be flagrant sin with a man much older than herself, continuing to shame him. He deserved to feel ashamed. She would never forget what he had done to her and her son. She wanted him to know it.

But soon she would have to say goodbye and make her way to New York. Once Ophelia left, Calli planned to leave, too.

She was terrified.

"He's in a better place," her mother had said, two days after Dorian was gone, when Calli had caught up to her at one of her cleaning jobs.

"Stop saying that! *He's not dead.*"

Her father could shout that lie until he was blue in the face, but Calli *knew*. Brandon's parents had offered her money to hand over the baby, claiming they had a nice family who would raise him to their standards, but she had to give up all claim to him. She had refused.

Then suddenly Dorian was gone and she knew, didn't have proof but she *knew* her father had taken the money and sold her son to them.

"Why are you doing this?" she had cried at her mother. "Why are you letting him get away with it?" It was more frankness than had ever passed between them, so many things always left unsaid to keep the peace.

"Look at you!" Her mother had turned on her with uncharacteristic sharpness. "You're a child. One turned willful and wild. What kind of mother would you make? And you want to bring up your baby in *this*?" She'd showed no pity as she waved at Calli's swollen eye and cut lip, the bruises on her shoulders and back, the dirt clinging to her clothes and hair from sleeping on the beach.

It was true she didn't want her son raised under the heavy hand of a hard, angry man like her father. She had learned an even uglier rage lived in him than she had ever feared or imagined.

"I'm going after him," she had declared.

"Don't. Those are powerful people, Calli. They can

offer more, but they can *take* more. *He is in a better place.* Accept it."

"What kind of mother are *you* to say that to me?" Calli had ducked the scrub brush that came flying at her, then had run out of the house to avoid a fresh beating on top of the one still throbbing black-and-blue under her skin.

She had numbly retraced this long stretch of ragged coastline on foot after leaving that stranger's house, fighting her mother's words. Calli had been a good mother, for the short time she'd been allowed to try.

But she'd been young enough to still put stock in the words of those who were older, those who seemed to know better. As she was forced into more and more desperate decisions simply to stay alive, she had started to wonder if her mother wasn't right. She was a terrible person. Not fit to be a mother.

Now it was six years later and she had tried several times to locate her son, but things had happened to prevent her. Each small failure had reinforced that she wasn't meant to have him.

He *was* in a better place without her.

But she would never rest until she knew that for sure.

It made moments like this bittersweet. As the road quieted and the cool, salt-scented air swept over her, she drank it in, trying to relax and live in the moment. To accept life's hard turns and just be.

But that made her hyperaware of Stavros's strong frame surrounding her.

It made her remember their kiss.

Think of Brandon.

That memory was a distant recollection of flattery and pretty lies that she had believed because she had wanted to. Those first stirrings of attraction were nothing compared to the way this man's aura glowed off him and sank through her skin, slanting rosy hues through her without even trying. He set her alight in ways she hadn't believed were possible.

She told herself the vibration of the bike caused her nipples to feel tight and her loins to clench in hollow need. She was hot because it was a hot summer day. She was flush against the front of his hot body while the hot sun beat down.

Still, it was all she could do to stop herself from inching back into the hard shape pressed to her butt. She knew what it was and it provoked an ache into her breasts and belly and the juncture of her thighs. It was maddening.

She told herself not to give him this power over her, but it wasn't voluntary. It simply *was*.

And now she was forced to slow and extend this ride. Up ahead, the road was plugged with sheep, the herd thick between the thornbush-covered hillside and the rail that kept traffic from dropping off the short, sharp ledge to the scrub-covered shoreline.

On impulse, she made a sharp right onto the narrow peninsula that jutted out into the sea. Might as well be a decent hostess if they were right here. At least she could take a break from the physical contact.

Behind her, Stavros said something, a curse or a protest, she wasn't sure. His hands seemed to harden on her hips, fingertips digging in, but not in a sensual way.

Worried about getting back to work?

"The sheep will be twenty minutes clearing the road. It would take that long to go back around the other way," she called back as she wound along the goat track to the end.

The motion rubbed their bodies together even more and she was relieved to finally stop the bike and climb off. "At least there's a breeze out here. And it's pretty."

It was spectacular. The jut of land provided a near 360-degree view of the horizon. As she took off her helmet, there was no sound except the whisper of wind in the long grass and the rush of foaming waves against the boulders that formed the tip of the spit.

The rugged beauty was deceptive, though. Sometimes people walked out on those boulders, tourists who didn't know better. One slip could be deadly. The currents were dangerous and if bad weather was headed for the island, it showed up here first, chopping the sea into crashing waves, then throwing itself against the land in mighty gusts and nasty pelts of rain.

When Stavros stayed by the bike, she glanced back. "Is your leg bothering you?"

He sent her a filthy look, one loaded with resentment and hostility, taking her aback.

She parted her lips, not knowing what to say.

The way he stalked behind her, toward the tip of the spit, had her stammering, "You can't swim here. It's too dangerous. People die."

"I know." The gravel in his voice made her scalp prickle.

Stavros paused where the end of the striated rock had been broken off by a millennia of waves, the pieces left jagged and toppled in the churning water below.

Part of her had disbelieved that he had ever lived here, but as he looked out as if he saw something in the rolling, shifting sea, she had the impression he had stood in that exact spot before. Searching.

Her heart dropped.

He seemed very isolated in that moment, with his profile stark and carved, his hands slowly clenching as though he was bearing up under tortuous pressure.

His anguish was palpable.

She moved without consciously deciding to, standing

next to him, searching his expression, wanting to reach out and offer comfort.

His flinty gaze seemed to drill a hole into the water, one that led directly to the underworld. He looked as though he was girding himself to dive straight into it.

His ravaged face made her throat sting. His posture was braced and resolute. Like he was taking a lashing, but refused to cringe. He accepted the castigation. Bore it, even though there was no end in sight for this particular punishment.

A clench of compassion gripped her, but he was a column of contained emotion.

"Stavros." It was barely a whisper. She wanted to say she was sorry. How could she have known this would be so painful for him?

His face spasmed before he hardened his jaw and controlled his expression. When he cut his gaze to hers, it was icy cold. His voice was thick with self-contempt.

"Man whore is the least of my character flaws."

Her heart lurched. She knew how deeply that word *whore* cut. She hadn't meant to sink to that level when she had called him a tomcat.

In that moment, she knew he was nothing like superficial Brandon who threw money at an unplanned child to make it go away. Stavros was as deep as the vast sea they faced, churning beneath the gilded surface he presented to the world.

"I didn't know—" She touched his cold arm, but he shrugged off her light fingers.

"Let's go. I have a job to finish so I can get the hell off this island."

CHAPTER THREE

THE WATER CURTAIN had been only a drawing and some footings when his father had died. Stavros was laying the tiles around the base of the two columns, standing back to assess his work, when Calli spoke.

"I've been making spanakopita. I thought you might like some."

He'd been trying to keep her at a distance these last few days, feeling exposed since she had blithely forced him to face what he had been avoiding for twenty years.

Swim for shore. I'll be right behind you.

He had always had a defiant streak. He came by it honestly. His father had flouted rules just as often.

Why do I have to wear a life vest if you don't? he had asked his father as they'd boarded the small skiff.

Do you want to go fishing or not? I'll be fine. Put on your vest or we're not going anywhere.

Sebastien had asked Stavros why he owned a boat he didn't use. That was why. Boating made him sick and it wasn't *mal de mer.*

He'd always had it in his mind that he would overcome that weakness, though. Perhaps he would even sail these waters one day.

To what end? So he could do this? Relive the day he

had, for once, done as he had been told and swam? Swam as if his life depended on it, because it had?

While abandoning his father to his death.

He kept thinking that Sebastien could have the damned yacht. He didn't want it. It certainly didn't bring him any sort of happiness, exactly as Sebastien had called it that night in St. Moritz.

He should have helped his father get to shore. That was the voice he used money and toys and women and death-defying feats to muffle. It wasn't only his opinion. That truth had been reinforced in his grandfather's interrogation after the accident and colored every word his grandfather had spoken to him since.

Use your American name. It's better for business. Translation: "You don't have the right to use Stavros. That was your father's name."

You want the company to succeed, don't you? Don't let your father's dreams die with him.

Think of your mother and sisters. Do you want them to be well supported or not? It's up to you.

Basically, "do as I say or I will turn all of you onto the street."

Despite Stavros saying nothing to Calli about the way his father had been killed, she had offered a doe-eyed empathy that had been too tender a thing to bear. He had brought her back here and worked until dark, only pausing when she had brought out a plate of ground lamb sprinkled over triangles of grilled pita, and a dollop of *tzatziki* with a salad of peppers.

"I'll have to start over with the moussaka tomorrow, but no sense letting this go to waste," she had said.

She was acting compassionate when he had only ever

seen grief in his mother and sisters and that well-deserved censure from his grandfather.

Yet, since that day on the spit, he hadn't been dwelling on the accident so much as how his grandfather had yanked them off this island and sold the house immediately after the accident. He had changed their names and refused to hear Greek under his roof, denying Stavros this connection to his roots. To his memories of a happy childhood.

"Keep the keys for the Vespa," Calli had told Stavros when he finished up that evening. "If I need it, I'll let you know."

Her generosity had been hard to assimilate against the criticism that had dominated his life for nearly two decades. He had taken the keys, but turned from her kindness like it was too hot, too bright.

He had worked half days on the weekend, spending the afternoons reacquainting with the island, allowing himself to remember more than his fatal mistake, all the while trying *not* to wish her curves were spooned against his back. He didn't need a woman cuddling him through this. He had to face it alone.

He had come to a decision among the seared hills and unforgiving water. He wasn't a boy any longer and his grandfather would no longer be his master. He would buy back his former home, if only to have somewhere to go when his grandfather made good on his promise to cut him off.

The decision eased the turmoil in him, put a fire in his belly. Put him in a conquering mood as he eyed the woman who moved with such unconscious grace. Her loose hair swung as she set the plate of triangular pastries on the low table next to the lounger. Her peach-colored shorts hugged her perfect ass and her breasts moved freely under her sleeveless pink top. The tails of the shirt were knotted above her navel, exposing a strip of skin he instantly wanted to touch. Taste.

He wanted her, wanted to lose himself in her. He wanted to imprint himself on her as if he could imprint himself on this island with the action. As if he could become the man he should have been by conquering *her*.

While she wanted to stroke his hair and say, "There, there."

He moved to the sink in the wet bar and washed his hands, shaking them dry as he said, "Quit feeling sorry for me."

She blinked. "I don't."

"What are you out here for, then?"

"I thought you might be hungry."

"I am." He advanced on her, watching her eyes widen. "But not for food." A small lie. He was starving and broke after using the wages he had been given last Friday to pay her back for the stitches. "No appetite for charity, either."

Calli scented danger, but held her ground.

"I'm just being nice." He'd been so haunted on the point. It had hurt her to see it. She knew what it was like to grieve and hate yourself. She struggled with it daily and she was facing it anew, not wanting to be so fascinated by him, tortured by their kiss, writhing every night on her sheets, caught in the grip of physical infatuation.

We react to each other. Why fight it?

Was it really the same for him? She searched his expression for the man who had seemed so human that day. So steeped in pain.

"You can talk to me, is all I'm saying."

His laugh held an edge that cut past her gentle tone to tighten her throat around any further offers of sympathy. "I don't want to talk. I want *you*."

She blushed, stung, while he kept coming forward. She backed up until she came to the wall of the courtyard, between the end of the lounger and the corner of the wet bar. His hands planted on either side of her head and she was trapped.

Her heart battered her rib cage, but her fear was the exhilarated kind.

He wasn't a spoiled rich boy like Brandon. Maybe she didn't know much about him, but she knew he was a man who understood regret and paid his debts and knew his own worth was intrinsic, not contained in a bank balance.

He also didn't lie and say he loved her. He looked her in the eye and spoke the truth. *I want you.*

An answering want had been pulling at her like a tide from the moment she'd seen him. She succumbed before he even touched her, letting her head rest against the wall and her lips part as she regarded him from beneath eyelids that grew heavy between one breath and the next.

Exultation flashed in his expression and he crowded closer, hot, damp hands finding the bare skin between her shirt and shorts.

The burning sensation was so acute, the electricity in his touch so sharp, she jerked in reaction.

His hands firmed, as though he was pinning her. Controlling her. He was. She was at his mercy. A distant voice in her head screamed that this was perilous, but there was pain deep down in her and she suspected he could soothe it. There was an ache in him, too, one that she longed to ease.

She was, after all, only human. They understood each other on a subliminal level. That was what she kept telling herself.

As he lowered his head, she slid her hands across his jaw. His stubble had softened as it grew in. She buried her fingers into the short, thick strands of his hair.

He took her mouth with ruthless command, stabbing his tongue and sliding his lips against hers with carnal passion.

It might have struck her as an abrupt shove into too much intimacy, but she'd spent the weekend reliving their kiss outside the clinic. Having the real thing, his taste of midnight and mystery on her tongue, his magnificent torso shifting against her, his knowing hands sliding up beneath her top to cup the undersides of her breasts, plunged her into a delirium of want. She wasn't wearing a bra and her nipples stung with longing, alert and needy, yearning for his touch, waiting.

He slid his knee between hers, positioned his hard thighs against the insides of hers to open her, then let her feel the hard ridge of his erection against the tender flesh pulsing between her legs. His thumbs swept across her nipples at the same time.

She shuddered at the onslaught of sensation, moaning into his mouth. Heat poured into the place where he rocked, making each of his mock thrusts that much more powerful. It was raw and raunchy, yet stoked such a white-hot fire in her she went blind with it.

She turned melty and shivery at the same time and kissed him back with a wild lack of inhibition or even skill. Pure reaction. The burn in her raged higher, engulfing her, threatening to slip beyond her control.

Clenching her fists in his hair, she dragged his head up, gasping, "I'm not on the Pill. I don't want to get pregnant."

"You don't get pregnant from this, *koukla mou*." He kept up the abbreviated thrust of his pelvis against hers, and stole one of her hands from his hair to pin it to the wall above her head. His fingers curled into hers, thick enough to cause a little stretch between them as he dipped his mouth to her neck.

Her skin tingled under the hot suck of his lips. He

splayed his other hand over her naked breast under her shirt. Her flesh felt swollen and hard. His palm abraded her nipple. Glittering lines of sensation shot into her abdomen and lower.

Her hips bucked of their own accord, answering his movements, seeking that hard, hard ridge against the bundle of nerves pulled so tight she couldn't bear it. So close. So hot. So tense. She felt as though she'd been ignoring thirst and suddenly, here was the water, promising a quench that was a type of absolution. She needed it, needed more of him. *Needed that*, the elusive thing hovering just out of reach, closer, nearly in her grasp.

She tightened her hand in his, urging him with her grinding hips. Begging.

She wasn't really letting this happen right here, against a wall, behind a rush of water with a man she barely knew, was she? Was she?

Oh, yes. She *was*.

Release struck in a flash of heat and a rush of shivery joy. She lost herself to the moment, falling apart, soaring and flying. She might have fallen down if not held in place by his strength and the hard pin of his weight and that relentless press of his hips that shot sensation through her again and again.

Distantly she realized she was making animalistic noises. Her free hand went to his lower back, encouraging his dying movements while he cupped her jaw and set nibbling kisses against the corners of her panting mouth, saying, "Beautiful. So gorgeous." His tongue slid against her bottom lip like he was taking a final taste of an excellent meal. His body was so tense he quivered with strain. The heady fragrance of male sweat surrounded her, sexy and compelling.

She felt drugged. Her breath was uneven, her pulse fluttering. She couldn't believe he had done that to her, fully clothed. Or that she was still so aroused. If anything her skin was more sensitized and desperate for his touch, her loins even more achy with want.

She opened her eyes and looked into the earthy brown of his, read desire, but humor, too. He wasn't as lost to passion as she was.

It was a blow. Even more of one when he said, "Are you a virgin?"

"I know *that's* not how you get pregnant!" She gave him a shove, but he barely moved. His thick, aroused flesh sat against her tingling mound, only the thin layer of his board shorts and the seam of her cotton ones between. "I thought you were as caught up as I was and might try to…" Her voice dried up. She had to strain to find sound again. "Apparently not."

She gave him another shove, not caring how good he'd made her feel physically. She wouldn't forgive him for playing with her like a toy.

He only cupped her throat, thumb moving with lazy eroticism beneath her ear while he told her in explicit detail what he wanted to do to her. "But I don't have a condom, so we'll have to find other ways to appease ourselves, won't we?"

His eyes were nearly black, they were so dark. His mouth held a line of wicked intent that bordered on cruel. But his kiss was tender and incredibly sweet after the storm of sensuality she'd endured. Her lips clung to his, encouraging him to linger. Inviting him. Capitulating…

The scrape of the screen door into the house sounded and a male voice called, "Calli." It was an equally harsh scrape across her nerve endings.

Stavros drew back enough to frown. "Who's that?"

"Takis." She looked past his shoulder, through the

blur of the curtain, to see Takis pause outside the door as though looking for her. She pushed at Stavros.

He didn't move. "Get rid of him."

Seriously? "He's my boss."

Stavros glared at her, backed off enough to glance down to where his shorts were tented and bit out a dissatisfied curse.

He threw himself through the thin waterfall into the pool.

Stavros came to the surface in time to see a flustered Calli moving toward a silver-haired man in a suit. He kissed her cheek, but it was a distracted greeting. His frowning gaze lingered on her blushing face before fixing on Stavros with open hostility.

"Who is that?"

"Stavros. He's fixing the tiles."

"From the water?"

It was a singular experience for Stavros to be spoken *about* when he was right here, listening, especially in such a dismayed, dismissive fashion. Like he wasn't good enough to be in this man's world, let alone his pool.

The denigration was enough to cool his ardor, but made him want to laugh at the same time. *Do you know who I am?*

Takis probably regarded himself as quite wealthy and powerful, but he would very soon be selling this country cabin to Stavros for what amounted to pocket change.

There was more that Stavros instantly disliked. The man kept his arm looped around Calli's waist as he watched Stavros climb from the pool.

Whatever he needs me to be.

A surge of something ripped through Stavros. Jealous rage? The thought scored a direct hit in a way the condescension hadn't.

He reacted reflexively, walking tall as he approached, shoulders set, oblivious to the water sluicing off his sopping T-shirt and shorts, puddling with each footstep as he advanced, about to go on the attack. Eager for it.

He was not only the heir to a fortune, but the bold, innovative president of a multinational corporation who had exponentially increased the reach and value of that entity into the stratosphere. In becoming *that* man, he had learned to exert his will over a tyrant whose autocratic nature matched his own. Nothing held him back. Nothing was unattainable. Men like Takis weren't even breakfast. They were a protein bar washed down with a swish of water on the way to a morning workout.

A frown of alarm pulled between Calli's brows, like she wasn't sure she recognized him.

In that second, he remembered the bet. Five more days of playing pool boy. He bit back an imprecation.

No matter which guise he wore, Stavros Xenakis was no lame quitter, but he wasn't about to bow and scrape before Calli's boss. Or pretend that Calli was anything except his. Takis could delude himself all he wanted. She had fallen apart against *him*.

Stavros conveyed that message as he extended his hand.

"Takis. Nice to meet you. Thanks for the dip. I needed to cool off." He let his gaze cut to Calli's, allowing them both to see he was remembering how she had climaxed from merely the tease of sex. How would she react when they were naked and he was inside her? Would she scream?

She blushed ferociously. "I'll leave you to show Takis your work," she choked. "Coffee?" she offered her boss.

"Thank you." He released her, face hard, eyes diamond sharp.

Takis didn't say much as he took in the work Stavros had completed thus far. The broken tiles were gone, Ionnes having removed the bin from the front late last week. Since then, Stavros had been laying the new ones, and he was taking as much care and pride as he would if the house were his own. He had already sent a text to Antonio, asking him to arrange an agent to appraise the house since he couldn't contact his own.

Takis went into the house and Stavros went back to work, chafing at the need to be patient. He was coming down the outer stairs with a load of tiles when he overheard voices through the small, shutter-covered window above him.

"—damned sure he's not a tile layer by trade, so who is he?"

"Ionnes wouldn't send anyone he didn't trust." Something snapped, like a towel. Calli, folding laundry perhaps. "If you have concerns, tell me and I'll relay them."

"My concern is that you were kissing him."

Stavros set down the tiles with care, straightening to scowl at the window.

"Are you sleeping with him? You are." The accusation held dismay. "I can see it in your face."

"I am not! And it's none of your business if I was. Do I ask you why your shirts smell like perfume?"

"He's a womanizer—"

"I know what he is." The words burst out in a hot voice. "I know he's only here on vacation, but there's more to him than that."

"I'm sure there is, but whatever it is, you haven't seen it. What happened to waiting until you married?"

"I said that for Ophelia's sake."

"You said that to *me*. And I did offer to marry you."

The green haze returned to Stavros's vision. His chest grew tight.

"Takis—"

"I'm not asking again," he said impatiently. "I'm past

wanting more children myself. But I expect you to shoot higher than a pool boy, Calli. You'll starve. Is it because he's American? I've told you, if you want to visit New York, I'll take you."

"I need more than— That's not why— Do you think I want to feel this way?" Something slammed, like the door on a washer. "About someone only passing through? But maybe I could do with a conquest, too. Did you think of that?"

"No." The word was flat and hard. "That is the furthest thing from who you are. He is a walk down a path you've already traveled. Learn from your mistakes..."

Their voices faded and Stavros picked up the tiles. He would have been amused by the blatant snobbery if it didn't sound so much like his grandfather.

Show me you're capable of looking to the future. Find someone worthy of carrying on our name.

Their *American* name.

What the hell was wrong with the name he'd been born under?

Edward Michaels had groomed Stavros to take over Dýnami Pharmaceutical, but on his terms. Stavros was sick of it. He had poured enough of his own blood and sweat into the company to have earned his place at the top, yet his grandfather kept pointing Stavros toward the bevy of potential brides in Manhattan, ordering him to select one if he wanted control of his birthright.

Stavros had been so resistant to the idea of marriage, he hadn't looked there or anywhere else.

Suddenly, however, he had a vision of Calli circulating through that social reef. Her thick black hair and elegant figure would look stunning in a burlap sack, let alone a designer gown. In fact, even without cosmetics or a high-end hairstyle, she would stand out as exotic against all those pale, blue-eyed blondes.

None of those overworked beauties possessed so much as a hint of warmth or passion, but when he had kissed Calli, she had matched his lust breath for breath. His blood ran hot as he recalled how responsive she was. Under the hand of a talented teacher, she would be incandescent.

That sort of passion would burn out, of course, but a marriage could be temporary, too.

It hadn't occurred to him to arrange both a marriage and a divorce when he'd been ordered by his grandfather to choose from their existing circle, but if she was a nanny from Greece with much lower expectations?

To hell with buying back his old house as a way of putting his grandfather on notice that his life was his own. There were better ways. *Greek immersion*, Stavros thought with wry delight. The kind that included sinking into a divine Hellenic figure every night and exchanging pillow talk in the language of his birth. He throbbed just imagining it, his skin growing tight, blood burning in his veins.

And when he considered the look on his grandfather's face as he presented a Greek wife...

A grim smile crept across his mouth.

Calli managed to sneak out of the house as Stavros was doing a final sweep of the courtyard. Takis had been quick to follow her outside all week, getting between them and not giving her a chance to have so much as a private word with Stavros, let alone private *time*.

Stavros hadn't made a concerted effort to see her, though, which had begun to erode her confidence. She was feeling bereft. Cast off, even.

It was silly. She and Stavros weren't even lovers! Not really.

"It's beautiful," she told him as she gazed in wonder at the transformed courtyard.

Whether he was a certified tradesman or not, he was meticulous and talented. He had managed to replicate the subtle pattern from the driveway, which was more complex than it looked on first glance. She had spied on him while he worked, absorbed by the way he carefully measured and cut each tile, turning it this way and that to get it exactly right.

Rather than replant the trees that had broken the old tiles, he'd suggested they order pots of fragrant wisteria that would eventually climb the walls and overhead trellis. He had hung strings of white lights and now, as dusk fell, the scattered pinpricks were like stars that were close enough to touch. Pure magic.

When she brought her attention back to him, she saw he was taking in her creased shorts and scoop-neck T-shirt, which amplified her insecurity. She'd been telling herself they were on the same level, that Takis was a snob, but she was very much an island peasant while Stavros was... She wasn't sure. *More.*

Somehow she knew she was outgunned.

"I, um…" Her nerve almost failed her, but each night she relived the way he'd made her feel and every morning she waited, hoping today would be the day she felt that way again. He was like a potent drug that only needed to provide one rush of ecstasy and she was hooked. It shocked her how atavistic this need was. How undeniable.

Her voice scraped from the narrow space between foolish courage and profound self-doubt. "I was going to suggest coming with you when you leave today, so I can drive the Vespa home."

Here is my self-respect. I brought it out of the vault. Please don't drop it.

Takis had *not* been impressed when he realized she was loaning out the Vespa. She hated that she had slipped a notch in his estimation, but she refused to dwell on it. She wasn't a child this time. Takis was not her father.

She wasn't being foolish. She was being a woman. Human.

Offering to go home with a man. For sex.

And maybe some give and take of the comfort she sensed they both needed.

"Tempting." A muscle ticked in his jaw and his gaze held memory and smug ownership as he swept it over her. "But Ionnes is coming to pick up the last of the equipment." He handed her the key for the scooter. "I'm riding with him, then leaving."

"For?"

"New York."

Déjà vu all over again.

She couldn't help a flinch of yearning at what he might see there, in ignorance, not the least bit aware it was everything to her.

"Want to come?" he asked in a way that suggested he knew she did.

She swallowed, feeling obvious and predictable. Why had she let him see this stupid sexual crush? Why let him distract her from her goals at all? She shook her head.

"Someday." The need to go to New York had been in every beat of her pulse for the last six years, but leaving Ophelia had grown harder over time, not easier. She hadn't been able to justify abandoning the girl for a wild-goose chase.

But she had never managed to confirm anything solid from this side of the world. Her only choice was to go to New York without a proper lead, which meant she would need time once she got there. She would have to get a job and support herself while she hunted, which meant getting a green card. She had started the process, but it wasn't easy, not when she was qualified for next to nothing. She had put her name in with some nanny agencies, but hadn't heard anything.

It was daunting and added to the old fearful certainty that she wasn't meant to be part of her son's life.

She lifted her gaze to look Stavros in the eye. The impact was like an arrow to the chest, but she hung on to that pain to ground herself. Dating was a luxury she couldn't afford. She had to remember that.

"Safe travels."

"I'll be back." His sensual mouth lost its skew of humor as he heard her words for the final goodbye it was. "I'll see you again. Soon."

She snorted, having played the game of waiting and wondering before. No. She would not let herself be that stupid again. A familiar trickle of humiliation invaded her bloodstream. *Fool.* Maybe she was still childish and immature.

"Don't bother. It wasn't meant to be." She offered a weak smile. "Take care."

As she turned away, he caught at her arm. "You're going to see me again, Calli."

Better not. Heart ripped from its moorings, she shrugged off his touch.

"Goodbye, Stavros." She went into the house.

CHAPTER FOUR

EVERY YEAR TAKIS celebrated his birthday with a huge bash. It happened to fall on the same day as a local festival that included fireworks on the water. He invited friends from the mainland and colleagues from his auditing firm. While he sometimes had a date for other events, for this one he always asked Calli to hostess. He rented her a gown and she stood at his side between keeping an eye on the local girls she'd brought in to serve the food she had prepared over the last two weeks. Ophelia had elected to stay with her grandparents on the mainland this year, claiming the event was hideously boring.

It was. Most of the conversation centered on finance or which hot car had been purchased by whom at what bargain price. At least Calli had done this enough times she knew most of the players and could inquire after a child or ask about the retirement party for so-and-so.

Many remarked on how nice the tiling looked around the pool, now it had been refreshed.

"Spending a lot this year, aren't you? Boarding school, now this." One of Takis's fellow auditors used a sharp gaze to add up the changes.

The game among Takis's workmates was always how *little* they spent, so she wasn't surprised by his response.

"I wouldn't have bothered, but Ionnes said he could do it at cost."

Calli had forgotten that was how the work had been approved. She'd pressed for it to happen later in the summer, worried it wouldn't be completed in time for this party, but Ionnes had insisted this was his only opportunity.

Because Stavros had been on his working vacation?

She was trying not to think of that man, but frowned up at Takis, wondering if he also thought it strange in retrospect.

He was looking past her, but not with his relaxed, charming host expression. He was stone-faced. Affronted.

She glanced, saw a new arrival in a tuxedo, then did a double-take as she recognized that the clean-shaven, gorgeous man was—

"Oh, my God!"

If the dry smile on Stavros's sexy lips hadn't given him away, the way her blood leaped in her arteries did. That was definitely Stavros. She didn't react like this to any man except him.

You're going to see me again.

She had refused to let herself even think it, let alone believe it.

"Excuse me," Takis muttered, and drew Calli toward Stavros, muttering, "Did you invite him?"

"No." Despite being as drawn as ever by Stavros's magnetism, she had an urge to bolt. Takis's arm across her back held her fast.

Another *zing* of electricity shot through her as her gaze locked with Stavros's.

"We meet again. As promised," he said, then lifted his gaze to her employer's. "Takis." It was a flat greeting. Arrogant and dismissive. Very nearly disdainful.

"What are you doing here?" Takis demanded.

She imagined he was taking note of the tuxedo. It was no rental. It was obviously made to fit Stavros's honed form to perfection. He looked like a secret agent in a spy film as he accepted a flute of champagne from a circulating tray and sipped.

"Men of my caliber are always invited." He reached into the pocket of his tuxedo and handed over a card.

"You run Dýnami Pharmaceuticals," Takis said with disbelief, handing her the card that proclaimed this to be Steve Michaels, president.

"I prefer my Greek name, Stavros Xenakis. Stav, if *you* like," he said directly to Calli.

Her heart took another leap while something slithery and wonderful curled deep in her belly under his regard. She had known he was more than he seemed. Now whatever shade he'd been standing under was gone and his full, glorious power was on display. He was both blinding and breath-stealing.

"Technically my grandfather, the director, has last say on our biggest decisions. But that will change very soon." His gaze stayed on Calli as though she was some kind of linchpin to that statement. "Let's discuss how you'll help me with that, shall we?"

Her heart ping-ponged in her chest. "*I* could never—"

"This can't be real. Get out of my house, whoever the hell you are."

Stavros lifted a gaze that was both weary and completely uncompromising. "You negotiated a generous offer with an agent this morning. This house is mine." The corner of his mouth twitched. "But I'll graciously allow you to continue your party."

"What?" A wave of shock slammed into Calli, leaving

her drained of all sensation, barely staying on her feet. She pulled from Takis's hold to look up at him.

Around them, the music and conversation continued. The lights sparkled and water splashed as a handful of couples laughed in the pool. A few faces glanced in their direction, making her conscious that she should keep her voice down and her expression neutral, but she couldn't take it in.

Takis wasn't able to hide his flash of culpability. "I countered by doubling it. I didn't think it would be accepted. I was going to tell you later. I can send you to New York, Calli."

Hot tears of panic filled her throat. It was one thing to want something with every fiber of your being, quite another to go after it. What if it didn't work out? What if she failed? What if she found her son and he wanted nothing to do with her? *She wasn't ready!*

"That won't be necessary." There was a possessive edge to Stavros's tone. "Calli will be coming to New York with me. As my wife."

"What?!" Calli didn't realize she'd been holding a champagne flute until it hit the tiles and smashed, leaving a wet stain spreading on the fancy new tiles Stavros had laid and now possessed. She swore under her breath and shot an abashed look around.

"Let's take this somewhere private." Stavros took her elbow. "Clean that up, would you?" he ordered one of the servers who came hurrying toward them.

Calli jolted under the impact of his light touch and wanted to pull away, but she'd already made enough of a scene. Takis was drilling holes into her with his gaze, and the weight of the crowd's attention made her even hotter with embarrassment.

Rather than tightening his grip when he felt her stiffen,

Stavros gentled his touch, so it became a caress that sent furls of disarming heat into her belly.

"I don't want to talk to you," she told him as he crowded close, urging her toward the house. "What are you even doing here? Why *were* you here, pretending to be a pool man, if you're actually some kind of drug tycoon?"

"Now, see? That sounds like you do want to talk. Come. All will be revealed."

She quickly moved ahead of him, folding her arms and trying to rub away the lingering sensation of his touch as she entered the den that served as a home office for Takis.

Stavros closed the door firmly behind them.

She swung around, her entire body prickling with fight or flight. "Explain, then."

He lifted one brow at her tone, but only shrugged.

"It was a bet." His attention shifted to assess the spare decor of his new workspace. "My friend has a sense of humor. He challenged a few of us to go two weeks without our credit cards, claiming we couldn't survive it. I did. Thanks to you." He shifted his weight onto one leg and flexed his foot to indicate where he'd had stitches.

"Congratulations," she bit out, watching him move to the liquor cabinet and help himself to the ouzo. "Why do you want this house?"

He didn't answer until he had poured and brought the small glasses across to her. She remembered thinking he would make an excellent poker player and thought it again as she tried to read his shuttered expression.

"Yamas." He clinked his glass to hers before throwing back his drink. "This was my home as a child. When my father died, my grandfather moved us to New York and sold it. I want it back."

His father. She recalled his anguish that day on the peninsula and knew it was his father he was still searching for, lost in that unforgiving water. Shadows of that old grief moved behind the shuttered stare he offered her now.

Her heart began to tilt toward him, like a flower reaching out to the sun, but she gave it a quick yank back. She couldn't afford to soften toward him.

"Must be nice to simply write a check and get what you want. You realize that means I'm shoved off without a job or a home? *Thanks*."

"Your *job* will be 'wife of a drug tycoon.' I'll admit that 'heir to a multinational pharmaceutical research and manufacturing conglomerate' is a mouthful, but let's try to find some middle ground. What do you say?"

"I say you're a dishonest person, *Steve*. And I'm not going to marry you. What on earth makes you think I would?"

Stavros lifted a scathing brow. "Shall I remind you what we left unfinished between us?"

A flood of heat washed over her. It was a mix of embarrassment and memory, pleasure and the pain of rejection. She set aside her untasted ouzo and folded her arms.

"Key word. You *left*," she stated flatly. "I've moved on."

Something hard and bright flashed in his gaze. "With whom?"

"Takis." She lifted her chin to deliver the outrageous lie.

"Nice try, but I already know you didn't marry him when you had the chance. He's a bit of a fool, asking when you were already living a fine life without putting out or getting pregnant in exchange for it."

She fell back a step. "What a horrible thing to say!"

He shrugged. "True, though. Isn't it?"

"No!" Takis had been kind to her in a thousand ways. She deserved none of it, but she had never felt anything toward him except gratitude and affection. "Well, it's true I didn't want to get pregnant. But I also said no because I didn't love him. Not the way a wife should love her husband anyway. Which is why I won't marry *you*."

"That's good news. The part where you don't love either of us." He poured a fresh ouzo for himself. "As is the fact you don't want children."

She hadn't said *that*. She just wanted to find the child she'd already had before she thought about having more. She swallowed the lump that came into her throat and shifted her stance. "Look, buy the house. I can't stop you. But why on earth would you suggest we marry?"

"My grandfather has been pressuring me to find a wife. He's holding off stepping down as director until I do. All the women I know would demand a real marriage. By that I mean years of my life. Children. Half of my assets if we divorce."

"You don't like children?" It suddenly became a pivotal sticking point in a conversation that was too outlandish to be happening, but she couldn't help jumping to a vision of finding her son and watching Stavros reject him. Her heart began to thud in painful tromps.

"I'm told I need an heir, but I'm in no hurry." He swirled the clear liquid in the bottom of his glass. "In fact, I plan to leave that up to my sisters, but I'm impatient to take the reins of the company. I need a wife to present to my grandfather. One who will act the part but leave on cue. Why do you want to move to New York?"

"How do you know that? Have you had me investigated?" She paled as she wondered what he'd found.

"I overheard you and Takis one day. Why? Do you have a deep dark secret you want to stay buried?" He narrowed his gaze. "Tell me now. I don't want a scandal popping up to smudge the family name."

She knew people whispered on the island that she'd had a teen pregnancy. They all thought the baby had died and Stavros might hear that same rumor if he sent someone to snoop, but he wouldn't find a headstone for the boy. Her father had refused to pay for one. Because her son wasn't *dead*.

He was somewhere in New York. At least, his father, Brandon Underwood, was in New York and he knew where the infant had been placed.

"I have a normal desire for privacy," she said, glossing over her alarm. "I don't like the idea you're prying." But it was starting to hit her that Stavros had the means to pry. That *she* would have the means.

With Stavros's name and social standing behind her, she would have the power to confront Brandon. The cache to meet him on a level playing field, face-to-face.

The thought made her dizzy.

"You live in New York? That's where you want to take me?" she confirmed, trying to keep from hoping. It was too big, too fast. Too *easy*.

"Manhattan, yes. Why do you want to go?"

She touched her neck where it felt as though her pulse would burst the skin. Takis had tried to help, taking her to a lawyer who had written a couple of letters on her behalf, but Brandon's family had been too rich and influential, exactly as her mother had warned her. There was a death certificate on file, so she'd been dismissed as everything from an opportunist to a loony. Brandon claimed to have no recollection of her. As far as he was concerned, their affair had never even happened, let alone the birth of a boy his family had *stolen*.

Paid for, they might argue, if they ever admitted he'd been conceived at all.

"It's just always been a dream of mine," she prevaricated, folding her arms again and feeling the spike of her fingernails into her upper arms. Could she do this? Pretend to be a society wife and confront an old lover to find her son?

"Surely you could have managed a holiday if you wanted one?" The deep timbre of Stavros's voice seemed to come through water, hollow and barely penetrating her swimming thoughts.

"I want to live there. I've started the paperwork, but…" She shook herself out of becoming too attached to this crazy idea. It would devastate her if it didn't pan out. "It would be a green-card marriage," she warned. "Is that the sort of scandal you'd like to avoid?"

"You won't be working. Even after we separate, I'll support you. My lawyers can handle all of that very easily."

Must. Be. Nice.

"I still don't understand why you would ask *me*." A lowly nanny maid with no skills. No worth to society beyond what Takis and his daughter had bestowed upon her.

"As I said. You'll agree to something temporary and not clean me out as you leave. There will be a prenup and a suitable settlement. That's *all*. You realize that's what you're agreeing to? Six months should be enough time to transition my grandfather out."

"You're really offering a marriage on paper so you can—"

"Oh, Calli," he cut in. "Don't be naive. We'll share a bed. *That's* why I'm choosing you."

A burst of excitement exploded in her, making her turn her face to try to hide her reaction. He must have guessed, or seen her blush. Knowing laughter scraped from his throat.

"You're assuming I would want that," she said in a thin voice.

"I'm quite certain you do."

"Your arrogance is a turn-off."

"So is your denial of the truth."

She swung a glare toward him, instantly anxious that she had caused his interest to wane. He was *such* a dangerous man.

He set down his glass and held up his hands, motioning her to come to him. "Let's seal the deal."

"I need time to think." She scowled at the carpet, blind to the pattern and only seeing a blur of blues and greens. "This is happening too fast."

"It *will* happen fast." He came toward her, clasping her upper arms before she could properly catch her breath. "It has to. But you'll be paid out by Christmas and free to do as you please. So will I."

Christmas. With her son...

She barely dared allow such a sweet dream to form.

"You want me to sleep with you for personal gain." She choked on the words as she said them.

"We're going to sleep together either way."

"Do you have a subscription for that level of confidence? Because I'd love to know where it comes from."

"Right here, *glykia mou*. In the way you respond to me." Stavros pulled her up against him and wiped her brain clean with the first touch of his mouth, sending a shock of pained excitement through her, like she'd slammed into a wall of lightning.

With a moan of angst, she tried to hold back her response, not wanting to be so easy for him. To prove to herself she could resist him. *This*. But her body betrayed her. Her arms couldn't resist climbing to twine around his neck so she could hang on as the rest of her wilted and softened.

He felt so good, his strong arms supporting her, his hands stroking her lower back in a way that made her scalp tingle. She found herself opening her mouth beneath his, hungrily returning his kiss and welcoming the intrusion of his tongue. Losing herself in the waves of pleasure that rolled with increasing intensity through her.

In a brutal move of forced deprivation, he set her back on her flat feet, wet mouth curled into a cruel smile of satisfaction. "Need more proof?"

He wasn't even breathing hard. Not like she was.

It was humiliating, but it was the education she needed. She hated him enough in that moment to feel no twinge of conscience over using him. Not if he was going to use her libido to manipulate her.

Her level of desire scared her, though. Hormones had led her into heaven and hell once before. The joy of a son, the grief of losing him, all because she'd wanted someone to kiss her and treat her like she was special.

"You don't love me," she said through lips that felt scorched and puffy. It was a needle of truth that she plunged into herself, before he could do it, as a vaccine. She was trying to undercut the way she reacted to him, form antibodies so he wouldn't leave her devastated in six months.

"No," he agreed blankly. "I don't."

The needle bent and she gave it a twist, snapping it off.

"Don't say it. You lied once. Don't do it again. Don't make promises you won't keep. Don't..." She looked at her hands where she tangled her fingers in agitation.

She wanted to say, *Don't hurt me*. Not because she was afraid for her physical self, but as much as she had learned to protect her heart, it was still a very thin-shelled, fragile thing.

A firm hand cupped her jaw and forced her to look into his eyes. "Don't?"

She pulled free of his touch before she melted and betrayed herself again. "This is a business agreement. Don't try to get inside my head."

He held her gaze and she tremored inside, wondering how anyone worked with a man this intense and powerful without incinerating under his laser regard.

"And I'm not sleeping with you until we're married."

A muscle in his cheek ticked. "Let's make it happen quickly, then."

Stavros had no best man. Alejandro was away on his challenge and Sebastien was witnessing Antonio's nuptials in Rome.

Antonio took the opportunity to provide sober second thoughts anyway, cautioning Stavros against taking a wife to appease his grandfather. "The first time I married, it was purely to serve family expectations. It was a disaster. Think twice, *amico*."

Stavros wasn't about to be swayed. "You're marrying for love this time, are you?" he challenged.

"I have a son." It was a face call and Stavros saw Antonio's jaw harden. His friend said nothing about the mother, Sadie.

Stavros had to wonder how a marriage like that could succeed, given the woman had kept such an explosive secret for so long, but he only said, "I want custody of my company. Same thing. And we've agreed it's only for six months."

"She said yes to that?" Antonio's brows lifted in surprise, then he shrugged as if to say, "Do what you like, then."

Stavros always did.

He ended the call, but soon heard from Alejandro. He thought he was about to get another warning, but aside from surprise, Alejandro passed no opinion on Stavros's marriage. He was more concerned with getting a DNA test for a horse.

What the hell was his friend facing in Kentucky?

Stavros had to wonder if Sebastien would think this challenge was worth the loss of half his fortune. It *had* turned out more mentally taxing than Stavros had expected, but it had only increased his desire to take control of his own fortune, not to seek a higher purpose with his life.

His desire to claim Dýnami was the only reason, he told himself the next day, that his heart fishtailed in his chest when Takis arrived at the *dimarchio* alone.

The mayor had gone into his chamber moments ago and was waiting for them.

"Where's Calli?" he asked Takis.

"Ladies' room. She's not usually concerned about fussing with hair and makeup, but…" He glanced at his watch, then his gaze came up, level and unflinching. "You realize that if you hurt her, I'll kill you."

Possessiveness seared through Stavros's veins like a hit of heroin. His knee-jerk reaction was to come down like a hammer on the man, but in the few dealings he'd had with Takis, he'd found him to be direct and genuinely interested in Calli's welfare. Stavros had to respect him for that.

So he only said, "My prospects are considerably better than a pool boy's. She'll be well taken care of."

"She was already well taken care of."

"If that was all she wanted, she would have married you when she had the chance." It was a bit of a low blow, but Stavros was fishing. He knew Calli was getting something more from their marriage than a trip to New York and a generous settlement. He wanted to know what it was. The answer might lie in her reason for refusing Takis. What had her employer failed to provide for her?

Takis had the grace to darken beneath his swarthy complexion.

"I knew she was too young for me." His voice sharpened

to defensive. "But I was running out of time to provide Ophelia with a brother or sister, and I knew what people were saying about Calli's presence in my house. They both deserved better."

His mouth grew so tight, a white line appeared around his lips.

"Regardless how she reacted to my proposal, I have to respect her decision to accept yours. Even if I have my reservations." His baleful glance was another warning. "She knows she has a home with us if it doesn't work out. Don't send her back to me in pieces."

Again Stavros told himself this catch of aggression was only because Calli leaving their marriage early could threaten his plan to take control of Dýnami, but there was more. There was something about the connection between her and this man that kicked him in the gut.

The sound of two pairs of high-heeled shoes approached and he lifted his gaze, then caught his breath as the image of his bride slammed into him.

The dress was simple, but Greek goddess–like in style. The front came down in a sharp V, hugging her breasts in gathered cups right above a wide band that emphasized her waist. Below it, the white silk draped gracefully to just past her knees. A handful of tiny white flowers had been woven into her hair and she held a bouquet of pink roses.

Her hand went to her middle as she saw him. "It's overkill, isn't it? I told you," she said to Takis, wincing self-consciously.

"No," Stavros insisted, shrugging on the suit jacket he had removed outside because of the heat. "You look beautiful." He held out his arm.

"I told you it was perfect." Ophelia wore pastel pink. She was coltish and pretty, not unlike Calli in her quintessential Greek looks, and glowed with importance as she took her father's arm and followed them into the mayor's office.

Minutes later, Stavros kissed his wife with a thrill of triumph. Strangely, the prize he most anticipated claiming was not the corporation. He was suddenly annoyed with himself that he had only booked a few short days—and nights—in Paris before he took Calli to New York.

It was an odd shift in priorities that he put down to sexual frustration, but these few days of making arrangements had been interminable. The last thing he had patience for was a drawn-out goodbye between Calli and her employer, especially when it put tears in her eyes.

"Thank you," she choked as she hugged Takis. "I'm sorry."

"For what? You silly girl." Takis rubbed her upper arms. "I'm the one who is sorry. I know I let you down. If I hadn't, you wouldn't be doing this."

"No! You gave me so much. Now I'm leaving like I don't appreciate it, but I do. I swear I do."

"All I ever gave you was a chance. You earned everything else. I wish you luck." His face grew grave and concerned. "Call me. Any time, for any reason. Understand?"

She nodded.

"I mean it."

"I know," she murmured and turned to his daughter. Ophelia sobbed openly and they hugged a long time, Calli murmuring reassuring noises to the teenager. "*You* call *me* anytime," she said as they finally broke apart. "For any reason."

"I love you, Calli."

"I love you, too. Stay out of trouble, *paidi mou*." There was such conflict, such an agony of torn loyalty in Calli's expression, Stavros felt guilty taking her hand and drawing her away, like he was wrenching her from her family.

If she felt so close to them, why was she marrying him?

He wanted to believe the answer was obvious. Money, of course, but she had seemed rather ambivalent about the settlement they had negotiated, saying only, "Wow. You really want this marriage. I'll try to live up to that."

She hadn't tried to negotiate the value higher so he had wound up increasing the ceiling amount himself. He hadn't lied to Takis when he had said she would be well taken care of, even if she didn't know how to do that herself.

He was still thinking about that, wondering about her reasons for wanting this marriage, when they were settled aboard his private jet. He watched her turn his rings round and round on her finger as though having second thoughts.

"What else did Takis give you besides a job?" he asked.

Her brows came together in dismay as she turned her head to look at him. After a surprised pause, she settled her hands in her lap and said, "I thought we agreed to keep this just business."

"We have to talk about something for the next six months. You didn't like the idea of my investigating you. Tell me yourself what you want me to know."

Her chin set and she rearranged the fall of her skirt. She was still in her wedding dress, but it didn't seem out of place. It seemed rather apropos, given the virginal nerves emanating off her.

In the back of his mind, he kept thinking of that overheard conversation, when Takis had said, *What happened to waiting until you're married?* She wasn't a virgin, was she? In this day and age?

"He gave me a home. Trust. Respect." He heard poignancy in her tone, like she feared she had lost those things all over again.

Stavros trusted her. To a point. He respected her as much as he respected any form of life. Maybe a little more, since she had the capacity for kindness and humor. Nevertheless, he was fairly sure his money was not her goal. She had other motives he had yet to determine. That produced a natural caution in him.

"He said he asked you to marry him because people were gossiping about your arrangement."

"They were. But I had already put up with it for two years. I didn't see the point in trying to change it just because I had turned nineteen. Frankly, they still would have talked. The age difference was that wide. And I didn't think of him that way."

He hadn't realized how young she was until he had filed for the marriage license. She didn't look more than the twenty-three she was, but there was a maturity in her demeanor that suggested she was a lot older.

"You were seventeen when you went to live with him?" Maybe she was a virgin. "Where were your parents?"

"They live on the island." Something in her tone warned him he was treading dangerous ground.

He had asked if her parents would be coming to Athens for the wedding. Her flat no had half convinced him they were dead.

"Did they disapprove of your living with Takis?"

"They disapproved of a lot of things."

He suspected that was a colossal understatement, given the marble-like smoothness of her profile. "Is that *why* you moved in with Takis? Did you run away?"

"They kicked me out." Her hands clenched into fists, crushing the delicate silk of her dress. "I was sleeping on the beach. It's a small island. Everyone knew my business. I thought it would be better to get to the mainland, but I didn't have ferry fare. Takis was the richest man on the island. I knew he was widowed. When I saw him waiting in his car for the ferry…"

Her mouth pursed. Bright red flags of shame rose in her cheeks as she turned her head to look at him, but she met his gaze without quailing. Defiant almost, while the shadows of anguish in her eyes made the honey gold of her irises hard as amber.

A spike of nausea went into his gut, anticipating what was coming, even though he somehow wanted to travel back in time and prevent the exchange she was about to admit to.

"I made him an offer he kindly refused." She tried to smooth the creases from her skirt as she realized how badly she had wrinkled it. "He knew there are plenty of men in this world who wouldn't hesitate to take advantage of a desperate teenager, though. He was on his way to pick up Ophelia from her grandparents and hire a new nanny. She was running through them like penny candy. He said he would give me a shot, but made it clear he wouldn't tolerate drugs or stealing or anything else like that. He's not a bleeding heart."

"Is that why your parents threw you out? Drugs? Stealing?"

"No." It took her a minute to continue. Her hands twined together so tightly her nail beds turned white. "I, um, messed around with a tourist. My father said I shamed him."

Ah. Not a virgin. He was disappointed, but not for possessive reasons. He sensed that experience had colored her view of men and sex.

"Is that why you wanted to wait until marriage to sleep with me? Because you had premarital sex and got thrown out for it?"

She hitched a shoulder. She was back to offering only her profile, and blinked rapidly. "I just didn't want to be used again. At least this time it's mutual." Her mouth quirked with distaste. "I won't be left with nothing."

That mercenary streak of hers shouldn't have chafed. He ought to find it comforting, he supposed, since it made her motives seem really straightforward, but he found himself saying, "I wondered why you were leaving him when you're obviously very attached. Money does make the girl turn round, doesn't it?"

She swiveled just her head, eyes wide with hurt and something else. Bitter astonishment. "Are you pointing out that I haven't risen very far from offering myself to Takis for ferry fare? I'm aware. But you married for money, too. If you find my behavior distasteful, it's because you're looking in a mirror."

Calli had already been reeling over what she'd done before Stavros had pushed a stiletto of an insult between her ribs.

She judged herself harshly enough, thanks. She'd married a stranger so he would take her to America. She was going to sleep with him and pose as his wife so she could search for her son.

Takis had nearly come apart at the seams when she had told him what she had agreed to. Ophelia's mother had been the love of Takis's life, but he cared for Calli. Under his blunt exterior, he had always been protective of her, which was sweet, but as time wore on, it had also begun to abrade. Ophelia had said her father smothered and controlled. It was his way of trying to prevent the people he cared about from being hurt, but even with the search for Calli's son, Takis had always been too quick to take the lead and make a call and act as go-between.

She had felt held back, but she had let him shield her for a number of reasons, not least of which was her belief, deep down, that she was to blame for what had happened. She feared she wasn't good enough to be a part of her son's life. Brandon's family hadn't thought so. Her own parents had berated her for going through with the pregnancy then orchestrated Dorian's removal from her custody. She had failed to hang on to him, had failed to even find out where he was.

She had failed as a mother.

So what right did she have to search for Dorian now? Would he even want anything to do with her? He was so young. Six. Was he in school? He might not even know he was adopted.

Was he adopted? Loved?

Takis had assured her more than once that powerful families didn't like surprises from the past cropping up. They controlled them from the outset, which was why they had taken their grandson and cut his humbly born mother out of the picture as ruthlessly as possible. People at their level didn't let their heir apparent marry an island girl knocked up during a holiday romance. They paid her off, then ensured their son's slip-up was given a silver spoon and an Ivy League education.

Takis was convinced Dorian was in a good situation. Brandon's family wouldn't have taken him if they only wanted to put him in foster care and forget about him. They could have left him in Greece if being raised by strangers had satisfied them.

But was he loved?

That was Calli's best wish for Dorian, but there was a dark side to that shiny coin. If he was happy, then having his birth mother arrive to disrupt things could be traumatic for him.

Until she knew exactly what kind of situation he was in, however, until she knew he *was* safe and loved, she would never rest easy. She would always be tortured by this sense that she had let him down.

"You don't like it?"

Stavros's voice startled her out of her introspection. "Pardon?"

"He's one of the top chefs in Paris, but you don't seem pleased. Shall I call back the staff and request something else?"

They'd been speaking to each other in stilted phrases since she had swiped back at him on the plane. Now she looked at the meal she had rearranged on her plate, but barely tasted.

"It's fine. Excellent. I'm just…distracted. I'm, um, sorry I was so bitchy on the plane. This is a big step I've taken. It's finally hitting me."

His brows twitched with surprise at her apology. His cheeks went hollow, then he made a dismissive gesture. "Your remark struck too close to home. And, to be quite honest, my time fixing the pool tiles allowed me to see what a nuisance it is to lack money."

"A 'nuisance,'" she repeated drily. "Do tell."

He shrugged off her sarcasm. "Even then, I had friends at the end of a telephone line and knew my dire straits were only for two weeks. I wasn't sleeping on a beach. When I think of you as a young girl in that situation…"

His sharp gaze was hard to bear.

She hated thinking about that time, too.

She sipped the very excellent white wine that had been paired with their meal for this private dining experience in a honeymoon suite with a view of the Eiffel Tower, then tried to lighten the mood.

"The beach was nothing. I've spent the last six years with a girl going through puberty. Forget two weeks without credit cards. I challenge you to survive *that*."

He chuckled into his own glass as he took it up. "Pass."

"That's what I thought." She took a bite and chewed slowly, awash in the conflict of leaving Ophelia. She didn't know about Dorian. Takis had left it to Calli to tell her if the timing ever felt right. It was such a very difficult subject. Calli had only ever opened up about it with Takis. Now she wondered if she should have explained better to Ophelia why she was marrying and moving to New York.

"You'll miss her," Stavros said.

"I will. When I first came to live with them, she was a nightmare. Did horrible things. Poured sand in my bed. Played dead in the pool. Got into Takis's liquor cabinet. The first sip made her cough and I heard her, so not much damage there, but still." Calli shuddered to remember those first months.

"She resented anyone in the house who wasn't her mother and wanted her father to stay home with her, but he couldn't. I was quite open about the fact I had nowhere else to go. I told her it didn't matter what she did, we were stuck with each other. Then one day we saw my mother as we were running errands."

Calli's appetite dried up again and she set aside her cutlery.

"Ophelia realized there could be something more awful than your mother dying. She could be alive and refuse to look at you." The agony of that painful moment caused a flinch she couldn't control, tightening her voice even though she attempted to sound unaffected.

Things had never changed and Calli doubted they ever would. Her mother had had opportunities to back her up about Dorian being taken, when Takis had first tried to help, but she had stuck with the story that the baby had died. She had aligned with Calli's father and Calli would never forgive either of them.

"Ophelia still pulled pranks after that, but they weren't so malicious. We started having fun together."

They had grown so close that by the time Calli first scraped together enough of her wages for airfare to New York, but *just* airfare, she had been reluctant to abandon Ophelia. She was finally settling down. Her grades had improved and Takis wasn't as worried as he'd been.

Calli had let Takis talk her into staying a little longer, unwilling at that point to confess to him her reasons for wanting to leave. It had been too humiliating, and it had felt good to hear how much she was needed by him and Ophelia. For the first time in her life, she had felt valued. Loved.

"She's excited to go away to school, but I know she's anxious, too. Now you've bought her home and I'm leaving for New York. It's a lot for her. I feel guilty." Torn.

"Regretful?"

"No." She was able to state that in a quiet, but firm tone of resolve. Whatever happened in New York would be painful. That was a given, but this was too much of a golden opportunity to get answers. She couldn't let anything hold her back. Not this time. "No, I'm quite committed to going through with this."

"I'll try to make it pleasant enough you don't have to simply endure it," he drawled.

"What? Oh, that did sound awful, didn't it?" She blushed and covered her hot cheeks. "I didn't mean it like that!"

"I know." His voice held humor, but confidence and anticipation, too.

It provoked a ripple of awareness, sending restlessness prickling through her. She had been avoiding thinking about sex. It had been a kind of denial as she focused only on what she would get with this marriage, not on what she would give up.

Or how easily he made her give up *so much*.

"Has there been anyone since that tourist?"

"No." She was struck with performance anxiety as she admitted it.

"Why would you do that to yourself when you're so sensual?"

"It was my first time. It was clumsy and awkward, not something I was excited to try again. Why do you feel a need to make conquests of women when you're barely interested in them?"

He snorted. "You do love to go on the attack when you feel threatened, don't you?" He threw his napkin onto his plate and rose. "Quit being so nervous. I was serious about making it good for you. And now I know how inexperienced you are, I'll take it slow." He drew her to her feet and into a close dance.

She stiffened, but couldn't, simply couldn't remain tense when everything in her was drawn to melt and soften against him. His touch made her shiver, especially when he found the low back of her dress and traced the edge, leaving a tickling line of fire against her skin.

With a wince that she hid with a duck of her head, she let herself succumb to his hold until she was resting against him.

"I have not stopped thinking about the way you moved against me that day, *koukla mou*." His voice was a low rumble in his chest. "How you ignited and made those erotic noises as you hit your peak."

"Don't remind me. It's embarrassing."

"It's arousing. Does it not turn you on to remember?"

It did. She was growing weak, even though they were talking about something that made her squirm. His body brushed against hers. They moved in a slow rock that didn't even match the muted instrumental music playing in the background. Was he hard? Was that what she had just felt as her stomach grazed his pelvis? All of her senses came alive to him. Attuned. All of her cells honed in like magnets attracted to the polarity in his. She held her breath, waiting for the next brush of contact.

"You don't want to hear that I relive it every night? That I can't sleep unless I let myself imagine I took you against that wall until we were both groaning and shuddering in a shared release?" His lips nuzzled her neck, making her whimper.

"Don't be graphic."

"Sex is graphic. You and I will have a lot of sex, *glykia mou*. Get used to the idea. Nerves are fine, but I can see you trying to resist what you feel and I don't like it. You're the one who said you don't want lies between us."

She stopped moving and glared up at him. "You really think you own me and the entire world, don't you?"

He lifted a hand to smooth back her loose hair, then slowly closed his fist into the mass at the back, not hurting, but holding her still as he lightly teased his mouth against hers, making her lips burn.

"You and your world. For the next six months. Beg me to kiss you."

"No."

He released a breath of hot laughter against her chin and lowered to almost but not quite kiss the side of her neck.

She tried to wriggle free, but his grip was implacable. He only lifted his head, leaving the skin at her nape tingling in anticipation, yet aching with loss. Everything in her wanted to beg him for that kiss, but she set her chin, refusing to.

"If you want me to stop, say so, but if it's yourself you're fighting then tell me why. Is it because you were raised to think it's wrong to like sex?"

"I don't have hang-ups, if that's what you're asking. I just don't like feeling manipulated by someone who treats my body like it's territory on a game board. You're not sensual at all. You're more turned on by the idea of conquering me."

His expression hardened and a bright light filled his eyes. "The only reason I didn't take you against the wall that day was because I didn't have a condom. Stop fighting how much you want me and I'll show you how much I want you," he promised.

Or was it a threat?

Either way, it was a huge risk. Scary. She didn't have a hang-up about sex, not really, but she didn't like letting her basest self overcome her rational brain. Biology was a powerful thing, designed by nature to perpetuate the species no matter the cost to the parents. The way Brandon had made her feel had been a tepid bath compared to the way she reacted to Stavros, but she had still allowed that bit of pleasantness to override her good sense.

The result had been a disaster, and she was terrified her life would spin out of control again, especially when the temptation to allow it was so strong.

"I won't beg, either," he said in a gravelly undertone, drawing a tendril of her hair across the base of her neck. "Even though I want you more than… I keep thinking it's because of the way we met. *Where* we met."

His gaze was fixated on the silk of her hair drawn across her skin, his voice a rasp.

"Don't imagine I could walk out of here and enjoy the next woman who comes along. I want *you*," he said.

She couldn't help the cut of her breath against the pressure on her throat. Her pulse leaped at the same time, while a flood of heat washed through her.

"I—" She tried to swallow. "I started a prescription, but

it's not working yet. You have to wear something until it is. I don't want to get pregnant."

It was a desperate attempt to slow things down, not that it had any effect on either of them.

"I won't forget."

They held a locked stare for a minute, something that was between a power struggle and a quest for reassurance. On her part, at least. She didn't know what it was for him. She didn't know *him*, which was distressing. But she looked into his eyes and sensed… Maybe she was projecting what she wanted to see, but she sensed that she could be his salvation in a way that she wanted him to be hers.

That reflection of herself in there, that sense that he wrestled in his own cage of agony, got to her every time.

Her gaze dropped to his mouth.

As if it was the signal he'd been waiting for, he set one brief, openmouthed kiss on her lips. A test. Was she ready for this? Would she respond as he'd asked?

She was. She did. Only this time she didn't just let her lips cling to his. When he came back for a longer kiss, she kissed him back. She didn't just let the wash of pleasure guide her reaction, she responded with intention. Encouragement. She revealed the hunger that had been prowling inside her from the first moment she had seen him.

A growl sounded in his throat as he took control of the kiss, deepening it.

She moaned, let him have his way, but splayed her fingers in his hair and massaged. His arms tightened, drawing her already hot body tight against the inferno that was his, making her breathless.

With each tiny reaction, the intensity pinballed tighter and faster between them. She arched into him; he gave her his tongue. She met the intrusion with a delicate suction and he made a ragged noise while moving wide, possessive hands over her back and hips. Her waist. When she rocked her breasts against his chest, both trying to ease the ache in the tips and incite his reaction, he caught one in his splayed fingers.

The sensation had her opening her eyes, but she saw nothing, all of her vision white. A flood of wet heat poured into the juncture of her thighs while he plucked and rolled her nipple through her dress and bra. A plea caught in her throat, begging him to strip her so she could feel that hot, sensual touch on her bare skin. *Please.* She thrust her pelvis into his.

He pivoted and stumbled her backward. They bumped an end table. A lamp hit the floor with a clattering smash, jolting her back to their elegant surroundings.

"What—"

"Forget it," he ordered, fingers working behind her. "Where is the zip?"

"It's here—" She lifted her arm, panting, but as her hand came up she couldn't resist cupping his jaw and chasing his mouth with her own.

He avoided her long enough to say, "Give me your tongue," then he kissed her, made a feral noise as she gave herself up to him and got her dress open enough to sweep his fingertips across the lace of her bra.

They fell to the sofa, angled and crooked, each with one leg hanging off. His knee dug into the cushion beside her hip and they both writhed a moment until he pulled back and guided her inside knee so he was between her legs. The skirt of her dress fell to her waist, baring her lacy white panties.

He took a moment to look from the scrap covering her hips to where her dress gaped at her shoulder. His carved features were more savage than ever. She shouldn't find it a turn-on, but her wetness increased. She shakily pulled her shoulder from her dress, then opened her bra, baring her breast.

She offered herself in the most blatantly scary way. *Please like what you see.*

His lips tightened across his teeth in something too feral to be a smile, then he covered her and took her nipple into his mouth, hot and assertive, sucking strongly so she bucked against him.

"Stavros!"

"Too much?" He drew back to circle with his tongue and scrape lightly with his teeth. "Or not enough? Tell me," he ordered in a guttural tone.

All she could say was a whispered *"More"* while she scored her nails across his shoulders, wishing she could tear open his shirt and feel his skin.

He kept teasing her while he lifted his chest enough to yank at his buttons, tearing open his shirt then making a noise of satisfaction as she slid her hands beneath it, stroking hot, flexing muscle, squirming with pleasure at the way he dallied at her breast and pulled at her other shoulder until both her breasts were available to him.

She was being utterly wanton, shocking herself, but the way he pulled back in a kind of sexual daze was incredibly exciting. How could she not thrill to the power in arching her back and hearing his breath grow ragged?

"Not scared now, are you? You should be," he said in a dangerous voice, stroking a hand up her inner thigh and catching at the damp fabric of her undies. His fingers went under and the backs of his knuckles grazed the seam of her lips, making her stomach muscles tense and jump.

He grunted approval. "Like that?"

She was trembling all over, unable to speak, to say she *loved* it. She moved one fingertip to his fly, tracing the ridge that pressed at the front.

He bit out a curse and, with a jerk of lace, he bared her to his avid gaze.

She squeaked in surprise, then caught her breath as he jerked open his fly with an equal lack of finesse and revealed himself.

Oh. That was… They were really doing this. He rolled a condom down his length, stroked himself with his fist as though ensuring a tight fit.

Her thighs twitched and she felt too exposed, too vulnerable. It was all happening so fast. Her hands went to his chest as he started to cover her.

His gaze flashed as he saw the hesitation in her eyes. "Say yes. Say yes, *please*."

She wasn't sure if he was ordering her to beg or pleading for her to give him permission. The hint of desperation in his expression reassured her, though. He looked like he thought he might die if they didn't do this. It was enough to convince her he was as engulfed in this experience as she was.

With a tentative touch, she slid her hand between them and guided him into place. Like it was a signal, he took control again, covering her mouth in a passionate kiss as he pressed into her.

There was a pinch and a stretch, but "Mmm…" She groaned in joy, stunned by the rush of sensation as he moved in a testing stroke. He trembled and lifted enough to look at her, his gaze intense, as though holding back took all his effort.

Nothing in her life had ever felt this good and she wanted more. Needed it. Demanded it. She arched, inviting a deeper penetration on his next return.

His breath rasped and he drove a little harder and drew back to do it again. From there they abandoned any attempt at propriety and gave themselves up to the wildness of it. It was primitive and raw. Graphic. But good. So sinfully good.

She heard herself urging, "Never stop. Never."

"Never," he growled, driving her higher with every powerful move of his hips. They clung and arched and moaned and, when the crisis arrived released jagged cries as they crested together.

CHAPTER FIVE

STAVROS LANDED ON his back on the floor when he rolled off her, knocking out what little breath he had left. His elbow bumped the coffee table when he eventually lifted his wrist from his eyes.

All he could see was one bare knee off the edge of the sofa cushion and a flash of torn white lace abandoned on the glass of the tabletop.

He licked lips that were dry from panting. His breath and pulse slowed, but remained unsteady. He swallowed and rubbed his hand down his face, trying to pull himself together.

What the hell had just happened? He had promised to take it slow.

He had known it would be good and had wanted to savor their first time, but damn. They were a seriously combustible combination. The part of himself that carried a million responsibilities, and remained in control while taking on crazy physical stunts, told him to step back and reassess. The other part, the part that went hang-gliding and ran with the bulls merely to keep from dying of boredom, that man was beating his chest and screaming a primal "Hell, yeah" from a mountaintop.

Her leg twitched and she made a noise. Discomfort?

Concerned, he forced his lethargic muscles to work and

rose on one arm. The rest of him came back to life as he came eye level with her landscape of curves *en déshabillés*.

"Are you okay?"

"Fine." She pushed her skirt down and tried to draw up her rumpled dress to cover her breasts.

He hitched his elbow on the side of the sofa, set his chin on his fist and patiently waited for her gaze to quit skittering in avoidance. She finally turned her head so mere inches separated her nose from his. Such adorable shyness after they'd been rapacious and lost to one another. Did she remember demanding *more* from him? Telling him to never stop?

He would never forget it.

His scalp tightened all over again.

"Do you think we could make it to the bed this time?" His voice came out more tender than he intended.

Her eyes widened. "You want to…again?" She swallowed.

He reminded himself she was the next thing to a virgin. "I did warn you we'd be doing it a lot." Say yes. *Please*.

Her pretty mouth drew into a moue and her lashes swept down. If she was physically uncomfortable, he would accept it, but if she was about to trot out one of her fibs about not wanting him, he would press harder. Surely they were past that now?

Surely she wanted to slake this voracious animal as much as he did?

"Perhaps if you gave me a head start?" She cut a dry glance toward him.

"Ha!" A rush of delight had him grabbing her and dragging her down atop him, laughing openly when she squealed in surprise. He caught at her dress, sweeping it upward and off as she wriggled to sit up across his hips.

They both stilled as he took in her naked figure.

She brought up a shy arm and he stopped her before she could cover herself. She blushed and bit her lip as she peered at him from behind hair that was loose and messy, framing her flushed face. Her curves were ample and soft, pale where she had protected herself from the sun. Mesmerizing.

He was humbled in that moment by her innocent beauty. By the feminine grace of her.

As he absorbed that this sensual, glorious woman belonged to him, it struck him that if he had grown up on their island, he might have been the one to take her virginity. Would he have married her? Had a lifetime with her?

It was a disturbing thought, like believing in fate, but it just went to show that the mistake he had made that day with his father continued to have repercussions.

He felt like a thief then, like he was stealing something he wasn't supposed to have.

He had long ago learned to live in the moment, however, not pine for what had been or what could be. He and Calli had an agreement. They had six months.

He would enjoy every one of them.

If it was possible to be punch-drunk from lovemaking, Calli was exactly that by the time they arrived in New York. They had even made love on the plane, since Stavros had a private jet with a stateroom.

When Calli thought back to her awkward fumblings with Brandon, something she'd done to feel close to a boy who had dazzled her, there was no comparison. It was the same act in name only.

Stavros took pains to make her soar, almost like it was a contest. Like every single time he was proving to her that he could make her feel like that. He seemed to take incredible pleasure in it, which was addictive in another way. She feared she was becoming infatuated, because how could she not fall for a man who provided such intense gratification with such delight in such an intimate way?

At the same time, the feeling that she was bought and paid for grew. When they had taken a break from lovemaking, their honeymoon had consisted of a lot of shopping. Obscenely decadent amounts of shopping.

She had protested, claiming the dresses, shoes and jewelry weren't necessary, but he had insisted. *We'll have a lot of appearances. You'll need to look the part.*

She wasn't his real wife. He wasn't spoiling her because he wanted to. He was paying her to be something he needed.

The number of parcels that had been loaded onto the plane had made her feel uncomfortable, especially when he had called for a particular bag from a lingerie boutique to be brought into the cabin.

I want to see you in the red set.

Try as she might to feel objectified by that, when he had skimmed his lips along the lace at her hips, drawing it down oh-so-slowly, she had begged for the pleasure of his tongue. Twice.

She was losing herself. It was especially disturbing because, despite the intensity of time they were spending together and the physical familiarity they had arrived at, she still felt as though he was a stranger. Especially once he dressed in a tailored suit on the plane and began firing orders at everyone from his driver to the people he spoke with on the phone as they drove into Manhattan.

Somehow she had failed to fully appreciate how rich and powerful Stavros was. Yes, he had bought her countless gowns and dresses from boutiques and salons in Paris, but she hadn't seen any price tags. She had told herself they couldn't be that expensive.

She knew they were. She read gossip magazines. She knew designer dresses could make mortgage payments for average people like her. One bra alone had been her weekly salary. Stavros had bought it in every color.

She was in a state of denial because she couldn't believe she was awake, not dreaming this ridiculous charade she had put herself in.

When they arrived at a freestanding mansion in the middle of the city, however, she began to fully take in what kind of family she had married into. What kind of *money*. The bricks of the three-story house were a mellowed, burnt orange in the fading sun of the summer evening. The white detailing gave it an elegant Mediterranean feel. It had a proper stone balustrade surrounding a private garden and a wrought iron gate that didn't make a sound as Stavros held it open for her, allowing her to precede him up the stone path lined with fragrant lavender and thyme.

"This is your home?"

"My grandfather's town house. He stays here three nights a week and spends the rest of the week upstate. I did the same until I had access to my trust and bought my penthouse."

"You have a penthouse? In New York?"

"I have several." He shrugged it off as no big deal. "Simpson." Stavros greeted the man who opened the front door before they finished climbing the steps.

"Master Michaels. Welcome." He greeted Calli with a nod and showed them down the hall. He knocked briefly, then entered a den, announcing, "Your grandson, sir."

The elderly man leaned forward to press a button that muted the television, not rising until he saw Stavros had company. He was heavyset with age, but moved spryly and had an old-world stateliness to his handsome features. The Xenakis genes aged well. Stavros would grow more good-looking over time, as if he needed any more advantages.

"Will you be dining with us, sir?" Simpson asked.

"No, we'll have a proper family dinner later in the week, with my mother and sisters. This is a courtesy visit. To introduce my wife. Edward Michaels, Calli Xenakis."

The old man straightened another inch, plainly astonished.

The rest of what Stavros said should have been directed at the butler, but Stavros's hard stare remained locked with his grandfather's.

"You'll refer to both of us by our Greek names from now on."

If Calli had landed in a state of denial, she was nursing white-hot anger by the time she stood in the lounge of one of Stavros's many penthouses. Uniformed staff finished unloading her parcels from a dolly, hurrying to finish before tugging their caps as they left.

She dragged her gaze off the open-plan main floor with its ultramodern furniture in masculine tones of charcoal and silver. The stairs climbed at different angles to multiple levels, pausing on a landing where a small sitting room provided a space to enjoy the expansive view over the city through the massive wall of windows. The uppermost flight of stairs ended in a loft she presumed was the bedroom.

"Don't worry about unpacking. People will be here tomorrow."

"People. More bodies you've purchased for use?" She stared with contempt at the mountain of parcels piled up like stacks of money against the wall. Another rich playboy who did as he pleased. She had pegged him right from the first, but had still fallen for his line. She really was the stupidest woman alive.

"Explain that remark." His tone might have scared her if she wasn't so appalled. And hurt. Profoundly hurt.

"You picked me specifically to annoy your grandfather!"

Greece? That's where you've been?

She had seen the disapproval in the old man's eyes. The flinch as Stavros revealed she had been born on "his" island, like he knew it would get at the old man as nothing else could. The way Edward had stood there, silent and baleful as some kind of silent war raged between them, had stung like a snakebite.

"I *paid* you to annoy him." He waved at the parcels. "And I've included a tip."

"Why would I wear any of that when the point is to embarrass him? To *be* an embarrassment." Humiliation choked off her voice, burning hotly behind her eyes. "That's an ugly thing to do to someone. I'm not going to be part of it."

She moved to stab the button that called the private elevator.

"We have an agreement." He pushed a button labeled Cancel, then leaned on the wall next to it, blocking her from hitting the call button again. "A legally binding contract."

"That's what happens when you shop the bargain basement, *Steve*. You don't get the longevity you expect from the item. Move." She jerked her chin, wanting to punch right through him to the button he was blocking.

"Don't call me that," Stavros growled, prickling with what might have been his conscience.

"Don't call you Steve? It's better than what I want to call

you. I'd take it, if I were you. *Move*." She dodged behind him, but he only flattened his back on the panel, aware he was being juvenile, but he hadn't expected this.

"You're overreacting."

"I'm reacting with the exact amount of outrage that is appropriate. You lied to me. You are exactly like the entitled, superficial jerk who ruined my life the first time." She pulled out her cell phone.

"Who are you calling?" As if he didn't know. It made him see red.

"I let myself believe you were better than you are." Disillusion put a ragged edge on her voice. "You knew I wanted to come to New York and you used that not just to advance your interests, but to belittle me."

He took her phone and her arm, turning her toward the sofa. "Come here."

"Don't you touch me." She shook free of his hold.

For one second, he stared down a look of genuine violence. He wasn't scared, precisely. He didn't expect she could hurt him beyond a few scratches or bruises, but he was taken aback by how deep her rage ran. How anguished she looked at the same time.

"You dragged me here with a promise of something that means *everything* to me—" She bit her lip, arms straight at her sides.

"Yes. Exactly what is that?" he demanded, looming over her so he could see into her eyes.

She ignored the question, throwing out her hand in a wild wave. "Just so you could parade me in front of your grandfather as something shameful. I can get that by going home to my father, thanks. Go to hell with your arrangement. *Steve*."

They had more to discuss, but "Last one." He pointed in warning. "I mean that." If he had come away with nothing else from Sebastien's challenge, he had at least reclaimed himself.

"Steve! Steve, Steve, Steve, Steve, Steve, Steve!"

He wanted to crush the word right out of her, but kept himself just this side of civilized as he gave her a deadly stare. "Use the name you call me when I'm inside you."

Her pupils expanded and a shadow of betrayal moved within them, dimming the angry light in her golden eyes. "Don't. Just admit you're a bastard."

"Not by birth, but definitely by nature," he agreed, moving closer. "Now call me by my proper name. My real name, *glykia mou*. Or I'll make you. You know I can." He was pretty sure he could. He had spent most of their honeymoon learning how to wring the prettiest noises possible from her.

Her jaw set and lifted as he came into her space. She glared up at him, mouth tight, hands still fisted at her sides. "Give me back my phone."

"You do not get to call your guard dog every time we have a disagreement."

"It's not a disagreement. You *lied*."

"I told you I wanted to marry you for this." He shaped the air closest to her body, deliberately keeping his hands in the space where the heat exchanged, but they didn't touch. Her nipples peaked as though he fondled her, though. Her breath changed and he knew by the way her thighs twitched that she pulsed in a way that echoed the tightening in his own groin.

"You said…" She swallowed, gaze clouding. "You said you wanted…"

He waited, feeling the pull of satisfaction in the corners of his mouth when she couldn't remember what they were talking about. Neither could he.

"I want *you*," he told her. Truthfully. With gut-wrenching honesty, if she only knew it. "Open your dress."

She breathed loud enough for him to hear it. Her mouth trembled.

"Why are you doing this?" she said with a helpless pang.

He cupped her cheek and stepped close enough to drop his head and capture her lips. No resistance, just pure, hot response as she welcomed him. He stole greedily past her teeth with his tongue, fingers dispatching her buttons with more urgency than finesse.

Her hands went into his hair as her dress fell open. He released her bra and took possession of her breasts, loving her groan of abject pleasure as he found both her nipples and rolled his thumbs over the pert tips.

Bending, he stole a taste of each one, wanting to linger, but wanting other things. The win. Total surrender. He turned her away from him.

"Put your hands on the wall."

She did, breath ragged as she placed each palm flat on either side of the call button on the brushed-nickel panel next to the elevator. As he ran his hands up under her skirt and caught at the lace that was soaked with her response, his breath hissed in, hot and fiery, burning his chest. He lingered to caress her slippery folds, watching her back bow and shudder, feeling her cling to his light penetration.

"More?" He barely choked out the word. "You want me?"

"Yes." She arched as he brought her skirt all the way up to her waist and caressed the smooth globes of her ass.

"Say it." He ruthlessly clung to control. Of himself. Her. But rationality was disappearing behind stark need. "Ask me for what you want. Ask *me*."

"Use a condom."

He tightened his fingertips into her hips, so aroused by

her words of permission he nearly went blind, but fought it, not certain he could keep himself from taking her without getting what he wanted first.

Then he heard her moan, "Please, Stavros…"

CHAPTER SIX

SHE WOKE ALONE in the bed. The humid scent of a recent shower drifted from the open door of the bathroom.

Her whole body protested when she sat up, muscles aching from exertion, brain lethargic from heavy sleep. She couldn't help a small whimper as she swung her feet to the floor and sat there naked on the side of the bed, feeling profoundly alone.

"Sore?"

She flashed a look into the dark cavern of the walk in closet, heart leaping in surprise. He was naked, but there was no reading his expression or even the tone of that one word. Concerned? Smug? She couldn't tell.

He'd been insatiable last night, but there'd been something in his desire for her that had made him undeniable. She knew there was something in his name, his relationship with his grandfather, something that pierced into the very heart of him.

She had felt him trying to exorcise it last night, as he had immersed himself in their lovemaking, not taking, but giving, again and again. His concentrated attention, his words of praise and pleasure, had been reassuring and compelling, but what had really kept her as lost to passion as he was had been that layer of inner pain she couldn't reach.

Succor. They had sought that together last night.

In the light of day, she still felt flaunted as something substandard, though.

She pulled the edge of the sheet across herself. It was a flimsy shield.

He finished pulling on his shorts and skimmed a white business shirt from a hanger. He shrugged into it as he came into the bedroom.

"I'll start a bath for you. Tell me next time if it's getting to be too much."

She snorted. "How does that go?"

"You say, 'Stavros, it's too much. Go to sleep.'" He moved into the bathroom and she heard the water turn on.

She hung her head in her hands, thinking that he might be able to turn his libido off and on like a tap, but hers wasn't so easily controlled. Not by her at least. By him... God, she hated herself right now, pleasures of the night notwithstanding.

She felt the weight of his stare as he returned. She lifted her head to see him buttoning his cuffs. He moved his sure fingers down the front of his chest.

"It's because you're Greek."

"The lack of stopping sense?"

He snorted. "That, too, since I don't possess any, either, but no. I meant my grandfather's disapproval."

He moved back into the closet, where he stepped into a pair of gray pants. He came out threading a belt through the loops, then stood before her as he tucked in his shirt.

"He's the son of an immigrant. Loves everything about being American. My father was visiting relatives when he met my mother. She's very traditional and wanted us raised in Greece. My grandfather wanted us here, so my father could help him expand the pharmacy chain his own father had started. They were developing laboratories, chasing patents." He zipped and buckled. "There was a lot of push-pull between them."

He fetched a blue tie and tied it without a mirror, inscrutable gaze fixed on her.

"After my father died, my grandfather brought us here and closed the door on Greece. My mother went back to see relatives every year and I've been to Athens for business, but my stint as your pool man was my first trip back to our island. My sisters and I spoke Greek to each other as a small rebellion growing up, and I purposely hired a Greek PA so I could keep up the language, but my grandfather has always insisted we speak to him in English. He wanted us to be American and made us answer to our American names. Steven. I've always hated it."

He disappeared into the bathroom and the rush of water stopped. He came back and smoothly picked her up.

"What— I can walk!"

"You can't sit there naked and not expect me to want to touch you, *koukla mou.*"

"I wasn't inviting you to."

"No, you were remembering how angry you are. You probably wouldn't have let me touch you at all if I had given you a choice." He gently set her on her feet beside the steaming tub.

She hugged herself, feeling horribly exposed, standing there naked, staring at his tie, knotted perfectly. All of him was perfect. On the surface anyway.

His thumb touched the corner of her mouth where it tugged down.

"I wasn't throwing you in his face so much as asserting my will. That always annoys him. I want you, Calli. I think I've made that obvious."

"And I can't resist you. A match made in heaven. For

you." She hated that she was so defenseless with him. She was raw and vulnerable while he had everything.

He made a noise and took her jaw in his strong hand. His touch was gentle as he forced her to look up at him. His thumb scraped lightly across her tender mouth.

"He and I have a contentious relationship. I can't tell you the number of times he has threatened to disinherit me—which means yanking the financial rug from beneath my mother and sisters. So I do as he wishes, but in my own way. Yes, I knew he would be angry that I'd gone to the island to find my wife. I didn't do it to hurt or humiliate you, though."

"You still accomplished both of those things." She pulled out of his touch. "But it's only for six months." She could endure it. What was a few months of insult against six years of missing her son? She stepped into the tub and lowered, exhaling as the warm water closed over her. She brought her knees up and hugged them.

Stavros hesitated with his hand in the air before he let it fall to his side.

"I have to go. I've been away from the office too long and I'm holding my grandfather to his promise, now that I've fulfilled his demand." His mouth pulled up, but he didn't show his teeth. It wasn't a smile. "Enjoy the city today."

Stavros deliberately went to his grandfather's office—the one he would claim, now that he was married. He arrived before the old man and waited there for him.

He hadn't lied to Calli. He had a ton of neglected work to clear up, much of it due to Sebastien's challenge. He should be at his desk, but he also needed this quiet few minutes to process his behavior last night. He wasn't an animal, but he'd been completely unable to leave her alone.

She had let him make love to her until they were both wrung out, so he shouldn't feel guilty, but he did.

Hell, he knew why he felt guilty. *You still accomplished both those things.* Hurt and humiliation.

He rubbed the back of his neck, arms aching, shoulders aching. He had held back his own pleasure again and again, determined to give her as much as he could. To bind her to him. He had thought she was with him every step of the way, but this morning she had made it sound like she hated herself for giving in to him.

That she looked down on herself for it.

When *she* talked of their six months, she made it sound like she couldn't wait for it to be over.

The door behind him clicked and he turned, ready for confrontation, fueled with Calli's dented self-esteem.

"Measuring the windows for new drapes?" Edward asked.

"You know me so well." Stavros went to the wet bar to pour the coffee Edward's assistant had started when she'd let him in.

"Long way to go for a wife," Edward said as Stavros brought the coffee over and took the chair in front of the desk.

"I was there on a dare. Sebastien bet me I couldn't go two weeks without my credit cards. A trial run of living without my fortune, if you will. Disinherit away. I'll survive."

"That's a bluff," Edward said confidently, adding under his breath, "Sebastien. When are you going to grow up and quit risking your life at whatever that man suggests?"

"Today," Stavros said, deeply facetious. "I'm married now and ready to take the Dýnami reins."

"Who is she?" Edward sipped his coffee.

Stavros couldn't bring himself to say "nobody." His

conscience wouldn't let him reduce Calli to that. "The love of my life, of course."

"Is she?" Edward drilled holes with his hard brown eyes.

It was a familiar look, filled with expectations Stavros could never meet. He wasn't his father. Never would be. It was his fault that his father wasn't sitting in this chair, staring into those eyes.

Stavros had been staring down that expression for nearly two decades, but today, quite suddenly, Calli's voice said in his head, *You're looking in a mirror.*

Which was disconcerting. It didn't even make sense.

Edward swore under his breath before nodding decisively. "Very well. I take you at your word, Stev— *Stavros.*" He flinched as he spoke the name that belonged to his dead son. "Pick a date for my departure and make the announcements. The company is yours."

The moment should have been a triumph. It was anticlimactic. Stavros was used to fighting bitterly to get what he wanted. Edward Michaels rolled over for no one.

So, even as his grandfather told him to put the wheels into motion to replace him, Stavros's knee-jerk reaction was to refuse. *I'm lying,* he wanted to say. *Fight me. Don't let me have it. Tell me I don't deserve it.*

He really was a perverse jackass.

He made himself stand and shake his grandfather's hand.

When had they last shaken hands? The old man's skin felt papery and his grip wasn't as strong as it used to be.

Quite suddenly, Stavros felt like a bully, like he was taking something from someone weaker.

"Thank you," Stavros said, disturbed, and left.

They had formal photographs taken on Friday morning, ones that would accompany the press release that afternoon. Immediately afterward, Stavros drove them to the family estate, Galíni, which was Greek for *tranquility*. The mansion, nestled on groomed grounds and surrounded by eighty-some acres of forest, was set apart and quiet, and it screamed of tasteful extravagance.

At only fifty years old, the house seemed even older, given the charm and attention to detail. Calli walked into a foyer of mosaic tiles and a stained-glass skylight over a grand staircase. "Only" ten bedrooms, Stavros told her, but each had a private bath, balcony and small sitting room. More of a suite, she deduced, as he showed her to the one they would share. He suggested she change into swimwear since they would join his sisters by the pool.

They spoke to his mother first. She was a stunning woman who welcomed Calli warmly. By the time they went outside to meet his sisters, who also greeted her with delight and natural curiosity, Calli was beginning to feel like a terrible fraud.

"You should tell them," she said to Stavros when they changed for dinner.

"Tell who what?"

"Your family. That I'm not...real. I mean, they acted so surprised. Shocked, actually. Like, even though your grandfather told you to get married, they didn't expect you would."

His mouth twitched. "He and I are renowned for our power struggles." It didn't sound like a lie, but she sensed it wasn't the whole truth.

"I meant that they seemed to think you wouldn't get married ever. Not for any reason." She waited, but he let that speculation hang in the air. "Is that *true*?" she finally prompted.

"Yes." He said it flatly. "But he was adamant he wouldn't

hand over the reins until I had a plan for the next generation. I found a workaround." He waved at her.

She wanted to ask why he was so dead set against marriage. Didn't everyone want to find a mate and form some kind of lifelong commitment?

But his dismissal of her as a "workaround" made her feel insignificant all over again. Like the fake she was.

"Well, they're tripping over themselves to be nice to me, acting like you must have really fallen for me. You should tell them it's not like that and they shouldn't get attached. Otherwise it will be hard when it's over."

"Is this because my sister offered to show you around the city? She paints. She loves walking around with a camera, scouting new subjects and locations. That is why you married me, isn't it? To see the city?"

Calli kept to herself that she could care less about sightseeing. As he glanced over his shoulder at her, she turned to fetch a different bra from the drawer, even though the one she wore was perfectly fine.

She let go of that conversation and was happy when they returned to the penthouse the next afternoon so they could attend their first public function as husband and wife.

A whirlwind of social engagements kept them busy for the next two weeks. They barely had a moment alone outside the bedroom, but at least she was able to advance her search for Dorian.

During the day, when she had the privacy of an empty penthouse, she stalked her paramour online, refreshing her knowledge of his family, searching his online photo albums for a six-year-old boy—all to no avail. If Brandon's relatives had taken him, they kept their privacy settings locked down tight. The connection wasn't obvious.

She made do with memorizing where Brandon grew up and where he had gone to school—Yale—along with the year he'd graduated and the names of his classmates and social circles. He bred thoroughbreds for racing, so there were a lot of references to tracks and derbies. She had just missed the Belmont Stakes and any chance of "bumping into him" there, damn it.

His family had made their fortune during prohibition, she learned, then turned their name into blue-blood, upper-crust American aristocracy. His father was a lawyer turned senator, his mother a homemaker and charity fund-raiser. They attended church, belonged to the right clubs, and knew the right people.

They *were* the right people. Four years ago, Brandon had kick-started his own political career with an interim council position. During the election, rumors had swirled about gambling debts and a thrown race, but they hadn't been proved. He was engaged to the daughter of a Washington insider and they lived in Manhattan. He had his sights set on the next election cycle for state representative and was currently on vacation at Martha's Vineyard.

If she could have gone there, if she could simply show up on his doorstep and confront him, Calli would have. Sadly, her previous attempts to contact him had resulted in cease-and-desist orders. A surprise face-to-face on neutral ground was her only choice.

She moved through the various cocktail parties and art exhibits, the ballrooms and living rooms, feeling as though she was playing one of those tile games that shifted one to make room for another. As she went along, she made a mental note of each name, trying to find a connection to Brandon, trying to figure out how she would rearrange these smaller abstract pieces into a bigger, clearer picture.

It wasn't easy when she also had to contend with sugar-coated glares of hostility from all the women who had thought they had a chance at the most eligible bachelor in America. If she had a dollar for every "Congratulations" that dripped poison, she would be as rich as her husband.

As for her marriage, it was the furthest thing from what she had imagined for herself. She hadn't aspired to marry, but when she had imagined such a thing, it had always been a love marriage that included romantic acts of intimate sharing, physical and emotional.

With Stavros, sex was a kind of delirium, the intensity growing rather than abating as time wore on. It was disturbing. Each morning, after giving up another piece of her soul to him during the night, she shored up her inner walls and distanced herself as much as she could.

If he noticed, he didn't let on. Perhaps it didn't bother him. He was focused on work and the new responsibilities he had taken on. He didn't talk to her about it and she didn't ask. She played her part, pretended she didn't feel the daggers or overhear the gossip about herself in the ladies' room. She went shopping when his sisters suggested she join in, and attended lunch when his mother invited her, all without prying beyond what they offered openly. Not because she wasn't curious. She longed to know more about her husband, but she also knew it was pointless. This was temporary.

She was here to find her son. If the emptiness of her marriage made her sad and bereft, well, she had lived in that state for a long time already. She could handle it.

Then finally, a breakthrough.

"I'm sorry," she said as she processed what the man next to her had just said. "Did you say your old rowing team would be there?"

"From my Yale days, yes. The regatta is our annual get-together. Heavy fines if you don't show for the kick-off party." He touched the side of his nose and winked.

"We all have to sail with a hangover. Otherwise it's not a level playing field."

Hilarious. She wondered how many people drowned each year.

"What a lovely tradition," she said with the social grace she had learned while hosting for Takis and had honed as Stavros's wife. "Who are your teammates? Have I met any of them?" Her heart began to thud and roll, like paddles hitting the water and pushing through the weight of waves.

Stavros couldn't take his eyes off the light in Calli's face—and his captivation had nothing to do with how attractive she was. Rather, it did, but it had its roots in the opposite side of admiration. Jealousy.

"What were you talking to Hemsworth about?" He skimmed off his tuxedo jacket and draped it over the chair near the window.

"Why don't you hang that?" She moved to do it.

"I pay the housekeeper to do it. She checks to see if it needs mending or cleaning. Leave it and answer the question."

Calli let go of the jacket and stiffened at his tone. "*Wally* Hemsworth?"

"Yes. You lit up like a Christmas tree. He was soaking it up. That was his wife with him, you know."

"Are you accusing me of flirting with a married man? In front of his wife?"

Her wide-eyed shock seemed genuine, but he only raised a brow. That was exactly what it had looked like she was doing. He still didn't know why she had married him and it was beginning to eat at him.

Her jaw moved in a small flinch. She slid her lashes down in what might have been an attempt to disguise hurt. She was the queen of disdain when she spoke, though.

"Last I checked, I was already married to the richest man in the city. What could Wally Hemsworth possibly have to offer beyond that? More sex? I don't think that's possible, is it?" She dropped her jewelry into a dish on the vanity.

"Is that a complaint? Am I making too many demands? You *respond*. If you ever turned me down, I might be able to control myself." He used a facetious drawl, but there was a hard core of truth in there. She flowered every single time he touched her and it was too enthralling to resist.

But that was all they had. Sex. He hadn't expected to find that infuriating, but it grated like sand in an oyster, always there, growing with layer upon layer of attempts to be ignored. She navigated a social event with ease, but gave up little about herself. When people asked him about her, he had few answers.

It left him feeling something he hadn't experienced even when he'd been in Greece, living on pennies. *Insecure*. He wasn't sure of her. It kept his gut in a state of tension and his libido at ten, constantly needing to reinforce their physical connection to ensure she was his.

His frustration sharpened his tone. "Then what were you talking about?"

"Nothing," she insisted, pulling the tie that had scooped her hair over her shoulder. "We talked about his time at Yale and the regatta next week. You said we were going to that, right?"

Her gaze ricocheted from the mirror to his like a bullet. "Yes. Why?"

She jerked a shoulder that didn't come off as casual. Not at all. "It sounds fun."

"Does it." His mind raced, looking for the missing puzzle piece. "Are you eager for some salt air? Because I notice you don't leave the apartment unless we have an engagement. Even then, you're resigned, not excited. I thought you married me so you could explore New York?"

She kept her back to him, gaze down, face stiff. "When I thought about living here, I always expected I would have to work. Since I don't have a job, I have no reason to go out."

"My sister said you turned down a shopping trip the other day."

"I didn't need anything. I wasn't trying to avoid her. I invited her to lunch."

She peeled off her gown, exposing her mouthwatering figure in a set of black lace shot with silver threads. A deliberate attempt to sidetrack him? If so, it was working. The way her thong framed her ass cheeks was positively erotic and nearly wiped his brain clean.

"Do you really want me to become BFFs with her? Maybe you should tell your family that this is a temporary thing, so they'll stop trying to form a relationship with me. That's why I don't enjoy our evenings out. I keep meeting new people, but a few months from now, I'll never see them again."

"You love to throw that in my face, don't you?"

"What?"

"How temporary our arrangement is. Is that what you were doing with Hemsworth? Putting your next paycheck in place?"

"For God's sake, no! And do you have any idea how offensive you're being? Every time we're out, I have to face ugly looks and snide remarks about how I'm your quaint little wife from the old country. I lack taste and polish. I'm a social climber. Your grandfather forced you to marry me, since you couldn't possibly have *chosen* me."

"Who said that?" He scowled, instantly affronted on her behalf.

"Do you think I bother to learn the names of the cats in the powder room who make sure I overhear them? *Do* let me put their curiosity to rest, though. How *do* you bring yourself to sleep with such a filthy immigrant?"

"Who said *that*?" His blood nearly boiled out his ears.

"You have quite the reputation. Did you really work your way through a sorority house in a weekend? Because that makes you quite the hypocrite for objecting to my *talking* to one other man."

She swung away and charged into the closet. He heard a drawer open and slam shut.

He swore and pinched the bridge of his nose. He had done some tremendously stupid things as a young man. He doubted he would earn any points by telling her it had been a bet and a dare, and the house had been only half full because the girls who weren't interested in testing his stamina had left.

"You should have told me that was happening," he said when she reappeared in a decidedly unsexy T-shirt and leggings that sent a loud message about her receptiveness to his advances tonight.

"Why? Those women are nothing to me." She hugged herself in the defensive way she did sometimes, like she was huddling against more rain than a person should be forced to endure. "In a few months, I'll never see them again. I'm not throwing that in your face. I'm reminding myself why it doesn't matter. I don't have any claim on you. This isn't my life."

His throat clogged with words, but he couldn't articulate them, couldn't agree or disagree.

"Our arrangement is a trade-off." Her brow flinched. "What do I care what small minds think of me, as long as I get what I want?"

"What *do* you want?" It wasn't the money he had promised her. It wasn't the most exciting city in the world.

For a moment she looked stark with hopelessness, then turned away. "What do you care, so long as you have what you want?"

She didn't wait for his response, only went into the bathroom to brush her teeth.

She made a good point. He stood there listening to the water run, wondering why he *did* care. Wondering why it felt like he *didn't* have what he wanted when, to the outside observer, he had everything.

CHAPTER SEVEN

CALLI WAS SO keyed up, she could hardly think straight.

She had obsessed over every detail of the coming evening. Her gown was the most quietly powerful in the closet, dark blue with an empire waist and a sheer white overlay on the bodice, suggesting royal elegance. She usually did her own makeup, but today she had splurged at a local spa, spending some of her allowance on a stylist who did her hair, as well. Wearing her tallest shoes, she was flawless and proud.

In the mirror.

Inside her clammy skin, her bones rattled with nerves.

Brandon, she would say, looking him right in the eye. *You probably don't remember me. We met years ago and I was deeply in love with the boy who left Greece with you. Dorian. How is he? Where is he?*

It almost didn't matter what he said or did after that. She just wanted to see his face. She wanted him to know she wasn't going away this time. He couldn't pretend he didn't know her, couldn't pretend they hadn't made a baby.

He couldn't even pretend ignorance about the way the adoption had happened. Letters had been sent since then. He *knew* she hadn't consented to the surrender of custody.

The jig was up. *Now* things would be different.

After tonight, she would finally have some answers.

It made her hands feel cold and disconnected from her body. Her heart raced and tripped in her chest. Her mouth was dry, her stomach in knots.

Nervously, she swept open her phone and checked Brandon's social media profile. His last post had been an exchange of comments with Wally Hemsworth, demanding Wally pony up a drink that was owed.

She scrolled to Brandon's profile picture, taking in the subtle changes six years had wrought. It was a professional headshot suitable for a politician. Handsome, she supposed.

Did her son resemble him? Her?

"Who's that?"

Stavros's voice startled her so badly, she let out a small scream and dropped her phone.

Stavros swept down to pick it up off the carpet and turned it over. His dark brows lowered into an accusatory line. "Brandon Underwood?"

It was Wally Hemsworth all over again. It was her father, with his repulsed glare as he pronounced her loose and shameful. She looked away from the sharp query in Stavros's eyes.

"I'm just—" She held out her hand, unable to think of a suitable excuse. Her hand shook. She swallowed. "Can I have that, please?"

"Do you know him?"

"Do *you*?"

"We cross paths sometimes." He didn't give her back the phone. The silence became deafening.

"I knew him a long time ago." She wiggled her fingers.

"Have you been in contact with him?"

"No."

He looked at the screen as though deciding whether to check her messages.

"I haven't," she insisted.

"This is it, isn't it? The reason you wanted to come to New York." He tilted the screen. "He's the tourist. The one who got you kicked out of your home. You're still carrying a torch? You seriously married me to get to him?" His voice tightened. "That's beyond obsessive."

"It's none of your business, Stavros." She held out her hand.

"You're my *wife*."

"By contract. You got what you wanted. Now give me what I want." She pointed at the phone, even though the phone had nothing to do with it.

He let his hand drop to his side, keeping the phone while he looked at her like some kind of veil had been pulled away and he didn't even recognize her.

It made her squirm, but she brushed aside whatever he was thinking of her. Her palms were sweating with anxiety. Tonight was her night. She *would* have it.

"I have to smile at your past lovers every time we go out. You can get through one night seeing mine."

"Like hell I do. He's *engaged*."

"I just want to talk to him." She stepped forward to take her phone.

He pulled back, yanking on her heartstrings with the movement so every part of her stung.

"Give me that."

"No."

He'd bought it for her, so she could hardly protest that it was hers. Tears smarted behind her eyes. She shrugged, trying to keep her control from shredding while her inner trembling grew worse.

"Fine. Keep it." She moved to pick up her handbag and made sure her credit card was in it. "Are we going? Or am I asking the doorman to call me a cab?"

"We're not going anywhere. You lied to me, Calli. That

was your rule. No lies. You didn't tell me why you wanted to come to New York."

"Because it's none of your business."

"It is *literally* my business. My grandfather would love an excuse to back out of the handover. I'm not watching you hook up with your old flame while putting my control of my *business* in jeopardy."

"Stavros." She turned to face him, elbows snapping straight at her sides as she turned her mind from anything but the tiny bridge she had glimpsed, the one that should take her to her son. Why was it starting to look like a mirage? Like the more she tried to reach it, the farther away it became. "This is not negotiable. I'm going to see Brandon tonight. That's happening."

It was the uncompromising tone she had developed as Ophelia's nanny, but Stavros was no adolescent girl.

He pocketed her phone, voice steely. "No. You're not."

"Watch me," she bit out, and turned to the elevator.

"Don't bother calling a cab. One word from me and you're off the guest list at the dinner. You won't be allowed in."

It was a slap. Yet another door slammed in her face before she could take two steps on her quest. She turned.

"Don't. You. Dare." Her ears rang, like they were straining for the sound of Dorian's cry. She could almost hear him. That was why she had woken, that last morning. She had heard him, but it was a distant sound and growing fainter. He wasn't dead. He was moving beyond her reach. Was that the thump of helicopter blades? Or her panicked heart?

She would *not* go through this again. Not when she was so close this time. Desperation pushed her forward, right up into his space.

"Do *not* stop me seeing Brandon or I will go directly

to your grandfather and tell him what a sham this marriage is." The words tripped and hissed, stumbling over a tongue growing thick in her mouth.

"Well, you've tipped your hand, haven't you?" He clasped her arms. "If you're going to make those sorts of threats, I'll put you on a plane back to Greece right now, and tell my grandfather whatever the hell I want."

"Oh, will you!" She slapped at his touch, shaking him off. "Like I haven't been *there* before. For the *same reason*. How dare you try to stop me? How *dare* you?"

"Calm down," he growled.

"Throw me out, then!" Fury erupted from the pit of her being, rising to consume her, just like that midnight confrontation with her father. "You want to tell me my baby is dead, too? Then blacken my eye? It adds a nice touch of ugly desperation when you offer to prostitute yourself. Go ahead! I'll need it out there." She pointed wildly to the window and the bleak streets below.

He recoiled. "What the hell are you talking about?"

She wanted to smash him in the face.

"What baby?" he ground out.

"*My* baby," she cried, hurling the words like hand grenades.

She stood outside herself. She'd been out of control in those early hours of the morning, too. Years of toeing the line around a father who was quick to correct with a swing of his arm had disappeared. She hadn't cared that she was pushing him past his limits. She had only wanted her son back. She had wanted her father to quit saying those awful words about Dorian being dead.

"Brandon *took* him. I've been trying to find him for *six years* and I finally have a chance to confront him, but you—"

She swiped at an irritating tickle on her cheek. Her

trembling fingertips came away smeared with black. She was crying. That was why her throat felt like it was made of broken glass. Her chest was under a piano, so tight she couldn't draw a breath that didn't hiss.

Her makeup was ruined and when she looked down, she saw little dots of charcoal had dripped to stain her dress. Even if she somehow pulled her appearance together, she couldn't confront Brandon with her emotions in tatters.

This latest chance was dissolving, just like all the rest. How had she let herself believe this time was different from the others?

Why did it always end like this?

She lifted her gaze, letting Stavros see how shattered she was. How betrayed she was by his refusal to compromise. His imposition of his will.

His act of cruelty.

"I got you what you wanted, but *you*... You're just like Brandon. Your precious life has to be protected at the expense of everyone else's, doesn't it? I knew what you were when I saw you, but I still—"

He jerked his head back, expression stunned, like she *had* punched him in the face.

She might have wondered how her words had struck so deeply if she hadn't been so devastated herself.

"I hate you. I hate *myself*."

He followed her to the bedroom. She had black tears dripping off her chin, and she yanked at her stained gown. Wisps of her hair were coming out of its upswept knot.

"Calli—"

"Leave me alone." Her voice was thick with rejection.

His heart lurched. He was at an utter loss. What the hell? Was this even real? A *baby*?

"Are you going to make me beg? You love it when I

do that, don't you? Fine. I'm begging you, Stavros. Please leave me alone."

Her broken words were the flash burn of a Molotov cocktail to the chest, leaving a hot, gaping hole where his heart resided. He stared at the traumatized woman before him and the look in her eyes snapped something in him. Something that had been golden and bright, something he hadn't even realized had come to exist between them, or even how precious it was.

It was gone now. Incinerated.

He could hardly breathe, but he made himself turn and leave. He made himself give her this one little thing she wanted. Had begged for.

Your precious life has to be protected at the expense of everyone else's, doesn't it?

His father had told him to swim for shore. He had said he would be right behind Stavros. But he hadn't been. The waves had been three feet high. After one glance back, Stavros hadn't risked another. His life vest had been the only thing that saved him, buoying him to the surface each time the waves plunged him under.

Calli couldn't know that she had scored such a mortal blow with her words, but Stavros reeled under the denunciation. *He* was to blame for his father's death. He knew that.

He was still as selfish as that boy who had saved his own life at the expense of his father's. Just look at his reaction tonight. He knew what he had with Calli was more than he had a right to. He kept telling himself it was a quid pro quo arrangement. That was how he justified enjoying her. How he justified playing house in a way he had long written off, not feeling entitled to it.

He poured himself a glass of the red wine that was open, bottle clinking against the glass as he relived that moment of seeing her interest in Brandon. Jealousy had seared through him. The depth that those talons had sunk into him unnerved him and he took a quick sip, wishing it was stronger, strong enough to burn the tension from the back of his throat.

He had ruthlessly shut down their evening because he had felt, yes, that his precious time with her was threatened.

He was still jealous. She had a son. With Brandon Underwood.

Once again he found himself wondering how his life would have been different if he had stayed on the island. Would that boy be his?

A fresh snap sounded and his palm stung. Red wine soaked past the shards of glass in his skin, changing shade as blood rose to mingle with the dripping liquid.

Stavros swore and went to find the first-aid kit, leaving bloodstains on the tile.

There had been days over the years when Calli had let herself hope. Times when she had a little money saved, or Takis sent a letter, or some other thing happened and she would let herself believe that her time of waiting was coming to an end. She would see Dorian again. Soon.

Then the other shoe would drop. Her dreams would be dashed and she would be overcome with grief all over again, crying so hard she was sure her lifetime allotment was used up.

Each time, once the storm passed, she was left hollowed out and desolate. Then, very slowly, she would gather herself and make a new plan.

So she knew it wasn't over. It would never be over. If she didn't have another chance tomorrow, she would make one for herself the next day, or someday far in the future. She had done this before, too many times to count.

It took courage to work herself up to taking action,

though, especially when the disappointment was so profound when it didn't work out. So she didn't try to make a new plan tonight. Tomorrow she would figure out how to proceed. Tonight was for accepting she had lost.

Again.

Footsteps sounded on the stairs to the loft. She remembered where she was, curled up in the corner of the settee in the dark of Stavros's penthouse bedroom. She had let her gown fall to the floor and stepped out of it, then wrapped a blanket around her while she cried. Now she was aching in the aftermath, filled with despair, blinking to focus her swollen eyes on the lights of the city laid out like a carpet of stars below her. Her heart weighed heavily in her chest.

Stavros had threatened to send her back to Greece, she recalled, which didn't sound so bad, actually. Takis would take her in. She could see Ophelia. At least she had that. She was terribly lonely here.

She glanced burning eyes toward the closet, wondering what she should pack. Her brain conjured nothing.

"It's late. I thought you'd be asleep," Stavros said.

She was tired. So tired.

So sad.

"I just wanted to ask him where Dorian was taken." Her voice barely functioned beyond a whisper, flaky and dry. "Where he is now. That's all."

She heard his breath hiss in, like her words had struck and hurt, but what did he know about pain?

"It wasn't about sex or getting back together with him. I would never see Brandon again if I had a choice, but he's the only one who can tell me what happened. His lawyers have been saying for years that nothing even happened between us, but a baby isn't nothing."

Stavros moved to stand behind her. She sensed his hand gripping the back of the settee near her shoulder.

"No," he agreed solemnly. "No, it's not."

"He can't say he didn't know how I got pregnant or by who. I called him and told him it was his. He offered to send money for an abortion. When I refused, he offered to pay me off if I kept quiet. He didn't want his parents to know, but my father contacted them once he realized I was pregnant. He figured they would pay more than Brandon had offered, and I guess they did."

She swallowed, recalling how sordid she had felt by it all, how she had begged her father to stay out of it.

"I didn't want *money*, especially when they said I would have to give him up. I thought Brandon loved me, that he would want to get married, but he just wanted me to go away."

"But he did want the baby?" Stavros spoke low and level, getting the facts. "He must have, if he took him."

She plucked her words from a maelstrom of deep, twisted emotions. Each extraction was agony. "Since he doesn't appear to have a son, I would say no, he did not want our baby."

"But you're certain he took him?"

"Someone did."

"Who?"

"Exactly." Her voice caught and she had to clear her throat. She snugged the blanket higher around her shoulders and neck. "Dorian was two weeks old and I woke up because I heard him crying. He wasn't in his bassinet. I went to the kitchen and my father was up, even though it was two o'clock in the morning. He said Dorian had died. I mean, really? I ran outside and I could hear a car engine. Our place was near the private airfield and a few minutes later I heard the helicopter. Papa stuck to the story and when I became hysterical, he let loose, then turned me out."

Stavros swore, stark and hard.

"That's when you wound up sleeping on the beach? For how long? You had just had a *baby*."

"Takis thought my pimp had worked me over. He wanted to take me to the police."

"You didn't go? For God's sake, why not?" His voice rang with disbelief, making her shrink all the more tightly into the corner.

"I was scared. Ashamed. My mother was standing by what my father had done. Said Dorian was *in a better place*. But where was the body? I accused Papa of killing him. That's when he really came after me. Not a man who will stand for being accused of murdering a baby, but he had no compunction leaving his daughter for dead on his front step."

"He abused you? Regularly?" His voice was steely and terrifying, making her tremble. She curled even tighter under the blanket.

"Mostly we knew how to keep from making him angry. I was just so upset about losing Dorian."

"Calli." The settee creaked as he leaned over her. "Being beaten wasn't your fault. None of this was."

She flinched at the way he was speaking, throwing the words down on her like stones. She leaned away, not really caring about that part of it anymore anyway.

"Takis took me to the police when I finally told him. By that time, Papa had used the Underwoods' money to buy a death certificate. The police refused to investigate. Takis had his lawyer send a few letters, but the Underwoods stonewalled. They called me an opportunist and said I was deluded." She shivered. "They said if I had a baby, it wasn't Brandon's. That given the way I was behaving, I wasn't a fit mother anyway."

"So you don't know for sure that—" He rubbed his

hand down his face. "Do you know if your son is alive?" he asked gently.

"In here." Her voice broke as she touched above her left breast. "In my heart, I know he's alive. Just as I'm sure that Brandon knows where he is. That's all I wanted to do tonight. Ask. But no one wants me to know what happened to my son. Even Takis didn't want me to know, not really. He didn't want me to leave him and Ophelia."

Her voice thickened and the tears threatened to come back, burning hotly and stinging the edges of her eyelids, thickening her throat.

"Calli—"

"I'm really tired." She forced herself to stand, numb fingers clinging to keep the blanket around her while she swayed on her feet. "Do you— Can I pack in the morning? I'm sorry. I'm just really tired." Her legs felt too weak to support her.

"No. I mean yes. I mean, go to bed." He spoke in a flat, gruff voice and followed up with a curse that made her hunch protectively again. "Do you need help?"

"No." She took the few steps to the bed and let herself drop onto it, eyes closed, cocooned in the blanket as she curled into a ball of misery and escaped yet another dark, hopeless night.

Stavros put on a fresh pot of coffee when he heard Calli stir. He was glad to finally have something constructive to do, having made as much progress as he could and was now just waiting until he would have to wake her.

She showered and came into the kitchen as he was scrambling eggs.

She paused when she saw him, face bare of makeup, eyes bruised, mouth pouted. She had slept late, but she looked like she could use another twelve hours. She pulled the lapels of her robe closed, sitting at the island when he set her breakfast there.

"Thank you," she murmured.

He slid her phone toward her. "Takis would like to hear from you."

"Is Ophelia okay?" She picked it up to check her history.

"She's the one who called. She had some questions about cosmetics. I asked her to put me on to him."

"Why?" Her honey-gold eyes flashed up, deeply defensive and wary.

His heart flipped over in his chest. There weren't words sorry enough for the pain he had caused her last night. He swallowed, helpless and furious and perhaps not as regretful as he should be, because she had been going about this all wrong.

He kept all of that to himself, though. He instinctively knew that any sort of strong emotion from him right now would send her shrinking into her shell.

"I wanted to know what steps he had taken to find your son."

Her sooty lashes fell and she set aside her phone. She tucked her hands in her lap and her voice cooled. "Why?"

He sighed, and pointed at her fork, urging her to eat. "Be thankful I did. My first instinct was to go beat the truth out of Underwood. Takis counseled me to use proper channels."

Actually, he had said, "Be careful. Once they knew she was looking for him, they closed ranks. I hired an investigator who found nothing. Meanwhile, steps were taken that nearly cost me my career, my daughter's future and my ability to support both of them. Nothing that could be traced back, of course, but the pressure stopped when the search was dropped. Calli doesn't know about that and I'd rather she didn't. She castigates herself enough."

That explained why Takis hadn't seemed to try as hard as Calli would have liked. Stavros remembered their wedding day, when Takis had said he had let Calli down.

"I can apply my own pressure," Stavros had told Takis. "And I'm a lot more impervious to threats and retaliation than you are."

"Why do you think I let her marry you?" Takis had said flatly. "I hoped she would ask you for help. Good job on getting her to open up. It took two years for her to tell me. This is not easy for her, Xenakis. She's not as tough as she acts. Use kid gloves."

Stavros saw that. Now. Her shoulders were incredibly slight. She was pale. Her hand seemed translucent and slender as she picked up her fork and nudged a bite of egg.

"I tried proper channels," she murmured. "I need to talk to Brandon face-to-face."

"Calli." He leaned his elbows on the other side of the island, so they were eye level. "Why did you marry me?"

She took a few grains of egg into her mouth and let the fork slide out from her sealed lips.

"So you could come to New York and have a conversation with Brandon? You could have come here for a week and done that years ago. That isn't all you want, is it? Why haven't you spent any of the money I've been giving you?"

Her lashes fell.

"Because you need to bankroll a legal battle. Right?"

"I need to know where he is first. That he's safe." Her gaze came up, fraught and urgent. "That's the most important thing. If I start with a letter from a lawyer, Brandon won't see it. I can guarantee you they won't even forward it. No one will confirm Dorian is alive. But if I look Brandon in the eye— Don't try to talk me out of this, Stavros!" Her eyes filled as she read his expression. "Is it because you think it will drag your family into a scandal? I won't go to the papers, I swear. I don't want to put my own son in the middle of something public and ugly. I wasn't going to make a scene last night. I had the words rehearsed in my head—"

"Calli." He reached across to cover her hand. "I need you to trust me."

"No!" She stood, yanked the tie on her robe tighter and stood there shaking. "No. I won't and I *don't* trust you."

It was a damned sledgehammer to the chest. He pinched the bridge of his nose. "Calli, listen—"

"No! Damn it, I know I was only seventeen." She pushed the heels of her hands into her eye sockets. "I know he might be better off where he is. He's probably with some rich, married couple who can give him a much better life than I ever could. I know I didn't deserve him." She dropped her hands to reveal the suffering in her eyes. "But I didn't give him up, Stavros. He was *taken*. I have to know he's safe."

He felt her pain in that moment. He felt it like knives in his chest and belly, like a tortuous ache that made his entire being throb. He felt pulled and anchored down at the same time, feet heavy as he went around to her and closed her cold fists in his bigger hands.

"I didn't say you didn't deserve him. Who said that to you?"

She pulled her hands from his and tucked them under her elbows, turning her face away as she fought to hang on to her composure.

He drew her into his arms, but she was as stiff and cold as marble. He set his lips against her temple. "Of course you deserved to keep your own son."

She flinched, pulling back in a way that clawed at him. He wanted to crush her, press reassurance into her so tightly she couldn't doubt it, but she was like spun glass in his arms. Not nearly as strong as she was trying to be, fighting back tears with that jagged, hissing breath. Her whole body was quivering like an animal run to ground.

"I have more resources than Takis," he said in a gentle, yet gross understatement. "The lawyers I hire will hire their own investigators. Good ones. Most important, contrary to what you just said, I am not afraid to use the press as a weapon."

"But what if Dorian doesn't even know he's adopted? It would be horrible to learn something like that on the schoolyard. What if—"

"Don't worry, *koukla mou.* I don't expect it would progress beyond a threat. The Underwoods do *not* subscribe to any publicity being good publicity. That's why they hushed up their son's mishap in the first place. That and they wouldn't want an heir to show up inconveniently in the future, seeking a piece of the Underwood pie. No. Better to place him in a suitable home where they can give him a measured slice, the way aristocracy has done for generations when they have a blue-blooded bastard to contend with."

"Don't call him that!"

"Apología." He drew her in, pressed his mouth to her hair, still trying to assimilate that she was the mother of a child. A fresh wave of jealousy overcame him as he absorbed that she would always have this connection to Brandon, her first lover. It was far more profound than losing her virginity to some man he'd never met. Brandon would always be a peripheral figure in her life and Stavros couldn't do a damned thing about it except loathe the piece of filth.

"Do you think he's with a family member? Because I've searched and searched online. I can't find a sibling or cousin or any other relative with a boy of the right age."

"Let me put my mothers and sisters on the job," Stavros said drily. "They'll have a list of possibilities in an hour. They know every top-tier familial connection in the country."

"I don't want them to know *this*."

"I don't have to tell them why." He glanced at the clock on the microwave. "But I'd like a starting point for our meeting."

"What meeting?"

"Lawyers, *koukla mou*. They'll be here soon."

"How—? It's the weekend!"

"Yes, they'll ding me for that, along with the fee for the house call, but…" He shrugged it off. "I wanted to let you sleep."

She drew back, brows pulled into a knot of worry. "Why are you doing this?"

"We have a deal, do we not?" *Now* it was quid pro quo and he grasped at the opportunity to justify their arrangement. Keep it going exactly as it was. "As you pointed out last night, I have not upheld my side of the bargain. You could have been more forthright in your reasons, but I am honor bound to give you what you sought when you agreed to marry me."

"No, you aren't," she mumbled, hair falling in a curtain down her cheek as she dipped her head.

"Oh, I am." He smoothed that wisp of hair behind her ear, mostly as an excuse to touch her. "You made a rather harsh comparison last night, *glykia mou*. I am not just like your faithless Brandon. I like being called *that* even less than Steven."

Her mouth quirked in a hint of leavening, but quickly skewed again with emotion. Her brow grew heavy. "I don't know what to say."

"You don't have to say anything. Sit. Eat. It's going cold and you missed dinner last night."

She went onto tiptoe and grazed her mouth against his cheek, filling his head with the scent of her freshly washed skin. Her voice rasped with emotion. "Thank you, Stavros."

She sat down and his tension bled out of him on a quiet breath of relief.

CHAPTER EIGHT

CALLI COULDN'T SEEM to move, barely able to lift her head as Stavros came back from seeing out the lawyers. She was emotionally exhausted. Hollowed out and raw.

But hopeful.

Which terrified her.

"I realize that wasn't easy for you," he said, lowering to sit on the ottoman in front of the armchair where she had huddled and cried, pouring out her soul along with the sordid details of her teenage affair.

"Which part?" She had covered everything, drawn out by the kind, soft-spoken Ingrid while she avoided the drilling glare from Norma unless the older woman interjected with a sharp-voiced question.

Oddly, it was that tag team of hard and soft, compassionate and ruthless, that had reassured her. Takis's lawyer had been at turns overwhelmed, distracted and impatient. Norma, Ingrid had informed her, was a champion of justice. Ingrid believed in her, which was why she worked with her—despite Norma's lack of bedside manner.

That gentle humor and candor had allowed Calli to open up to Ingrid, but shame had colored every word. Shame for how she'd got herself pregnant and how shame had kept her hiding it as long as she could, waiting for Brandon to come back and marry her. Shame that she'd been stupid enough to believe he would and deep, deep shame instilled by her parents when they'd learned. Shame that they hadn't loved her enough to overcome their own embarrassment, rejecting her and refusing to keep Dorian, then shame that she had trusted them. Shame that she hadn't suspected her father could go to the lengths he had. Shame that she had lost her son. Mothers were supposed to protect their babies at all costs, right?

The shame had continued well after she had offered herself to Takis. Askance looks around the island had kept it going as rumors swirled of her giving birth out of wedlock and losing the baby to crib death, then living with Takis as his presumed mistress. She was ashamed that she had taken so long to tell him, to fight for her son, only to lose.

"The part where they asked you for time." Stavros set his elbows on his thighs, hands linked between his splayed knees. "You've already waited too long."

She twitched a shoulder. What did a couple more weeks matter after six years?

"Can I ask— You said that you didn't tell Takis right away because you didn't think you would stay with him that long, and that you were embarrassed, but what made you finally tell him after keeping it secret for two years?"

She sighed and gathered up the balled tissues that had collected in her lap and around her legs. "He asked me to marry him."

"Ah." His hands closed a little more tightly together.

"He knew he was too old for me, but he wanted a brother or sister for Ophelia. We gelled as a family in a lot of ways. For the first time in my life, I felt...wanted. Ophelia was a brat, but she loved me. Does."

She smiled with affection, missing her girl. Feeling the distance, especially today, when her emotions were so spent and heavy.

"She helped me so much and doesn't even know it. On my worst days, when I felt like an utter failure for not having my son, she would cuddle up to me, or give me something she'd made at school, and I would realize I was the only mother she had. It made me want to..." She cleared her throat. "I always thought... Somewhere out there, someone is looking after *my* child. Ophelia's mother would want to know *her* child was being loved and looked after well. I couldn't rob Ophelia just because I was missing my son. I had to give her my best and hope my son was getting the same from the woman he was calling mama."

She grabbed a fresh tissue and swept it across her damp lashes, impatient with this unending leak. Her eyes were beyond raw.

"I made it clear to Takis that I was saving my wages to go to America, but little things kept happening with Ophelia that made it hard to leave. Every time I brought it up, Takis would offer me more money. I would sock it away, thinking I was buying more time in America, more time to plan my attack, more money for lawyers."

She sighed and propped her head in her hand. It was too heavy for her neck.

"Then we went to Athens for my birthday and he took me out to dinner and proposed. I was stunned. Didn't see it coming at all. And when he told me he wanted to make a baby... I fell apart. It all came out and he was so shocked, but he tried to help and..."

"Didn't get very far," Stavros finished softly.

"You're sorry you picked me now, aren't you?" He had to be, which made her sad. "I should have told you. I just don't like talking about it. It hurts."

"I know."

The concern in his expression undid her. It took those passionate, deeply fascinated feelings she had for him and made them flower into something more poignant and permanent. Love. She had probably been in love with him for a while now, but this was the moment where it blossomed and became real. He knew her deepest secret and didn't judge her for it. He wanted to help her.

She dropped her gaze, trying to hide the glow of yearning that dawned in her heart and swelled to suffuse her whole being.

"Come here." He leaned to gather her up, then shifted them onto the sofa so she was in his lap. "You worry me when you're looking so vulnerable like that. We're going to find him, Calli. I'm going to do everything I can to make this right for you."

She wanted to believe him. She believed *he* believed it, which was deeply reassuring. Sliding her arm around his neck, she buried her face in his throat, moved beyond words. Her throat closed, trying to hold back revealing how much his support meant to her. How much *he* meant to her.

She turned her lips against his skin instead, telling him with her openmouthed kiss and the small shift of her body how she felt about him.

He stilled and she felt him swallow. He drew back to look down at her, thoughts unreadable when his eyes were slitted like that, his lashes a forested line.

He usually made the advances, but she took the initiative, pressing her mouth to his, letting him know she was interested. Receptive.

He kept the kiss brief, pulling back a little to keep staring down at her in that inscrutable way. "You don't owe me anything, if that's what you're thinking."

That's not what this was, but— Oh, God, now she felt like a fool. Perhaps her messy personal life had completely turned him off. "You don't want to?"

She drew her arms from around his neck, tucking them

protectively against her chest. She must look like hell, too. What was she *thinking*?

"Calli." He adjusted her position in his lap so she felt the hardness of his erection against her butt cheek. "That happens when you're not even in the room. All I have to do is think about you. It's inconvenient, if you want the truth. I *always* want you. But I don't take advantage of women when they're at a low point."

"Stavros—" She dropped her head against his collarbone. "I'm not trying to compensate you. I want to feel something besides pain." She let her head fall back. "Do you mind?"

He snorted and gathered her high against his chest as he stood. "In that case, I'm your man."

Stavros was at a loss as he set Calli on her feet beside the bed. Sex was a playful pursuit for him. A sport. Not the game-hunting kind. More a good-natured set of tennis. He liked to control the play, definitely kept track of how many points he scored and he was always willing to take instruction and hone his skills.

With Calli, a new bar had already been set in terms of intensity and endurance, not to mention sheer level of enjoyment. Plus, given how frequently they came together, he knew exactly how aggressive he could be while keeping her with him through the whole act. It was mind-blowing how great the sex had become with her.

But this was different. There was no room for dominance when she was so completely defenseless. She needed healing, and he was capable of gentleness, but he didn't know how to be tender. Not without opening his heart.

That shift terrified him. He was a man who thrived on risk, but he was taking a huge one here. He couldn't turn away from her, though. If ever there was a time to be self-less, this was it.

A strange instinct guided him, something that had its origins near last night's jealousy, but wore the flipside of it. Humble gratitude, maybe. A sense of privilege that he could be the man to touch and heal.

His hands moved of their own accord to carefully sweep her hair. As much as the need to consume her gripped him, he ached to absorb her in smaller ways. Savor her. He found himself lingering with his lips against her cheek, appreciating the softness of her skin and the delicate scent that reminded him of Greece.

As he turned her to help her shed her top, he pressed tiny kisses against her nape. They were small stamps of reassurance. He wouldn't rush her. They had all the time in the world.

They didn't, he acknowledged distantly, gut knotting with tension, but in this moment, time was at a standstill. He smoothed his lips against the warmth of her shoulder, murmuring how lovely she was.

She chuckled softly and reached to cup his jaw, turning her head so they were nose to nose, lip to lip.

"We've been speaking English so much I didn't understand you right away," she said in Greek. "I like it when you use our language." She pressed her mouth to his, lips clinging in the way that went straight to his head.

He tamped down on the animal that rushed up in him, turned her and drew her slender form into his front, forcing himself to keep the kiss from raging out of control.

It was incredibly powerful regardless, fracturing all the walls inside him. He tasted the emotion on her lips. The enormity of all that she was, all the expansive feelings she hid within that sweet, calm exterior she showed the world.

He was the only one she showed this side of herself, he

realized with a fresh rush of dizzying excitement. This passion of hers, these depths, they were all his. No one else caught more than a glimpse. It made him that much more possessive, yet careful, as he unwrapped the gift that she was. And when they were naked on the bed, he let her press him onto his back and slither her soft form and flowing hair over his skin.

"You're making me crazy," he growled, cradling the sides of her head. Her hair spilled from between his fingers, forming a tent around them as they kissed. The rest of him was a line of primed muscle, holding still, acutely aware of her straddling him, teasing his shaft with her nest of curls, breasts swaying lightly against the plate of his chest. He was damned near levitating, wanting so badly to be in her.

"I want to make you crazy," she told him, smiling the sly grin of a woman exalting in the power of her femininity. She was both beautiful and terrifying. He swelled with pride at being the man who gave her this confidence while he feared what he had unleashed.

He had stopped worrying about his mortality years ago, but in that moment of glorying in the goddess that held him in thrall, he was petrified. At some point, this would end. Not just their faux marriage, but their lives. They would age and die, and this woman was far too precious not to live forever. He was far too greedy not to demand an eternity with her.

If only...

He tamped down the thought. Rather than grow urgent, he slowed his movements even more. Drew out every caress and cherished every sensation. He tasted her gasps of pleasure and listened for the music beneath her skin as he stroked her. He gave himself up to whatever she chose to take, watching, experiencing her wrench of climax like it was his own, even though he held back, stunned by her glorious release as she rode his hips.

Then he rolled her beneath him and gave more. More of himself, more attention and assurance and assuagement. Everything in him was hers. And when he finally gave up the last piece of himself and poured himself into her, as she clenched and cried out her own joy, it was not only the most potent and satisfying climax of his life, it was worth all that it would cost him when he had to let her go.

As if Stavros hadn't already pulled her apart and put her back together a million times, he did it again when he asked her to go to the anniversary party for his friend Sebastien.

"Antonio and Alejandro will be there. They're all good friends. I'd like to see them."

He wasn't saying he wanted her to meet his friends, precisely, but it seemed significant. Although he had introduced her to his family despite their marriage having an expiry date. Maybe he was just as blasé about bringing her into his social circle.

Things had shifted since she had told him about Dorian. Stavros was the same dynamic man who didn't stop working unless it was to make love, but he scaled back their appearances to a few smaller dinners with people she had already met. When Friday came, he drove them out to Galíni, where much of the weekend was spent lazing by the pool with his family, talking about everything and nothing.

As relaxing as it was for her, Stavros kept working, drawing his grandfather into several conversations about this or that initiative.

"You always make Edward sound like such a hard case, but he seemed really supportive of all the things you're planning," she remarked as they drove back to the city.

"Things were a lot different when I was younger. Even a year ago." His expression was difficult to read behind his sunglasses, but she had the impression he was somewhere between perplexed and concerned. "I guess he's retiring from riding my ass along with the rest."

She snickered, but he didn't.

"Why did he tell me to bring you back in one piece from Oxfordshire?"

He scratched his cheek, saying drily, "He might have had reason to ride my ass. Sending me to Greece is one of the tamer things Sebastien has goaded me into."

That made her curious, but now she was thinking about the trip itself. "England seems a long way away," she murmured.

"Norma knows to call if something turns up with Dorian."

The way he spoke her son's name as if he was a real person and not some dirty secret turned her inside out all over again. It made her all the more susceptible to him. She reminded herself daily that he was only holding up his side of their bargain by hiring Norma, but she couldn't help wondering if it was a signal he was growing to care for her.

It had been two weeks since she'd told him, and she jumped every time her phone buzzed with a text or he took a call in front of her. She agreed to the anniversary party simply because she needed the distraction of another weekend away.

Waldenbrook, the two-hundred-acre estate in Oxfordshire, was certainly a distraction. She nervously double-checked her appearance in the mirror behind the visor as the car slowed to amble up the long drive toward Sebastien's majestic estate house. It was right out of a period drama, lovingly maintained since its erection in Georgian times, and scrupulously groomed for a weekend celebration of their hosts' first wedding anniversary.

"I'm nervous," she admitted as he parked before the waiting footmen.

"Why? It's a garden party with a few friends." He set the brake and turned off the engine.

She bit back a blurted "Pah!" because her door opened.

This particular "garden" would host five hundred "friends" tomorrow night. Of course she was intimidated. The feeling grew worse as they were shown to the suite of rooms that Stavros said he always used, pointing out the ones reserved for Antonio and Alejandro, bringing their bride and fiancée respectively.

Flowers and a basket of wine, fruit, cheese and crackers put the finishing touch on a beautifully decorated apartment with a balcony overlooking the pool and a huge four-poster bed beneath a pair of Gauguins.

"He doesn't greet *me* like this," Stavros said, handing her the envelope from the flowers.

Calli opened it to read their hostess's elegant script.

Calli,
I hope you will join me in the Rose Room for breakfast at eight tomorrow morning. I've invited Cecily and Sadie. I'd like to take this opportunity to get to know all of you better.
Monika

"Don't they know our marriage isn't…?" *Real. Forever.* She handed him the note and gripped her elbows.

"It's only breakfast. If you don't want to go—"

"She's the hostess. Of course I'll go. I just feel like I'm misleading her. It doesn't matter," she insisted, snapping into unpacking her few things. "This is the role I agreed to."

* * *

Stavros didn't know what their roles were anymore. When he had first begun parading Calli on his arm, he had experienced simple pride in having such a beautiful woman at his side. She carried herself well and he had enjoyed the lack of politics. She didn't fish for compliments or act possessive. They were already married, so there was no fishing for that, either. It was easy.

Now he knew the pain she hid behind her quick wit and unassuming demeanor. There wasn't a mercenary bone in her, and playing the role of his wife plagued her conscience. It left him seeing her as far more human than he had at first credited her as being. In fact he saw her as quite fragile, which shifted him into the role of protector.

The last thing his friends would call him was anyone's knight in shining armor.

Still, as they moved downstairs and onto the terrace for cocktails with the guests, Stavros stayed close to his wife. She had already introduced herself to Antonio and Sadie, when she had run downstairs in search of the phone she had misplaced.

Sadie was a stunning blonde with eyes that tracked back to her husband as though magnetized, and Antonio gave her the same close attention when she spoke. His friend was in love?

The obvious chemistry surprised Stavros. He had understood the marriage to be a convenience so Antonio could have access to his three-year-old son.

"You were right," Sadie assured Calli as they chatted. "I checked in with the nanny and Leo is fine. I'm worrying for nothing."

"You're a mother. It's your job to worry," Calli said with a reassuring smile.

All of Stavros's defensive hackles rose. He started to

make an excuse to draw her away, but Alejandro arrived with his fiancée. Cecily was a leggy blonde and Stavros couldn't fault his friend's taste. No wonder they had been necking in the hallway when Stavros had brought Calli down. They still wore a glow.

Their arrival defused his tension until he overheard Alejandro murmur something to the waiter about bringing Cecily a sparkling cider. Cecily was pregnant? She wasn't showing, but it explained his friend's sudden desire to marry.

In another life, Stavros would be pleased for his friends and hopeful that all their wives could become as close as they were. As it was, he was too intent on shielding Calli from further heartache. He drew her into a quiet corner.

"I didn't mean to do that to you."

She frowned with incomprehension. "What?"

"It must be hard for you. Talking to women with children. I didn't mean to set you up for that."

"People have kids," she dismissed, sweeping her lashes down to hide her gaze, but he saw her flinch. "Envy doesn't change my situation. They can talk about them and I can be happy for them. That's just life."

Stavros was still worried and was relieved to go back to a familiar dynamic when she turned in early. He retired to the snooker room with the usual suspects, where Sebastien toasted their successful completion of their recent challenge.

Their friend seemed determined to be smug about having "won," even though he was now committed to giving away five billion dollars.

Stavros dodged Sebastien's attempts to make them admit what they had "learned" from their challenge and muttered, "I think your real intention was to get us married off so you're not the only one wearing a ring."

"And I managed it."

"How is yours working out? With your grandfather?" Antonio asked Stavros.

"Most of the handoff is completed," Stavros replied as he circled the table, planning his next shots. "He's officially retiring at the end of the month, staying on the board in an advisory role."

His grandfather was surprisingly comfortable with all the changes, the marriage included. He must know it was a ruse. The old man wasn't stupid, but he had actually asked if Calli was pregnant the last time they'd spoken, saying, "She looks pale."

Since she was on the Pill and they'd only just stopped using condoms, Stavros would have to be superhuman to have gotten her pregnant, but his grandfather had seemed genuinely disappointed to hear she wasn't.

And even though he had long decided his sisters could continue the Xenakis dynasty in his stead, Stavros had felt like he'd let the old man down. Again.

Sebastien was topping up drinks and Stavros heard Antonio say something about being grateful to have found his son.

"I always assumed my grandfather was the fallback if anything happened to me," Stavros admitted. "He kept such an iron grip, I thought the company would be his forever. Now I see why he was so determined to whip me into shape." He sipped, inhaling the oaky bite into the back of his throat. "And why he held back letting me have control."

The other men smirked, well aware that Stavros had been a loose cannon in his youth.

Stavros was seeing the old man's heavy-handedness in a new light, though. Over the years, Edward had railed on about how people would depend on Stavros for their livelihood and, given the types of drugs they manufactured, even their lives. It had sounded like rhetoric, but as Stavros took his grandfather's chair, he was seeing the old man's perspective more clearly.

All the responsibility was his and it was enormous.

He wasn't one to entrust such responsibility to others without due regard, either. He could appreciate why his grandfather had been so determined that Stavros's father come home to help him run it, and that his grandson prove his dedication.

He kind of understood why his grandfather was hopeful he would make a baby with Calli, but still felt the kind of empire-building his grandfather had in mind wasn't for him. Stavros was the outlier, the strain of the bloodline that shouldn't be replicated.

He had promised Calli a son, but it was the one she already had.

Calli woke to cold hands pulling her into chilled, naked skin. She reflexively squirmed to get away. "Stav— What?"

"Warm me up." He dragged her into a tight spoon against his damp body. "I asked Sebastien what he wanted for a bottle of sauterne and he threw it in the pool. Bastard." He pressed cold lips to her neck. His hair was wet.

"There's a bottle of wine in that basket," she reminded, wriggling her backside into him, hoping the friction would take the sting out of contact with his cold skin.

"It's not a Château d'Yquem 1921. I need that vintage for a vertical I'm compiling. One more and I could auction it for a million. Do you want to make love?" His hand slid to cup her breast, cool fingers fondling gently.

"Do you?" She rolled to face him and ran her hand down to where he was hardening. Growing warm and ready.

His response was wonderfully reassuring when she had

spent an evening growing more and more aware of how completely she didn't belong in his world. The people here weren't just business contacts, but friends. People he liked.

"Always." He climbed her nightgown up her body, hands caressing along the way.

She moaned approval, slithering against him to help expose her naked skin, opening her legs so he could nestle into place between them.

In this way, at least, she felt confident and cherished. She felt like this was exactly where she belonged.

They fell asleep still joined. He woke when she disentangled herself some hours later and pinned her in place with a heavy arm.

"Where are you going?" His voice was muffled in the pillow.

"Breakfast."

He grunted a noise of dismay. "I can't think about food right now." He let her go and rolled away.

She smirked, showered, then tentatively made her way to the appointed room. She had taken care with her appearance and wore one of her prettiest day dresses. It had a floral pattern suited to a weekend brunch, but she hadn't realized how much she had begun to rely on Stavros's presence at her side until she didn't have him to lean on.

Sadie was already there. When Calli had met her yesterday, with Antonio, she had thought them an intimidating couple, utterly beautiful in the way Italians managed without effort, then she had realized Sadie was English, but still very poised and elegant.

Cecily arrived. She was a firecracker who was obviously deeply in love with her fiancé. It made Calli feel even more of an outsider to be the only one in a loveless relationship. The women were incredibly warm and welcoming, though. They were the kind of women she would have very much enjoyed developing long-term friendships with, but she held back, knowing there was no point.

She kept the conversation light, mentioning Stavros's midnight swim for lack of other topics.

Monika chuckled. "That's the sort of thing they do. They thrive on challenging each other. Of course, this most recent challenge takes the cake."

Calli realized all three of their men had been set up to go without credit cards for two weeks. Antonio had posed as a mechanic in Sadie's garage and Alejandro had gone to work as a groom at Cecily's stable.

Calli exchanged looks with the other two women, who both seemed shocked, especially Cecily.

"This is something they do a lot?" Sadie asked, astonished.

"For years," Monika told them. "Sebastien's first real venture was a zip line in Costa Rica. He was in his last year of university. In order to get the company off the ground—pun intended—he sent out invitations to specific students at different universities here and in the US. He chose the risk takers, but the ones with money. He comes across as impulsive, but he's shrewd. He *dared* them to try it, knowing full well most young men can't resist something like that. He made some excellent connections as well as enough profit to start his next business. That original zip line expanded into the extreme sports club they all belong to today."

"What were the stakes in the bet?" Cecily asked Monika, clearly still dumbfounded.

"If Sebastien won, the men would give up one of their most prized possessions. Alejandro's private island, for instance. If Sebastien lost, he promised to donate half his fortune to charity."

"And all three men completed their challenges?"

Monika nodded. "Sebastien will be making the announcement of the donation in a few weeks' time. He plans to set up a global search and rescue team with it, something that's close to his heart given his near-miss last year."

He'd been caught in an avalanche, Calli learned, and his friends had saved his life by digging him out.

The conversation moved along to the horse trials that would be run today.

"Will you ride today?" Sadie asked Cecily.

Cecily was a show jumper, but she dismissed the idea, saying something about preferring to spend her time getting to know the three of them, but she looked out the tall windows at the dew-laden grass and bright blue sky like a prisoner longing for freedom.

Pregnant, Calli suspected, and experienced a pang, then turned her attention to Sadie's question about what she and Stavros would do today.

"I promised his sister I would take some photos of the grounds, but I imagine we'll wind up joining the crowd watching the show."

Calli was still thinking about the club and the bet and whether Stavros was a horseman when she returned to the room.

He was sitting on the love seat, feet propped on the ottoman. He was showered and had pants on, but was barefoot and his shirt was open. He had a cup of coffee steaming on the side table and was flicking through messages on his phone.

"Sunglasses?" she teased. "Feeling poorly?"

"Just a headache. Sebastien wanted us to try some port after we'd been drinking whiskey all night. I know better." He set aside his phone and motioned her to come to him. "How was breakfast?"

"Fine." She let him draw her down to straddle his thighs

and splayed her hands across the fresh-washed planes of his chest as she kissed him. He tasted faintly of mint and more strongly of coffee. "Monika told us how the club was started. I didn't realize your swim was the latest in a long line of stunts. What else have you done?"

He let his head relax onto the back of the sofa, expression rueful behind his sunglasses. "Swimming after a bottle is nothing. We're usually rock climbing without gear or scaling vertical ice slopes. Cave diving. Whatever tests of intestinal fortitude Sebastien can dream up. This past winter was a paragliding ski event. I expect wing suits will be next."

"And you'll do it? *Why?* Wait, let me guess. Peer pressure. Listen, if all of your friends jumped off a bridge, would you?" She took on her best nanny voice, fists on her hips, elbows akimbo.

"Too late. We *have*," he drawled, sidling his hands up her thighs under the skirt of her dress. He lightly traced the edges of her thong. "Blindfolded."

She laughed, wriggling with pleasure at his touch, but astounded at his audacity. "Ophelia wanted me to go on a ride with her at an amusement park once. It went upside down so I refused. I can't even jump off the diving board into our pool."

His pool, she recalled.

"You have a healthy sense of self-preservation. Me, I've never had a reason to live, so I push the limits every time."

They both sobered.

"I hope that was a joke." She lifted his sunglasses and saw something dark move behind his eyes. Ghosts? He was looking past her, wearing the agonized look from that day on the spit. He was such a devilish, assertive man, it was easy to forget he had his own demons.

She cupped his jaw in her two hands, waited until his

gaze met hers. "You have very good friends and a family who loves you. Please don't say you have nothing to live for."

"I'm not suicidal, if that's how it sounded." His hands tightened on her hips and she thought he might try to set her aside.

"Stavros." She let her weight settle onto him, signaling her intention to stay exactly where she was. "What happened in Greece? The first time."

His jaw hardened.

"I told you my secret," she reminded softly. "I know your father died. How?"

His hands came out from beneath her dress. "I wanted to go fishing and he made me wear a life vest, but didn't put one on himself. The wind came up, we went over and he told me to swim for shore. I did. He didn't make it."

She drew a breath, one of the heavy, aching kind filled with empathy for his terrible loss. Very carefully she let it out. It moved like powdered glass in her windpipe, straining her voice when she spoke.

"You can't blame yourself. Everyone on the island knows how rough the water can be on that side."

"I was never one to do as I was told, but I did that day. The one time I should have rebelled and stayed."

"And drowned yourself? You can't think that."

He set her aside and rose. "I'm hungry. Are you coming down with me?"

She shifted on the love seat, pulling her skirt down and smoothing it, watching him settle his sunglasses into place and button his shirt, firmly locking her out.

Her heart continued to ache. She knew all about guilt and grief, regret and self-loathing. What she didn't know was how to reach for someone trapped in that same bubble and bring him out of it.

"Ophelia texted a while ago. I'm going to have a quick face call with her, then I'll come down. I promised your sister I would send her a few pictures from the grounds. Do you want to walk with me?"

"Find me in the dining room." He closed his cuffs and left.

"Stavros..." Calli was speechless as she stared into the mirror, throat closing above the heavy, cool lump that sat just below her collarbone.

She couldn't even make herself reach for the matching earrings. The prenup had outlined his responsibility for providing a suitable wardrobe and accessories, but she had never expected it to include a square-cut yellow sapphire surrounded by diamonds, suspended from two ropes of flat-linked, twisted gold.

He had put it on her himself, after zipping her gown—which was the most form-fitting she'd ever worn. Burnt red satin plunged from spaghetti straps to show off her cleavage, forming a perfect frame for the necklace. Then the gown hugged her waist and hips, covering her backside like a coat of paint before falling away in a flare of sparkle-dusted silk.

He eyed her, standing behind her reflection. "It suits you. Brings out your eyes."

"It's making them fall out of my head! What do you mean it's *not* on loan?"

"Well, it's not stolen, if that's what you're implying. I was shopping for an anniversary gift for Sebastien and Monika when I saw it. I wanted you to have it."

Many moons ago, she had dreamed of being whisked into a rich boy's world, but that aspiration had long died, replaced with a simple one where she knew her son and he knew her. For the first time in a long time, she wistfully yearned to be part of a man's life, but not for this. She wanted so much more than a cut stone from this man. Things she couldn't bring herself to ask for.

He'd been remote all day. She had tried to respect his desire to retreat emotionally. She did the same all the time, so she didn't try to get past his shuttered expression, had only asked him whether he wanted to take this path or that.

It had been a gorgeous day. From across the grounds, the sounds of horse hooves and cheering carried from the trials they were conducting. Where they walked, the air was filled with the sounds of nature. Birds and bees. A soft breeze caressed her skin and the air smelled sweet and fresh.

They happened across a stone bridge that crossed a brook and she paused to take several photos of the sun slanting through the trees onto the water.

When she lowered her camera, Stavros turned her into his arms. He didn't say anything, only held her close so her ear was pressed to the steady thump of his heart while the run of water moving under the bridge sounded below.

She hugged his waist, offering the comfort she wished she could have given him earlier. Her insides trembled like the leaves quivering and whispering around them. When he kissed her and took her hand, tugging her along in silence, her heart was so loose in her chest she could hardly walk.

It made this gift all the more surprising, yet profound, completely unraveling her.

She made herself turn and press her mouth to his. "I'm overwhelmed. It's beautiful. Thank you."

They didn't speak about his father or anything else very serious for the rest of the night. They made their way out to the marquee that had been set with round tables, white cloths, crystal and china, then decorated with candles and roses.

It was pure magic and Sebastien and Monika were clearly ecstatic in their marriage. They started the dancing, then Antonio and Sadie joined in, making a fetching couple as Sadie's daring black-and-white gown mirrored the crisp tuxedo her husband wore. What must it be like to be so in love? Calli wondered.

Despite how in sync they seemed, however, Calli thought there was a flash of conflict as Sadie said something and Antonio seemed to stiffen.

Before she could decipher it, Cecily came alongside her. She wore a gold affair that made her look like a gilded angel.

"You look stunning," Calli told her.

"So do you," Cecily said, eye catching on the pendant. "Wow. That's gorgeous."

"Oh, um, Stavros gave it to me," Calli murmured, self-conscious as Cecily's expression softened.

"He loves you," she said, and there might have been a glint of despair or longing in her eyes, but her lashes swept down, disguising her thoughts.

Calli bit back protesting that Stavros didn't love her at all and reassured instead, "Your fiancé is obviously crazy about *you*."

"Because of this afternoon?" Cecily made a face and darkened with a small blush. "That wasn't…what it looked like."

It had looked like Alejandro had thrown her over his shoulder and carried her from the horse trials to their room to make love. What else could it be?

The men joined them at that point and they all moved onto the dance floor, at which point Sadie abruptly left.

"Oh. Something to do with her son, do you think?" Calli asked, watching her with concern.

Monika followed Sadie while Antonio moved off the dance floor and into conversation with Sebastien.

"They'll let us know if it's an emergency," Stavros said, sharp gaze on his friend.

A short while later, Sebastien assured them everything was fine, that the couple had simply gone into the house.

It became a night to remember and Calli knew she always would. She would look back with nostalgia in her golden years to this time when she had been young and married far out of her league, invited to a party she had no business attending, dancing like Cinderella with the most handsome man at the ball.

The man she loved.

"How's your head this morning? Do you need anything?" she asked as they returned to their room after breakfast. He had disappeared in the middle of the night, leaving her to wake alone, telling her he hadn't been able to sleep and wound up having a beer with Alejandro.

She wondered if he had been regretting being so candid with her about his father, but this morning he was his regular self.

"I'm fine. Why? Are you suffering? You only had a couple of glasses of Champagne last night."

"I only asked because I was just about to get my pill and—" It struck her that she didn't remember taking yesterday's. She frowned and hurried into the bathroom to find her makeup bag, quickly spilling out the eye drops she used for a pollen allergy, and the bottle of over-the-counter pain relievers, before pulling out her blister pack of birth control.

Then she said a word she *never* used.

Stavros came to the door. "What's wrong?"

"I always wait until after breakfast." She was shaking,

she was so shocked by what she was seeing. "I have it in my head that medication is better on a full stomach. But when I came back up here yesterday morning…" They had talked and she'd been consumed by what he had told her about his father. She had completely forgotten to take her pill and had carried on with the day.

"It's just one," he said as he looked at the dates on the packet. "That's not usually an issue."

"Except…" She swallowed, feeling nauseous. "Before we left New York, I popped out my pill and left it by the sink, then packed this and went down for breakfast. We ran out to catch the flight right after. I honestly don't remember if I went back and took it."

She was almost certain she hadn't. *Damn it!*

When they had first discussed birth control, Stavros had suggested something like a patch or one of those capsules under the skin. She had never used anything before so she had wanted something temporary, to see how her body responded.

Realizing she had missed *two* made her heart plummet through the earth and into the void of space on the other side.

"We've been having unprotected sex." Her voice trembled and she hardly recognized herself in the mirror. She was white as a sheet.

"We'll get a morning-after pill."

"That's for the *morning after.* It's been three days, Stavros." She slapped the little packet down, but it made only a tinny rattle of a noise, nothing resounding enough for the magnitude of this mistake. Her world, already upside down, began to rend and tear at the seams. "What if I'm pregnant?"

His pupils seemed to explode, turning his eyes midnight black.

"Don't you dare say I did this on purpose," she warned through lips that started to buzz. Her throat burned. "Don't you *dare*."

"I didn't."

She pushed past him to the bedroom, pacing, feeling trapped. She could hardly breathe and the pressure in her skull was so great, she cupped the sides of her head.

"I need to think." But all she could grasp was that they'd been having sex without protection. Lots of it. "Why can't I control myself around you? Why am I so *stupid*?"

Stavros had been dodging this sort of thing from the moment he'd become sexually active. He'd always been diligent about protecting himself as well as his partner, using condoms every single time he had sex. He might have a reckless streak, but he wasn't stupid.

Given how adamant Calli had been that she didn't want children, he had trusted her to take her pills. For the first time in his life, he'd started going bareback. He loved it.

Now he was reaping the consequence. And he might have suspected her of doing this deliberately if she hadn't looked so much like a loved one had died.

"Is this really such a disaster?"

He never would have gotten her pregnant on purpose, but by accident? His hunger for her was showing no signs of abating and, as his mind raced through the ramifications, it hit him that an accidental pregnancy could be a really convenient way of prolonging their arrangement. It wasn't selfish. It was *decent*. Right.

"Make another baby with a man who thinks I'm in it for the money? Who plans to divorce me in a couple of months? What then, Stavros? Do I find myself someone even richer than *you* so I can have access to my child?"

She was like a cat, swift in her turn and swipe of sharp claws. "*Yes*, this is a disaster!"

"We could stay married," he growled.

"Do you love me?"

He instinctively recoiled. Why the hell would she even want him to?

She made a noise too injured to be classified as a laugh. A sharp inhale that dragged over razors. "That's what I thought."

"Calli—" He took a step toward her.

She held him off with an outstretched arm. Her fingers were white at the tips and trembled. "I can't do this again. I *can't*."

"I don't think you planned this," he said through his teeth.

"Yes, you do." Her voice throbbed with such profound defeat it made his heart clench. She looked to the ceiling. "And there I would be, stuck in a marriage with a man who resents me, just so I could be part of my child's life. I'm really making progress on making better life decisions, aren't I? God, I hate myself right now."

"Calli." He tried to take her by the arms, but she shrank away.

"Can you…" Her voice thinned to nothing and she swallowed. "Can you go arrange the car or something? I need a few minutes."

CHAPTER NINE

THEY BARELY SPOKE all the way back to New York. It wasn't an angry silence, just a thick, significant one. They had no sooner landed and she picked up a text from his sister, reminding Calli she had promised to help with her art-exhibit preparations.

While Stavros's middle sister played an active role in the company, coordinating the many women's health interests, his youngest sister painted. Beautifully.

"No, you have to come," she insisted when Calli tried to get out of it. "You had such a good eye for that mat on my seascape."

Calli had had dumb luck when she had set a sample next to the painting, picking up an understated tone so the entire piece popped in a fresh way. She had only agreed to help with the rest of the framing because she hadn't known how to say no nicely.

"You have to tell them," she said to Stavros when she got off the phone. She meant that he had to explain their marriage was temporary.

"We don't know, do we?" he said without inflection.

Even without shades of anger or blame, it was an arrow through the heart.

She had stopped taking the pills altogether and was waiting for her cycle. Please, God, let her get her period.

And since she didn't want to take any further risks of a pregnancy, she supposed disappearing for a few days to the family estate and not sleeping with her husband was a good thing. At least it was something to occupy her mind, rather than obsessing over the child she had and the imaginary one that terrified her because she couldn't say outright that she didn't want it.

She returned to the penthouse a few days later, in time to accompany her husband to his grandfather's retirement party. Once again, she felt like the biggest con artist alive when Edward Michaels singled her out for praise.

"The recent addition of Calli to our family has been a breath of fresh air. I have often believed I knew better than my grandson, but in marrying her, he has proved to me his decisions are sound."

Everyone chuckled while Calli stared at the single drop of red wine that stained the tablecloth in front of her.

"I miss my son every single day," Edward continued. "But I could not be prouder of the heir he gave me in his stead. I know the future of Dýnami is in good hands and I have no qualms leaving it for him to steer."

Stavros seemed a little stunned by what sounded like heartfelt praise. He made a warm and respectful toast, his voice just a tiny bit unsteady. Most wouldn't have noticed, but his mother leaned in to say, "Those two. All I ever see when they're at each other's throats is my husband. They act like they hate each other, but their love runs so deep…" She blinked and small tears hit her lined cheeks.

Calli waited until the applause had died away, then asked, "Did Stavros fight with his father?"

"Oh!" She rolled her eyes. "He was the most headstrong boy. Even before he could speak, he was challenging the both of us. I honestly didn't know what to do with him. And he has never forgiven himself for the accident. I genuinely feared for what he would do to himself without a strong man in his life. When Edward said he wanted to bring us here, of course I went along. It was my children's future. I didn't agree with everything he did, of course. He was hurting, too. We often had words about his decisions."

"In front of the children?"

"Oh, goodness no. The Xenakis men do not enjoy being challenged in front of an audience. They will dig in just to be perverse. No, you pick your time and attack when they least expect it." She made a jabbing motion, as though wielding a pocketknife. "A little advice from a mother who knows." She winked.

Calli chuckled, surprised by this sly side in such an elegant woman. "Stavros told me Edward refused to hear Greek in the house."

"Because our English was terrible! If we were going to live here, we needed to assimilate. Before my husband died, I was so afraid he would take me away from everything I knew, but even I agreed with Edward when it came to giving the children their best advantage. Stavros likes to make out that Edward is some kind of tyrant, but..."

"It takes one to know one?" Calli guessed.

His mother laughed with great enjoyment. "You've met my son! If he only knew the number of times Edward begged me to take him back to Greece and leave him there." She smiled, but it wobbled. "We used to laugh and cry then, both of us missing my Stavros so badly."

Calli squeezed her arm and tilted her head against the woman's shoulder in a show of compassion.

Stavros returned to their table, brows raised in query as he saw the affection between them.

"We're bonding," his mother said, catching at Calli's face and pressing a kiss to her cheek. "Your grandfather isn't the only one who is pleased with at least *one* of your decisions."

He made some dry remark and the evening continued, but he brought it up when they came into the penthouse after midnight.

"What were you and my mother talking about?"

"Your father. And that she didn't regret bringing you here because she thought you needed your grandfather's influence growing up."

He made a face, one that suggested he might have to reluctantly concede that.

"I'm going to bed," she said, and halted when he said, "Where?"

She turned back, not saying anything. She'd been sleeping in the guest room.

He sighed. "I can wear a condom."

"I won't relax until I know."

The restless look he gave her made her skin tighten. He was thinking about seducing her.

"Don't." It was more plea than order and made him look away.

He hissed out another breath. "Go to bed, then."

Stavros had mountains of work ahead of him, now that he had achieved the pinnacle position in the company. He ought to be immersing himself in it, but found himself with palms flat on his desk, staring discontentedly at the email from Norma.

A letter was forwarded a week ago to the family we believe adopted Dorian. No response yet.

A letter. What kind of letter? To whom exactly? If he was this impatient for answers, he could only imagine how Calli felt.

Calli. He hit Forward on the email, sent it to her, then

sat down, prickling with tension. Along with due process, Mother Nature was also taking her time providing news.

Did he want her to be pregnant? It meant they could take up where they'd been and he could keep her longer than a few months.

Not that she was as warm to the idea.

Do you love me?

He had shied away from answering when she had thrown the question at him and still wasn't ready to explore what he felt toward her. It didn't matter. He couldn't ask for her heart either way.

His phone buzzed, snapping him out of his introspection.

He started to set the device to Ignore, but saw it was an unfamiliar number. A premonition made him swipe to answer. "Yes?"

"Mr. Xenakis? It's Ian. The weekday doorman at your building. I see there's a notation on your account that you'd like to be notified if—"

"Underwood is there?" Stavros nearly leaped out of his skin.

"No, sir. But a woman was here in the lobby just now. Wanda Abbott. She asked me to ring your wife, but Mrs. Xenakis came down before I could reach her. She was going out, but I overheard Mrs. Abbott say she and your wife shared a connection through Mr. Underwood. Your wife took her upstairs. I wasn't sure if that was something you wanted to be informed about?"

"Definitely," Stavros said, already on his feet and striding for the door.

Calli was grateful when Wanda Abbott refused coffee or tea. She was shaking too much to pour so much as a glass of water without soaking herself in the process.

Wanda wasn't doing much better. She wore a tailored

pencil skirt with a classic sweater set, looking very much an Underwood, even though she explained that she was only a second cousin by a half sister who had married into the Underwood family. She had at least fifteen years on Calli and even though she was perfectly made up and obviously took very good care of herself, she looked every one of those additional years. Her lipstick stood out on her pale features and her eyes were not only weary but tortured.

"I had no idea there was anything about the process that wasn't completely aboveboard," she said after dropping the bombshell that her son, James, had been adopted shortly after his birth six years ago. "I knew Brandon had fathered him, but we were told the mother had given him up because she was too young. Brandon was only nineteen. I understood why he wasn't ready to be a parent. I had had surgery in my teens that left me sterile and we wanted children so badly…" Her eyes filled.

"My signature was forged," Calli blurted, needing to impress that into the woman.

"So the letter said. It didn't even occur to me such a thing could happen. I was just too happy to have a baby." Wanda's gaze pleaded with Calli for understanding. "We had already been on wait lists with agencies for several years. I didn't take him because the Underwoods set up a trust for him. I wanted *him*. He was such a gift."

Calli searched Wanda's expression, seeing again that plea for understanding. That vulnerability that a baby created in his mother. She probably wore the same expression. *Don't take him from me.*

"Brandon had his whole life ahead of him, they said. A career in politics. That's why they wanted us to keep James's paternity confidential. Brandon's mother comes to see him a few times a year, but not even my sister knows." She dug in her handbag for a tissue, pushed it up against her nose. "When the letter from your lawyers arrived, I was beyond stunned. Devastated."

"I tried once before—"

"So my husband admitted, once I showed him the letter. He said the Underwoods would make it all go away, that they had before. He was furious I opened it. I thought it was about whether we could access James's trust for our daughter's hospital bills. I haven't been myself since she was diagnosed."

"I— What? What do you mean?" Calli pinched her clammy fingers between her knees.

"Our youngest has leukemia. We're not... Well, we're trying everything. It's been difficult." Her eyes filled. "And then to get this news, that we might have to fight to keep James—" She choked and jammed her fist against her mouth.

Calli felt as though she stared down a train, but she was paralyzed. Couldn't move. It was going to flatten her and leave her in pieces, but she was tied to the tracks, unable to avoid it.

"My husband is going to kill me for coming here, but I had to. I had to tell you that I didn't *know*. I would never do that to someone. And I came to beg you, Calli. *Beg you*. You have every right to want to see James, but now is such a bad time. I'm trying so hard to keep things normal for him. He's usually such a happy boy, but lately he's been acting out and he's not sleeping... He's worried about his sister."

The train whistle filled her ears. The clatter of its wheels grew deafening.

"He knows he's adopted. I've braced myself for this sort of thing, always imagining I would graciously welcome his birth mother into our lives..." Her tears overflowed and her shoulders began to shake. "I knew people's feelings could change. But I just can't do this right now. And if you started picking apart the adoption, tore him from the only home he knows… It could do lasting damage. I'm begging you not to do that to him, Calli."

And there it was. At least now she knew he was loved. He had a mother who would do *anything* to spare her son pain.

"Could…" Calli had to clear her throat. "Could I see a photo of him, at least?"

Stavros was damn near propelled up the elevator by fury alone. It coursed through him like rocket fuel. The door opened and he charged into the penthouse to the anticlimactic sight of Calli curled up in the armchair, looking at her phone.

"Where is she?"

"Who?"

"Underwood's minion."

She was inordinately pale. Her eyes were rimmed in red, but there was a strange acceptance in her. She looked sober and grave, but resolved. Like one of those religious icons who accepted life's brutality with grace and humility.

"He did go to a loving family." She held out her phone. "She gave me some photos. He looks really happy."

Stavros took it and glanced at a boy with a cheeky grin, his eyes endearingly familiar with their brown-gold color. He swiped to the next one and saw the boy with his arm looped around the neck of a fuzzy-headed, brown-skinned toddler.

"That's his sister. She's sick. Really sick." She took back the phone, swept to another photo, adding in a small voice, "I hope he doesn't lose her. It sounds like they're really close."

"She might be lying," he warned, still battle ready.

"She's not." She swiped for another photo, gaze greedily eating up the image of her son. "She said she would send me updates. That she would try to find a way for me to meet him, but that it probably wouldn't be until they knew what was happening with her daughter."

"You're going to accept that?"

Her gaze came up. "She *begged* me, Stavros. She doesn't have any pride where his well-being is concerned. Mothers sacrifice themselves for their children. The most loving thing *I* could do for him, as his mother, is not pursue my own interests over his. He's in good hands. At least I know that now." She swiped the inside of her wrist against her cheek, clenched her eyes hard then opened them wide, trying to clear the wetness so she could see the screen.

"Calli." He sat on the ottoman and reached to circle her ankle with a comforting grip.

She clicked off the phone and tucked it against her breast. The sound was oddly loud. Significant.

"I'm not pregnant."

A wash of something went over him, far more profound than disappointment. Dread. Portent of pain.

"I see." He didn't know what else to say. He felt sick.

"It's for the best," she said without inflection.

His hand was still on her ankle, but he felt as though he was waving his hand through smoke, trying to catch at her. She was nothing but vapor.

"I think..." Her brow flinched and she cleared her throat. "I think it would also be for the best if we ended things here. Now." Her gaze came back to focus on him, but it held an emptiness that made a protest rise in his throat.

"You agreed to six months." His voice had to push past gravel in his chest.

"I don't care about the money. I don't want it. We both

have what we really wanted from this marriage." She clicked her phone and gazed at it again. The yearning in her face was too acute to bear.

She didn't have what she wanted. Not really.

"Calli—"

"I have to leave before I get hurt, Stavros. Before I start believing I belong here and that you and I have more than sexual attraction. Before I fall in love with you."

He flinched at the word again, part of him thinking, *Do it. Fall.* But he couldn't say it aloud. Couldn't ask that of her. Couldn't accept it, even if she offered it.

"Take pity on me," she begged softly, touching his hand in a caress that made all the hairs on his body stand up. "I'm not as strong as you are."

Was that what he was? Strong? He felt weak as a kitten. Utterly helpless.

Very slowly, very reluctantly, he released his hold on her and let his empty hands hang between his knees.

"Whatever you want," he said in a rasp.

An hour later, she had packed a single bag and the apartment was empty. She was gone.

CHAPTER TEN

"WHAT THE HELL do you mean, she's gone?" Edward Michaels demanded a week later, when he called Stavros to the town house, apparently planning to hand over this mansion to his grandson as a belated wedding gift.

"I mean she left. Went back to Greece." Stavros stuffed his hands into his pockets and rocked his heels on the carpet where he had taken more stinging lectures from this old man than either of them could possibly recount.

"What the hell did you do?"

"Nothing." Stavros looked to the reds and golds he knew so well, bit the bullet and came clean. "I only married her to get the company."

"Yes, I know that," his grandfather said scathingly. "But why did you let her go?"

Of course his grandfather had seen clear through it. He was sharp as a tack.

"There's this thing called 'unlawful confinement.' Even I have my limits."

"Steven—"

"Don't call me that."

"Damn you, what does it matter what I call you?" Edward's hand slapped the antique desk that was pure decoration now. No longer used by that man, and would remain unused because Stavros couldn't stomach moving into this mansion and living here alone. He would rather be in the penthouse, where he could still see her rising to greet him, or walking up the stairs with a flash of her legs, or inviting him with a glance over her shoulder into the bed they had shared.

"*Imbecile.* All I have ever wanted was for you to quit throwing away your life like it doesn't matter and you do *this*?"

"I didn't throw her away. She *left*."

"Because you didn't hold on to her!"

"I *couldn't*! She deserves better. You think I don't know what matters? I was thinking of *her*."

"The hell you were. Are you feeling good, wallowing in the misery you created for yourself? I thought it was bad when you kept trying to kill yourself as punishment. Now you're going to carve out your heart and let her take it back to Greece?"

"It's where I left it," Stavros ground out.

"Your father would have wanted—"

"Don't tell me what he wanted. I know what he wanted." *Swim. I'll be right behind you.*

"He would have wanted you to live, Stavros. Properly. Not with a death wish. He would want you to love and have a family. Children. That's what *I* wanted for *him*. It's what I have always wanted for *you*."

"You wanted him to come back here and grow the company," Stavros reminded hotly. "You fought all the time about his staying in Greece."

"I wanted my son in my life. I wanted him back here to work with me, yes. I was creating a legacy and wanted him to be part of it. But I was…" Edward made a noise and waved a dismissive hand. "I was jealous. All right? Of your mother's hold on him. Your grandmother was a good woman, but I didn't love her the way your father loved your mother. I grew up a son of immigrants. We had nothing when we started. Money and success were always more important to me than love. I thought he should feel the same."

Stavros thought back to the latent anger in his father's voice, his mother's mollifying tone as they talked about the power struggle between the two generations. The conflict of loyalties.

"I regret that I was so hard on him for putting his wife and children ahead of me. I resented his buying a home in Greece and spending so much time with you there. I will always be sorry that he died before we resolved that. It was worse when you came to live here. I learned what a truly generous and loving person your mother is. They should have had more time together."

Stavros winced.

"I'm not blaming you for that! I'm telling you I blame myself. I shouldn't have made him feel as if he had to choose. You don't own the patent on being hardheaded, Stavros. We're all guilty of it. If I had asked him, rather than ordered, you might have been on an airplane to come here, rather than on the sea that day."

Stavros shook his head. "I'm the one who wanted to go fishing. It was my fault we were out there."

"And he indulged you because he wanted a better relationship with his son than he'd had with his father. It took me a long time to see that. To recognize the mistakes I had made with him and continued to make with you."

"You had every right to be hard on me. I was a little bastard."

"You were," Edward agreed without compunction. "And when you showed up with Calli the way you did, I saw myself in that cutthroat tactic. I realized I had raised you to be exactly like me, and I was not proud of myself. Then

I got to know her and she doesn't give a damn about our money. The way she looked at you... Even I could recognize it as the furthest thing from avarice. She loves you. And, damn it, as much as you wanted the directorship, you left by five every night. You wanted to get back to her. I thought you were finding the kind of happiness I denied your father."

Stavros pinched the bridge of his nose, thinking about how he had watched the clock, eager to get home to his wife. Since she had left, time crawled. He worked late and woke early in an empty bed. It was a meaningless way to start a day.

Do you love me?

He had never felt he deserved such a thing. He had certainly done his best to make his grandfather reject him. Only his mother and sisters were allowed to love him, and then only because he couldn't bear to hurt them by cutting them from his life.

Calli wasn't allowed to love him.

But when she had said her little speech about showing her love for her son by bowing out of his life, Stavros had known he had to let her go. He had been so certain he was doing right by her. Letting her go because he *loved* her.

"I am an imbecile."

"Finally we agree on something." His grandfather slapped his shoulder. "Go get her, son."

The knock at the door had Ophelia sitting up from her slouch on the sofa. "Pizza!" She clicked to pause the movie.

"You did not order pizza," Calli protested. She was going to gain three hundred pounds before this girl left for school.

Ophelia's expression blanked. "I thought you did."

"No. I said we're not charging anything more to your father's card."

"He's fine with it." Ophelia groaned, pushing to her feet and sending Calli a scowl of impatience. It turned to a frown of curiosity. "If not pizza, who's at the door?" She moved to go on tiptoe, peering through the peephole. "Oh, my God!" she hissed. "It's your *husband.*"

"What? Don't—"

Too late. Ophelia swung the door open. "*Geia.* What are you doing here?"

"Ophelia…" *Don't be rude*, Calli wanted to say, but the sight of Stavros nearly knocked her off her feet as she tried to stand. How could he have grown more handsome in a handful of weeks? While wearing stubble and a wrinkled shirt with a loosened tie?

At the sound of her voice, his gaze swept to slam into hers. "What are *you* doing *here?*"

"Girls' night," Ophelia volunteered with a wave at the litter they had accumulated. "Popcorn. Ice cream. Movie without nudity because she thinks I'm still *nine.*" She folded her arms and lifted her brows in disdain.

Stavros came into the flat and closed the door.

"I mean, why are you staying here?" He didn't take his eyes off Calli. "I gave you the codes to our flat before you left." For the Xenakis penthouse, he meant. The one that provided views of both the Acropolis and the horizon on the sea, rather than being tucked on the edge of that posh address and overlooking the red lower rooftops of middle-class districts in Athens.

"Takis had to travel. Ophelia didn't want to stay with her grandparents." And their marriage was a farce. He was divorcing her. Had he forgotten? She hadn't.

"So he's not here?" Stavros cut a swift, sharp look around what had always seemed a luxurious flat to Calli, but compared to the way Stavros lived was only very nice. There were three bedrooms, but they were quite small. The decor was professionally selected, but the wall art was prints, not originals. The rugs weren't hand-loomed.

"He'll be gone the week. Why? Do you need to speak to him?"

"No. You're not working for him again, are you?"

"Kind of." She scratched her elbow. "I took his things to the dry cleaners and brought in some groceries, so I'm not freeloading. Mostly I just wanted to spend some time with Ophelia before she goes to school."

She had told Ophelia about Dorian. All of it. Ophelia was at an age where boys were beginning to occupy a lot of her thoughts, and it had seemed a sensible cautionary tale. It had also been cathartic, and Ophelia's reaction, so defensive on Calli's behalf, had been incredibly sweet. The empty calories and mindless movies had been Ophelia's attempt to spoil her, trying to help her heal while Calli figured out her next moves.

"We're homesick," Ophelia announced, moving to throw her arm around Calli. "I wanted her to take me back to the island, since technically she's still your wife and owns half of our old house, but she said it wouldn't be right." Ophelia wrinkled her nose at him. "Care to weigh in with a different opinion?"

"You may use the house anytime," Stavros offered with an offhand shrug.

"See?" Ophelia beamed smugly at Calli.

"If you could give us a few minutes of privacy right now."

"Oh." The girl's smile fell away. "Fine. I'll go to my room and put in my earbuds so you grown-ups can talk."

Don't go, Calli wanted to say as Ophelia went down the hall and a door firmly closed. She wasn't prepared for this. She had convinced herself she would never see Stavros again.

And she had felt like she was slowly bleeding out because of it.

"Calli—you don't have to work." He touched his forehead, pained, adding impatiently, "Of course, you don't know that because you're not at the penthouse. If you were, you would have received the courier envelope from Norma, explaining that the Underwoods have made you a settlement offer. For what it's worth, Brandon will have to give up his own babies—those precious horses of his—to even approach the number I suggested was a good opener."

"What?"

"Do not sign anything until you discuss it with me or Takis. You sell yourself way too short in these kinds of things. Soak him, damn it. Give it all to charity after, if you can't stand to take it, but wring him dry."

He sounded positively bloodthirsty. "Is that why you're here? To discuss that? Because—"

"No." He frowned. "I'm here because…"

"Oh, were there other papers I should have signed?" Something worse occurred. "Your grandfather didn't back out, did he? Oh, Stavros—"

"Calli, be quiet." He ran a hand down his face, then held out his palm as if requesting patience. "I shouldn't be snapping at you. It's frustration. You weren't answering my texts and you weren't at the flat. Until I actually clapped eyes on you, I was quite worried something had happened."

"I'm fine. I changed my number when I got a new phone, but my email is still the same. You could have tried that."

"Why did you change your phone? I can afford to keep

paying your bills. I told you to use our flat." He was back to snapping.

"It's your family's flat. It didn't seem right."

"It's *ours*. Yours and mine." He stared at her, lips a white line. "I'm not used to being erased from a person's life like this."

Was that hurt in his tone? She dropped her gaze to his polished shoes. "You did a lot for me. I didn't want to keep taking advantage."

"I paid to have *one* letter written. You're not even wearing the clothes I bought for you. You left the necklace. Everything." Both his empty hands came up, like he couldn't fathom it.

She became acutely aware of her oversize T-shirt and striped leggings, her bare face and feet, the hair she had let air dry after her shower. Her lack of a bra.

She folded her arms.

"Do you love Takis? Is that it?"

"What? No. I told you. I love him like a father or a brother, not like that."

"Do you love *me*?"

"What?" She had the feeling of a hot spotlight finding her and glaring mercilessly, giving her no place to hide.

He knew. Behind his frustration was a glittering knowledge. Certainty. He was nodding like it was a foregone conclusion.

Her eyes stung and she looked away. "Stavros," she protested weakly.

"You do. You love me 'like that,' but you won't let *me* take care of you. That doesn't make sense, Calli."

"You don't love me." The words came out thin and dry.

"You're completely content to love in one direction. You love your son without his even knowing you're alive. You love that girl even though she pushes all your buttons." He pointed toward the hall. "I would bet my entire fortune that deep down, you still have something like love for your parents, even though they don't deserve it. You love unconditionally and without reserve, Calli. And you love me. I know you do. But you left me and I finally figured out why. It's because there's one person you *don't* love. *Yourself.*"

She flinched as though he had struck her and started to turn away, but he caught her back, his hands warm and strong on her arms.

"It wasn't your fault, Calli."

"Don't." She tried to twist out of his hold, but he made her look him in the eye.

"Stop blaming yourself. You think I don't understand? I'm a piece of walking garbage. That's how I've felt since I outswam my father and made it to shore without him. You asked me if I loved you and I couldn't bring myself to saddle you with this." He tapped the place over his heart. "Who could possibly *want* my love? It's worthless."

"Don't say that."

"I let you go, didn't I? I let you walk away thinking I didn't love you. That you weren't worthy of love. You are. So very much. My love for you takes up so much room in me, I can barely breathe."

"Stavros."

"You're not tainted. You're not a bad mother. You're a warm and loving woman." He cupped her cheeks, filled her vision with the tender look on his face. "Redeem us both, Calli. Tell me I'm worthy of love and let me do the same for you."

Her vision began to blur. She blinked. The hot drops of her tears leaked onto her cheeks. "I've made a lot of mistakes."

"Me, too. But I love you exactly as you are. Now admit you love me, flaws and all."

"I do. I love you." The words hurt, tearing a hole in her heart that immediately filled in a rush, swelling it to painful capacity. She could hardly draw breath, especially when his lips touched hers.

The light kiss was benediction. A cool satin ribbon of touch, then a warmer press. Love. Sweet, sweet love that gently opened to passion. His hand moved into her hair. She stepped into his heat. Their mouths melded, deepening the kiss by increments until they were one being, sharing themselves with the other.

On and on they kissed. Her arms were around his neck, his heart beating so hard in his chest she felt it against her breast.

He drew back to dry her cheek with the pad of his thumb. *"S'agapó gynaíka mou." I love you, my wife.* "I refuse to divorce you. What do you think of that?"

"I think you're saving me from myself." She tucked her face into his shirt and hugged him tightly. "I'm scared to love this much. To want."

"I've thrown myself off cliffs with less terror than I felt coming after you. Failure was not an option." His hand clenched in her hair. "I told you once that I didn't have a reason to live, but I do. *You* are that reason, Calli." His arms banded her to him like he would never let her go.

"You have a lot of reasons, Stavros."

"You have a lot of modesty, *glykia mou.* Do not underestimate what you mean to me."

She drew back, the vastness of it all lodging in her chest. "I wanted to be pregnant," she admitted huskily, laying bare her deepest longing. It was a small test, perhaps, but he passed, easily.

"I wanted that, too." He caressed her jaw. "When you're

ready, *agápi mou.* When you're sure of me, we will make as many babies as you want. And we will always have room for your son."

How did she deserve him? Her face crumpled. "I love you, Stavros."

"I love you, too."

EPILOGUE

OF ALL THE death-defying stunts Stavros had pulled over the years, nothing had left him as keyed up with adrenaline as watching his wife give birth. He'd been utterly helpless, forced to watch her suffer the pain and conquer her fear and push through a feat devised by nature as the ultimate test.

She and his son had come through with flying colors, but ten days later, Stavros was still dry-mouthed and quite certain he would never try *that* again.

"Is he awake?" Calli murmured drowsily, stirring from her nap on their bed.

Stavros looked from the growing discontent in the face of their swaddled infant to his wife. Her color was good, her smile well rested. Joy shone from beneath her heavy eyelids. She was so beautiful, she flipped his heart.

"He woke a little while ago, but has been trying to latch on to my arm the last few minutes. I thought I'd better bring him to the source. Company will be here soon anyway."

He sat on the edge of the bed and used his free hand to help her sit up. He waited while she arranged a few pillows and sat back, then handed over Lethe, watching as she took him to her breast as though she'd been doing this all her life.

He stole a slow, shaky breath. The boy didn't even weigh

eight pounds, but the heft of responsibility he had thrown onto Stavros was profound. He was still coming to terms with it.

"Did I hear the phone earlier?"

"Ophelia. Exams went well. She's flying to Athens tomorrow and Takis will bring her next week. Then I talked to Takis and told him we'd like her to stay the summer if he's willing. He said at her age, extended time with a newborn could go either way in terms of curbing impulsive behavior."

They both chuckled and Stavros cocked his ear. "There's the doorbell."

Simpson would get it. They had settled into Edward's mansion last year, once her pregnancy had been confirmed, and had quickly adopted his grandfather's routine of spending half their time here and the rest at Galíni. In fact, they had gone there straight from the hospital and had only come back to the city last night.

Stavros went to greet their guests while Calli finished nursing, then made herself presentable.

When she came down the stairs, James—whom she still called Dorian in her heart—was hanging off the newel post at the bottom, waiting with barely contained impatience. His wide grin was missing all four front teeth. He extended a stuffed bear wearing a blue ribbon around its neck.

"Is that for me?" She stooped for a hug.

"It's for my brother." He was reaching the age where shows of affection were brief, even with his mothers, but he lingered in her looped arm, staring into Lethe's sleeping face. "Is that him?"

"This is Lethe, yes. He'll love it. Thank you." She tucked the bear against Lethe's freshly swaddled chest. "How is your sister? How was her appointment yesterday?"

"She's sick. She couldn't come."

"Just a cold," Wanda quickly provided as Calli shot her a look of concern. "Her counts were exactly where they should be." She crossed her fingers. "But we didn't want to get Lethe sick, so she stayed home with Daddy."

"I hope she feels better soon." Calli rose to hug Wanda.

Wanda smiled at Lethe with the melting expression most women wore when they gazed on a newborn. "Oh, he's beautiful. Look at that mouth. It's yours, same as James's."

They had become fast friends, she and Wanda. Calli had only been back in New York a few weeks when Wanda had invited her to visit James. She was a woman with a strong conscience who had been torturing herself since asking Calli to back off. "You obviously love him," she had said. "Who am I to deny my son more love in his life? What if something happened and I had kept you apart?"

Calli had sat with Wanda more than once as she waited for her daughter to come out of treatment. They shared a son and so much more.

"We've been very excited all morning," Wanda said ruefully, as James went on his tiptoes, trying to see Lethe again.

"Lethe, too." Stavros was completely straight-faced as he teased James. "He's been asking for you. All morning."

"He's a baby!" James protested, giving Stavros a you-can't-fool-me look.

Those two had their own special relationship characterized by discussions of heavy equipment and debates about superheroes and spirited wrestling matches over possession of a foam football.

"Do you want to hold him?" Calli sat down on the sofa and patted the cushion beside her. James wriggled his bottom into position beside her, right up against her side.

Her heart melted every time she was with him, every time she gazed into his bright, cheeky expression.

Gently she set her newborn son in the arms of her first-born, keeping one hand lightly on the infant, securing him on James's lap. She was so happy in that moment, she could hardly bear it.

Lethe yawned and opened his eyes, making James jolt with excitement. "He's looking at me."

"He is." Her throat was nearly too tight to speak. "Say hello."

"Hello, Lethe. I'm James. Your brother." Then he leaned down to whisper. "I love you."

Calli's eyes filled.

"This is too cute for words," Wanda said, voice throbbing with emotion. "Stavros, sit down with them. I need a photo."

He sat on the far side of James, arm outstretched so his fingers caressed Calli's shoulder. She lifted her gaze from her children to meet her husband's warm, dark eyes. She saw so much love reflected back at her, she thought she would combust.

"Do you know how happy it makes me to see you this happy?" he said in a quiet rumble.

"You must be pretty happy, then," she choked.

He gave her cheek an affectionate brush with the back of his finger, sweeping away her tear. "I am."

Later, when the house was quiet and their son was settled in his bassinet, and they were naked in the big bed they shared, she snuggled into Stavros and said with a tiny throb of old anxiety, "I sometimes wonder what would have happened if Sebastien hadn't sent you to the island."

Sebastien was still setting up his extreme challenges, but Stavros was picking and choosing, just as happy to schedule a ski trip or another more mainstream vacation with his friends. Calli had developed wonderful friendships with all the wives, which was another thing she would have missed if Stavros hadn't taken that dare from his friend.

The happiness she enjoyed seemed so tentative sometimes.

But his low rumble was reassuringly confident. "You would have come here for Dorian and I would have seen you. We would be exactly where we are right now."

"In a city this huge?" She lifted her head from his shoulder, trying to see him in the dim light from the clock. "You really believe you would have noticed me?"

"I do. Even if you had been able to keep him, our lives would have found another way to intersect. We were meant to be together, Calli."

"Oh." His words panged her heart. "When you say things like that, I believe you." She cuddled into him again, squeezing her arm across his waist, eyes closed against emotive tears.

"No one could love you the way I love you." He cradled her close, lips against her hair, then her cheekbone, searching for her mouth. "No one else could love me the way you do."

They kissed. The passion between them hadn't abated, staying strong between them right up to the evening before she delivered. He'd been a perfect gentleman since the birth, but she could feel how aroused he became, and stroked him.

He groaned. "I miss making love to you."

"We'll have to find other ways to appease ourselves, won't we?" she teased. "Lucky for you, I'm an inventive woman."

"I'm fairly innovative myself. Let's see what we come up with."

He pressed over her and she made a noise of indulgence, already sinking into the world of pleasure he gave her. The joy.

He was right. Something this perfect must have been fated. She never worried about it again.

* * * * *

WEDDING NIGHT
REUNION IN GREECE

ANNIE WEST

Dedicated with thanks and affection to
the people of Corfu,
whose warmth made my first visit to that
beautiful island so memorable.

CHAPTER ONE

'CONGRATULATIONS, CHRISTO.' DAMEN grinned and gripped his friend's arm in a hard clasp. 'I didn't think I'd ever see the day.'

'You didn't think I'd invite you to my wedding?' Christo smiled. Who else would he ask to stand up as his best man but Damen, his friend since childhood?

'You know what I mean. I never expected to see you married till you'd played the field for another decade and decided it was time to breed some heirs.'

The look that passed between them revealed their shared understanding of what it meant to be the sole male heir to a family dynasty—Damen's in shipping and Christo's in property. There were expectations and responsibilities, always, even if they came with the cushion of wealth and privilege.

At the thought of his newest responsibility, Christo rolled his shoulders. The stiffness pinching the back of his neck was familiar. But now he could relax. With the wedding over, his plans fell into place. He'd had a problem and he'd fixed it, simple as that. Life could resume its even course. The glow of satisfaction he'd felt as he'd slid the ring onto Emma's small hand burned brighter.

Everything had worked out perfectly.

'I'm glad you could get here at short notice.' Despite Christo's lack of sentimentality, it felt good to have his old friend with him.

Besides, it would have looked strange if there'd been no one from the groom's side, even at such a small wedding. Damen had arrived in Melbourne just in time for the private ceremony. Now, in the gardens of the bride's home, this was their first opportunity to talk.

'She's not what I expected, your little bride.'

Christo raised an enquiring eyebrow.

'She's besotted with you for a start. What she sees in you...' Damen shook his head in mock puzzlement, as if women didn't swarm around Christo like bees around blossom. It was another thing they had in common.

'Of course Emma's besotted. She's marrying *me*.'

Christo had no false modesty about his appeal to the opposite sex. Besides, he'd wooed old Katsoyiannis's granddaughter carefully, taking his time in a way that wasn't usually necessary to win a woman. Having his proposal rejected hadn't figured in Christo's plans.

He'd done an excellent job. A spark of heat ignited at the memory of Emma's wide-eyed gaze and the eager way she'd returned his perfunctory end-of-ceremony kiss, tempting him to prolong it into something more passionate. Christo's hands had tightened on her slender waist and he'd found himself looking forward to tonight when he'd take her to his bed for the first time.

Damen huffed out a laugh. 'There speaks the mighty Christo Karides, ego as big as the Mediterranean.' He frowned and glanced back at the house, as if confirming they were alone. Everyone was at the wedding breakfast on the far side of the building. 'But, seriously, I was surprised. Emma's lovely. Very sweet.' Another pause. 'But not your usual type.' His look turned piercing. 'I'd have thought her cousin more your speed. The vivacious redhead.'

Christo nodded, picturing Maia's pin-up-perfect curves in the tight clothes she favoured. Her confidence, her sexy banter as she'd tried to hook his attention. She would have succeeded, too, if things had been different.

A twinge of pain seared from Christo's skull to his shoulders and he rubbed a hand around his neck.

'You're right, she's gorgeous. In other circumstances we'd have had fun together.' He shook his head. His situation was immutable. Regrets were useless. 'But this is marriage we're talking about, not pleasure.'

A muffled sound made Christo turn to scrutinise the back of the large house. But there was no movement at the windows, no one on the flagstone patio or sweeping lawn. No sound except the distant strains of music.

He'd have to return to the celebration soon before his bride wondered what was taking him so long.

A beat of satisfaction quickened Christo's pulse. 'Emma's not sexy and sophisticated like her cousin, or as beautiful, but her grandfather left her the Athens property I came to buy. Marriage was the price of acquiring it.'

Damen's smile faded. 'You married for *that*? I knew the deal was important but surely you didn't need to—?'

'You're right. Normally I wouldn't consider it, but circumstances changed.' Christo shrugged and adopted a nonchalant expression to camouflage the tension he still felt at the profound changes in his life. 'I find myself in the bizarre situation of inheriting responsibility for a child.' Saying it aloud didn't make it sound any more palatable, or lessen his lingering shock. 'Can you imagine *me* as a father?'

He nodded as his friend's eyes bulged. 'You see why marriage suddenly became necessary, if not appealing. It isn't a sexy siren I need. Instead I've acquired a gentle, sensible homebody who wants only to please me. She'll make the perfect caring mother.'

Emma's hands gripped the edge of the basin so tight, she couldn't feel her fingers. That was one small mercy because the rest of her felt like one huge, raw wound throbbing in acute agony.

She blinked and stared at the mirror in the downstairs rear bathroom. The one to which she and her bridesmaid had retired for a quick make-up fix as the bathroom at the front of the house was engaged. The one with an open window, obscured by ivy, that gave onto the sprawling back garden.

In the mirror, dazed hazel eyes stared back at her. Her mouth in that new lipstick she'd thought so sophisticated was a crumpled line of colour too bright for parchment-pale cheeks.

Around her white face she still wore the antique lace of her grandmother's veil.

Emma shuddered and shut her eyes, suddenly hating the weight of the lace against her cheeks and the long wedding dress around her shaky legs. The fitted gown, so perfect before, now clasped her too tightly, making her skin clammy, nipping at her waist and breasts and squeezing her lungs till she thought they might burst.

'Did you know?'

Emma's eyes popped open to meet Steph's in the mirror. Instead of turning into a wax doll like Emma, shock made Steph look vibrant. Her eyes sparked and a flush climbed her cheeks.

'Stupid question. Of course you didn't know.' Her friend's generous mouth twisted into a snarl. 'I'll kill him with my bare hands. No, killing's too good. Slow torture. That's what he deserves.' She scowled ferociously. 'How could he treat you that way? He must know how you feel about him.'

The pain in Emma's chest intensified from terrible to excruciating. It felt as though she was being torn apart. Which made sense, as she'd been foolish enough to hand her heart to Christo Karides and he'd just ripped it out.

Without warning.

Without anaesthetic.

Without apology.

'Because he doesn't care.' The words slipped through numb lips. 'He never really cared about me.'

As soon as she said the words aloud Emma felt their truth, despite the romantic spell Christo had woven around her. He'd been kind and understanding, tender and support- ive, as she'd grappled with her grandfather's death. She'd taken his old-fashioned courtesy as proof of his respect for her, his willingness to wait. Now she realised his patience and restraint had been because he didn't fancy her at all.

Nausea surged as the blindfold ripped from her eyes.

Why hadn't she seen it before? Why hadn't she listened to Steph when she'd spoken of taking things slowly? Of not making important decisions while she was emotion- ally vulnerable?

Emma had been lost in a fairy tale this last month, a fairy tale where, as grief struck yet again, her Prince Charming was with her, not to rescue her but to be there for her, making her feel she wasn't alone.

Everyone she'd loved in this life had died. Her parents when she was eleven, abruptly wiped out of her life when the small plane they'd been in went down in a storm. Then her grandmother four years ago when Emma was eighteen. And now her opinionated, hopelessly old-fashioned yet wonderful Papou. The sense of loss had been unbearable, except when Christo had been beside her.

She drew a sharp breath that lanced tight lungs, then let it out on a bitter laugh. 'He doesn't even know who I am. He has no idea.'

Wants only to please him, indeed!

A homebody!

Obviously Christo had believed Papou, who'd insisted on thinking she studied to fill in time before she found the right man to marry!

Maybe Christo thought she lived in her grandparents' house because she was meek and obedient. The truth was that, despite his bluster, Papou had been lost when her grandmother had died and Emma had decided to stay till he recovered. But then his health had failed and there'd been no good time to leave.

The tragedy of it was that Emma had thought Christo truly understood her. She'd believed he spent time with her because he found her interesting and attractive.

But not as attractive as her *vivacious, gorgeous* cousin Maia.

Pain cramped Emma's belly and her breath sawed from constricted lungs.

Bad enough that Christo viewed her as a plain Jane compared with her *sexy siren* cousin. But the fact he hadn't noticed that Maia was warm-hearted, intelligent and funny, as well as sexy, somehow made it worse.

Christo was a clever man. According to Papou, his insightfulness had made him phenomenally successful, transforming the family business he'd inherited. Clearly Christo didn't waste time applying that insight to the women he met.

Because we're not important enough?

Because he thinks we're simply available for him to use as he sees fit?

What that said about his attitude to women made Emma's skin shrink against her bones.

He had a reputation as a playboy in Europe, always dating impossibly glamorous, gorgeous women. But in her naivety Emma had dismissed the media gossip. She'd believed him when he'd assured her his reputation was exaggerated. Then he'd stroked her cheek, his hand dropping to her collarbone, tracing the decorous neckline of her dress, and Emma had forgotten her doubts and her train of thought.

She'd been so easy to manipulate! Ready to fall for his practised charm. For his attentiveness.

Because he was the first man who'd really noticed her.

Was she really so easily conned?

Emma lurched forward over the basin as nausea rocketed up from her stomach. Bile burnt the back of her throat and she retched again and again.

When it was over, and she'd rinsed her mouth and face, she looked up at her friend. 'I *believed* in him, Steph. I actually thought the fact he didn't respond to Maia was proof he was genuinely attracted to *me*.' Her voice rose to something like a wail and Emma bit her lip.

She'd been gullible. She'd brushed aside her friend's tentative questions about the speed of Christo's courtship. At the time it had made sense to marry quickly so her Papou could be with them. And when he'd died, well, the last thing he'd said to her was how happy he was knowing she had Christo and that he didn't want her to delay the wedding.

She should have waited.

She should have known romantic fantasies were too good to be true.

'I've been a complete idiot, haven't I?' She'd always been careful—cautious rather than adventurous, sensible rather than impulsive—yet she'd let a handsome face and a lying, cheating, silver tongue distract her from her career plans and her innate caution.

'Of course not, sweetie.' Steph put her arm around her shoulders, squeezing tight. 'You're warm and generous and honest and you always look for the good in people.'

Emma shook her head, dredging up a tight smile at her friend's loyalty. 'You mean I usually have my head in the sand.' Or in books. Papou had regularly complained that she spent too much time with her nose in a book. 'Well, not any more.' She shuddered as ice frosted her spine. 'Imagine if we hadn't heard…'

'But we did.' Steph squeezed her shoulder again. 'The question is, what are you going to do about it?'

The question jolted her out of self-pity.

Emma looked in the mirror, taking in the ashen-faced waif dressed in wedding lace. Suddenly, in a burst of glorious heat, anger swamped her. Scorching, fiery anger that ran along her veins, licking warmth back into her cold flesh and burning away the vulnerability she'd felt at Christo's casual contempt. The flush of it rose from her belly to her breasts and up to her cheeks as she swung round to face her friend.

'Walk away, of course. Christo can find another *sensible* woman to care for his child and please him.'

Silly that, of all the assumptions he'd made about her and the games he'd played, what rankled most was that he'd recognised her longing for physical pleasure. For *him*.

A shudder ran through her at the thought of how she'd looked forward to pleasing him and having him reciprocate with those big, supple hands and that hard, masculine body.

Now the idea of him touching her made her feel sick.

Especially as the reason he'd abstained from sex clearly hadn't been out of respect for her and for her dying grandfather. It had been because sex with the dowdy mouse of the family hadn't appealed to him. If Christo had been engaged to the beautiful Maia, there'd have been no holding back. They'd have been scorching the sheets well before the wedding.

A curl of flame branded deep inside Emma's feminine core. In the place where, one day, a man she loved and who loved her back would possess her. She'd thought she'd found him in Christo Karides. Now all she felt was loathing for him and disappointment at herself for believing his lies.

'I'm so relieved.' Steph's words tugged her into the present. 'I was afraid you might think of staying with him and hoping he'd eventually fall in love with you.'

Emma shook her head, the old lace swishing around her shoulders. Papou had been proud that she'd wear the same veil his bride had worn to her wedding. This marriage had meant so much to him. But it was a sham. Christo hadn't only made a fool of her but of her grandfather too. She'd never forgive him that.

'I might be the quiet one in the family but I'm not a doormat. As Christo Karides is about to find out.' She met her friend's eyes in the mirror. 'Will you help me?'

'You have to ask?' Steph rolled her eyes. 'What do you have in mind?'

Emma hesitated, realising she had nothing in mind. But only for a second.

'Can you go up to my room and grab my passport and bag? And my suitcase?' The case she'd packed for her honeymoon. The thought was a jab to her heart. She sucked in a fortifying breath. 'You'll have to come down the back stairs.'

'Then what?'

'I'll book a flight out of here. If I can borrow your car and leave it at the airport—'

'And leave Christo Karides to face the music when his bride disappears? I love it.' Steph's grin almost hid the fury glittering in her eyes. 'But I've got a better idea. Forget the airport. That's the first place he'll look. With his resources, he'll be on your trail within hours. Head to my place and wait for a call.' She reached into her purse and pulled out her key ring, pressing it into Emma's hand. 'I'll get you out of Melbourne but so he can't trace your movements. I'm not the best travel agent in the city for nothing. It's going to be a real pleasure watching him stew when he can't find you.'

For the first time since overhearing Christo's conversation, Emma smiled. It didn't matter that her cheeks felt so taut they might crack, or that the pain in her heart was as deep as ever. What mattered was that she had a way out and a true friend.

Suddenly she didn't feel so appallingly alone and vulnerable.

'Thank you, Steph. I can't tell you what it means to have your help.' Emma blinked against the self-pitying tears prickling the back of her eyes.

She'd cried when she'd lost Papou. She refused to shed tears over a man who wasn't fit to speak her grandfather's name. A schemer who'd played upon the old man's love and fear for his granddaughter's future.

'But you'll have to be careful not to give me away.' Emma frowned at her friend. 'One look at your face and Christo will know you're hiding something. He may be a louse but he's smart.'

Silly how speaking of him like that sent a fillip of pleasure through her. It was a tiny thing compared with the wrong he'd done her, but it was a start.

Steph shook her head and put on the butter-wouldn't-melt-in-her-mouth expression that had fooled their teachers for years. 'Don't worry. He won't suspect a thing. I'll tell him you need a short rest. He'll accept that. He knows this has been a whirlwind, plus you're missing your grandfather.'

Steph's words sent a shaft of longing through Emma for the old man who'd been bossy and difficult but always loving beneath his gruff exterior. She blinked, refusing to give in to grief now.

'Great. You go upstairs while I get this veil off.' There was no time to get out of the dress, but she couldn't make her escape in trailing lace. 'I'll hide it in the cupboard here, if you can collect it later and look after it for me?'

'Of course. I know it's precious.' Steph put her hand on Emma's arm, squeezing gently. 'Just one more thing. Where are you travelling to?'

Emma turned to the mirror and started searching for the multitude of pins that secured the veil. 'The only place that's still home.' Her aunt and uncle, Maia's parents, had inherited this house and Papou's Australian assets. She'd got the commercial property in Athens that had then been signed over to her husband to manage. She'd have to do something about that, she realised. Plus, she'd inherited her grandparents' old villa in Greece. The one where she'd gone each year on holiday with her parents till they'd died. 'I'm going to Corfu.'

It was the perfect bolthole. She'd never mentioned it to Christo and, anyway, he would never look for her on his home turf of Greece.

She could take her time there, deciding what she planned to do. And how she'd end this farce of a marriage.

CHAPTER TWO

EMMA STEPPED THROUGH the wrought-iron gates and felt the past wash over her. She hadn't been to Corfu for years, not since she was fifteen, when her grandmother had grown too frail for long-distance travel.

Seven years, yet it felt more like seven days as she took in the shaded avenue ahead curling towards the villa just out of sight. Ancient olive trees, their bodies twisted but their boughs healthy with new growth, drifted down the slope to the sea like a silvery green blanket. Nearby glossy citrus leaves clustered around creamy buds in the orchard.

Emma inhaled the rich scent of blossom from lemon, kumquat and orange trees. Her lips tightened. Orange blossom was traditional for brides. It had been in short supply in Melbourne during autumn, unlike Greece in spring.

She shivered as something dark and chilly skipped down her spine.

What a close shave she'd had. Imagine if she hadn't learned of Christo's real agenda! She cringed to think how much further under his spell she'd have fallen. Given his reputation, she had no doubt his skills at seduction were as excellent as his ability to feign attraction.

Swallowing down the writhing knot of hurt in her throat, she grabbed the handle of her suitcase, hitched her shoulder bag higher and set off towards the house.

She was sticky and tired and longing for a cold drink. Silly of her, perhaps, to have the taxi drop her further down the road, near a cluster of new luxury villas that had sprung up in the last few years. But she didn't want to take the chance of anyone knowing she was staying here, in case word somehow got back to Christo.

She'd confront him in her own time, not his. For now she needed to regroup and lick her wounds.

Emma trudged down the drive, the crunch of her feet and her suitcase wheels on the gravel loud in the quiet. Yet, as she walked, her steps grew lighter as memories crowded close. Happy memories, for it was here her family had gathered year after year for a month's vacation.

Drops of bright colour in the olive grove caught her eye and she remembered picking wildflowers there, plonking them in her grandmother's priceless crystal vases, where they'd be displayed as proudly as if they were professional floral arrangements. Swimming with her parents down in the clear green waters of their private cove. Sitting under the shade of the colonnade that ran around three sides of the courtyard while Papou had taught her to play *tavli*, clicking the counters around the board so quickly his hand seemed to blur before her eyes.

They were gone now, all of them.

Emma stumbled to a halt, pain shearing through her middle, transfixing her.

She took a deep breath and forced herself to walk on. Yes, they'd died, but they'd taught her the value of living life to the full, and of love. Even now she felt that love as if the old estate that had been in Papou's family for years wrapped her in its embrace.

Rounding the curve in the long drive, she caught sight of the villa. It showed its age, like a gracious old lady, still elegant despite the years. Its walls were a muted tone between blush-pink and palest orange that glowed softly in the afternoon light. The tall wooden window shutters gleamed with new forest-green paint but the ancient roof tiles had weathered to a grey that looked as ancient as the stone walls edging the olive grove. Despite being a couple of hundred years old, the place was well-maintained. Papou wouldn't have had it any other way.

Nor would Emma. She was its owner now. She stood, looking at the fine old house and feeling a swell of pride and belonging she'd never felt for her grandparents' Melbourne place. This was the home of her heart, she realised. With precious memories of her parents.

A tickle of an idea began to form in her tired brain. Maybe, just maybe, this could be more than a temporary refuge before she returned to Australia. Perhaps…

Her thoughts trailed off as the front door opened and a woman appeared, lifting her hand to shade her face.

'Miss Emma?'

The familiar sound of Dora Panayiotis's heavy accent peeled the years right back. Suddenly Emma was a scrawny kid again. She left her bag and hurried forward into sturdy, welcoming arms.

'Dora!' She hugged the housekeeper back, her exhaustion forgotten. 'It's so good to see you.'

'And you, Miss Emma. Welcome home.'

Emma flicked her sodden hair off her face as she reached for the towel, rubbing briskly till her skin tingled. Early rain had cleared to a sparkling bright afternoon and she hadn't been able to resist the lure of the white sand cove at the bottom of the garden. Turquoise shallows gave way to teal-green depths that enticed far more than the pool up beside the house.

Since arriving she'd sunk into the embrace of the villa's familiarity, feeling that, after all, part of her old life remained. How precious that was.

For four days she'd let Dora feed her delicious food and done nothing more taxing than swim, sleep and eat.

Until today, when she'd woken to discover her brain teeming with ideas for her future. A future where, for a change, she did what *she* wanted, not what others expected.

A future here, at the villa that was her birthright.

For the first time since the funeral and her disastrous wedding day, Emma felt a flicker of her natural optimism.

Her training was in business and event management. She was good it and had recently won a coveted job at an upmarket vineyard and resort that she'd turned down when she married because she planned to move to Athens with Christo.

Emma suppressed a shiver and yanked her thoughts back to her new future.

She'd work for herself. The gracious old villa with its private grounds and guest accommodation was perfect, not only for holidays but as an exclusive, upmarket venue for private celebrations. That would be where she'd pitch her efforts.

Corfu was the destination of choice for many holiday makers. With hard work and good marketing, she could create a niche business that would offer a taste of old-world charm with modern luxury and panache.

It would be hard work, a real challenge, but she needed that, she realised.

Wasn't that what she'd always done? Kept herself busy whenever she faced another loss so that she had no choice but to keep going? It was her way of coping, of not sinking under the weight of grief. She'd adapted to a new life in a new state with her grandparents after her parents had died. She'd taken on the challenge of supporting Papou after her grandmother's death.

It was easier to focus on the ideas tumbling in her brain than the searing pain deep inside. To pretend Christo hadn't broken her heart and undermined her self-confidence with his casual dismissal.

Emma's mouth set in a tight line. She was still angry and hurt but now she had a plan, something tangible to work towards. That would be her lifeline. Today for the first time she no longer felt she'd shatter at the slightest touch.

Today she'd contact a lawyer about a divorce and getting back her property and—

'Miss Emma!'

She turned to see Dora hurrying around the rocks at the end of the private beach. Her face was flushed and her hands twisted.

Emma's heart slammed against her ribs. She knew distress when she saw it, had been on the receiving end of bad news enough to recognise it instantly. Foreboding swamped her. She started forward, hand outstretched, her beach towel falling to the ground. Was it her aunt or uncle? Not Maia, surely?

'I came to warn you,' Dora gasped. 'Your—'

'There's no need for that, Mrs Panayiotis.' The deep voice with its bite of ice came from behind the housekeeper. 'I'm perfectly capable of speaking for myself.'

Then he appeared—tall, broad-shouldered and steely-eyed. Christo Karides.

Emma's husband.

Her heart slammed to a stop, her feet taking root in the sand. The atmosphere darkened as if storm clouds had covered the sun. Was it the effect of his inimical stare? For a second she couldn't breathe, an invisible band constricting her lungs as she stared into that face, so familiar and yet so different.

Then, abruptly, her heart started pumping harder than before. She sucked in a faltering breath.

He was still the most handsome man she'd ever seen with his coal-black hair and olive-gold skin contrasting with clear, slate-blue eyes. Eyes that right now seared her right down to the soles of her feet.

Desperately Emma tried for dispassionate as she surveyed those proud features that looked like they'd been etched by a master's hand. Strong nose, square jaw, the tiniest hint of a cleft in that determined chin. Only the small silvered scar beside his mouth, barely visible, marred all that masculine perfection. Perversely, it accentuated how good-looking Christo really was.

Handsome is as handsome does. She could almost hear her grandmother's voice in her ears.

This man had proved himself anything but handsome. Or trustworthy. Or in any way worth her notice.

Wrangling her lungs into action again, Emma took a deep breath and conjured a reassuring smile for Dora. 'It's okay. Perhaps you'd like to organise some tea for us in the main salon? We'll be up shortly.'

As acts of hostility went, it was a tiny one, ordering tea when she knew Christo liked coffee, strong and sweet, but it was a start. Emma preferred conciliation to confrontation yet she had no intention of making him feel welcome.

Silence enveloped them as Dora hurried away. A silence Emma wasn't eager to break.

She told herself she was over the worst. The shock, the disillusionment, the shattered heart. But it was easier to believe it when the man she'd once loved with all her foolish, naïve hopes wasn't standing before her like an echo of her dreams.

Yet Emma wasn't the innocent she'd been a week ago. Christo Karides had seen to that. He'd stripped her illusions away, brutally but effectively. She was another woman now.

Pushing her shoulders back, Emma lifted her chin and looked straight into those glittering eyes. 'I can't say it's good to see you, but I suppose it's time we sorted this out.'

Christo stared at the woman before him, momentarily bereft of words for the first time in his adult life.

He told himself it was the shock of seeing her safe and healthy, after almost a week of worry. It had been uncharacteristic of gentle, considerate Emma to vanish like that, as all her friends and relatives kept telling him. He'd worried she'd been injured or even kidnapped.

Till she'd called her aunt and left a cryptic message saying she was okay but needed time alone.

Time alone!

His blood sizzled at her sheer effrontery.

What sort of behaviour was that for a bride? Especially for the bride of Christo Karides, one of the most sought-after bachelors in Europe, pursued wherever he went.

That had been another first—finding himself frantic with anxiety. Christo recalled the scouring, metallic taste of fear on his tongue and the icy grip of worry clutching his vitals. He never wanted to experience that again.

Nor did he appreciate being made a laughing stock.

Or enduring the questioning looks her relatives had given him, as if her vanishing act was *his* doing! As if he hadn't spent weeks carefully courting Katsoyiannis's delicate granddaughter. Treating her with all the respect due to his future wife.

Christo clamped his jaw, tension radiating across his shoulders and down into bunching fists.

It wasn't just discovering Emma hale and hearty that transfixed him. It was the change in her.

The woman he'd married had been demure and sweet-tempered. She'd deferred to her grandfather and been patently eager to please Christo, with her ardent if slightly clumsy responses to his kisses.

The woman before him was different. She sparked with unfamiliar energy. Her stance, legs apart and hands planted on hips, was defiant rather than placating.

The Emma Piper he knew was a slight figure, slender and appealing in a muted sort of way. This Emma even looked different. She wore a skimpy bikini of bright aqua. It clung to a figure far more sexy than he'd anticipated, though admittedly he'd never seen her anything but fully dressed. Her damp skin glowed like a gold-tinted pearl and those plump breasts rising and falling with her quick breaths looked as if they'd fill his palms to perfection.

A feral rush of heat jagged at his groin, an instant, unstoppable reaction that did *not* fit his mood or his expectations.

Christo dragged his gaze up to her face and saw her eyebrows arch in query, challenging him as if he had no right to stare.

As if she wasn't his runaway wife!

'You've got some explaining to do,' he murmured in the soft, lethal voice that stopped meandering board meetings in a second.

But, instead of backing down and losing the attitude, Emma jutted her rounded chin, lifted her cute, not quite retroussé nose in the air and planted her feet wider, drawing his attention to her shapely legs.

The heat in his groin flared hotter.

Slowly she shook her head, making her tangled, wet hair slide around her shoulders. Sunlight caught it, highlighting the dark honey with strands of gold he'd never seen before. But then they'd spent most of their time indoors, in her grandfather's house or at nearby restaurants. The bright Greek sunshine revealed details he simply hadn't noticed.

'You've got that the wrong way around.'

'Sorry?' Christo drew himself up to his full height, looking down on the slim woman before him. But, extraordinarily, she simply stared back, her mouth set in a mulish line. Her stare was bold rather than apologetic.

For a second he was so surprised he even wondered if the impossible had happened. If this wasn't Emma but some lookalike imposter.

But Christo Karides had never been one for fantasy. He'd been a pragmatist since childhood, with no time for fiction.

'Have you any idea how worried everyone was?' His

voice was gruff, hitting a gravelly note that betrayed the gut-deep worry he'd rather not remember. 'I even called the police! I thought you'd been abducted.'

He'd mobilised the best people to scour Melbourne and the surrounds, praying something terrible hadn't happened to his quiet little spouse.

There were ruthless people out there, including some ready to take advantage of a defenceless woman. His brain had kept circling back to the possibility that when he found her it would be too late. He'd never felt so helpless. The memory fed his fury.

'I rang my aunt to explain that I was safe.'

'You didn't ring *me*!' Christo heard his voice rise and drew a frustrated breath.

Was she wilfully misunderstanding? The woman he'd wooed had seemed reasonably intelligent and eminently sensible. Not the sort to disappear on her wedding day. He leaned into her space, determined to get through to her. 'I half-expected to find your abused body abandoned somewhere.'

He saw shock work its way through her, making her eyes round and her shoulders stiffen. Then she shook her head again as if dismissing his concern as nothing. 'Well, as you can see, I'm fine.'

'Not good enough, Emma. Not nearly good enough. You owe me.' An explanation to start with but far more after that.

'Oh, that's rich coming from you.' Her mouth curled up at one corner.

Was she *sneering* at him?

Christo covered the space between them in one long stride, bringing him close enough to inhale the scent of sea and feminine warmth that made something in his belly skitter into life.

Shackling her wrist with his, he tugged her close enough to feel the heat of her body.

'Stop it, Emma. You're my wife!'

Her voice when it came was so low he had to crane forward to hear it. Yet it throbbed with a passion he'd never heard from her. 'And how I wish I wasn't.'

Christo stared down at her. Never, in his whole life, had he met a woman who wasn't pleased to be with him. He'd lost count of the number who'd vied to catch his attention. Yet this one, the one he'd honoured with his name and his hand in marriage, regarded him as she would a venomous snake.

Had the world gone mad?

Where was his sweet Emma? The woman who revelled in his smiles, the gentle, generous woman he'd selected from all the contenders?

Her mouth twisted into a tight line as she stared down at his hand on her wrist. 'Let me go now. Marriage doesn't give you the right to assault me.'

'Assault? You have to be kidding.' His brow knotted in disbelief. As if he'd ever assault a woman!

'It is if I don't want to be touched and believe me, Christo, the last person on this earth I want touching me is you.'

Her voice was sharp with disdain and her nostrils flared as she met his stare. Something thumped deep in his chest at the unexpected, unbelievable insult.

Deliberately he dropped her hand and spread his empty fingers before her face. Anger throbbed through him. No, fury at being treated with such unprovoked contempt.

'Okay, no touching. Now explain.'

At last Emma seemed to realise the depth of his ire. The combative light faded from her eyes and her mouth compressed into a flat line. Abruptly she looked less fiery and more…hurt.

Christo resisted the ridiculous impulse to pull her close. He'd met enough manipulative women not to fall for a play on his sympathy.

'I know, Christo.' Her voice was flat, devoid of vigour. 'I know why you married me. There, is that enough explanation?'

'It's no explanation at all.' Yet the nape of his neck prickled.

It wasn't possible. He'd spoken of it to no one except Damen and then he'd ensured they were out of earshot. He'd left his blushing bride with her beaming family on the other side of the sprawling house.

He wasn't ashamed of what he'd done. On the contrary, his actions had been sensible, laudable and honourable. He'd offered marriage and the promise of his protection and loyalty to this woman. What more could she want? His actions had been spurred by the best of motives.

Except, looking into those wide, wounded eyes, Christo recalled her untutored ardour. Emma's shy delight at his wooing.

He'd told himself she didn't expect his *love*.

The old man had made it clear his granddaughter would marry to please him. Christo assumed she understood that behind the niceties of their courtship lay a world of practicality. That he'd wed for convenience.

But you never spelled it out to her, did you?

Christo silenced the carping voice.

No one who knew him would believe he'd been bowled over by little Emma Piper.

But Emma didn't know him. Not really.

For a second he wavered, surprised to feel guilt razor his gullet.

Till logic asserted itself. She'd chosen to marry him. He'd never spoken of love. Never promised more than he was willing to give.

Emma had flounced off in a huff and made him look like a fool. It was a part he'd never played before and never intended to play again.

Indignation easily eclipsed any hint of culpability. 'Nothing excuses what you did, Emma.'

'Don't try to put this on me, Christo. You don't even *want* me. You'd prefer someone beautiful and vivacious, like my cousin.'

Was that what this was about? He shook his head. He should have known this would boil down to feminine pique.

Emma was such an innocent that she didn't understand a man could be attracted to a woman and not act on that attraction. That a man of sense chose a woman who'd meet his needs.

Emma was that woman, with all the qualities he required of a mother for his ward. Even her defiance now just proved she had backbone, something he admired.

Plus she was more, he acknowledged. He met soft hazel eyes that now sparked with gold and green fire, feeling his blood heat as he took in her delectable figure and militant air. Christo acknowledged with a fillip of surprise that he wanted his wife more than he'd thought possible. Far more than he recalled from their restrained courtship.

There was a vibrancy about her, a challenge, a feminine mystique that called to him at the most primitive level. Gone was the delicate, compliant girl so perfect for his plans. This was a *woman*. Obstinate, angry and brimming with attitude. Sexier than he'd realised.

Lust exploded low in his body, a dark, tight hunger so powerful it actually equalled his fury.

'I married *you*, Emma. Not your cousin. I gave you my name and my promise.' How could she not understand what those things meant to him? 'That's far more important than any fleeting attraction.'

But Emma refused to be convinced. She shook her head,

wet hair slipping over her shoulders. Trails of sea water ran down from it to the miniscule triangles of her bikini top. Christo followed those wet tracks to the proud points of her nipples. Another wave of lust hit him and his flesh tightened across his bones as he fought the impulse to reach out and claim her.

'You're mine.' The words emerged as a roughened growl.

She stiffened, her chin jerking higher. 'Not for long. I'm filing for divorce.'

Like hell she would!

He'd carefully chosen Emma after considering all the options. Every reason he'd had for making her his wife still stood.

He needed her to make a real home instead of the bachelor flat he'd lived in for years. He needed her to be a mother to Anthea, providing a stable, caring environment for the little girl who was a stranger to him and with whom he had no hope of building a rapport.

Besides, Emma was *his*, and what Christo possessed he kept. It was in his nature.

Then there was today's revelation. That he wanted his wife with a hunger more powerful than he'd thought possible. That just standing here, fully dressed while she wore nothing but a bright bikini and a frown, brought him closer to the edge of his control than he'd been in years.

He intended to have her.

On his terms.

'File away, *wife*.'

He saw her flinch at the word and vowed that one day soon she'd purr at the sound of his voice. The thought of his runaway wife, eager for his touch, offering her delicious body for his pleasure, made the blood sing in his veins.

'But, before you do, I'd advise you to investigate the consequences. Divorce isn't an option.'

CHAPTER THREE

EMMA GROUND HER TEETH.

She was tired of men trying to rule her life. At least Papou had acted from love, not self-interest, wanting to see her 'safe' with a 'good' man before he died. Christo Karides had no such excuse. Her battered heart dipped on the thought but she refused to crumble as the familiar hurt intensified.

Instead she watched the tall figure of her husband turn and saunter back along the beach without a glance in her direction.

He should have looked out of place, ridiculously over-dressed, wearing a tailored dark business suit on a sandy beach. Instead, as she watched his easy stride, the latent strength in those broad shoulders and long legs, a thrill of appreciation coursed through her.

What a terrible thing desire was.

Her love, still fresh and new, had been battered away, swamped by pain and outrage. Yet standing in the sunlight, shivering not with cold but with a heat that she tried to label fury, Emma realised in horror that things weren't so simple.

She despised Christo Karides.

She loathed the cold-hearted way he'd set out to use her.

She vowed never to trust a word he said.

Yet as she watched him disappear around the end of the beach honesty forced her to admit she still desired him. That hadn't disappeared with her trust and her fool-ish dreams.

In Melbourne she'd thought the slow pace of his wooing sweet, proof he was considerate to her grief. At the same time she'd hungered for more than gentle caresses.

Now that hunger coalesced with the white-hot ire in her belly, producing an overwhelming mix of emotion and carnal need. She wanted to hurt him for the hurt he'd inflicted on her, yet at the same time she wanted...

Emma gritted her teeth and forced herself to breathe slowly.

She did *not* want Christo. She refused to allow herself to want him.

What she wanted, what she *needed*, was to free herself of him and this appalling marriage. She had plans, didn't she? An exciting scheme that would require all her energy and skill and which promised the reward of self-sufficiency in this place she loved.

Who did he think he was to decree divorce wasn't an option?

He might be the expert negotiator, the consummate sleazy liar who thought her easy pickings, but he was about to discover Emma Piper couldn't be steamrollered into compliance!

Forty-five minutes later Emma made her way from her bedroom to the salon with its expansive views of the sea.

Instead of hurrying to shower and dress, she'd taken her time, after having checked with Dora that Christo was, in fact, still on the premises. With that knowledge she'd locked her door and set about deciding what to wear.

Ideally she'd have worn a tailored suit, severe and businesslike. But Steph had persuaded her to splash out on new clothes for her honeymoon, reminding her that Papou would have wanted her to enjoy herself.

There was nothing businesslike in her wardrobe here. In the end, Emma gave up worrying about what impression her clothes might give Christo. She'd dress for herself.

The swish of her lightweight sea-green skirt around her bare legs reminded her of the holiday she was supposed to be enjoying. That she intended to enjoy as soon as *he'd* left. Her flat sandals were beach-comfortable rather than dressy and she wore a simple top that was an old favourite.

But she pulled her hair up into a tight knot at the back of her head and put on make-up, feeling that armour was necessary for the upcoming confrontation.

Ignoring the way the door knob slipped in her clammy palm, Emma opened the door and walked in.

To her surprise, Christo wasn't on his phone, absorbed in business, or pacing the vast room in obvious impatience.

Instead he stood at one end of the room, perusing the family photos her grandmother had collected. Generations of photos, mainly taken here on the Corfu estate to where Papou had brought his Australian bride before they'd decided to live full-time in her home country.

Christo swung around. His pinioning stare brought all the feelings she tried to suppress roaring into life.

After a moment Emma gathered herself. *She* had nothing to answer for.

She opened her mouth to ask if he needed another drink, then shut it again, annoyed that innate politeness made her even consider making the offer. Instead she crossed to a comfortable chair and sat.

'We need to talk.' Good. She sounded calm yet cool.

Silently one black eyebrow rose with arrogant query. The effect might have made her squirm if she hadn't been prepared.

'Or, if you prefer, I'm happy to finalise this via our lawyers.'

To Emma's chagrin that didn't dent his composure in the least. He strolled the length of the room, stopping to tower over her long enough to make her wonder if she'd made a mistake, taking a seat. Then, just before she shot to her feet, he settled into a chair, not opposite her but slightly to one side.

Emma silently cursed his game-playing and shuffled round to face him. Her skirt rode up at one side and she tugged it down, wishing she'd worn jeans instead.

Annoyingly, Christo looked utterly unruffled.

Until she saw the fire in his eyes and the determined set of his jaw.

Clearly he wasn't used to being crossed.

Good. It was time someone punctured his self-absorption.

'I'll file for divorce in Australia. I assume that's easiest.' Her tight chest eased a fraction as she spoke. It would be a relief to take action after days of doing nothing but grapple with disappointment and hurt. It was time to stop the self-pity.

'That's not a good idea, Emma.'

She frowned. 'I can't stay married to a man I despise.'

For an instant she thought she read something new flare in those heavy-lidded eyes. Something that sent a shiver tumbling down her backbone.

Emma sat straighter. What did she care if he wasn't used to hearing the truth about himself? He'd behaved appallingly and she refused to pretend otherwise.

'I know you're upset by your recent loss, so I'm willing to forgo the apology for your behaviour. But—'

'Apology for *my* behaviour?' She barely got the words out, she was so indignant.

Annoyingly, Christo simply nodded. 'Disappearing from your own wedding breakfast is hardly good form.'

She goggled at him.

'But your aunt and I convinced everyone you were completely overwrought. That the wedding had come too soon after the loss of your grandfather.' He spread his hands. 'I took the blame for wanting an early wedding, but your family understood and were very sympathetic.'

Emma opened her mouth then closed it again, feeling pressure build inside like steam in a kettle.

This was unbelievable!

'You made it sound like I had a breakdown? And they *believed* you?'

He shrugged, the movement emphasising the powerful outline of his shoulders and chest. 'What else could they believe? Your suitcase was gone, with your purse and passport.' His eyes narrowed to glowing slits that belied his relaxed pose. As if he were even now calculating how she'd managed to get away. Did he suspect Steph of helping? Had he bullied her into confessing? Steph hadn't mentioned it, but then she wouldn't.

'Once your aunt got that nonsensical message from you, of course she wondered.'

Emma shot to her feet. 'It wasn't nonsensical. I explained I needed time alone to think things through.'

Christo merely lifted those sleek black eyebrows and leaned back. 'Exactly. What sane woman would do that when she had a caring family and a brand-new husband to share her problems with?'

'Except *you* were the problem!' Emma heard her voice rise on a querulous note and swung away, pacing across to the window.

The view across the terrace to the private cove and bright sea did nothing to calm her fury. No one, not even her *papou* at his most obstinate, had got under Emma's skin the way this man had. Had she ever been so furious, her thoughts skittering so wildly?

How straightforward her world had been, how easy to be calm, before Christo Karides had slithered into her life.

Emma's heart hammered high in her chest at his gall, implying she was an emotional wreck who'd had a breakdown.

With a huge effort she pushed that aside. 'You said you'd worried I'd been abducted. But you knew I'd taken my luggage.'

Another nonchalant shrug. 'That wasn't clear at first. Your friend Steph didn't seem quite sure. And, even if you *had* left of your own free will, you could still have got into trouble. You're not used to being by yourself.'

Emma blinked. Christo made her sound like a child. Clearly he had no concept of the fact that she'd run Papou's house and some of his local investments for years. She'd chosen to live there for Papou's sake, not because she lacked independence.

Pride demanded she set the record straight.

She swung round and met that complacent, slate-blue stare, feeling the instant buzz of reaction as their gazes clashed. Immediately she changed her mind. Why explain to a man who'd soon be out of her life?

The notion eased the tightness cramping her chest and shoulders.

'We're wasting time. What's done is done.' It was time they moved on.

'I agree.' Yet the way Christo surveyed her, like a cat poised outside a mouse hole, warned her the next step wouldn't be so simple.

It was on the tip of her tongue to demand an apology but the way he sprawled there, ankles crossed nonchalantly, arms spread across the upholstery as he surveyed her, Emma knew she had no hope of getting satisfaction on that front.

The only satisfaction she'd get from this man was knowing she'd never have to see or hear from him again.

'It's in both our interests to end this quickly,' she began. 'Would an annulment be faster, do you know?'

'You think I'm an expert on unconsummated marriages?' For the first time Emma saw more than a flicker of annoyance in Christo's preternaturally still expression. Did he think she impugned his manhood by mentioning an annulment? She wouldn't be surprised. 'But I can tell you it would be a mistake.'

'How so?' Maybe annulments weren't simple after all.

'Because I refuse to consider it. Can you imagine the press furore if it became public?' He shook his head with grim disapproval.

'Frankly, I don't care. All I want is to be shot of you.'

His eyes narrowed to steely slits and his stare turned laser-sharp, scraping her throat and face. Emma crossed her arms and refused to look away.

'You've led a sheltered life. You have no idea how disruptive media attention can be till you've lived in the public eye.'

He was right. Emma had seen the articles about his business prowess, defying the odds when Greece's economy had faltered and his global investments had continued to return so spectacularly. And more, about his private life, all those assignations with beautiful women.

She shrugged one tense shoulder, her lips twisting in distaste. 'I'll cope, if it means ending this marriage quickly.'

'You really think you'd be able to deal with paparazzi camped at your door? Following you wherever you go? Digging up dirt—'

'There's no dirt to dig up!' At least not about her. Who knew what secrets Christo guarded?

'They'd invent something. The press are good at that.' He paused. 'Unless you have the power to keep them in check. As I have.'

Emma shuddered at the picture he painted of her hounded by photographers, of scurrilous stories in the tabloids, of friends and family pestered for interviews.

'If not an annulment, then a divorce.'

Christo spread his hands in mock sympathy. 'You'd still be hounded relentlessly.'

Emma lifted her chin. 'Maybe I'll sell my story to them

instead. Have you thought of that? I could make big bucks and then they'd leave me alone.'

For a second Emma thought he'd surge to his feet. She read the quickened pulse throbbing at his temple and the severe line of his mouth and knew Christo Karides wasn't used to such defiance.

Did people always do as he demanded? It was time someone broke the trend. Satisfaction filled Emma at the thought of being the one to disrupt his plans. She wasn't a pawn to be played to suit his schemes.

'Good try, Emma, but you won't do it.'

'You think you know me so well?' She sucked in a rough breath, trying to control the wobble in her voice. It didn't matter that fury, not hurt, made it unsteady. She hated the idea of seeming weak before this man. 'You have no idea who I really am. You never did.'

For what seemed an age, her surveyed her. 'I know you're a private person. You don't wear your heart on your sleeve.' He paused and she wondered, choking down hurt, whether he realised he was rubbing salt on her wounds.

For she *had* worn her heart on her sleeve. She'd been gullible, believing the unbelievable—that handsome, charming Christo Karides, with the world at his feet, actually cared for mousy little Emma Piper.

She spun on her heel and hurried across to the window, feigning interest in the view she knew as well as the back of her hand. It gave her time to deal with the honed blade of pain slicing through her.

Silence swallowed the room. When Christo spoke again his voice had lost that easy, almost amused cadence. 'What I mean is, you have more pride and integrity than to share anything so personal with the gutter press.'

Was he complimenting her? Emma blinked out at the sunlight glittering on the Ionian Sea and told herself it was too little and far, far too late.

'Coping with the press is a problem I'll deal with when I have to. My priority now is getting a divorce as quickly as possible.'

'That's not going to happen, Emma.'

Was that *pity* in his voice?

Her hackles rose. She swung round and was relieved to find she'd been wrong. That tight jaw spoke of impatience, nothing softer.

'You can prolong the process but you can't stop it.' That much she knew.

'You're my wife. We made vows—'

'Vows that meant nothing whatsoever to you!' Hearing her voice grow strident, she paused, hefting a shallow breath. Emma needed to stay calm, not fall apart. She'd run from him once, overwhelmed by the disillusionment that had rocked her to the core. She refused to give in to emotion now.

'I vowed to honour you, to cherish and look after you.' He'd never looked more proud or more determined. 'I have every intention of doing just that. This misunderstanding—'

'There's no misunderstanding. You cold-heartedly set about marrying me for a property deal.' As if she were a chunk of real estate! 'And to get a carer for your child.' Emma dragged in another breath but couldn't fill her lungs. 'Your baby is your responsibility. Yours and your lover's.'

An image filled her mind of Christo as she'd imagined him so often, sprawled naked in bed. But this time he wasn't smiling invitingly at her, he was kissing another woman. Their limbs were entwined and…

Emma banished the image and ignored the sour tang on her tongue that might, if she thought about it, be jealousy.

When she spoke again her voice was ragged. 'Together you need to look after the baby, not foist it on someone else.'

Her heart pumped an unfamiliar beat as adrenalin surged. Emma wasn't used to confrontation. She was a negotiator, a people pleaser, not a fighter. But something inside her had snapped the day she discovered Christo's motives and she still rode that wave of indignation.

She didn't know which was worse—that he'd played on her emotions and callously made her fall for him, or that he'd tried to palm his baby off on someone else. An innocent child deserved its parents' love.

What sort of world did the man inhabit? Surely one far removed from hers, where family and friends were everything.

Suddenly she realised he was on his feet, prowling towards her. Emma swallowed but stood her ground.

Fortunately he stopped a couple of paces away, so the illusion of distance held, though she caught a hint of the aftershave he used—cedar, spice and leather mingling with warm male skin. To her dismay, a little shimmy of appreciation shot through her.

'*Not* my child.' His voice was silky and soft but she heard the edge of anger. 'I would never be so careless.'

No, she realised, Christo was careful and calculating. Everything planned. Even down to choosing a suitable bride without a trace of sentiment or true feeling.

'And not a baby but a little three-year-old girl. The child is my stepsister's. She died recently.'

'I'm sorry.' Emma felt herself soften. She knew about loss, knew the struggle to keep going when everything seemed bleak.

Was it possible grief had made Christo act out of character? Could that explain…?

No. One look into those severely set features disabused her of that notion. She'd been right the first time. Christo didn't act in passion. He was a schemer who plotted every move.

'I barely knew her. Only met her once, years ago.'

'Yet you're now responsible for her child?' It made no sense.

He shrugged. 'There's no one else.'

It was on the tip of Emma's tongue to say that must be the case because no sane person would entrust an innocent child to such a man. But she bit the words back. She processed his words—*no one else*. But that was right: he was an only child and his parents were dead.

'The father?'

'If she knew who he was, she never said.' He paused. 'No one is going to come along and claim the girl.'

The girl.

He didn't even call the poor kid by her name.

Sympathy flashed through Emma. She understood what it meant to lose your family young. One day her parents had been there, seeing her off to school. The next, they'd been gone.

But she had her own battle to fight. She couldn't be swayed by emotion. That had been her downfall before.

'You both have my sympathy. But that's no reason to prolong this marriage.'

'Can you think of a better reason than to nurture a motherless child?'

How dared he talk of nurturing when his plan was to palm the child off on her?

'Of course I can. What about—?'

'Yes?' He leaned closer.

'Love', she'd been about to say. Marrying for true love.

But it hadn't been true and it hadn't been love, at least on his side. It had been a marriage of convenience.

As for her own feelings, Emma was ashamed of them. Especially since, despite everything he'd done, she wasn't as immune to this man as she wanted to be. Just as well there was no chance of him turning around and trying to persuade her he loved her. Even now she dreaded to think how effective he might be, given how he'd conned her the first time.

'I'm not getting into an academic discussion about marriage. I'm sorry for your niece…' *in more ways than one* '…but she's your responsibility. Take care of her yourself.'

Again, Emma felt that pang of sympathy for the little girl with no one but Christo to care for her. But he had money with which to bring in the best nannies. Once they were divorced, he'd find another wife. He'd proved how easy that was.

'Either agree to a divorce or leave. I have business to attend to.'

'Business?' His eyebrows shot up and for the first time she felt she'd truly surprised him.

'I have arrangements to make. A future to plan. A future without you.'

Stormy eyes surveyed her and she felt the force of his disapproval. No, more than disapproval. Sheer fury, if she read the thickening atmosphere correctly.

Once she would have hurried to placate, or at least redirect, that anger. Years living with Papou had made her adept at averting storms, finding ways of making him change his mind over time.

Today Emma stood her ground and rode the wave of displeasure crashing around her. If anything it buoyed her higher, knowing Christo could fume to no avail.

'These arrangements, do they require capital?' he asked finally.

'That's none of your concern.' He was stringing this out, hoping to undermine her confidence. Clearly he'd swallowed Papou's line about her needing to be looked after and guided.

As if part of her degree hadn't been in business management! Clearly Christo had missed that part of their conversation, probably distracted by planning how to tie her to his niece's nursery.

'On the contrary, it is my concern, if you're hoping to use your grandfather's property as capital.'

Something dropped hard through Emma's middle, like a stone plunging into a pool of arctic water. Chill splinters pricked her body.

She didn't like the triumph in Christo's eyes. As if he knew something she didn't.

But that was impossible. She already knew control of the valuable real estate in Athens had been handed to Christo on her behalf. Emma intended to change that, along with her married status.

'It's not my grandfather's property now. It's mine.' Her gaze swept the gracious room. This place, so full of precious memories, was her solace now, her home.

And more. It was her future. Her one asset, given her savings after years studying and looking after Papou were negligible. She'd get a loan using the property as collateral and invest it in the business she'd establish.

'If only that were true.' A deep voice cut through her thoughts.

She swung her head round to face him.

Either Christo had the best poker face in the world or he really did have bad news for her. Emma had a horrible feeling he was about to pull the rug out from under her feet…again.

She hiked her chin up, ignoring her stomach's uneasy roiling. 'If you have something to say, say it. I've had enough games.'

That sharp gaze held hers an instant longer then he shrugged. 'It seems your grandfather didn't tell you everything.'

That did it. Emma's stomach was now in freefall. She shifted her feet wider, bracing herself for the axe she sensed was about to drop, curling her hands into each other behind her back where Christo couldn't see.

'Go on.'

'He believed you needed a guiding hand. Which is why he left me in charge of the Athens property.'

'And?' Was he dragging this out to torment her?

'And your other inheritance, the estate here, is yours with the proviso that for the next five years any decision to sell or develop it, or take a loan against it, is subject to my approval. I have the right to veto any change of use if I don't believe it's in your long-term best interests.'

He smiled, a baring of white teeth that looked carnivorous rather than reassuring. 'Look on me as your business partner.'

Emma had been prepared for something but not this.

The blow struck at her knees, making them shake and threaten to collapse. Frantically she redistributed her weight, standing taller and hauling her shoulders back to glare at the man surveying her with that smug hint of a smile on his too-handsome face.

'I'll fight it. I'll challenge it in court.'

'Of course you will.' If she didn't know better, she'd almost have believed that soothing tone. 'But do you know how long that will take, or how much it will cost? How it will eat into your inheritance?' He paused, letting her digest that. 'You could lose everything.'

Main force alone kept Emma where she was. If she thought she had a hope of doing it, she'd have slammed a fist straight into Christo's smirking mouth.

She was still reeling, her brain whirring fruitlessly because, outrageous as it sounded, it was just the sort of thing her old-fashioned Papou might have done. Especially as he'd known his grandson-in-law-to-be was a commercial *wunderkind*.

He'd wanted to protect Emma. Instead he'd tied her to a man who wasn't fit to enter this house.

Belatedly she realised she should have insisted on reading every line of every legal document herself. More fool her!

'I'll still fight it.' Her voice was strained, her vocal cords pulled too tight.

'That's your prerogative.' Christo paused, that searing gaze stripping her bare. 'But there's an alternative.'

'What is it?' She didn't dare hope but she had to know.

'Simple. Meet my terms and you can do as you like with this place.' His mouth lifted at one corner in a hint of a smile but Emma knew in her very bones this would be anything but simple. 'I'll sign your inheritance into your control. All you have to do is fulfil your vows and live as my wife for a year.'

CHAPTER FOUR

'LIVE AS YOUR WIFE? You've got to be kidding.'

A flush climbed Emma's pale cheeks and her greenish brown eyes glittered more brightly than he'd ever seen.

She was a pretty woman but indignation made her arresting.

Christo surveyed her curiously. She vibrated with energy, her breasts heaving and her mouth working. She looked...full of passion. That hadn't been on his checklist.

The news he'd become responsible for his stepsister's child had come just before his visit to Australia. He'd picked Emma as a suitable bride because she'd make a good mother and a compliant wife.

But Emma was far more than either of those things, he realised. Instinct had drawn him to her with good reason. Her allure was more subtle and intriguing than surface glamour. His body tightened in anticipation.

He wanted his wife.

Wanted her more by the minute.

And he intended to have her. To salvage his pride after being dumped like an unwanted parcel at his own wedding. Because he had a score to settle. But above all because he'd desired her ever since their first gentle kiss. Her breathless ardour had unlocked something deep inside that had grown and morphed into something very like need.

'There are two things I never joke about. Business and family.' The first because it was his lifeblood, the second because he never made light of anything with such power to destroy.

'I *know* why you married me, remember? I *heard* what

you told your best man.' Emma's lips thinned as she pulled her mouth tight and the colour faded from her cheeks.

Christo didn't like her pallor. That drawn look made her seem fragile. Vulnerable. Reminding him that she looked that way because of him. He was responsible.

'I never lied to you.'

'Not specifically, but you made me believe—' She bit her tongue and looked away.

Christo could finish her sentence. He'd made her think he was falling for her. That he was a man capable of love.

Something dark slithered through his belly, drawing nausea in its wake. Without a second thought Christo stifled it. He didn't have the time or inclination for feelings. Nor for pointless self-recrimination.

'It's done now. And my offer is on the table.' An offer she *would* accept.

Her face swung round and the impact of all that barely contained emotion slammed into him. To his surprise, Christo welcomed it.

Because he'd rather have his wife angry than sad and defeated. It was a new concept. He filed it away for later consideration. Along with the dark shadow edging his conscience.

'You can't want me to live with you. I despise you.'

If Emma expected that to derail his plans, she really was an innocent. But then she hadn't come from his world but from what appeared to be a close, loving family. For a second Christo pondered what that would be like.

'You might be surprised at what I want and what I can live with. Besides, you owe me.'

'*I* owe *you*?' There it was again, that shimmer of defiance, that surge of energy that made his wife the most interesting woman he'd met in years. Even the fact that her vibrancy was due to inconvenient *feelings* didn't deter him.

'You gave your word. You made promises to me, Emma.' He even enjoyed the taste of her name on his tongue.

How would that pale golden skin of hers taste?

'You really expect me to share a house with you?'

'And a bed.'

She goggled up at him as if he spoke Swahili instead of English.

'You're not serious.' For the first time since he'd arrived he saw her falter, grabbing the back of a nearby chair.

That hint of vulnerability ignited a trail of gunpowder right through his considerable self-control. Was the idea of sex with him really so appalling? He refused to believe it.

Christo enjoyed women, within strict parameters, and he knew sexual attraction when he saw it. A week ago his demure bride had been counting the hours till they were naked together. Soon she would be again.

'But I am. You're mine, Emma, and I intend to have you. At the very least you owe me a wedding night.'

Emma gripped the carved back of the antique chair and willed the room to stop spinning.

This was crazy. Impossible.

Yet Christo Karides stood there looking as implacable as ever. More so. Before the wedding she'd seen a gentler, more restrained man. Now she saw the real Christo, haughty and demanding. Over the top with his outlandish demands.

'You'd force me into sex?'

For the first time since he'd stalked along the beach—sexy, brooding and starkly dangerous—she saw him recoil.

'I'd never force a woman. What sort of man do you think I am?' He even had the temerity to look outraged!

'I know exactly what sort of man you are and the question stands.' Stronger now, Emma let go of the chair back and slid her hands to her hips, adopting a combative attitude to hide her nerves.

'The answer is no. Sex with an unwilling woman… Never.' He shook his head, grimacing with distaste, and Emma felt the knot of tension in her chest loosen.

Then his gaze zeroed in on hers and suddenly she was short of breath.

'But you want me, Emma.' His certainty was infuriating and devastating, because it tapped into a weakness that shouldn't exist any more. She despised herself for feeling a tiny tug of response to his words. 'And I'll make sure you enjoy every single minute of it.'

His searing look clogged the protest in her throat. Or maybe it was her body's reaction to the images his words evoked. Heat blasted her. She reminded herself she hated him.

'If nothing else, I expect to share the wedding night we missed.' Something shifted in his eyes, something that spoke of calculation and determination. Emma shivered and rubbed her hands up her arms.

'You're demanding a year living with you and one night of sex? That's totally bizarre.'

He spread his arms, palm up. 'I need a wife to help my niece settle in. I have no skills with children.' His mouth twisted and for a second Emma thought she read something else in those slate-dark blue eyes. But it was gone before she could identify it. 'Even I know she needs more than a nanny. She needs a kind, caring parent figure to help her through the worst of the change. Don't forget, she's been through the trauma of losing her mother. *You* know how important it is that she has someone there for her.'

Damn the man. He was right. Emma didn't want to get involved. Yet she couldn't prevent a pang of sympathy for the little girl who'd lost her mother. And who apparently only had Christo to rely on! Poor kid.

Emma's bruised heart squeezed on the girl's behalf. At least when she was orphaned she'd had her grandparents, aunt and uncle. They'd closed ranks around her, a tight circle of love and support.

But she couldn't afford to be swayed, no matter how sorry she was for the child.

'As for us enjoying each other sexually...' Christo's deep voice cut through her thoughts. 'Once we begin, I'm sure we'll both want far more than one night. I'm confident we're well-matched physically.' His voice lingered on the last word, drawing unwanted heat from Emma's midsection down to the aching hollow between her legs. The sensation was new and unnerving. 'But I demand at least one night. Those are my terms.'

Despite her intention not to show weakness, Emma shuffled back half a step. 'It's preposterous!'

Christo said nothing, merely folded his arms over his chest and lifted one eyebrow.

Emma cast a look around the dear, familiar room. It would break her heart all over again to leave the family villa. But better that than what Christo proposed.

'I'll see you in court.' Her voice was crisp and decisive, despite the jittery whirl of emotions. 'Even if I have to walk out of here with only the clothes on my back. I'll go back to Australia, to my family and friends, and begin legal action to divorce and get back what's mine.'

Even if justice took years. Even if her inheritance was depleted in the meantime. She'd work and support herself.

She couldn't contemplate the alternative.

'That would be unfortunate.' Christo's arms fell to his sides, fingers flexing, and Emma wondered if he was restraining the impulse to reach for her. She pushed her shoulders back, meeting him eye to eye, knowing she had no alternative than to face him head on.

'I understand your uncle's business is dangerously over-extended. Even with the recent inheritance from your grandfather. If one of the investors were to withdraw it would be disastrous. The repercussions would impact not only him but your aunt and cousins. They could lose everything.'

Words choked in Emma's throat as her larynx tightened. She stared, wide-eyed, absorbing the threat in those softly spoken words.

Papou had said Christo was clever and daring. That he had a nose for business and a ruthless edge. Would he really be so ruthless as to destroy her family out of pique because she'd turned him down?

Emma wanted to doubt it but she couldn't take the risk.

'Are you *threatening* my family?'

She couldn't read anything in those arrogant features but determination.

'Do I need to?' He shook his head. 'There'd be no threat to them if you simply abided by your vows. With you as my wife I'd feel obliged to support your uncle if his company was in danger of floundering.'

Emma sucked in a breath. It was true her uncle's construction company had been through rough times. Now she thought about it, there'd been talk of Christo investing in it. But her head had been so full of other things that she hadn't paid much attention.

Now she was paying attention, far too late!

The walls pressed in on her. Or maybe it was the net this man had cast around her drawing tight.

Had Christo really invested in her uncle's company to ensure she complied? Or was it an empty threat?

Emma stared into eyes the colour of a stormy sky and felt something inside shrink. He was implacable, as merciless as a winter storm that wrought destruction on everything in its path.

Whether Christo had put money into the business for

purely financial reasons or as shrewd emotional blackmail didn't matter. Emma couldn't let him destroy her family.

'My grandfather was right about you. You really are utterly ruthless.' She grimaced, remembering Papou's enthusiasm for this man. 'To think he actually *respected* that. I'm glad he never had to find out what sort of man you truly are. You're a bully, Christo Karides.'

He didn't even blink, just stared back, eyebrows slightly raised, as if waiting for her to capitulate.

Emma swallowed hard, tasting a coppery tang. She realised she'd bitten down on her lip so hard she'd drawn blood and hadn't even felt the pain.

Frantically she ransacked her brain for an out. Something that would free her from this nightmare. But her luck had run out the day she'd fallen for this wolf in a tailored suit.

Why, oh, why had she broken the habit of a lifetime and acted rashly, marrying so quickly?

Because you fell for him. Hook, line and sinker.

The knowledge was acid, eating at her insides.

'I want to live here, in Corfu. Not in Athens.' Emma refused to let herself stop and think about the implications of what she was agreeing to.

'That works. My Athens apartment isn't designed for a child. This is much more suitable.'

If she needed anything to remind her of Christo's priorities, this was it. His first thought, his only thought, was for the child he expected her to mother. Everything else, even the sex he said he wanted, was secondary. But then he'd never really been attracted to Emma. The demand to share a bed was just male pique, because she'd escaped becoming another conquest.

She crossed her arms, clamping her fingers hard into bare flesh.

'Don't tell me you're willing to leave Athens?' Was

there, perhaps, hope that the threats had been a ploy? That he had no intention actually of living with her?

'It's only an hour by plane. I'll spend week nights on the mainland and the weekends here. That way Anthea will have a chance to get used to me.'

For the first time he'd called his niece by her name.

And for the first time that Emma could recall, Christo looked uneasy. His voice lacked its usual confident tone.

At the thought of spending time with Anthea? It didn't seem possible. Christo was the most assured man she knew.

Emma didn't understand this cold-hearted stranger. He showed no compunction or remorse about threatening her in the most outrageous way, yet one little girl unsettled him?

But Emma had enough to deal with. Firmly she pushed aside curiosity about the girl and her relationship with Christo.

'I need time to consider.'

He shot his cuff and sliced a glance at his designer watch. 'You have ten minutes.'

'Ten—'

'I have business to attend to. I need this wrapped up.'

As if she were an item on a meeting agenda, to be crossed off before he moved onto the next matter.

Once, Emma would have murmured something placatory and avoided further direct confrontation. But that had been with her darling Papou, whose quick flares of impatience had masked genuine worry for her future and fear that his failing heart would give out before he saw her settled.

Settled! With this arrogant...

'Of course making money is far more important than dealing with real people.'

Her words brought that laser-sharp gaze back to hers. Emma swallowed hard at the impact of that silent scrutiny.

Did he see past her bravado to the woman grappling with hurt and shock?

'Talk to your uncle, Emma. He and your aunt are real people, aren't they? Ask him how strong his business is.'

In the past Christo's deep voice had sent a thread of molten heat trailing through her insides. This time it created crackling frost along her bones.

Of course she'd talk to her uncle, but she knew he'd confirm what Christo said—that his company was vulnerable. One thing she'd learned, when Christo Karides wanted something, he didn't leave anything to chance.

'If I agreed to stay with you for a year...' Emma forced down bile '...how do I know I can trust you to keep your word?'

His eyebrows shot high, as if no one had ever questioned his integrity. She found that hard to believe.

'I'll have a contract drawn up.'

A contract setting out such a...personal deal? Her mind boggled. Yet she couldn't trust his word. Look at how he'd fooled her with his suave, persuasive ways.

'I won't sleep with you.'

He merely smiled. The man was so full of himself.

'It's not sleep I have in mind.' This time, despite every shred of indignation, despite his insufferable arrogance, Emma felt a tell-tale flutter in her belly. As if the woman who'd loved and longed for this man was still here, eroding the foundations of her anger.

'The contract will arrive tomorrow.' He looked as if he was going to say more then shook his head. 'Anthea and I will be here on the weekend.' Then, before Emma could find any words, he strode from the room.

Sure enough the next afternoon a courier arrived.

Emma was dishevelled after hours trying to quell her fury and fear by exploring the estate from top to bottom.

She'd checked out every inch of the villa, its outbuildings and the neglected villa next door which Papou had bought and hadn't got around to renovating. If Emma was to turn this into an exclusive small function centre, that second villa would be a wonderful asset.

If she was still here in Corfu.

If she didn't cut her losses and go home.

Except she'd called her uncle and knew she had no choice. He'd confirmed that Christo had invested heavily in the family construction company. He'd even added that things would be tight without Christo's support.

Support!

Emma shivered and looked down at the sealed envelope in her hands. It felt like a ticking time bomb. Her hands were clammy and, despite the cool breeze through the open front door, she was overheated.

The sound of the courier's car accelerating onto the main road broke her stasis. She tore open the envelope.

There it was, in excruciating detail. Christo had signed over control of the Corfu property, and a sizeable share of the expected profits of the Athens redevelopment. In return she'd live as his wife for a year. She'd take no lovers. She'd appear with him as necessary in public and behave with expected decorum. She'd accommodate his niece. She'd grant no media interviews about their relationship, ever.

And she'd have marital relations with Christo Karides at least once.

He'd actually had the gall to include that in the contract! His signature slashed the page just below it.

All Emma had to do was sign and she'd have the property that should already be hers.

For long moments she stared at the document. Then something snapped. Emma shoved the contract back into the envelope, breathing hard.

Dared she?

But what alternative did she have?

She'd keep this safe as proof of her husband's intentions and manipulations in case she needed it in a future court case. She'd delay filing for divorce till the twelve months was up. She'd give his niece a home, poor little kid. She'd even put up with Christo staying every weekend.

But as for the rest... She might be cornered but she had her self-respect. Emma refused to sign. She and Christo Karides would be married in name only.

If that wasn't good enough, she'd swallow her pride and go to the press. It was a distasteful last resort. Emma valued her privacy and shuddered at the thought of laying herself bare for the world to read about. But selling her story might provide enough money to tide her family and her over till she won back what was hers.

For the first time since Christo had sauntered back into her life, all arrogance and outrageous demands, hope stirred.

She could do this. She *would* do it.

She'd throw herself into creating her business and at the end of the year she'd get her property back. Christo was bluffing about them having sex. He had to be. It was just bruised masculine pride talking.

He'd only drawn up the contract to satisfy her concerns that he'd renege on the deal. Now she had his signature proving he intended to hand over the property, she was safe. She had to believe that.

All she had to do was endure fifty-two weekends without trying to kill her infuriating, selfish, diabolically annoying husband.

CHAPTER FIVE

THE FOLLOWING SATURDAY morning Emma and Dora stood in the villa's entry, watching a driver open the back door of a long, black limousine.

Emma's breath snagged in the back of her throat and her pulse pounded, waiting for Christo to emerge. But it wasn't he who appeared. Or a little girl.

It was a woman, and what a woman.

Emma had told herself nothing Christo did now could surprise or hurt her.

She'd been wrong.

Watching long, toned legs appear, narrow feet in high-heeled sandals and a tall, sinuous figure in a tightly fitted dress, everything inside Emma stilled. Then the woman turned to look about her and the sun danced on glossy sable waves that cascaded around slim shoulders and framed a face so beautiful it belonged on a magazine cover.

Emma felt as though she'd been slapped in the face.

He'd brought his lover with him. To her home.

Her home!

Abruptly the nerves making her anxious melted away, replaced by incandescent fury.

Emma's gaze locked on the woman, so she didn't even notice Christo emerge from the car, or the little girl who stood awkwardly between the two adults, until Dora started forward with words of welcome.

Emma blinked and looked again, taking in the tableau before her in freeze frames.

The beauty was looking tentatively at Christo, who frowned mightily. But he ignored the woman, his attention fixed on the child who must be Anthea. A little girl with tight brown plaits and pale, skinny hands clasped before her. She didn't look at either of the adults beside her, but stared warily at Dora, who smiled and welcomed them.

Finally Christo turned, his eyes locking on Emma's. Even braced for it, she was stunned by that sudden sizzle of connection. No, not connection, she told herself. Fury.

She stalked forward, intending to confront him, only to falter when Anthea shrank back, not towards Christo or his girlfriend, but towards the solidly built driver.

Emma's anger ebbed as other emotions rose. Guilt for scaring the kid with her sudden surge of movement. Sympathy and remembered heartbreak. Memories of grief and insecurity. Of feeling alone in a world that didn't make sense after her parents had died.

Emma dropped to a crouch before the little girl, discovering soft brown eyes, a smattering of freckles and a mouth that hooked up at one side as she bit her cheek.

'Hello,' she said quietly. 'I'm Emma. You must be Anthea. Is that right?'

Silently the girl nodded, her eyes wary and huge. Emma's chest tightened as if her ribcage shrank around her heart. She watched Anthea's hands tighten convulsively on each other and repressed a frown. At the very least the poor kid should have a teddy or something to cuddle given none of the adults with her could be bothered offering comfort.

'Do you like rabbits?' Emma asked impulsively, thinking of the toy rabbit she'd rediscovered in the room she'd used as a girl. Washable and soft, it had survived years of snuggling almost intact.

Anthea didn't answer, just lifted her shoulders in a tiny shrug and bit her lip harder. Emma waited for one of her companions to step in and reassure her. But a quick glance showed Christo standing back as if the girl had come with a health warning. The woman was no better, busy surveying Christo through her lashes.

'Would you like to come inside and see one?' Emma smiled. 'He can't hop or eat grass but he likes spending time with little girls and he loves being cuddled.' She paused. 'Do you like giving cuddles?'

'I don't know.'

The whisper stilled the last buzz of Emma's dying temper. She forgot about her unwanted adult guests and focused totally on the too-serious face of the girl before her. The girl she hadn't wanted to build a close relationship with, because she knew it could only lead to pain when they went their separate ways after twelve months. Emma had told herself it was up to Christo to forge a bond with his niece, not her.

Now that notion died an abrupt death. Emma couldn't ignore this little girl whose reserve and tension told its own sorry tale. She wanted to wrap her close and tell her everything was going to be okay. Instead she kept her tone light.

'Then let's find out, shall we? I'll take you to him if you like.' She rose and reached out her hand.

Anthea stared at it as if she'd never held an adult's hand in her life. She shot a swift, upward glance at the others, almost as if expecting reproach, then reached out and touched Emma's fingers.

Anthea's tiny hand was cool in hers but Emma was careful not to betray surprise at that or the tremor she felt pass through the little girl. Instead she smiled and turned towards the door, catching Dora's eye. The housekeeper would see to the adults. Right now the priority was this little waif and making her feel comfortable.

The enormity of the situation hit Emma again, making her falter for a second. She was about to take on responsibility for a child, a child who, obviously, needed love and lots of it.

But Emma couldn't turn her back on the girl. This had nothing to do with Christo's threats. It was about recognising the blank shock on Anthea's face, the feeling of loss and fear, the dreadful uncertainty.

Emma had been there. She couldn't treat the girl as a pawn in some power play.

She stepped into the house, Anthea tentatively returning her grasp. 'He's a very special rabbit, you know. He's lived here for a long time. I hope you like him.'

Christo surveyed the spacious bedroom suite he'd been given and tried to turn his mind to practicalities, like Wi-Fi access. Instead he found himself staring at the perfect curve of blue-green sea in the cove, his thoughts in turmoil.

Not only his thoughts. His gut roiled with unfamiliar emotion.

It wasn't the Ionian Sea he saw. It was Emma crouching before his niece, cajoling her into a response after hours of the kid being silent and withdrawn.

He'd known all along that Emma would make a great carer. She was warm-hearted and generous. Her body language around the girl had been fiercely protective, yet her expression had been soft, something that he was sure would turn into love one day.

His gut clenched.

Christo couldn't remember ever being so close to such naked maternal tenderness. Any sort of tenderness, come to that. Except the fleeting sense of intimacy he got from sex. The short afterglow that made the mirage of emotional intimacy seem almost as tangible as physical closeness. Until logic kicked in, reminding him it was a fantasy.

Impatient, Christo marshalled his thoughts, ignoring the unfamiliar pang as he recalled Emma's expression and his unwarranted reaction.

He opened the French doors and stepped onto the wide terrace.

Emma's reaction might have been all he could wish for but Anthea's nanny was another matter.

He gritted his teeth at the thought of the woman who'd been recruited so carefully to provide the best care for his step-niece. He'd left the recruitment to experts. After all, what did he know about selecting a child minder?

Now he saw he should have taken a hand, vetting the applicants himself. The woman with such excellent experience and references—the woman who had been soberly dressed and devoted to her charge, the time they'd met previously—had transformed utterly. He'd been confronted at the airport by a siren more interested in batting her eyelashes at him than caring for Anthea.

He sighed and shrugged out of his jacket, dropping it over the back of a chair. He'd sometimes had the same problem with temporary office staff. Women who were all business till the day they found themselves alone with the boss. A boss who regularly featured on those 'hottest, richest bachelor' lists.

The question was, did he fire her effective immediately or give her notice? It would take time to replace her. And even he, used to others doing his bidding, didn't expect his wife to take sole charge of Anthea.

Anthea. Who looked so like her mother.

Christo shoved his hands in his pockets and stepped out onto the grass. He'd deal with the nanny later. With everything later. For now he needed fresh air.

Ever since he'd boarded the plane and seen Anthea with her big brown eyes, Christo had felt claustrophobic to the point of nausea.

It was pathetic. It was all in his head. Yet he felt the tension notch higher with each breath.

Being with the child brought back memories he hadn't revisited in years.

Turning his back on the house, he lengthened his stride.

* * *

'Where have you been?'

Christo stopped in the shade of a wide, twisted olive tree, locating the source of the question.

Emma. His wife.

Heat ignited low in his abdomen. Satisfaction. And more besides.

Instead of being pinned up, her hair was around her shoulders in a drift the colour of wild honey. Was it the sunshine that made it glow? In wintry Melbourne the colour had been more subdued. Like the woman.

Maybe the difference was her bright, summery clothes. In a sleeveless wrap-around dress the colour of apricots, she looked good enough to eat. Especially as the light fabric skimmed breasts and hips and that narrow waist which had so fascinated him when he'd held her close.

Christo's groin grew heavy. She stood with arms folded and hip jutting in a confrontational stance that triggered a reaction deep in his psyche. Something he could only describe as very primitive and utterly masculine.

'Walking,' he murmured, watching her eyes flare brighter. As if she struggled to contain her emotions.

Was that what she'd done before? Kept her emotions under wraps?

The woman he'd courted in Australia had been reserved and eager to please. Christo had thought he wanted the quiet, compliant Emma. But there was a lot to be said for vivacity. For passion.

'You don't think it would have been helpful if you'd stayed with Anthea? Helped her settle in?'

Christo settled his shoulders back against the rough bark of the tree and slowly crossed his arms. 'You were doing a fine job. Better than I could have done. My skills don't lie in that direction.' Give him business any day. Wrangling a profit in a difficult commercial environment was far easier than dealing with family or feelings.

Emma shook her head gain, dark blonde waves slipping around her shoulders. 'That's no excuse. You should have been there. You're her uncle.'

Step-uncle. But Christo didn't correct her.

'It's not me she needs. It's someone like you, with a knack for dealing with children.'

'Don't think you can get out of your responsibilities so easily.' Her voice was low and even but determined. 'You need to build a relationship with her. When we divorce, I won't be around to take care of her.'

There'd be no divorce.

Christo planned to keep Emma as his wife. Once she got used to the idea, once he'd taken her to bed, she'd change her mind. It might be his money and looks that initially attracted women, but he knew how to satisfy them.

Pleasure stirred at the memory of Emma on their wedding day. Her breathless anticipation. The flurry of nerves that barely concealed her desire for him.

All he needed was patience, time to remind her how much she wanted him.

There'd be pleasure too in having what she'd denied him when she'd run off, leaving him to explain the inexplicable to her friends and family. Runaway bride, indeed! Did she really think she could make a fool of him and not pay? Did she think he had no pride?

'I have every intention of developing a relationship with her.' Though the thought of it made him feel...

No. Better not to examine that too closely. He knew his duty and he'd do it.

'Well, you haven't got off to a good start.'

Christo shrugged. 'Some things take time.' Such as seducing a woman who needed the reassurance of a gentle touch. He read more than anger in Emma's obstinate stance and quickened breathing. There was awareness. How could he not notice when it crackled in the air between them?

'They'd go far better without your girlfriend here.' The words emerged through clenched teeth. Emma bit the words out.

Jealousy?

Despite the tension he'd fought these last hours, Christo felt delight unfurl.

'She's not my girlfriend.'

'She sure fooled me.'

Emma's chin swung higher. It wasn't Christo's companion who'd made a fool of her. It was her own husband. How she hated that word. Husband. Almost as much as she hated the fact she'd been stupid enough to marry him. She must have been out of her mind!

Now he'd brought his lover here. She'd heard about open marriages but this was the man who just days ago had demanded sex as his marital right!

As if all that weren't enough, there was yet another sting in the tail.

Despite the different colouring, one brunette and one redheaded, there was a strong similarity between the woman who'd stepped out of the limo and Emma's cousin, Maia. The gorgeous cousin with whom Christo had admitted he'd like to have an affair.

Both women were tall, sexy in a sultry, almost earthy way, yet with a sophistication Emma couldn't hope to match.

Plain Emma. Ordinary Emma. Emma the 'nice' girl. Emma who played by the rules and didn't like to upset people who cared for her.

She dug her fingers into her upper arms, fighting a wave of reckless anger. Losing her temper wouldn't help.

Yet, now she'd met Christo's 'type' and realised how far she was from the sort of woman he wanted, it was a battle to retain some surface calm. Because it brought home how ridiculous her dreams of happy-ever-after had been.

'Emma?' He straightened from the tree and moved closer, forging a path through scarlet poppies and smaller wildflowers. In the dappled light of the olive grove she almost believed that was regret on Christo's face. Except she'd had enough of self-delusion.

'That's far enough.'

He halted before her, his gaze clear and open, as if he'd never deceived her.

'She's Anthea's nanny, not my lover.'

Emma snorted. 'Even I'm not that gullible.'

'But I was. Or at least, the recruitment expert was.'

Something about his tone of voice, the jarring note that sounded like discomfort, as well as annoyance, stopped Emma's scornful reply.

This was the first time Christo Karides had admitted being anything other than in control. Was it a trick?

He curled his hand around the back of his neck. The action dragged his casual shirt up, stretching it across his wide chest.

Emma stared then raised her gaze to his face, telling herself it was the drowsy afternoon heat of the sheltered grove that made her feel warm.

'You're telling me she really is a nanny? She doesn't look or act like one.'

'The only other time I met them, she wore flat shoes, hair pulled back and her outfit was sensible, not—'

'Sexy?' Emma arched her eyebrows. 'Surely you noticed she couldn't take her eyes off you? She didn't even glance at Anthea.' Outrage on behalf of the bereaved little girl cut through Emma's hurt. They were both victims of this man.

'Oh, I noticed. *Today.*' His tone was grim. 'But she wasn't like that the other time. Then she was wonderful with

Anthea. Attentive and reassuring. She perfectly matched her excellent references.'

Emma frowned, finally registering what Christo had said a moment ago. *The only other time he'd met them.*

It wasn't just the nanny he'd met only once. It was his niece too. No wonder Christo and Anthea behaved like complete strangers. Yet did that explain his grim expression as he'd surveyed the little girl?

Slate-blue eyes caught and held hers. 'Today I saw a different side to her.' He lifted one shoulder in a half-shrug and Emma realised he was still talking about Anthea's nanny. 'It happens. Women deciding to make a play for a rich man who'll be a meal ticket. But I confess this time I was taken completely by surprise.'

Emma stared back at this man who took such things in his stride. A light breeze riffled his jet-black hair and the shifting shadows cast those high, carved cheekbones in stark relief, accentuating his hard male beauty.

She knew they came from different worlds but to accept such games as inevitable? 'If that's normal in your world, then I pity you.'

Something shifted in his face. His expression closed, turned still. For just a second Emma sensed she'd hit a nerve. Or had she imagined it?

'I'm not interested in sleeping with the hired help.' His voice was chill, sending a shiver tracking over her bare arms and neck. 'I never mix sex and business. Besides, I have a wife. Remember?' The way his voice dipped suddenly took Emma's stomach with it, diving low in a giddy swoop. 'What I want is someone I can trust to care for Anthea. She needs it, poor kid, after what she's been through.' He paused, as if side-tracked by his thoughts.

'You mean more than losing her mother?' Emma didn't know what prompted her words. A parent's loss would make any kid withdrawn and wary. Emma was certain her own early losses had affected her that way too. Yet after just a short time with Anthea she wondered at her level of self-containment, and the bruised expression in her eyes, as if expecting the worst at any moment.

Christo fixed her with a hard stare, as if daring her to go on. For answer she simply stared back.

Finally he sighed and shoved his hands deep in his trouser pockets. 'It's as well you know.' He paused and paced away, as if too restless to stand still. 'Anthea was living with her mother, my stepsister, in the USA.'

'Not in Greece?' But then that would explain why Anthea had responded easily when Emma had spoken to her in English.

'My stepmother and stepsister were American. It was decided Greece didn't suit my stepsister.' To Emma's astonishment, she saw Christo's mouth work, tugging down in a grimace before flattening into a grim line.

Her curiosity rose. She was about to ask what that meant when Christo continued. 'She went to live with relatives in the States.'

'Instead of staying with her mother and your father?' It seemed odd.

'Yes.' His tone put off further questions. 'She lived there till she died recently. Sadly, it wasn't a settled life. She was…troubled.' There it was again, that slight hesitation that made Emma more rather than less curious about his choice of words.

'Put plainly, she became addicted to drugs and alcohol. As far as I can tell, she never lived with Anthea's father, whoever he was.'

'You weren't in contact with her?'

Christo shook his head and turned to survey the villa through the trees. Was it her imagination or did he deliberately avoid her eyes?

'I only ever saw her once, years ago. I never heard from

her after she left.' He opened his mouth then closed it again. Had he been going to add something?

Emma pushed the idea aside. The issue now was Anthea, not Christo's relationship with her mother.

'Anthea lived with an addict?' Her heart sank as she imagined the sort of life the little girl had experienced.

Christo nodded, the movement abrupt. 'They moved a lot and I suspect she was neglected.'

Emma looked at that hard face, the profile made severe by tension, and realised that behind the adamantine stillness of his features Christo was distressed.

It made him suddenly, unexpectedly, human.

A flurry of warmth rushed through her. An unwanted stirring of sympathy.

She'd thought of him as a liar and a cheat. Seeing evidence of a softer side was unsettling.

'I should have followed up. I shouldn't have assumed she was okay.' The words were so quiet they melded with the sigh of the breeze through the silvered olive leaves.

Emma was puzzled. She'd assumed Christo and his stepsister had been young when they'd met. That Christo hadn't been responsible for her.

He turned back, those dark blue eyes searing in their intensity. 'Anthea hasn't had the advantage of a stable home or family. That's one of the reasons I want her settled with someone who can nurture her.'

Emma, in other words.

Indignation stirred anew. She wasn't some mail-order bride to be brought in to fill a gap. Yet her anger was muffled this time by the story she'd heard.

She understood Christo's desire to look after his niece. She even applauded it. Except for the ruthless way he'd lied to her, making her believe he wanted *her*.

'In that case, you need an excellent nanny. You can't rely on me long term.'

To her surprise, Christo inclined his head. 'Before you arrived I was debating whether to dismiss this nanny immediately. But that would leave you in the lurch when I go back to Athens.'

'You were concerned about me?' His consideration surprised her. Hadn't he acquired her for that very purpose?

Familiar hurt jabbed her. That was all she was to him, a convenient business acquisition, bringing him property and the mothering he wanted for Anthea. Even his demand for sex had been an afterthought, driven by annoyance that she'd defied him. She knew one thing for sure. She wasn't his type.

'Of course.' His gaze held hers. 'I never expected just to foist Anthea onto you. It would be unreasonable to expect you to care for her twenty-four hours a day. As my wife, you'll have other things to do with your time. And Dora is already busy enough.'

For a moment there Emma had actually started to warm to Christo. Until the reference to her being his wife. As if she had no other purpose in life.

'Actually, I'm going to be busy setting up my business. I won't have time for much else.'

Those penetrating eyes surveyed her for silent seconds and Emma wondered what he read in her face.

'All the more reason to find reliable help for Anthea.' Emma couldn't argue with that. 'The difficulty is that when I dismiss this nanny it will take time to find someone suitable.'

'You could look after her yourself.'

Black eyebrows winged up that broad forehead. 'I'm many things, Emma, but experienced in caring for traumatised children isn't one of them. Even if I trashed my schedule for the next several weeks to be with her, I wouldn't be suitable.'

'It's not a matter of being suitable. It's about providing warmth and love.'

Christo didn't answer. Didn't so much as blink.

He was right, Emma realised with icy clarity. Christo didn't do love. Little Anthea needed more than he could provide.

'Don't sack the woman. Give her another chance.' She surprised herself with the words.

'Are you serious?'

'You said yourself that she did a good job before. Maybe today was an aberration she's already regretting. We all make mistakes.'

Emma should know. This man had been the biggest mistake of her life. She knew how he could turn a woman's head.

'I could put her on notice. Spell out the boundaries to her,' he said slowly, as if thinking through Emma's suggestion. 'After all, she's the only one of us that Anthea has known for more than a couple of hours.'

'In that case, definitely give her a second chance. For Anthea's sake.'

He frowned. 'We'll have to keep a close eye on the situation. I won't allow Anthea to be neglected again.'

Did he notice that he'd said 'we'? It sounded as if he intended to take an active role in monitoring the situation. Perhaps he wasn't as cold-hearted as he seemed.

'If she doesn't live up to expectations, you can hire someone else. You could even tell your recruitment people that you may need a replacement if this one doesn't work out so they can check their books.'

'This time I'll vet the applicants personally.' Christo nodded. 'Thanks, Emma. It's a good, practical suggestion.'

Suddenly he smiled, a grin that transformed his features from sombre to breathtakingly attractive. It made Emma's pulse trip and stumble, then continue erratically.

'See how well we work together when we try? It just proves how perfectly matched we are.'

CHAPTER SIX

PERFECTLY MATCHED!

How dared Christo pretend they were any such thing?

Emma lay on her bed, fuming. No matter how she'd tried, she hadn't been able to sleep.

To her dismay she'd shared dinner alone with Christo. Anthea was too little to stay up and, after an interview with Christo, her nanny had elected to stay and watch over her. Dora had refused, point blank, to break a lifetime's habit and join them in the dining room.

Christo had been all easy charm, reminding her of their courtship in Australia. He'd complimented Emma on the villa and won Dora over with praise of her food and her home-made kumquat liqueur. It was hard to believe he was the same man who'd threatened blackmail to get Emma into his bed.

But she'd been taken in by him before. She refused to fall for that charade again. He might seem considerate but beneath lay a heart as cold as a steel trap.

Except where his niece was concerned. And, Emma suspected, his stepsister. There'd been something about his expression when he'd spoken of her...

Emma rolled her eyes, disgusted at her eagerness to find good in the man. She turned over and punched her pillow, trying to get comfortable.

It was impossible. Christo Karides kept invading her brain. It was bad enough when he'd been in another country, or on the mainland. Having him under the same roof made her edgy.

She told herself she felt indignant at him making himself at home, as if he were an invited guest instead of an unwanted husband.

There it was again. That shudder of repugnance at the word 'husband'.

But Emma was always brutally honest with herself, even if she'd spent years smoothing over prickly issues with her *papou*. That wasn't all she felt. There was a sliver of something else.

It had been satisfying this afternoon, discussing Anthea and her needs with him, hearing his thoughts and having him take her input seriously. That reminded her of their time in Melbourne, when he'd been not only solicitous but interested. She'd thought that had all been false. Now she wondered.

Emma bit her lip. She was going around in circles. She couldn't trust Christo Karides. The truly unnerving thing was that, despite everything, part of her wanted to.

On a surge of impatience, she flung back the covers and got up, grabbing the robe from the bottom of the bed.

Her mouth twisted as she put it on and cinched it around her waist. Steph had helped her choose it, and the matching nightgown of champagne silk and gossamer-fine lace for her trousseau. Emma had never owned anything like them in her life.

She'd imagined wearing this on her wedding night. Imagined Christo peeling it off as he kissed her in places she'd never been kissed before.

The thought raised gooseflesh on her skin, from her thighs to her hips and abdomen.

Spinning on her heel, Emma marched across the room and wrenched open the door to the balcony. She needed to think about something other than Christo. She'd count stars. That would keep her busy for the next hour or two.

There wasn't much moon and as the village was around the headland there was no light pollution. Just the inky-dark sky, the sigh of the sea and thousands upon thousands of stars.

Emma crossed to the railing and breathed deep. Funny that she'd never realised how much she missed this place till she returned. The scent of the sea was so evocative, mingling with the perfume of blossom and something else she couldn't name. A spicy aroma that tugged a cord low in her belly. She closed her eyes and inhaled through her nose, her brow crinkling in concentration. It was tantalisingly familiar and deeply attractive. She just couldn't place it.

'Hello, Emma.' Christo's voice, warm as melted chocolate, enveloped her. 'Couldn't sleep?'

She spun, one hand grabbing the railing for support, the other automatically closing the neck of her robe.

He stood a little way along the balcony. The private balcony accessed only by the master suite and one extra room where Papou had occasionally slept when Grandma had been ill and easily disturbed.

Emma blinked, but he was still there. Christo Karides, looking as she'd never seen him before. The light was too dim to read his expression but there was still a lot to see. A lot of naked flesh. He wore only loose, low-slung trousers that rode his hips and looked on the verge of sliding down long, hard thighs.

She swallowed abruptly and yanked her gaze up. But there was his bare torso. The starlight picked out sculpted lines and curves that spoke of power and pure eroticism.

He looked wonderful fully clothed. But half-naked, he was stunning. She'd dreamed of him nude so often but it was a shock to discover how compelling the sight of that bare body was. How it smashed through her anger and drilled down to the burning truth within her. That physically, at least, she'd never stopped craving this man. Even the rounded angles, from shoulders to arms and the symmetry of that tall, muscular frame, were too much.

Emma's breath disintegrated in an audible sigh and she swung away to stare at the sea. But her precarious calm was gone. She heard nothing over her pulse's catapulting rhythm.

And the tiny voice in her brain that spoke of want.

'What are you doing here?' She turned her head in his general direction, but not far enough to see him. This blast of weakness was too appalling. She refused to feed it.

'Like you, I had trouble sleeping.' He paused but only for a fraction. 'Perhaps we should find something to do together that will tire us out.'

Emma ignored the amusement in his tone and the blatant innuendo. That didn't deserve an answer.

But she couldn't ignore the unnerving hollow ache low in her body. Or the spiralling heat. It was as if at twenty-two her body had suddenly lost all connection with her brain, or with that part of it devoted to rational thought. She despised this man. She never wanted to see him again. But her long-dormant libido hadn't got the message yet. Once roused by him, it was still alive and eager.

'I mean, what are you doing here, in this part of the house? We prepared a different suite for you.'

'And it was charming. But totally unsuitable.'

Emma was on the point of swinging round to look at him when she changed her mind. Instead she anchored her fingers on the decorative ironwork railing and clenched her teeth.

'Why?'

'Because I asked Dora where your room was and told her I wanted to be next door. I refuse to sleep in the wing furthest from my wife. As you said, we have a relationship to forge.'

'I was talking about you and Anthea.' Her fingers tightened till they felt numb.

'Us too, Emma.' His voice slid easily to that *faux* intimate note that in the past had drawn her in so easily. The note that she'd innocently thought signalled genuine caring. She knew better now.

'There's no need for that. It's a marriage in name only and it will last just twelve months.'

'You know that's not true. You know there's more between us.'

Unable to contain herself, she spun round to face him. He'd moved closer, so close she could almost touch him. She jerked her gaze up and caught the glitter in his eyes.

'There won't be anything more. I'm not signing that contract.'

Slowly, annoyingly, he shook his head. 'I wasn't talking about the contract. I was talking about the fact that we want each other.'

'Not any more.' Emma curled her fingers, fighting the restless urge to reach out.

'Liar.' It was the merest whisper yet the accusation tolled through her body like a chiming bell.

He was right. That was the horrible truth.

Here in the intimate darkness, Emma felt the thousand proofs of it. The thrust of her pebbled nipples against the silk of her nightgown. The way that fine fabric grazed her bare flesh as if every nerve ending was suddenly too sensitive. The liquid heat between her legs. The edginess that made her want to shift and wriggle and, worse, press herself up against that hard body and discover how it would feel to…

'I don't want you, Christo.' It was the first bald-faced lie she could remember telling. But she refused to let him think she was so pathetic.

'Really?' He didn't sound at all dismayed. 'I could prove you wrong.' He shifted his weight, as if to step nearer, and Emma's heart leapt.

'No closer!' Emma flung her arm up, palm out. It took

everything she had to draw air into her lungs and find her voice but she did it. She'd learn to resist him if it killed her. 'I don't want to go to bed with you.'

Could he hear the lie?

At least he didn't move closer. In fact, to her astonishment, he turned and leaned his weight on the balustrade, looking out to sea. Her gaze roved his profile, from that strong nose to the hard angle of his jaw and up to the dark hair that looked rumpled, as if he'd dragged his hands through it.

Christo in a suit had been handsome. Christo pared back to basics and ever so slightly dishevelled made Emma's belly squeeze in longing.

Abruptly she turned away, sucking in a deep breath and placing her hands on the same railing.

'Don't look so scared. I told you I'd never force a woman. I'll wait till you come to me.'

She opened her mouth, to say that would never happen, then closed it again. The words would wash off him like water off a rock. She'd just have to demonstrate she meant what she said.

'So you don't want a contract now?' He sounded mildly curious, as if the issue of her sleeping with him was only of minor interest.

That, surely, would feed her determination? She'd never been brash or loud, demanding attention, but he'd already made her feel insignificant and taken for granted. She refused to settle for that.

'I don't want *that* contract.'

'Ah. But you still want everything else.'

'"Everything else" being property that's mine by right.' Adrenalin pumped through her blood. 'Or should have been if you hadn't inveigled your way into my grandfather's trust.'

How a wily businessman like Papou had been taken in

by Christo Karides, Emma would never understand. His health might have been failing but his mind had been sharp right till the end. It was he who'd warned her uncle that he'd over-extended, expanding his construction business so rapidly.

'Tell me about this place.' Christo's low voice drew her back to the present.

Instantly Emma stiffened as suspicion reared. 'Why do you want to know? I thought your company handled commercial property. Isn't that where you invest?'

'Relax. I only want to know because it's important to you. I heard it in your voice when you talked about it in Australia.' He paused. 'And you seem different here.'

She frowned. 'Different?'

'More assured. More confident.'

Emma shook her head and, standing straighter, turned to face her nemesis. 'I'm the same woman I always was. Nothing's changed.' Except she'd lost the last person she held dear. 'You were looking for a quiet mouse so you believed everything Papou told you about me.' Maybe *this* time he'd believe her.

'And your grandfather didn't get it right?' Instead of sounding annoyed, Christo's tone was merely curious.

She shrugged. 'He thought I was more delicate than I am.' Emma paused, wondering how much to share. But maybe this would convince Christo he was mistaken in thinking she could ever be the sort of wife he wanted. 'I had asthma badly as a kid and I was on the small side. Even though I grew out of the asthma, Papou never quite believed it. He was over-protective. He used to worry, so I learned not to confront him over things that didn't matter.'

Which had led to her taking the path of least resistance a lot of the time. Maybe if she'd stood up to him more often he wouldn't have persuaded Christo that she'd make the perfect homebody.

'I'm not a dutiful doormat.'

'So I've discovered.' Was that approval in his voice? She had to be imagining it. 'Now, about the villa…'

Emma stared up into that bold, shadowy face and wondered why he really wanted to know. On the other hand, talking with Christo was better than fighting him. Even with right on her side she found that unsettling.

She'd never enjoyed confrontation, but arguing with him was simultaneously frustrating and—Emma hated to admit it—exhilarating. As if the pulse of energy between them gave her a rush she'd never experienced before.

That was just plain crazy.

Finding her gaze straying down to those broad, straight shoulders and the muscled body limned by starlight, Emma swung away. She planted her palms on the railing and fixed her eyes on the view.

Which wasn't nearly as fascinating as the view of the man standing beside her.

She closed her eyes, willing herself to find the resolve she needed to pretend he didn't affect her.

Yet when she spoke her voice had a hoarse edge that she feared betrayed her. 'My grandparents met on Corfu. Papou had come back for a friend's wedding and my grandmother was on holiday from Australia. After a week, they were engaged. Three months later they were married.'

'Your grandfather was a decisive man.'

'Love at first sight is a family tradition. My aunt and uncle married after four months and my parents after two.' Emma snapped her mouth shut, belatedly seeing the connection to her own disastrous wedding. She'd fallen for Christo in record time. Because she genuinely believed in him, or because she'd been programmed to think love at first sight was utterly reasonable?

Now she knew to her cost how perilous that illusion was.

'And your grandfather owned this place?'

'It was his grandfather's.' She opened her eyes to survey the familiar coastline, the fragrant garden and behind it the silvery sweep of olive trees rising up the slope towards the hills. 'My grandmother adored it from the moment he brought her here. She was a horticulturalist and loved seeing what she could grow.'

'So they lived here.'

Emma shook her head. 'Only for a short time. Mainly they lived in Athens, then Australia. Papou was a businessman with interests on the mainland. In those days telecommuting wasn't an option. But this was always their favourite place. They'd come here several times a year. Even when they moved to Australia they came back regularly. We all did.'

'It had sentimental value, then.' He paused. 'For you too.'

Silently she nodded, surprised at the understanding in Christo's voice. She couldn't believe he had a sentimental bone in his body. Some of her happiest memories centred around this place. Of those precious years before her parents died. Of course there were other memories of them, of their day-to-day lives in Australia, but here at the villa there'd always been more time together as a family. Time Emma treasured.

She drew a breath and made herself focus on the present. 'It's a nice old place.' She wouldn't admit exactly how much it meant to her. Who knew how Christo would try to use that to his advantage? 'It's also an asset I can use to support myself.'

'Because you're determined to be independent.' His tone was non-committal but Emma heard the question.

'That's always been the plan.' Though she hadn't originally envisaged herself building a business here, in Greece. 'I've got a degree in business and event management. Plus experience in the field.' Okay, it was part-time experience, first with a major event organiser and later with a small but up-and-coming wedding planner. But full-time work had been impossible while she studied and looked after Papou. 'Of course I'll work.'

'Some would say marrying a wealthy man is a great career move. You need never lift a finger to support yourself.'

Emma's breath sucked in so sharply, pain shafted behind her ribs to radiate out and fill her chest.

She swivelled to face him, outrage obliterating caution. 'You…' She was so furious, the words backed up in her throat. In frustration she pointed a finger at his chest. 'You…'

Warm fingers enclosed hers and a thread of fire traced from his touch along to her elbow, then up to her shoulder, making her quiver.

'You're accusing me of marrying you for money?' Finally the words poured out, high and harsh.

'It's not unknown.' Christo's voice was matter-of-fact. His utter lack of expression was fuel to the fire of her anger. Did he think she'd been on the *make*?

'My family might not be as wealthy as yours, but we're not stony broke. At least, we weren't, before you weaselled your way into my grandfather's good graces.' For now Christo controlled her assets. 'But even if I didn't have a cent to my name—' scarily, she wasn't too far off that now '—I would never marry a man just to get his money.'

Vaguely Emma was aware of heat encasing her fingers as his big hand surrounded hers. But she was more concerned with convincing Christo he was utterly wrong about her.

'What proof have you got?' His tone was infuriatingly calm. 'Women do it all the time.'

That, Emma realised with a jolt, was the second time he'd referred to women cold-bloodedly targeting men as meal tickets. Suddenly she had a glimpse of the down side of being a mega-wealthy bachelor. Christo would never know how much of his appeal was down to his bank balance.

Tough! That didn't give him the right to use her for his convenience. Or accuse her of being a liar.

'Well, I don't. *I* didn't come looking for *you*, Christo Karides. *I* didn't deliberately set out to con you into marriage.' That had been him, targeting her and playing up to her hopes and vulnerabilities.

'So, if you didn't marry me for my money...' his words were slow and warm, like sun-drenched honey dropping onto her skin '...why *did* you marry me, Emma?'

It was only as the darkness pulsed between them and the silence grew heavy with waiting that Emma recognised his trap. To tell the truth meant admitting that she'd fallen in love with him. Or at least fallen for the mirage of love.

'This conversation's getting us nowhere. That's in the past and—'

'On the contrary, this conversation is just getting interesting.' He lowered his head, as if trying to read her face in the darkness. 'Tell me why you married me, Emma.'

That voice, honey now mixed with rumbling gravel, scraped through her insides. But, instead of leaving painful grazes, it stirred something altogether unwanted. Something she needed to banish. If only she knew how!

Suddenly she realised the danger of being this close to him. Of his flesh on hers. 'I want to go inside.'

'Could it be,' he went on as if she hadn't spoken, 'Because of *this*...?'

He tugged her hand, pulling her against him. Emma's hissed breath was loud as she planted her other palm on his chest to push him away.

But before she could he'd raised her captured hand to his face and pressed his lips to her palm. She felt surprisingly soft lips and the delicious abrasion of his hair-roughened jaw, a reminder of his masculinity, as if she needed it!

Instantly sensation juddered through her.

Desire.

Delight.

Weakness.

Shivers reverberated through her and Emma knew she had to fight this. But then Christo moved, bending lower to kiss the sensitive flesh of her wrist, creating a shower of sparks in her blood.

The trouble was Emma had so little experience. There'd been a guy at university when she'd been eighteen but that had never progressed beyond a few kisses, because her grandmother had died and suddenly, more than ever, she'd been needed at home. She had no experience withstanding such powerfully erotic caresses. Or the demands of her own body, finally woken after so long.

Firming her mouth, she pushed that unyielding chest with her free hand. It made no impact.

Or perhaps she didn't push very hard. For now Christo was kissing his way along the bare flesh of her forearm where the wide sleeve of her robe fell back.

His grip wasn't tight. She could yank her hand free. If only she could find the willpower to do it.

But, oh, the lush sensations spreading from those tiny yet incredibly intimate kisses.

Her breath sawed and in her ears blood rushed helter-skelter.

He'd reached her elbow and she stiffened like a yacht's sail snapping taut in the wind. Taut but trembling too, at the sensations he evoked. Her hand on his chest no longer pushed. Instead it splayed, fingers wide, absorbing the sultry heat of his hard chest and the teasing friction of the smudge of dark hair on his pectorals.

'Stop that now.' Because, heaven help her, she couldn't. 'I'm not sleeping with you, Christo.'

That caught his attention. He looked up and even in the

gloom she caught the brilliance of his eyes as he looked down at her. Then, without uttering a word, he put his mouth to her arm and slowly licked her inner elbow.

Emma's knees all but gave way as a frighteningly potent shot of lust punched her. She made a sound, a soft, keening noise that she wouldn't have thought possible if she hadn't heard it slide from her lips.

She cleared her throat, ready to demand he release her, when she felt the scrape of teeth nipping the soft flesh in the crease of her elbow. Then almost immediately the strong draw against her skin as he sucked the spot.

Emma bit down hard on her lip to prevent a groan escaping into the night. She'd had no idea something as ordinary as an elbow could be so sensitive. That it could make her feel...

Ready for sex. That was how she felt. With her trembling limbs and that pulsing point down between her thighs that urged her to move closer to Christo. There was an aching hollowness inside and her breasts seemed fuller than before, eager for contact, her nipples impossibly hard. If she followed that animal instinct she would rub herself against him, purring and pleading for follow through.

Her own weakness terrified her.

'I said I don't want to go to bed with you.' Her voice was too loud and too wobbly.

For answer he released her hand which wavered uselessly in the air then slowly dropped to her side. Instead of moving back he stroked his fingertips over her cheek. All she had to do was pull her head back a couple of centimetres to sever the contact but she couldn't do it. Instead she stood as if mesmerised by the caress of long, hard fingers that worked magic with each touch.

'I don't believe you.'

Why should he?

That was what terrified her. Not Christo's practised seduction but the fact that, after all he'd done, she still had no defences against him, or more precisely against her wilful body's craving for satisfaction.

The breath shuddered through her lungs. She felt herself sway, but managed to pull back at the last moment.

Christo followed.

Emma felt his warm breath on her cheek, the heat of his frame close to hers. She dragged in that leather, wood and male spice scent that made something inside her fizz like champagne bubbles.

Then those warm lips brushed her jaw. So lightly she almost wondered if she'd imagined it. But there was no mistaking the scorching trail of heat curling from her chin to her ear and then along to her mouth.

Emma had stopped breathing, stopped thinking. Her hands pressed to Christo's bare body which was part of the spell he wove. His smooth flesh and springy muscle invited exploration.

He kissed his way to the corner of her mouth then paused, hovering half a breath away.

Her lips tingled with want as she waited for him to kiss her properly. Not as he'd kissed her in the church, just a brief salutation to satisfy custom. Not as he'd kissed her when they'd got engaged, tenderly but too short and too chaste.

What Emma wanted, what she craved, was full-blown passion. She wanted to fall into that whirlwind of rapture she'd read about, and that her body assured her was waiting for her if she'd just let go and give herself to Christo.

She might detest him but she had no doubt he could allay the terrible gnawing hunger inside. The hunger *he'd* created. All she had to do was…

'Say it, Emma. Invite me into your bed. You're aching for me. I'll make it good for you.'

Of course he would.

But then, afterwards, what about her self-respect?

How could she hold her head up?

She'd let this man sweep her off her feet into a hazy romantic cloud that had about as much link to reality as unicorns prancing along the white sand of the beach below.

Seconds later Emma found herself in the doorway to her room, hands braced as if to stop herself reaching for Christo. She couldn't remember telling herself to step back. It must have been some primal survival instinct so deeply buried as to be almost automatic.

For there was no doubt now that Christo was the most dangerous man she'd ever met. He wasn't just cunning and ruthless, he'd introduced her to desire, and now her frustrated body had imprinted on him as the one man who could satisfy her.

It was ludicrous and appalling.

It scared her witless.

She grabbed the handle of the French door.

'I don't want you. I'll never want you.'

He stood, arms folded, watching as she tugged the door closed. In the instant before it snicked shut, she heard his voice, soft, deep and, oh, so sure.

'We both know that's a lie, Emma. But take your time. When we finally have sex it will be worth the wait.'

CHAPTER SEVEN

CHRISTO PULLED HARD through the water, forcing his body to the limit in an effort to weary himself. Anything to douse the frustration that had him wound so tight.

How had he ever thought winning Emma over would be simple? She had more determination, more sheer obstinacy, than any negotiator he'd ever confronted.

Her insistence on resisting him, despite the fact she clearly wanted him, was infuriating. He told himself if it weren't for the fact he was committed to her he'd walk away.

Christo had given her more than he'd ever given any woman. His name, his word, his promise for the future. Yet she looked at him with those glittering hazel eyes as if he were the devil incarnate.

Christo gritted his teeth and quickened his stroke till his shoulders and legs ached and his lungs were ready to burst.

Treading water, he hauled in a needy gulp of air and turned. In the distance the villa nestled into the curve of the bay, gracious and charming.

He'd thought Emma was just like that too, a mix of gentle ways and unobtrusive prettiness. An easy fit for his needs.

His harsh laugh echoed across the water.

Easy!

Anyone less easy he had yet to meet.

Oh, she certainly did her best to avoid direct confrontation. These last three weekends, whenever he'd arrived from Athens, she'd been the perfect hostess.

Christo ground his teeth. It was true he'd wanted a woman who could do him proud when entertaining, but it was something far more personal he wanted from her.

Far more personal. Despite the cool water and his fatigue after the sprint swim, he still felt that frustration low in his body.

Three weeks! He couldn't believe she'd held out for three weeks. He'd thought she'd break by now. For, try as she might, she couldn't hide her desire for him.

That first night here he'd almost had her in his arms and in his bed. She'd been like a fragrant summer rosebud, unfurling into his hand, velvet-soft and exquisite. His groin throbbed at the memory. But his little bride had an unexpectedly thorny resolve. Besides, he'd given his word. He'd promised to wait till she was ready.

The taut weight in his lower body testified to the toll his self-imposed patience was taking on him.

At least in one area she'd lived up to expectations. Her relationship with Anthea. Whenever he saw them together the brittle aura of containment around his niece chipped a little more. As for Emma, her policy of not getting involved had lasted about two seconds. Increasingly Anthea turned to Emma rather than the nanny paid to care for her.

Despite her obstinacy, Emma had a soft side. She was ruled by emotions. Plus she suffered from the same sexual frustration he did.

Christo's mouth curled up. All he had to do was take advantage of the opportunities that arose. Ignore his pride and chagrin that she hadn't already come to him and *make* those opportunities happen. Remind her again of the unfulfilled desire sizzling between them.

He lowered his head and began a steady overarm stroke towards the shore.

Half an hour later, a towel slung over his shoulder and his body warm from the sun, he strolled up the path from the cove and through the garden. A fat bee droned in the sunshine and the smell of roses caught his nostrils.

The irony of it didn't escape him. The drowsing villa

with its secluded garden and scented roses might have been
Sleeping Beauty's bower. Somewhere inside was Emma,
his bride, waiting to be woken by his touch.

She'd never admitted it but he suspected she was a virgin. Those tell-tale blushes and the slight clumsiness of
her kisses had raised his suspicions. Which was one of the
reasons he hadn't pressed her too hard.

Once they were lovers, once they'd shared intimate physical pleasure, he knew there'd be no more holding back.

He rounded a corner and stopped. It seemed his imagination was more accurate than he'd suspected. For there
was Sleeping Beauty herself.

Emma lay fast asleep on a sun lounger.

His gaze tracked her from her honey-toned hair splayed
around her shoulders to her bare feet. Afternoon sun gilded
her toned legs where her lacy white skirt rucked up high
above her knees. Christo's pulse quickened and his throat
dried as he imagined exploring that satiny skin.

With each gentle breath her breasts swelled up against
the vivid red of her sleeveless top, riveting his attention.

Even in sleep she was more striking than she'd been in
Australia.

Because of her bright clothes? Or because he'd begun
to appreciate she was far more than the docile bride he'd
assumed?

A couple of children's books were tumbled across her
lap, making her look as if she hadn't intended to fall asleep.

That was when he saw movement beside her and stiffened. At the same moment little Anthea, who'd been sitting
on the flagstones half-hidden by the sun lounger, looked
up.

Big brown eyes met his and Christo felt again that sti-
fling sensation in his chest. It was as if the years scrolled
back and he was looking into the wary eyes of his new
stepsister, Cassie. Cassie had been older, almost a teenager,

yet those eyes were the same. And so was the suffocating shadow of guilt that chilled his belly.

He hadn't been able to help Cassie all those years ago. In fact his casual attempt at kindness to the nervous little girl had backfired spectacularly. Because of him her whole future had been blighted. Was it any wonder he found it difficult being with Anthea? She might be tiny, but she was so like Cassie he couldn't look at her without remembering.

Christo waited for Anthea to turn away as she usually did. Proof again that he'd done the right thing organising a new mother and a nanny to care for her, since patently he wasn't cut out for it.

To his surprise, instead of shrinking back, his step-niece took her time frowning down at something she held then looked up at him again. Her eyes were bright and her look trembled between excited and tentative. As if she wanted to share with him but was afraid of being rebuffed.

Slowly she lifted a large piece of paper for him to see. It was covered in green crayon scrawls.

Christo felt something give deep in his chest, like a knot suddenly loosening, cutting the tension that stiffened his body. His breath drifted out, making him realise he'd been holding it.

He told himself he should leave her be, simply walk away. For he knew, even if she didn't, that he wasn't the person she needed.

But her expression, turning now from expectation to disappointment at his lack of response, slashed through his caution.

How could he resist?

He padded barefoot across the warm flagstones to Anthea. Her brow wrinkled in concentration as she tilted her head up to look at him.

Christo's heart gave an unsteady thump. How his business competitors would laugh if they could see him now,

scared of a little girl, or more precisely of somehow doing
the wrong thing for her. He didn't know children. He had
virtually no experience of them. And the one time he'd actually bonded with one it had ended in disaster.

Breathing deep through his nostrils, he hunkered down
before her. It was a relief to look away from that intense
brown stare and focus on her drawing.

Amongst the swirl of circles he discovered four downward strokes that might have been legs. 'You drew this?'
he said, buying time. He still hadn't a clue what it was.

Gravely Anthea nodded, watching expectantly.

Christo frowned, his brain racing. Clearly she expected
more.

'It's very good.' Did he sound as stilted as he feared?

'Nice dat.' They were the first words Anthea had spoken
directly to him and he should have celebrated this sign of
thawing, except he had no idea what she meant.

Till she lifted one dimpled hand and pointed. 'Dat.'

Christo followed her hand and saw a white cat stretched
out in the shade of a tree, one ear twitching, as if following their conversation. He looked back at the drawing and
enlightenment dawned. There, he spied two triangles that
might have been feline ears and a curling line that could
be a tail.

'You drew the cat?'

She nodded emphatically.

'Do you like cats?'

Another nod.

Now what? Clearly he was meant to contribute more.

Briefly Christo thought of the work he could be doing,
the calls he should make. Of waking Emma or rousting out
Anthea's nanny to take over.

Was he really so craven?

'Would you like me to draw a cat for you?' He wasn't
consciously aware of forming the words but suddenly they

were out and she was nodding again, a hint of a smile curving her mouth. Warmth trickled through Christo's chest.

He settled more comfortably on the flagstones and took the drawing she held out. But, instead of turning it over and drawing on the back of it, he chose a purple crayon from those scattered nearby and wrote her name on one corner, sounding out the letters as he went.

'There, now everyone will know it's yours.'

Fascinated, Anthea traced the letters with her finger, one dark plait falling forward and brushing his arm. It seemed she'd forgotten to be wary of him.

'Now you.' She pointed to the blank pages nearby. 'A dat.'

Once more Christo was rocked by a moment of déjà vu. It had been years since he'd drawn. Since that weekend when he'd amused his shy young stepsister with sketches and cartoons to make her smile. In those days drawing—or doodling, as his father had scathingly called it—had been a habit. A hobby that had distracted him from the pressures of his father's demands and their uncomfortable family life.

But not after that weekend.

Christo swallowed the sour tang of bile as old memories stirred. Setting his jaw, he shoved all that aside. It was over, dead and buried.

He took a sheet, glanced at the cat, now sitting up watching them, and began to draw.

At his side, Anthea watched, apparently entranced, as a few swift lines became a cat half-asleep in the sun. Another couple of lines and the cat was dozing over a book that looked rather like the picture book beside Anthea's stack of crayons.

Christo heard a childish giggle and added a striped sun umbrella similar to the one behind Emma. Anthea giggled again but shook her head when he went to give it to her.

'Put your name.'

This conversation was the most she'd ever said to him

and it felt like a victory. Not that he had any illusions about ever being particularly close to Anthea. She'd already bonded with Emma and that relationship would strengthen with time.

Christo would provide a comfortable home, protection and support, but as for being a close father figure... He shook his head even as he wrote his name in clear letters for Anthea.

He'd never known love from either of his parents. To one he'd been a convenience and to the other something to be moulded into the perfect heir to the Karides commercial empire. The heir to a man who married trophy wives and expected his son to be as ruthless and successful as he.

Christo's lips twisted in a shadow of a smile as he thought how proud the old man would be if he were still alive. For Christo was far more successful than his father had ever been, having expanded the family business to a completely new level. As for ruthless—he'd always tried to be more humanitarian than his father. But when the pressure was on, when he really needed something, like a mother for Anthea, it turned out he was every bit as unrelenting as the old man.

The knowledge was a cold, hard lump in his belly.

He ignored it, for there was no point pining over things that could never change. Instead he leaned over the paper and concentrated on a new drawing for his eager audience.

Emma drifted out of her doze to the sound of Anthea's excited voice. She heard another voice answer, a deep, reassuring blur of sound that soothed her back towards slumber.

Blearily Emma tried to summon the strength to move, fighting the fog that enveloped her. She never napped during the day but last night, knowing Christo was in the room next to hers, she'd been unable to sleep.

It was like that each weekend when he returned to the island. In the beginning she'd wondered if he'd break his word, try to 'persuade' her into his bed. But as the days and nights had passed and he'd kept his word that fear had subsided.

Yet she was still on tenterhooks.

Because it's not Christo you're afraid of.

It was herself. She hadn't yet been able to banish that simmering attraction she felt. The physical awareness whenever he was near. For, despite his promise to wait, Christo was often near, not crowding her or touching her, but *close*. She'd feel his stare and look up to discover she had little defence against the heat in his eyes. Inevitably answering need flared.

She told herself again and again he didn't really want *her*, except as a convenient child minder. But her besotted self, the one who'd once tumbled headlong into the romantic mirage he'd created, refused to listen.

Finally she forced her eyelids open to squint at the sunlight. She moved and the books on her lap slid sideways. Panic stirred. Anthea. Was she okay? Emma was supposed to be minding her while the nanny had her afternoon off.

'Dog now. *Pease.*'

Emma turned towards the little girl's voice and would have fallen off the lounge if she hadn't been lying down.

For there was big, bad Christo Karides, down on the pavement with his niece.

Emma blinked and rubbed her eyes, wondering if this was some hard-to-shake dream. But the image remained. The little girl in her shorts and T-shirt, looking up earnestly at the man beside her.

Christo Karides in nothing but damp, black swim shorts and acres of bare, muscled body, was spectacular. A shot of adrenalin hit Emma's blood, making her heart kick into a frantic rhythm. Ever since the night on her balcony she'd been haunted by thoughts of his body. But he looked even more impossibly delicious in broad daylight.

It struck her that for the first time he didn't wear the closed expression that usually clamped his features when he was around Anthea. He seemed at ease.

Almost. He leaned over a sheet of paper, his brow furrowed in concentration, his expression intent.

Moving slowly, not wanting to draw his attention, Emma sat higher to get a better view. What she saw held her spellbound. Using a crayon, Christo deftly sketched a couple of lines that turned into a whiskery, canine face wearing an almost comical expression of longing. A few more sure strokes and a body emerged with short legs and a curling tail. Finally he completed the picture by adding a large bone, almost as big as the dog, which explained the animal's hungry look.

He was good. Very good. The dog had such character, she could imagine it trotting around the corner of the villa, dragging that oversized bone with it.

Anthea laughed with delight, the sound as bright as sunshine. Emma's lips curved in response. The little girl was gradually relaxing here in Corfu and smiled more often. But she was still withdrawn and shy. Hearing her so exuberant was wonderful.

Emma shafted a curious glance back to Christo.

For once he wasn't aware of her scrutiny, focused instead on the girl beside him.

'More!' Anthea was so excited she knelt beside him, her tiny hands on one muscled knee as she leaned over to look at the drawing.

'Why don't you draw a friend for the dog?' He pushed the paper towards her and held out the crayon.

After a moment's consideration she nodded, her small fingers plucking the crayon from his broad palm.

Emma's chest squeezed at the sight of them together. It

wasn't that she was eager for a baby, but she *had* imagined Christo as the father of her children some time in the future. Had imagined those powerful arms cradling their baby.

Seeing him now, gentle and patient as Anthea scribbled what looked like a woolly sheep across the rest of the page, Emma couldn't prevent a pang of loss. Silly to pine for a man who wasn't real. The Christo Karides she'd fallen for was a façade, deliberately constructed to gull her into marriage.

Yet, watching her husband, she couldn't help mourning the loss of what might have been. If only Christo had been genuine.

'Tell me about what you've drawn,' Christo murmured.

''Nother dog. See?' Anthea leaned in, the tip of her tongue showing between her teeth as she added another figure, this time with an oversized head and stick legs. 'And me.' Another lop-sided figure appeared. 'And you.'

She sat back, beaming, and Emma had a perfect view of Christo. His face changed, an expression of surprise and pleasure making him look years younger than thirty-one. It made her realise how often he looked older than he was— still devastatingly attractive, but as if he carried an unseen burden that kept him too serious. That was, she supposed, what came of running a successful multinational company.

Then he seemed to collect himself. 'Wonderful! Should we put in anything else?' He looked across the terrace to where Dora's old cat watched them.

'Emma!' Anthea leaned across Christo, chose a blue crayon and held it up. 'Put in Emma.'

At the little girl's words, he lifted his head, his gaze colliding with Emma's.

This time the impact wasn't so much a sizzle as an immediate burst of ignition. Emma felt it like a whoosh of flame exploding deep in her belly.

But now there was more too. For Anthea followed his

gaze and saw her awake. Immediately she grabbed the picture and brought it over, excitedly pointing out the dog and identifying the figures she'd added. As Emma smiled, nodded and praised the little girl, her gaze met Christo's in a shared look of understanding and pleasure. A mutual relief that Anthea was starting to come out of her shell.

Perhaps it was crazy, but to Emma it felt like a rare, precious moment of connection.

As if, for once, she and Christo were on the same side. As if their shared purpose in providing for Anthea drew them together.

As if they weren't really enemies.

Except thinking like that had got her into this mess in the first place.

The spell was broken as Anthea held out the paper to him. After a moment he took it. But, instead of adding another figure to the crowded page, he turned it over.

She watched, fascinated, as he began to draw. Random lines coalesced and separated. Shapes appeared, familiar features. When he was done Anthea clapped her hands.

'Nice Emma.' The little girl crooned the words and held the page up.

It was a remarkable piece, considering it was executed with a thick child's crayon on cheap paper. Christo really was talented. But what held Emma's attention was the unexpected beauty of what he'd drawn. Not merely that the portrait was well-executed and recognisable as her. But that, for the first time in her life, Emma *looked* beautiful.

Her brow crinkled. What had he done to make her appear different? It looked so like her and yet on the page she was…more.

'Beautiful Emma.' His words feathered across her bare arms and wound themselves down her spine.

'Hardly.' She lifted her eyes to his, angling her chin. 'There's no need to exaggerate.'

He didn't so much as blink. 'I never exaggerate.'

No. He just implied more than was true. Such as making out he cared for her to get her to agree to marry him.

Swinging her legs over the side of the lounger, Emma got up, belatedly catching the spill of Anthea's books.

'It's a lovely picture, Anthea, but I like the one you drew better. Perhaps you could make another one for me to keep while I go inside and work? I'm sure Christo would love to help you.'

She didn't even look at him, just waited to see Anthea happily settled down with another sheet of paper, then turned on her heel and headed indoors.

Christo could look after his niece for once. Emma needed to work on her plans if she was ever going to turn the villa into a viable business.

But it wasn't business on her mind as she walked away. It was that strange moment of connection she and Christo had shared over Anthea's head. The instance of common purpose and understanding. It had felt profound. Even now Emma felt its echo tremble through her, making her skin shiver and her insides warm.

Or perhaps, more dangerously, it was a reaction to Christo's assessing stare that she felt trawl down her body as she walked.

She told herself she imagined it, yet her step quickened. She needed to get inside. Away from the temptation to turn back and see if she'd imagined the spark of something new in Christo's eyes.

To Emma's surprise, he stayed with Anthea for the next hour. Whatever had held the little girl back from him earlier had vanished. Whenever Emma looked out—and, to her chagrin, that was often—the pair had their heads together, poring over drawings then Anthea's books.

She heard the deep murmur of Christo's voice, a rich

velvet counterpoint to Anthea's higher voice, and satisfaction stirred. In the couple of weeks Anthea had been
there, Emma had grown fond of the girl. It was good to
think that she was beginning to build a relationship with
her only relative.

Curiosity stirred about that family. Emma sensed there
was more to their story than the death of Anthea's mother.
She recalled the dark edge to Christo's voice as he'd talked
of his stepsister and couldn't douse her desire to know more.

Desire. There it was again. That word summed up too
many of her feelings for Christo.

'Emma?' She jerked round to find the man himself in
the doorway, still almost naked in black swim shorts. Why
didn't he put on some clothes? Emma hated the way her
heartbeat revved at the sight of all that bare, masculine
flesh.

She looked past him but saw no sign of Anthea. Instantly she was on alert, hyperaware that her visceral response to him made her vulnerable. Emma tried to spend
as little time as possible alone with Christo but somehow
that never quite worked.

'Anthea is with Dora, having a snack.'

Had he read her nerves? The thought was intolerable.
Emma got up from the desk where she'd been working on
her business plan but Christo was already padding across
the room towards her.

'We need to talk.'

Her brow pinched. His tone and his watchful expression
told her she wasn't going to like this.

'About Anthea?' A couple of weeks ago her thoughts
would have gone instantly to their tenuous marriage arrangement. Strange how even the outrageous could seem
almost normal after a while.

'No.' He paused and she sensed he marshalled his words
carefully. The idea sent a premonition of trouble skitter-

ing through her. 'About our marriage. The paparazzi has got hold of the story.'

Surely he'd been prepared for that? Christo had insisted on fencing the estate with high-tech security infrastructure to keep out trespassers. He'd been convinced news of their very private wedding would score media attention. When she'd protested he'd spoken of protecting her and Anthea, which had ended her arguments. The little girl had been through enough without being hunted by the press.

'Is that all? It had to happen some time.' The tension pinching Emma's shoulders eased.

Christo stopped so close, she saw herself in his eyes. She hitched a silent breath and shoved her hands into the pockets of her skirt.

'Unfortunately it's not just the wedding they know about. There are reports that you ran away before the honeymoon and that we've separated.'

Storm-dark eyes bored into her and Emma realised Christo had just received this news. The last three weeks he'd been annoyingly at ease while she'd fretted about their impossible relationship. Now he hadn't had time to bury his anger under a façade of calm.

'It's close enough to the truth.'

His mouth tightened. '*Not* the story we're going to give them.'

Emma frowned. 'Do we have to give them any story? Surely you don't have to comment? You're Christo Karides. I thought you were above worrying about gossip.'

'I will *not* be pilloried in public as a deserted husband, or as some sort of Bluebeard who frightened off his bride.'

Even if you did?

The words danced on Emma's tongue but she didn't say them. She read his implacable expression and knew there was no point saying it. It would only inflame the situation.

Papou had taught her that no Greek male worth his salt

would allow a slight to his masculinity. Being seen as an undesirable husband clearly fitted under that heading.

'You'll need to start wearing your rings.' His gaze dropped to her bare left hand.

Emma froze on the spot, remembering the day she'd last worn them. Her wedding day.

'That's not necessary. Besides,' she hurried on when he opened his mouth to speak, 'I can't. I left them in Melbourne.' She'd dragged off the dainty gold band and the enormous solitaire diamond and left them with Steph for safekeeping. The memory of that moment of disillusionment and despair left a rancid taste in her mouth.

Christo's eyes narrowed but instead of berating her he merely paused. 'They can be replaced.'

Which proved just how little those symbols of their vows to each other meant to him.

Emma swallowed, hating the scratchy sensation as her throat closed convulsively.

'Me wearing a wedding ring won't be enough to convince anyone all's well with our marriage.'

'Of course not.'

The look of calculation on his face made her nervous. Emma crossed her arms.

'So how are you going to convince everyone?'

Christo's mouth curled up in a slow smile that simultaneously set her hormones jangling and sent a cold chill across her nape.

'Not me. *We*.' He paused, watching her reaction. 'You're coming with me to Athens this week. Together we're going to present a united front as a pair of deliriously happy newlyweds.'

As Christo's words sank in, Emma realised two things. That he was utterly serious. And that it wasn't just determination she read in his face—it was anticipation.

CHAPTER EIGHT

EMMA PROTESTED. SHE flat out refused to go.

But Christo was as immovable as Mount Pantokrator looming imperiously over the island. He refused to countenance her refusal.

She'd been ready to fight him over his need to appear macho and perfect. The adoring public saw him as a shining light in difficult economic times, a beacon of hope for the future. Frankly she'd enjoy seeing him taken down a peg.

But to her chagrin he cut off her arguments quickly. His character and status were inseparable from the success of his company. Especially now he'd turned from his usual international focus to concentrate on a major redevelopment in Athens. Persuading investors to come in with him was tough when Greece still suffered hard economic times, but he was determined to contribute to a resurgence.

If it came out that she'd run from him, the scandal could undermine confidence in his character and decision-making. His business would be affected. So would the livelihoods of his employees and contractors. As would others who relied on his continued success. Like her uncle.

But if they gave the paparazzi opportunities to see them as a couple the press would soon shift to other stories.

The prospect of being hounded wherever she went chilled her blood. And Anthea would be caught in the media circus too. It was in everyone's interest to minimise gossip.

Which was how Emma found herself staring across the Athens skyline from Christo's penthouse. The silhouette of the Acropolis was reassuringly familiar, as was the distant bright metal shimmer of the sea in the early evening light.

Yet Christo's Athens bore little resemblance to hers.

First there'd been the private jet. Then the discreet security detail. Emma had been prepared for the plush limousine, but not to have it waved through a stationary traffic snarl by a policeman who'd all but saluted as they'd passed. Then the no-expenses-spared shopping trip which had made Emma's eyes bulge.

Now this. The expansive sitting room seemed all glass and marble against that multi-million-dollar backdrop.

Emma had been into luxurious homes, assisting with lavish celebrations. She knew quality, and this was it.

Everything spoke of wealth, but not ostentatiously. No over-gilded ornamentation or fussiness here. Just the best of the best, from the soft furnishings to the custom-made furniture and original art.

She wandered through the room, past a modern fireplace which was in itself a work of art, to stop before a wall hanging that turned out to be a traditionally woven rug in deep crimson and jewel colours. The richness of its tones and tactile weave drew her hand. But she didn't touch. It was probably worth a fortune.

Emma's pulse skipped. Speaking of fortunes…

The hand she'd raised dropped to the delicate fabric of her dress. She'd never worn a designer original.

Involuntarily her gaze darted to the mirror above the fireplace. A stranger looked back.

The sheen of dark green silk accentuated the dress's close fit. Emma blinked. The change wasn't just that, or her newly styled hair. Nor the prohibitively expensive shoes.

She tilted her head. Was it the subtle smokiness of her new eye make-up? Or the lustre of the almost nude lipstick she'd never have chosen on her own?

When Christo had mentioned shopping for clothes, Emma had wanted to refuse anything bought with his funds.

But she knew the importance of appearances. The casual

clothes she'd packed for her honeymoon would look rustic in a sophisticated city venue. She wanted to scotch the stories about their mismatched marriage, not add to them.

Yet she'd resented being foisted on a cousin of Damen, Christo's best friend, whom Christo had lined up to take her shopping. But for once her husband had been right. She'd needed someone like Clio, with an eye for fashion and experience navigating Athens' most exclusive boutiques.

To Emma's surprise the other woman, despite her dauntingly glamorous appearance, had proved to have an irreverent sense of humour, a warm heart plus an unerring eye. She…

Her thoughts skittered to a halt as footsteps sounded from the corridor. Firm, masculine footsteps.

Everything inside Emma stilled, except her fluttery pulse that beat shallow and fast, like a moth trapped against glass. She spun round, lifting her chin.

Christo was a tall figure in the shadows at the far edge of the room, his expression unreadable. Was it a trick of the light that made that firm jaw look tense?

The air surged with sudden energy, like a giant heartbeat. She felt her nerves quicken, waiting.

Till she realised this was all her reaction to Christo. Freshly shaven and wearing a made-to-measure tuxedo, he looked good enough to eat. Her mouth dried as her imagination detoured in that direction and she forced herself to concentrate.

Did he like what he saw?

Furiously she told herself it didn't matter whether he did or not. While she wouldn't adopt this look every day, *she* liked it. That was what mattered. And that she looked sophisticated enough to pass as the wife of Greece's sexiest billionaire.

Christo had refused to be made a laughing stock in public. But how much worse for her to be the woman everyone knew he'd married for convenience, not love?

The thought sent a judder of revulsion through her. Come hell or high water, she'd play her part in this masquerade. She refused to be a figure of pity.

Still Christo said nothing. That brooding silence got on her nerves.

She turned towards the lounge where she'd put the wispy wrap and tiny evening bag that matched her jewelled green shoes. 'Are you ready to go?'

'Unless you want a drink to fortify yourself?' Out of her peripheral vision she saw him step into the room.

'I'd rather have a clear head, thank you.' Emma felt the familiar knife-twist of pain in her middle. The pang of hurt that even now she couldn't kill her attraction to him.

'I have something for you.'

Emma turned sharply, alerted by a note of something she hadn't heard before in Christo's voice. She couldn't place it.

But she did recognise the flare of heat in those dark blue-grey eyes. A thrill shot past her guard to resonate deep within her core. Her fingers curled into her purse, digging like talons into the fragile silk.

'A gift?' Emma strove for an insouciant tone. She already wore a new wedding band and a stunning gold filigree and diamond engagement ring. The latter was beautiful but felt like a brand of ownership. 'Not divorce papers, by any chance?'

One coal black eyebrow rose in a look that should have been annoyingly superior but, in her flustered state, seemed appallingly sexy.

Emma shut her eyes, praying for strength. This physical infatuation was supposed to disintegrate the longer she was exposed to him, not intensify.

'Emma?' The low burr of his voice rippled to her womb.

Opening her eyes, she fixed her gaze near his bow tie. But that was a mistake because above it was that oh-so-masculine jaw and stern chin with just a hint of an intriguing cleft.

'Are you all right?'

Surprised at his concern, Emma jerked her eyes up to his. A mistake, for she was instantly captured by a steely stare that this time seemed softer, like dawn mist over mountains.

'Of course. Why wouldn't I be?'

Christo read doubt behind the defiance in her fine eyes and felt protectiveness stir. He knew how tough it could be to maintain a smiling façade when in private all was turmoil. But he'd had a lifetime to master the art. He'd plucked Emma from the shelter of her home and thrust her into his world. He owed her his support.

'How about a truce for tonight? I'll keep the wolves at bay. All you need to do is smile and follow my lead. I'll look after you.'

Her head tilted to one side. 'That's supposed to make me feel better?'

It was a cheap jibe that should have annoyed him. Yet, like the crack about divorce papers, it had the opposite effect. Christo could weather a little snarkiness and he'd developed an appreciation for Emma's resilience.

Once he'd thought he wanted a quiet, docile wife. Now he discovered he preferred spirit to automatic obedience. Emma's eyes blazed brilliantly and he was pleased to see there was colour in her cheeks.

When he'd walked in, she'd looked pale. Beautiful, surprisingly so, but a cool stranger.

Even now he was unsettled by that first impression of her, standing like a glamorous stranger in his home. She'd looked sexy, svelte and sophisticated in the strapless fitted dress. He'd known in that instant she'd be accepted without question by his acquaintances and the press, for she had the appearance of so many other women in that milieu. Glossy. Confident. Gorgeous.

Strangely, that knowledge was undercut by disappointment. Even concern. That the Emma he'd begun to discover on Corfu had disappeared.

Tonight was about public perception, yet Christo hated the idea of the real Emma being lost or transformed into just another glamorous socialite.

'I may not be Prince Charming, but this time you can rely on me. I promise.'

Her gaze snagged on his and something beat hard in his belly. Something more than sexual desire or anticipation about tonight's performance.

Christo's breath frayed as he read her expression, saw defiance and annoyance and—could it be yearning?

Abruptly she turned away, as if to leave. 'Well, I can't promise this Cinderella won't turn into a pumpkin at midnight, but I'll do my best.'

Relief buzzed through him. Any fear that Emma had been subsumed by her new, sophisticated look died at her words.

'Wait. Don't you want your gift?'

'Gift?' She was half-turned away, but he saw her frown.

'For tonight. I want you to shine.' He withdrew a flat box and held it out to her.

Weird that he actually felt nervous, giving Emma jewellery. As if he hadn't given girlfriends jewellery before. Only this time it felt imperative that he got it right.

Maybe he was still smarting over the perfunctory glance she'd given the new rings he'd ordered. As if the exquisite filigree work, modelled on ancient designs and studded with flawless diamonds, hadn't impressed her in the slightest.

Annoyance flared. Christo wasn't used to questioning his emotions. He held out the leather box and flipped the lid open.

His anger died at Emma's long sigh of appreciation.

'I've never seen anything like it. What sort of stones are they?'

'Tourmaline.' The dark green was richer than emeralds, in his opinion. As soon as Clio had called him to describe Emma's dress, he'd known what he wanted. Finding it had been another matter. This set had just been flown into Athens for him.

'They're stunning. But I don't wear much jewellery. I don't want to look—'

'You'll look perfect,' Christo urged. Why wasn't he surprised that Emma, of all the women he'd known, should hesitate to accept beautiful jewels? 'Everyone will expect you to wear something spectacular. I'm supposed to be doting on you, remember?'

He watched as his words had their inevitable effect, cutting through her hesitation and stiffening her spine. For a second he regretted the loss of that misty smile of wonder on Emma's face. But, as she put on the long tourmaline and diamond eardrops, he was too busy maintaining his expression of gentle teasing when everything inside turned hot and urgent.

The elegant Art Deco style earrings swung against her slender throat. The colour intensified the green in her hazel eyes, making them glow.

Or was that something else in her expression?

Need pulsed through him. Not the need to put an end to public gossip, but the need to haul his pretty wife close and bury his face in the scented hollow of her pale throat. To smash down the barriers between them and make love to her.

'Now the necklace.' His voice hit a gravelly note.

'No.' She shook her head. 'It would be too much. On some other woman maybe, but not me. I'm not...'

The furrow of uncertainty in Emma's brow cut through his libidinous thoughts.

'Not what?'

Emma looked away and he sensed she was going to prevaricate. Then, instead, she shrugged and met his eye. 'I'm not a model or a sophisticate. I'm not...' Again that telling pause. 'Gorgeous and glamorous.'

Christo heard the hitch of her breath and realised that despite her defiant stare, as if daring him to judge her, Emma really couldn't see her own attractiveness.

But then, he hadn't in the beginning. Originally he'd thought her pretty and charming, but not in a league with the beauties he knew. Somewhere along the line, though, Christo had come to appreciate his wife's character and fire, her unique beauty.

'Who'd want a model?' he murmured, stroking a fingertip down her cheek. 'Most of them are scrawny and too afraid to enjoy a proper meal.' He paused, holding her eyes. 'You're beautiful, Emma. I defy any woman tonight to outshine you.'

Her eyes widened and a flush rose up her throat and into her cheeks. She swung away. 'Don't lie, Christo.' Her voice sounded muffled, twisting something in his belly. 'I've had enough lies from you to last a lifetime.'

Stymied, Christo stared at her profile, proud and, he realised, hurt. He was damned if he told the truth about her beauty and damned if he didn't. He should drop the subject, yet he was reluctant to leave it.

Emma hadn't struck him as a woman with hang-ups about her looks. Then memory pierced him. She'd admitted some time ago that she'd heard his conversation with Damen about why he'd married her. He recalled saying she wasn't his type. That her cousin was more his style, sexy and flamboyant.

Christo dragged in a slow breath, battling self-loathing. He plucked the necklace from the case and stepped behind his wife. Carefully he draped it around her neck, feeling her shiver as his hands brushed her nape. His own hands were unsteady. From the thwarted lust that had stalked him for weeks, or something else?

The clasp closed, he palmed her bare shoulders, fingers splaying across warm, satiny skin, and turned her to face the mirror.

'Look.'

Her chin jerked up, her narrowed eyes meeting his in the mirror.

'Not at me.' He let his gaze drift over the woman before him. 'You're stunning, Emma.' And it wasn't just because of the magnificent tourmaline and diamond collar around her slender throat. It was because of the woman who stood before him, trembling but as stiff as a soldier on parade.

Emma's eyes locked on the reflection of the man behind her as she battled not to lean back against all that delicious heat.

Christo Karides had treated her appallingly. He'd used her for his own advantage. Yet sometimes, like tonight, she fought to remember he was the enemy. He seemed too much like the caring lover she'd once believed him to be.

Take the expression in his eyes. Despite his stern tone, his eyes caressed her, made her feel warm and fuzzy inside. It wasn't the glaze of sexual possessiveness she'd seen in the past but something more tender.

Her thoughts terrified her. Hadn't she learned her lesson, reading emotions and motivations into Christo's actions that just weren't there?

She made to pull away but his hands stopped her. Not because his grip was hard, but because at that very moment those long fingers swept wide over the bare curve of her shoulders, massaging gently.

'Look, Emma.' His voice was soft.

Oh, she was looking. Her gaze swept from those broad shoulders to that solid jaw, past the tiny nick of a scar to his mobile mouth. Then up that decisive nose to eyes that glowed the colour of the sky at dusk.

Emma dragged in an abrupt breath and found herself inhaling that heady signature of cedar, leather and spice with that underlying note of male skin.

The scent shot to her brain, and her womb, and suddenly Emma wasn't looking just at Christo but at the pair of them. He with his hands on her body, she canting back towards him as if drawn to a magnet.

Suddenly she saw herself as others would. Wearing couture clothes and fabulous gems because Christo Karides demanded the best. A swift glance confirmed what she'd seen before. The makeover turned her into someone else. Someone glossy enough to match a billionaire, if only for an evening.

Heart hammering, Emma broke away. Tonight she'd play the doting bride and counter any negative press stories. But she'd be herself, not some puppet on a string dancing to Christo's tune. If he didn't like that, then that was entirely his problem.

CHAPTER NINE

CHRISTO COUNTED THE final items to be auctioned as the charity event drew to a close. Only half a dozen more.

He set his jaw and concentrated on keeping his touch light as he drew his fingertips across the soft skin of Emma's shoulder. She leaned close, her tantalising honey scent teasing his nostrils. The press of her hip on the seat next to his and the rounded contour of her breast against his side stirred a libido already at breaking point.

Telling himself she only did it to play the besotted bride didn't help. His body didn't care about her motivations, just the imprint of her warm curves and how much closer they could get once they left here.

No one bid on the next item. Christo frowned at the delay as Emma turned from speaking to the entrepreneur sitting on her other side and eased back into his embrace.

Fire stormed through his body, drenching him in heat.

Still no bids. Christo raised his hand, nodding to the auctioneer, who beamed back. It was past time they moved on to the final items and ended this. The event had dragged intolerably.

It had begun well enough. Emma had played her part admirably, sticking by his side and not flinching when he pulled her close. The fact she trembled when he did, Christo read as a positive sign. Emma had always been responsive to him and that hadn't changed. Did she know her body's reaction gave her away every time?

She'd been an enormous hit with his acquaintances. Far from being a shy mouse, she'd been quietly assured, conversing easily with everyone. She had the knack of drawing people out, truly listening to what they had to say and keeping the conversation rolling, even when it wasn't about her. She'd been everything he could have hoped for and more. As well as being articulate and sociable, she was…nice.

It seemed such a paltry word. But to Christo, having grown up in a world where appearances were everything, where trust was rare and self-interest dominated, Emma's sweet honesty and generous spirit felt precious.

He wasn't the only one to think so. All night he'd been congratulated and envied. In fact, he'd noted a few guys considering her a little too warmly. Till Christo had warned them off with a speaking stare.

Now he was heartily sick of the crowd. Of being congratulated on his lovely bride when that bride still kept her guard up against him. When this nearness was for show and she'd re-erect the barriers between them as soon as they were alone.

He wanted more. Much more.

He wanted his wife. Frustration grew with every minute and every brush of his hand against silky bare skin.

'You're bidding? I didn't think you'd be interested in this item.' Emma sounded surprised and he shrugged, willing the auctioneer to hurry.

'It's an important cause and no one else was bidding.'

Finally someone else did. The auctioneer caught Christo's eye and he read a mix of doubt and expectancy that indicated the man would drag this out in the hope of securing a much bigger profit. So much for Christo's scheme to end this quickly.

Supressing a sigh, he raised his hand and made a bid calculated to win. Whispers rippled around the room.

The auctioneer looked stunned, but recovered quickly to ask for more bids. There were none. Christo's price was too high for anyone else.

With a slam of the gavel, bidding closed.

Five more items to go. Christo stretched his legs and

tried to stifle his impatience. Emma moved, her body twisting against his, and the molten heat through his lower body turned to forged steel. His skin felt too tight and his lungs cramped.

'What are you going to do with it?'

'Sorry?' He turned to meet her eyes and felt the pause in her breathing as their gazes meshed.

Oh, yes. This desire was definitely mutual. She couldn't conceal the minute, give-away proof of her body's reaction to his.

All the more reason to get out of here as soon as possible and persuade her to put an end to this intolerable sexual frustration.

'The prize. Are you going to use it?'

Despite the confusion in Emma's expression, Christo read the glaze of heat in her eyes. Anticipation slammed into him. Tonight the waiting would end.

Strange to think that originally he'd viewed her as passably pretty. Merely a convenient spouse. She was anything but convenient and far, far beyond merely passable. Had he ever wanted a woman like this?

'Christo?'

'I'm not sure.'

Suspicion dawned in her fine eyes. The corner of her mouth curved into the tiniest hint of amusement. Christo's gaze locked on those glossy lips that had driven him to distraction all night.

Emma leaned close, her words whispering heat across his face as she murmured, 'You do *know* what you bought, don't you?'

He shrugged. 'I was more interested in helping them get through the programme quickly.'

Her breath hitched, her eyes widened and then she was laughing. The sound brought an answering smile to his mouth and an intense feeling of wellbeing. But at the same time that husky chuckle curled around his belly like a lasso, drawing tense nerves even tighter.

Beyond Emma heads turned. People leaned forward to hear the joke but she was totally focused on him. Just the way he liked her.

'That's very noble of you.' Still she smiled. No shadows in her expression now, just mirth and approval.

Christo was surprised at how good it felt when Emma looked at him that way. With shared understanding and humour.

'Don't you want to know what you spent all that money on?'

He shrugged. 'A car?' There'd been a sports car coming up for auction. When she shook her head he tried again. 'A boat?' Not that he needed another cruiser.

Emma shook her head, amusement and approval continuing to dance in her eyes. It struck him he could get used to her approval. It made him feel good.

'So, enlighten me, Emma.' His voice slowed on her name, savouring it. Or, more correctly, savouring the flicker of awareness in those bright eyes that shone tonight more green than brown.

She tilted her head down, whether to keep their conversation private or to avoid his eyes, he couldn't tell. 'An all-expenses-paid trip for a family of four to France, including a couple of days at Euro Disney.' Abruptly she looked up, her eyebrows rising. 'Are you excited to go on all the rides?'

His laughter shouldn't affect her like this. As if he'd turned her insides to melted caramel and added a huge dollop of sexual desire.

People laughed all the time. But Christo's deep, uninhibited chuckle affected her in the strangest way.

Not so strange. You've lusted after him all night.

All night? Far longer!

Just because he could afford to donate a small fortune to a children's charity didn't make him a decent man. Just as his smile didn't make him any less dangerous.

But it was hard to keep him in a box marked 'ogre' or 'blackmailer' when she saw him like this. Or head down with Anthea, working together on a crayon drawing.

Emma released a silent sigh and felt another layer of her defences slip away.

Face it. You've enjoyed being with him tonight. You like snuggling up against him, feeling his arm around you.

You like the admiration in his eyes.

Even if the admiration was for a glossy façade that wasn't the real Emma. Underneath the couture gown and priceless gems she was the same as always—ordinary. No makeover could change that.

'Hey.' A warm finger curled under her chin, tilting her face up. 'What's wrong?'

For the briefest moment, Emma contemplated telling her husband the truth. That she still cared for him despite her attempts not to. That part of her wanted him to care for *her*, not because she brushed up well enough to attend a gala social event but because he found her interesting, because he liked her for who she really was.

'Nothing.' She paused and summoned a smile, pulling back a little till his hand fell away. 'What are you going to do about the prize?'

For a long moment Christo studied her, as if probing to discover what went on inside her head.

'Give it to Giorgos.'

'Giorgos?'

'Our building's concierge. I introduced you to him today. His wife lost her job two weeks ago and their youngest is just out of hospital. They could do with a treat.'

Emma nodded as Christo turned to the event organiser who'd come up to talk with him.

Every time she reminded herself Christo wasn't worth pining over, he surprised her. Such as now, with his plan to give the holiday to his concierge. How many people who lived in the luxury apartment building even knew the man's name? Christo knew it and far more. He was genuinely interested in people. It wasn't the attitude of a man who viewed others as pawns.

Then there was his willingness to give Anthea's nanny a second chance. His patience with his little niece, despite his initial reserve. Plus there'd been his surprise gift for Dora, a bright-red motor scooter she now used whenever she needed to travel the several kilometres between the villa and the nearest town.

Emma had been stunned by his thoughtfulness. And by her lack of perception. Dora had mentioned she didn't like driving Papou's big car that sat gleaming in the garage. But Emma had forgotten the local bus only went by twice a day. Nor had she noticed the older woman was often fatigued or that she often made the trip on foot. Being distracted by her own problems was no excuse. Nor was the fact she'd grown up thinking Dora indomitable. That she'd come to rely on the housekeeper too much. It was Christo who'd arranged extra staff to assist Dora now the villa was occupied.

It was discomfiting, discovering her husband was more perceptive and generous than she'd credited. That he'd taken it upon himself to help out with something she should have dealt with.

The trouble was, Christo wasn't just a ruthless tycoon. There were times when he was plain likeable. That made him hard to resist. Especially when tonight all her not so dormant longings reawakened.

His arm tightened around her shoulders and he leaned in, breath tickling her ear and sending shivers of erotic awareness rippling through her.

'Ready to go?'

'But the auction?' She swung around towards the stage, belatedly registering the wave of applause that signalled the end of the event.

'We can skip the final speeches. I want to be alone with you.' Christo's eyes locked onto hers and the sizzle in her blood became a burst of fire.

Emma opened her mouth to protest. But what was the point? She'd tried and tried but resisting had become impossible.

Maybe it was time to reach out and take what she wanted. She was a woman with a woman's needs. Surely she could satisfy this physical craving and reduce the stress of trying to resist the irresistible?

She couldn't love Christo after what he'd done but she wanted him. She had nothing to lose by sleeping with him.

In fact, that contract he'd signed made it a condition of her escaping his influence. Though right now she had no thoughts of escape.

Nervous, she licked her lips. Instantly his attention dropped to the movement. Emma heard his breath catch.

Suddenly it was so easy. Because for the first time they were equals.

'I'd like that.'

The words were barely out of her mouth when he scooped her up to stand against him. Their farewells were rushed and she saw knowing glances as she grabbed her bag and wrap and said goodnight.

She'd liked the people at their table and enjoyed their conversation, but she was as eager as Christo to leave. So eager that she didn't protest as he guided her through the crowd with one arm still round her, his broad palm on her hip. Heat splayed from the spot, up her side, round to her breasts and straight down to her achy, hollow core.

Emma didn't even mind when photographers pressed close as they left the building and got into a waiting car.

All her attention was on Christo and the charge of erotic energy sparking between them.

Finally they were alone, a privacy screen cutting them off from the driver.

'At last.' The words were a groan, as if from a man exhausted. But Christo didn't look worn out. He looked taut, thrumming with energy.

When he reached out his hand, palm up, she put her fingers in his and felt that pulse of power race through her. It was like thunder rolling in from a massive storm front, a deep vibration heavy with building promise.

Emma couldn't prevent a shiver of reaction. She'd never experienced the like.

Christo nodded as his fingers clamped round her hand, as if he too felt that overwhelming inevitability. His smile of understanding looked strained.

That strain on his severely sculpted features flattened any final hesitation. This wasn't Christo seducing her. This was the pair of them caught in something elemental and all-consuming.

'Come here.' His voice was a rough whisper that did crazy things to her insides. Yet, despite the peremptory command, even now Christo didn't haul her close or try to force her. This was Emma's choice, as he'd promised.

She slid across the seat till she came up against the steamy heat of his big frame. One long arm wrapped around her, turning her towards him. She needed no urging. Her palm slipped under his jacket, moulding the rigid swell of his chest muscles through his fine shirt. Emma shivered at how good that felt. How much more she wanted to feel.

For a second those thundercloud eyes held hers, then Christo lowered his head and took her mouth.

Despite the urgency thrumming through them, his kiss was restrained, as if he fought to control the elemental storm that threatened to sweep them away.

He tasted of black coffee and something indefinable that set Emma's senses ablaze. Her hands clutched and she leaned in, needing more, far more than this gentle caress. Inside she was a threshing mass of need.

'Kiss me properly,' she hissed against his lips. She'd craved this so long. All that time he'd been carefully courting her she'd yearned for the taste of his unbridled passion. 'Please.'

Christo pulled back just enough to look deep into her eyes. Then, as if reading the hunger she could barely express, he planted his hands at her waist and hoisted her up to sit sideways across his lap. Emma had a bare moment to register his formidable strength, to lift her so easily in such a confined space. Then he kissed her again and nothing else existed but Christo and the magic he wrought.

There was fire. Emma felt it lick her insides, flaring brighter by the second. Frenzy. Rough demand and eager response. Tongues sliding together and mouths fused. Hearts thundering in tune. The roar of blood in her ears and bliss in her soul. Steely arms binding her to him.

This was the kiss she'd dreamed about in her virginal bed. No wonder she'd been frustrated and jittery all this time, unable to settle to anything useful after nights with too little rest and too many hours imagining Christo making love to her.

He tasted glorious. He felt even better. But there was more. Passion far beyond her experience, beckoning her deeper, simultaneously satisfying her desire and increasing it.

Emma's ribs tightened around her lungs as she forgot to breathe. But she couldn't have stopped if her life had depended on it. She clutched him as if she could meld their bodies through sheer force of will. She twisted closer, stymied by her fitted dress. There was something she needed even more than his lips on hers and those satisfyingly hard arms pinioning her close.

Emma shifted on Christo's lap, trying to ease that compelling restlessness.

Then without warning he tilted her back so she was no longer upright but supported only by his arm. Foggily she wondered why this felt so insanely perfect when at any other time she'd chafe at a show of superiority by her husband.

Her husband.

The word snapped her brain into a belated stir of worry, till Christo's hand on her bare knee obliterated extraneous thoughts.

Instantly that restless, needy feeling between her legs intensified. Her breath stalled as Christo plunged his tongue into her mouth in a lascivious swirl that made her nipples ache and tighten. At the same time his big, warm hand stroked up her thigh, rucking the silk dress higher and higher till air wafted...

A sudden hubbub erupted. Christo jolted upright, taking her with him as he ripped his hand free of her dress. She heard strange voices, questions and, like a dark undercurrent to the unfamiliar noise, the sound of Christo cursing quietly but ferociously.

For a second nothing made sense. Then out of the darkness a light flashed and then another.

Emma realised the back door of the limo was open. An attendant stood holding it wide. Behind him a huddle of people surged close, cameras snapping.

Paparazzi. Taking photos of her lying sprawled across Christo, his tongue down her throat and his hand up her dress.

In that instant glorious elation turned to wordless embarrassment. She shrivelled and couldn't quite get her body to move, to cover herself.

But Christo was already doing that. Not covering her, since there was nothing at hand to drape over her, but leaning forward, putting himself between her and those avid faces.

He said something she didn't hear and moments later the door slammed.

As if that movement released her from her shocked stasis, Emma suddenly found the strength to slither off his lap and onto the seat, scrambling to put some distance between them.

Eyes wide, she stared up at Christo. They were parked outside a brightly lit building and there was enough light to see his face. Far from being distressed or self-conscious at finding himself photographed in the act of making love in the back seat, he looked as solid and calm as ever.

As if making love to her *had* been an *act*?

Pain stabbed her heaving chest, transfixing her. Desperately she searched for some sign of annoyance or embarrassment on those proud features. She found none.

Had he *expected* the intrusion on their privacy?

Could he really be so calculating?

Everything inside Emma froze. She'd have sworn the moisture in her mouth turned to icicles as the idea hit.

Christo was breathing heavily, but that was understandable, given how their mouths had just been fused together. His hair was rumpled where she'd tunnelled her fingers along his scalp. His bow tie was undone and his shirt askew. But he looked unfazed by the furore outside the car. Unfazed and insanely hot.

Eyes on her, he pressed a button and gave instructions to the driver. His voice was crisp. Emma knew if she tried to talk right now it would emerge as a breathless squawk.

He watched her closely, as if trying to read her reaction. Was he wondering if she realised this had been a set up? Just like their wedding?

Had he really used her so callously? But then, given his track record…

The last shreds of heat inside Emma disintegrated, leaving her chilled to the marrow.

Even her fury, emerging from that white-hot sear of mortification, was cold. It whipped through her like the icy winter wind that swept Melbourne from the Antarctic.

'I apologise, Emma. The driver's original instructions were to take us to a restaurant where the press would be waiting to take photos.' Christo lifted his wide shoulders a scant centimetre. 'I was distracted when we left the auction and forgot to tell him to take us straight home instead. It was my mistake.'

'How very convenient.'

'Pardon?'

Emma lifted her hand to her hair, hauling up the soft waves he'd dislodged as he'd kissed her and jabbing in pins so hard Christo almost winced, imagining the grazes on her scalp. He wanted to reach out and grab her wrists, tell her the haphazard attempts to rectify the sophisticated hairstyle weren't working, and that besides he preferred it down. But she was upset enough. She wouldn't thank him.

The horror on her face smote his conscience. He shouldn't have let it happen. Should have protected her better. Even a woman who'd grown up in the public eye would cringe at the sort of pictures he knew would cover the tabloids in the morning.

Emma had looked wanton, beautiful and thoroughly aroused and the thought of anyone but him seeing her that way was like a knife to his gut. She was *his* and his alone.

'How incredibly convenient that you should *forget* to change the instructions. And that the doorman from the restaurant should open the car without a signal we were ready.'

Christo registered the acid in her tone and frowned. 'That's what doormen do. They open doors.'

He tamped down annoyance at her implication. She'd had a shock.

Emma's mouth turned mulish and her chin reared high in an attitude he knew too well. Stubborn defiance. 'And I suppose you had no idea we were outside the restaurant, even though you know Athens so well?' Her voice dripped shards of sarcasm that grazed his already smarting conscience.

'Let me get this straight. You're accusing me of luring you into a compromising situation just to embarrass you publicly?' Christo picked the words out slowly, barely crediting her implication.

'Of course not.' The vein of righteous indignation pulsing through him slowed. He'd been mistaken to think Emma could believe... 'Not to embarrass me specifically. I'm sure that was just collateral damage as far as you're concerned.' She dropped her hands to her lap and belatedly snicked her seatbelt closed as if to reinforce the distance between them. 'You did it to prove we're hot for each other, didn't you? That all's well between the bride and groom and any rumours that I'd left you were laughable.'

Her voice wobbled on the last word, but Christo couldn't feel sympathy.

Her accusation impugned his integrity. What sort of man did she think he was? So desperate he'd let the world into such a private moment?

A ripple of distaste coursed through him, starting from the bitterness filling his mouth and ending down at the soles of his feet.

He'd been vilified and taunted by his father whenever the old man thought he wasn't callous or committed enough to shoulder the mantle of the Karides corporation. He'd grown accustomed to press reports that misinterpreted or even invented facts about him. He accepted as inevitable that there were probably only a handful of people in the world, like his PA and his old friend Damen, who really knew him. But that didn't mean he'd shrug off such a deliberate insult.

An insult from the woman who, fifteen minutes ago, had all but begged him to take her in the back of this car.

A woman who'd driven him crazy these last weeks with lust and frustration.

A woman whose actions in running from him after their wedding had left him using all his influence and ingenuity to avoid a scandal that would damage them both.

The limo glided down into the underground car park of his apartment building. The increased lighting showed Christo a woman who was not only defiant but sneering.

Something cracked inside him.

'We'll continue this in the apartment.' He opened his door and got out, leaving the driver to get Emma's door.

The trip to the penthouse was completed in thick silence. The sort that wrapped around the lungs and squeezed mercilessly.

What was it about this woman that made him feel so furious, so resentful, so blindsided?

So *gutted*. As if, despite being in the right, he could have done better?

Christo had spent a lifetime learning to be top of his game, top of *any* game he played. He'd survived thirty-one years riding the rough with the smooth, learning never to expect too much. But nothing had prepared him for Emma.

Christo held the front door open to let her sweep past, nose in the air, green jewels swinging from her ears with each step. She crossed the foyer and entered the sitting room with an undulating sashay of her hips in that tight dress that might have been due to her high heels but which instinct told him was a deliberate provocation.

Did she know she played with fire?

In the car she'd driven him to the brink of insanity with her untrammelled eagerness. His wife kissed like an angel, but a woefully inexperienced one. He'd bet his last dollar Emma hadn't thought through the effect of such blatant sexual challenge. If she had, she'd probably run and lock herself in her bedroom.

The separate bedroom he'd arranged because he'd fool-ishly agreed to let her make the first move.

Christo gritted his teeth but made himself close the door quietly before following her.

She swung around, face flushed, eyes febrile and hair a delectable mess that made her look as though she'd just got out of bed.

His belly clenched painfully, re-igniting frustration. Even now his wife couldn't conceal the fact she wanted him. She devoured him with her eyes, her tongue darting out to slick her lips. Her breasts rose so high with each breath they strained the strapless bodice and her hard nip-ples signalled arousal. Anger, yes, but desire too.

It struck him that her indignation was a convenient shield for other emotions.

Christo shoved his hands in his pockets, rocking back on his heels. 'I've had enough, Emma.'

'*You've* had enough? I—'

'It's my turn to talk.' His tone was even but held the note of authority he'd honed over years as a CEO.

She took another hefty breath that made him wonder if her breasts might pop free of the green silk, then nodded.

'Maybe I should have been more upfront with you.'

Emma's eyes rounded, as if stunned at his admission.

'Maybe I should have spelled out exactly why I wanted to marry you.'

Not that it would have changed anything. He'd been de-termined to find the right woman and Emma was definitely it, despite her annoying habit of throwing up obstacles and questioning his motives.

'Maybe I shouldn't have assumed you knew there was

a business element to the arrangement. I shouldn't have assumed, wrongly, that your grandfather had discussed that with you.' He paused. 'I could have told you myself about Anthea.'

Except he'd been worried news of a ready-made family might deter Emma and he'd been utterly focused on putting his ring on her finger.

'But since then I've been completely upfront. From the moment I found you in Corfu I've been utterly honest with you.' Christo felt a bubble of mirthless humour rise. 'So honest, it shocked you.' The look of horror on her face when he'd mentioned sharing a bed had been both a blow to his ego and a spur to his determination.

Emma opened her mouth to speak but he shook his head. 'I told you we were going to the auction then to an exclusive restaurant so we could be seen together.' Christo drew a slow breath, still finding it hard to believe he'd so lost control that he'd been unprepared when the limo door had opened.

He never lost control. Never.

'I also apologised and explained how it happened. I forgot to tell the driver to bring us here because I was concentrating on you. Specifically, how I was going to strip you bare and make love to every centimetre of that delectable body.'

Emma's shocked hiss was loud in the quiet room, reminding him that she was a sexual innocent. That didn't excuse her accusations. Except that it was convenient for her to distort the truth.

Christo stalked closer. She couldn't hide the shimmer of nervous excitement in her eyes. But he wasn't in the mood to play to her tune any more.

'Tonight was an honest mistake. I have no more interest than you in having compromising pictures of us spread across the news. I prefer to keep my love life private.'

Not that he *had* a love life now. Because he'd given his word not to push her. This woman drove him mad!

'Don't imagine conspiracies where there are none. I don't operate like that, as you'd know if you'd paid attention lately.' Christo drew in a calming breath, but to little effect. He was past the point of no return.

'What's between us is real, Emma, and I'm not talking about a marriage certificate. I'm talking about desire, lust, attraction—whatever you want to call it. You can't run from it, though that seems to be your style. Instead of facing me after the wedding, you ran off like a hurt child.'

Her mouth dropped open at the jibe but he kept going, driven by the need to slash through all the pretence.

Christo closed the space between them, feeling the inevitable shimmer of awareness as he stepped up against her. It intensified to a riotous clamour as he touched his fingertip to her chin and tilted it up.

Bewildered eyes met his and he might have felt sorry for her if her games weren't driving him to the edge. It took every scintilla of control not to haul her close and kiss her into mindless abandon. No doubt then she'd claim he'd forced her. That she hadn't really wanted him.

'It's time you faced what's between us instead of pretending it doesn't exist or inventing excuses not to trust me.' Christo's voice ground low as his patience frayed. 'I've been patient. I've given you my name and my word. I want to give you my body too. But I won't be the butt of your lame excuses or manufactured obstacles because you're too scared to take what we both know you want.'

He stepped away, ignoring the confusion in her face.

'When you grow up, when you're ready to follow through, let me know.' Christo turned on his heel and strode away.

CHAPTER TEN

EMMA WRENCHED OFF the taps and grabbed an oversized towel. The shower had done nothing to relieve her distress. Warm water usually relaxed her. But tonight the fine spray had needled her skin like Christo's words needled her conscience.

She hadn't run away like a child!

Had she?

But why should she have stayed? He'd behaved monstrously, making her believe he loved her.

Except most of that had been wishful thinking. He'd been considerate and kind to her, so she'd *wanted* him to love her because she'd fallen for him.

As for making excuses or throwing up obstacles...

Emma briskly rubbed the towel over her body. But instead of expensive plush fabric, it felt like sandpaper. Like the graze of Christo's accusations.

Firming her mouth, she stepped out and dragged off her shower cap. Her hair fell around her shoulders but, instead of its familiar weight, she imagined his touch, so strong yet so tender, as he held her to him and kissed her.

Breathing heavily, she slung the towel over a rail and turned to get her nightwear. Except she'd been so furious and distressed, she'd stomped into the bathroom without grabbing anything to wear.

As she turned the beautiful green dress, discarded over a chair, caught her eye. Then the exquisite jewellery on the marble bathroom counter, sparkling under the light so much she could almost imagine it winked mockingly. As if reminding her that tonight's outfit wasn't her style. She was no glamorous sophisticate. She and Christo didn't fit.

Or was she doing it again? Making excuses and manufacturing obstacles?

Emma's mouth crumpled and her heart dived towards the honey-toned marble floor as suspicion solidified into something like certainty.

Christo had done the wrong thing, no doubt about that.

But shouldn't she at least have faced him and called him on that straight away? Shouldn't she have had more gumption than to run and hide like a child?

Misery curdled her belly. Her disappointment had been so acute, her heartbreak so painful, she'd needed to escape. But there was no escaping the complicated truth between them now.

Christo was right. Remarkably, she wanted him every bit as much as he seemed to want her, physically at any rate.

Desire fizzed in her blood whenever she saw him, or thought about him. But instead of doing something about it she'd looked for distractions to avoid facing it. Taking umbrage when she'd thought he'd brought a lover to the villa, though if she'd thought about it for even a second she'd have known Christo had more class than that. Accusing him of engineering that scene for the press tonight when that was laughable. Especially as she had perfect recall of his erection, steely hard against her hip.

Christo hadn't pretended to desire her. And she knew how vigorously he protected his privacy. One of his first actions after having found her in Corfu was to arrange perimeter security to stop intruders and prying press.

He'd wanted her. Plus he'd made her feel wonderful tonight in so many ways. His interest in what she had to say. The pride in his voice as he'd introduced her, and the way he'd kept steering conversations away from people she didn't know and into general areas so she could contribute. The warmth in his eyes as they'd shared amusement at some of tonight's auction items.

His possessiveness when men had got too close.

Emma shivered despite the warmth of the steamy bathroom and realised she was still naked.

Her gaze caught her reflection in the mirror that took up one wall. She was still the same old Emma. Not stupendous in any way. An average body and an ordinary face. Nice legs, she'd been told, but she'd always wished they were longer. As she'd wished for wheat-blonde hair and an elegant nose instead of one too close to being snub.

The only real difference she saw, apart from hair a shade lighter from the Greek sun, was the way her eyes glowed. Had they been so bright before?

It didn't matter. What mattered was why they glowed.

Christo. He had a talent for getting under her skin and making her feel more for him than she should. Once it had been love. She hurried to assure herself she was cured of that. What she felt was simple animal attraction.

Inevitably her mind turned to the salacious, outrageous demand he'd made that first day on Corfu. That she spend at least one night in his bed to claim her inheritance.

No matter how she'd told herself he couldn't force her, she'd never been able to forget it completely. She wanted to be with him and that need to discover how it would be grew daily. As if the seed, once planted in her mind, had grown till it obliterated all else. Now was her chance to satisfying her craving and her curiosity. Then afterwards, if she wanted to, she could walk away.

She shook her head. This wasn't about her inheritance or Christo's outlandish proposition. It was about satisfying her needs.

What would she do? Run and hide, as he expected? Play safe and try to avoid him?

Or throw herself into the fire and hope she survived?

Emma knew a moment's terrible self-doubt as inclination fought a determination to stand up for herself, not with words this time, but action.

Then she grabbed a plush robe from a hook and shrugged it on, cinching it around her waist.

The rap of her knuckles on the door of the master suite sounded over-loud. Emma waited, heart pounding, head tilted forward to listen. Nothing. Was Christo asleep?

Surely not. They'd only parted twenty minutes ago.

Firming her lips, she turned the doorknob and entered. Predictably the master suite was vast and luxurious. What surprised her was how comfortable it felt. She had an impression of parchment walls and splashes of rich teal that reminded her of the deep sea off Corfu on a sunny day. There was a book-lined wall and a leather lounge.

But what drew her eye was the filmy curtain riffling in the breeze at the open door, and beyond it the tall shadow on the terrace.

'Christo?' With numb fingers she shut the door behind her. That was all the time it took for him to step inside.

He still wore dress trousers but his tie was gone and his feet bare. Rolled sleeves revealed strong forearms that looked so good, her insides gave a needy leap. His formal white shirt gaped to reveal a slice of dark olive skin dusted with black hair that made her mouth dry.

Emma had seen him almost naked in his swim shorts, but somehow that V of tantalising flesh seemed just as decadently tempting. She gulped and lifted her gaze, noting the way his hair stood up, as if he'd clutched it. And the glitter of dark, assessing eyes.

'What is it, Emma?'

'I came to apologise.' She sucked in a quick breath. 'I was wrong to accuse you the way I did. I'm sorry.'

He pushed his hands into his trouser pockets, drawing her attention to his powerful thighs.

'Apology accepted. Thank you.'

Still he stood, simply watching.

She couldn't work out if that was anger emanating from him or something else. A voice in her head told her it was time to leave before she made a fool of herself or did something irreversibly dangerous.

Instead she stood her ground. Adrenalin shot through her blood in a classic 'fight or flight' response to this big, bold, provoking man who watched her as if he had all the time in the world.

'I didn't think before I spoke,' she offered.

He inclined his head, as if that was obvious.

Emma shifted her weight from one foot to another. He wasn't going to make this easy for her, was he?

Finally he spoke. 'It's late. Was there anything else?' His tone wasn't encouraging. He made no move towards her and Emma knew a craven urge to whip round and escape to the guest room.

But she was stronger than that.

Or perhaps just needier.

'Yes.' The word emerged too loud. 'I came because I want you to make lo—' She stopped. That wasn't what either of them wanted to hear. 'I want to have sex with you.'

Emma didn't know what she'd expected but it was more than she got. Christo didn't seem to move a muscle. Did he even blink?

What was he waiting for?

Then it struck her. She'd already said yes to him once tonight, only to turn on him after that mistake at the restaurant.

Maybe words weren't enough.

Or—the devastating thought sliced through her—maybe he'd changed his mind.

'If you still want me?' Ignoring the slight unevenness in her voice, she lifted her chin.

'I do.' The two words in that slow, deep voice sounded like a vow. Her nape prickled as she recalled their wedding vows. Then she shoved the recollection aside. This was different. She felt that here, now, there was only honesty between them.

Gathering her nerve, Emma paced forward, not stopping till they stood toe to toe.

The heady scent of virile male tantalised her nostrils and the breeze through the open door stirred her hair. What she read in those smoky eyes made heat flare across her skin. The dazzle of hunger was so potent, so raw, it dried her mouth and made her tremble.

Christo read Emma's nerves in her wide eyes and the racing pulse at her neck. She swallowed and he wanted to lick his way down her throat. He'd hungered for her for so long. He'd made allowances for her inexperience and hurt. He'd denied himself because he'd understood she needed time. Tonight his patience had reached its limit.

Which was why he wouldn't make a move till he knew she was absolutely committed. That she wouldn't change her mind again.

Swathed in an oversized bathrobe, Emma looked vulnerable, yet sexy and determined. It was a contradiction he didn't understand but he was fast losing the capacity for thought as she stared up with that provocative pout and her body clearly naked beneath the towelling.

He was torn between protectiveness and rampant lust.

'Show me.' His voice was a harsh whisper through lips that barely moved. His whole body ached from being held in check. From fighting the need to take.

He blinked when she stepped closer. He felt her warmth against him, her breath a puff of heat against his chest as she reached for his shirt and began to undo it.

Christo sucked in a desperate breath as her knuckles brushed his skin in a delicate, moving pattern designed to unstring his tendons and loosen his resolve. She leaned in and the honey scent of her hair infiltrated his brain, sending it into overload.

Abdominal muscles spasmed at she reached his trousers and paused.

Glowing eyes met his. Questioning eyes.

'Are you sure?' It cost him to speak. 'If we start this there'll be no turning back.'

She dropped her hands and stepped away. Disappointment smote him, so severe, he tasted it like poison on his tongue.

Christo was silently cursing his restraint when Emma tugged the belt of her robe. With a defiant tilt of her head, and a sensuous little shimmy that undid him, she let the material drop.

Naked, she was perfection.

Christo's heart beat so fast, it tripped and stole his breath.

Pale skin, pink nipples, and a V of darker hair nestling between her slender thighs, accentuating the impossibly sweet curve from waist to hips.

He'd wanted her when she was a convenient bride, acquired for purely practical reasons.

He'd been hot for her as she'd confronted him wearing only attitude and a blue bikini.

These last three weeks he'd ached for her at an even deeper level, haunted by her laugh, her sweetness with Anthea and Dora and, tonight, with him. Even when she defied him and drove him crazy, it only raised the scale of his wanting.

'Christo?'

He dragged his gaze up and saw her bottom lip caught between her teeth. Hesitation in her eyes.

Emma was about to turn away when his eyes met hers and blue fire welded her soles to the floor. Heat drenched her and suddenly doubt fled.

Big hands took hers and hooked them into the front of his trousers above the zip.

'Don't stop now,' he drawled as he dragged that snowy shirt up from his trousers and shrugged it off, leaving her in possession of a view that dried her mouth.

For ages she stared at the shift and play of bare, taut flesh over muscle. Then her brain kicked into gear and onto the task of undoing his trousers. It was tricky, possibly because her hands shook.

Finally, with a sigh that swelled her chest, she got them undone, but not before her knuckles brushed the tantalising length of his erection. She shivered, trying to imagine herself accommodating all that hardness. But the shiver wasn't all anxiety. Mostly it was excitement.

His trousers fell to the floor and still Christo stood, unmoving. Swallowing, Emma crooked her fingers into the top of his boxers and slid them down. The place between her legs throbbed with heat as she watched the reveal of yet more golden skin. Then his shaft sprang free and she jumped, staring.

As if reading her moment of panic, Christo lifted his hand to her cheek in a butterfly caress that eased her riot of nerves. But the riot started again as his finger trawled down, over her chin and collarbone to her breast, where delicately he circled her nipple. Emma shifted, trying to assuage the edgy sensation inside when his other hand captured hers and brought it against him.

'There's nothing here to be afraid of.' His voice wound around her as his eyes held hers.

Instinctively her fingers curled round his length, slowly exploring the fascinating velvet over steel combination. At the movement, Christo's eyes flickered, the corners of his mouth pulling down as if with tension. Gripping a little tighter, she slid her hand again and watched that tell-tale drag of his lips.

The realisation that she did that to him boosted Emma's confidence.

'I'm not afraid.'

But her smile ended in a gasp as his other hand flirted across her thighs, then slipped between her legs, right up against folds that felt swollen and wet. Gently he slid his fingers down, arrowing to the exact spot where sensation centred. He pressed, and she jolted as a current of electricity snapped through her.

Emma swayed forward, needing more, almost sighing with relief when his hand at her breast opened to mould her more firmly. In answer her fingers tightened around Christo till he murmured, 'Easy,' and she loosened her hold. Needing more, she planted her left hand on his chest, solid with muscle and tickly with that smattering of dark hair.

His heart beat steadily beneath her touch, the rhythm reassuring as she found herself in completely new territory.

The big hand between her legs moved again, sending sparks showering through her, then dipping even further till one finger slid home and Emma gasped at the shocking unfamiliarity of it. But shock turned to eagerness as he withdrew, then slid home again, evoking wonderful sensations. She found her pelvis rocking with the movement.

Another slide and the friction made her breath stop. Stunned, she stared into Christo's eyes and couldn't look away. Surely they should be in bed, lying down before…?

'We can't.' Her words faded as his thumb pressed that sensitive nub and she trembled all over.

'Believe me, sweetheart, we can. We can do whatever you like.' His words would have reassured Emma, except she read excitement in his dark eyes and determination in the angle of his jaw and knew he was as aroused as she. 'Hang on to me.'

He took his hand from her breast and lifted her fingers from his erection to his shoulder. Instinctively she held tight there. Just as well, because her knees threatened to buckle as he returned to caressing her breast, his other hand working between her legs.

Now she moved with every slide of his hand, finding the rhythm and forgetting her inhibitions. This felt so good, so perfect, she...

'Christo!' It was a desperate shout, half-muffled by the wave of ecstasy enveloping her.

She had half a second to see him smile, then he bent his head to hers. His kiss was lavish, demanding yet reassuring, connecting them even as she shattered, her soul shooting towards the heavens as her body shuddered and almost collapsed.

Christo took her weight, drawing her against him and hugging her tight. His warmth enveloped her and soft words rained down, soothing her gradual descent from that acute peak of pleasure.

Finally the shudders became random trembles and the burning white light dissipated as she clung to him, limp with satiation. Dimly Emma wondered that she felt no embarrassment at climaxing in front of him. She'd imagined finding release with Christo in bed with the lights off, not flaunting her pleasure before him. But it had felt perfect.

'Thank you. That was...'

Emma couldn't find the right words so gave up. Instead she smiled against his muscled chest and let herself sag in his arms, knowing he had her.

His erection hard against her belly reminded her that Christo hadn't found satisfaction. She wanted him to enjoy what she had and slid her hand between them.

'Not yet, *glyka mou*. Let's get you somewhere comfortable.' He stepped clear of his clothes, then scooped her up in his arms.

Emma's eyes snapped open and she fell into his slate-blue gaze. Was that satisfaction she saw? Or anticipation?

As he laid her on the bed a shiver shot through her at the prospect of what lay ahead. Still languid from that intense orgasm, she felt a scurry of nerves as Christo opened a nearby drawer then rolled on a condom.

'I haven't done this before.' The words jerked out of her and she licked her lips, torn between fascination, eagerness and just a touch of apprehension.

He paused, kneeling on the bed, arms braced beside her. Something flared in his eyes, something she couldn't decipher. 'But you want to?'

It was the second time he'd asked. It struck her that, far from being the domineering, macho bully she'd pegged him for when he'd made that demand about her living as his wife, Christo was careful with her. The tension riding his bunched shoulders and clenched jaw was obvious, but he held back. Did he feel the urgency she'd felt just minutes ago? Her mind boggled at his control.

Emma lifted her hand towards him and nodded. 'Show me how to make it good for you.'

Zeus preserve him. How to make it good for him!

Christo grimaced. 'It's already far too good.' He'd been so close to the brink that, even when he'd removed her hand, he'd almost come just watching and feeling her climax. And when she'd snuggled into him like a living blanket...

'But it could be better.' Her eyes were enormous but he read that obstinate mouth and felt his own curve.

'Oh, definitely.' He moved to straddle her legs, getting high just from the sight of her lithe, beautiful body laid out for his enjoyment.

Christo wanted Emma badly. He needed to possess her, fill her and claim her as his own. The urge to spread her legs and take her was so strong. But she was a virgin. He had no experience of virgins but he knew he needed to make this as easy for her as possible.

Instead of pushing her legs apart, he bent and pressed a light kiss to her hip bone. She jolted, as if still wired from her orgasm. The scent of feminine arousal wafted to him and he smiled. He'd give her a first time she'd never forget.

With that silent vow, Christo set about learning her body.

Emma protested. In between her sighs and gasps as he found a particularly sensitive spot to kiss or lick or stroke. He discovered a place at her ankle that undid her. A spot near the small of her back. Her inner elbow where he'd driven her to the edge that night on Corfu. And the more obvious places. Her breasts that filled his palms so sweetly. The sweep from neck to shoulder. And her inner thighs. By the time he'd finished she was trembling with need and he felt as if he'd been forged from pure, burning steel.

When he nudged his knee between her legs they fell open instantly and elation surged. He'd waited so long. He braced himself on one arm and, sliding his other hand beneath her, tilted her.

Blazing eyes met his. 'Finally!'

'Don't tell me you didn't enjoy yourself.' His mouth rucked up at one side at the memory of exactly how much Emma had enjoyed his caresses. Her skin was flushed and there was a dreamy look in her eyes that contradicted her attempt at brusqueness.

'It was wonderful.' She sighed. 'But I want *you*.'

Strange how her words reverberated within him. How long had he wanted to hear that? Emma wanting him, not running or fighting him.

Her fingers curled around him and his breath hissed. He'd done his best to prepare her but, at her touch, he could hold back no longer.

Christo leaned in, letting her guide him till he was positioned at her slick entrance. She gave a little wriggle at the contact and he rolled his eyes. He was never going to last; that was a given.

'Lift your knees.' His voice was as rough as gravel, but she understood, and he felt her legs lift to cradle his hips. He pressed into the most exquisite, firm heat. His breath stalled and he had to fight not to pump hard. Instead he kept his eyes on Emma and saw her brow wrinkle, as if in confusion.

'Okay?'

She blinked up at him but he saw no sign of pain. 'Odd but okay.'

'Odd?' He shook his head as he allowed himself to slip a little further. The sensations were overwhelming now. The feel of Emma taking him was so good Christo shook with the effort of restraint.

A soft hand touched his face. 'Are you all right?'

Christo grimaced. 'That's my line.' Clearly he wasn't doing this right if Emma felt nothing but concern for him.

Lifting one hand, he cupped her breast then bent to lower his head and suck at her nipple.

'Ah!' She lifted off the bed, drawing him further into that enticing heat. Fingernails dug into his shoulders as he caressed her and inexorably drove home.

Christo lifted his head and read Emma's glazed eyes. No pain there, no fear, just the same wonder he felt as he withdrew and forged home again.

With slow deliberation, Christo set a pace that had her rocking against him. Then, as she licked her lips and said his name, he reached his limit. Christo felt the bunch of tightening muscles in his arms, legs and backside. His rhythm changed, became urgent and inescapable, and the tingling began, racing down his spine and round to his groin.

There was just time to recognise the convulsive clasp of

Emma's tight muscles around him when rapture slammed into him, a rolling tidal wave that went on and on. She curled up, her climaxing body jerking and trembling in unison with his.

Blindly he dropped to one elbow, protectively scooping her close as together they plunged off the edge into oblivion.

CHAPTER ELEVEN

EMMA WOKE TO a sense of luxury and warmth. She lay, savouring the feeling of wellbeing. Opening her eyes, she discovered it was early morning, pale, rosy light spilling through the open window.

She was in Christo's bed.

Unreadable eyes watched her and she discovered that luscious sense of comfort came from the fact she was cuddled against him, lying on her side with one knee hooked over his hip and his arms around her.

'How are you?' His words caressed her mouth and, strangely, that seemed almost as intimate as the way their lower bodies were aligned, his powerful erection a reminder of what they'd shared last night.

Her face flushed. Even her ears tingled. What they'd shared went beyond everything she'd imagined.

'Fantastic.'

His mouth crooked at one corner. 'You are that.' Then dark eyebrows angled down. 'Not hurting at all?'

'I don't think so.' Emma shifted slightly, registering a slight heaviness between her legs, more an awareness than anything.

It wasn't any change in her body that concerned her. It was the consequence of sharing Christo's bed.

She couldn't pretend any more that he was a despicable monster. Yet was sex any solution to their convoluted relationship?

'So you got your wedding night after all. Just as you specified in the contract.' What made her say it, Emma didn't know. Except belatedly she realised she didn't have a clue where they went from here.

That hint of a smile vanished in an instant.

Christo's muscles stiffened around her. 'You're saying last night was about the contract? Giving yourself for a piece of property?' The abrupt change in him was shocking, his tone scathing.

'It was you who insisted I owed you a night in your bed!' Emma pushed against that solid chest and reared back, but he kept her where she was. Close enough to read, for a second, what seemed like disappointment in those smoky eyes.

She stilled, intrigued, telling herself it couldn't be. Christo wore that look again, the steely one that spoke of severe disapproval. His mouth was tight and the pulse at his temple drummed too fast. Yet still there was something in his eyes...

'Why did you sleep with me, then?' she challenged, her throat tight. 'Because I *owed* you? Was I some trophy? Was last night payback for me leaving you?'

'You think I collected a debt for pride's sake?' Christo's nostrils flared. 'I slept with you because you drive me crazy with wanting.' The words carried the lash of accusation. As if he held her responsible. 'Because there's a connection between us. You felt it too. Don't tell me you didn't.' He drew in a deep breath. 'Last night was about you and me, nothing else.'

Emma's breath jammed in her lungs. She couldn't doubt his sincerity, not when she was so close she read every change in his body.

'Why did you come to my bed, Emma?' The look in his eyes told her the answer was important to him.

She didn't want to reply but what was the point in trying to hide the truth?

'I couldn't fight myself any more,' she finally admitted. 'You're right. There *is* a connection.' It was growing stronger all the time. Emma tried to tell herself it was just sex but it was more complicated than that.

'You want to be with me.' He pulled her closer and she let him, because this was where she wanted to be, even if she had no idea where it would lead.

'I do.' She sighed. Once that would have been an admission of defeat. Now it was the simple truth. She was tired of hiding from it.

'And I want to be with you.' He nudged her chin up and she read his sincerity.

Excitement pulsed through her. Whether this was a mistake or not, at least in this they were equals. Emma couldn't find it in herself to turn away from him again.

She shrugged, feeling a little foolish. 'I only mentioned the contract because I'm a bit out of my depth.'

At her words he lifted his hand to stroke her hair back from her face. The gesture was so tender, almost loving. Emma felt a pang of regret that this could never be love. But she was an adult. She'd accept reality. Take the pleasure they both wanted and move on when it ended.

'I'm sorry. I overreacted.' Christo's mouth compressed to a crooked line. 'It's my own fault for spelling it out on paper. That *was* hurt pride.' Emma blinked at the admission and the apology. More and more, the Christo Karides she'd despised was transforming into a man she liked.

Emma nestled against that solid chest, inhaling his rich, salty male scent. After just one night she feared she was addicted to his body. His hugs banished the loneliness she'd felt since Papou's death. But it wasn't only that. In Christo's arms she felt wanted, cherished.

'It's a hot button of mine,' he continued. 'Women who trade their bodies for gain.'

'I suppose you've met a few, being rich.' And handsome.

'Enough.' Then, to her surprise, he went on. 'My mother was like that. She married my father for his money.'

Emma pulled back, searching Christo's face. Behind the scowl she was sure she saw hurt. It made her insides twist.

'Are you sure? Maybe she just—'

'No mistake.' Slate-blue eyes held hers. 'My father was good-looking and successful but he didn't have a loving nature.' Again that quirk of Christo's lips that looked more like pain than amusement. 'He had an eye for stunning women and my mother was a beauty queen. They married because she got pregnant with me.' Christo shook his head. 'He was a hard man, but honourable and faithful, whereas her main interest was spending. She admitted she'd never wanted me. Pregnancy was just her way to secure her future.'

'That's appalling! How could any mother say that to her child?' The thought sickened Emma.

Christo shrugged. 'She was furious at the time. She blamed me for my father finding out she'd cheated on him.' At Emma's questioning look, he added, 'I walked in on her with her lover and didn't react well. My father eventually heard about the fuss, I assume from the staff.'

Emma tried to imagine what it would be like, discovering your parent with a lover. She wondered what Christo meant by her not reacting well but, given the stark line of his clamped jaw, thought it best not to ask.

'So she spoke in the heat of the moment.' Emma didn't like the sound of Christo's mother but she hated seeing the lines of pain bracketing his mouth when he spoke of her.

'You're trying to excuse her? Don't bother. She never spoke to me after that. I haven't seen her since. She's living in Brazil now, married to a mining magnate, probably pretending she doesn't have an adult son.'

Emma digested that in silence. With a mother like that, and a father he'd described as hard, Christo began to make more sense. He was an only child and love had clearly been in short supply in his family. She wondered with a pang if he'd ever had tenderness from his father. Or anything approaching a happy family life.

Was it surprising he'd held back from Anthea, admitting he didn't have the skills to care for a child? There was even a lop-sided logic to his plan to acquire a convenient bride to fill that role, if he had no experience of a loving family.

What mattered, she realised, was that he hadn't shirked his responsibility. He was determined to make a good home for Anthea. She couldn't fault him for that.

Honourable, he'd called his father. Surely Christo had inherited that trait, or at least a strong sense of responsibility?

Emma surveyed him under her lashes. He could be a hard man. Look at the way he'd set about acquiring a wife. But there was more to him. Christo felt deeply. That was clear from everything she saw in his face and from the tightly contained voice as he'd relayed that horrible story about his mother. Obviously he held back a dam of painful emotions.

He didn't just feel responsible for his niece, either. He cared for her, even if he was just learning how to express it. That was why the sight of them bonding had fascinated Emma. It was as if he got as much out of being with Anthea as she did.

Plus, he cared for Emma. Last night at the reception he'd smoothed her way, ensuring she was at ease. His smiles and laughter had been genuine. She'd *liked* him as well as desired him. Then there was the way he'd taken time to ensure her first experience of sex was spectacular. Emma knew that wasn't always the case. Christo had put her needs above his own.

Perhaps the man she'd fallen for in Australia hadn't been a total mirage. Christo Karides was more complex than she'd credited.

'What are you thinking about?'

His words drew her attention back to his face. Their eyes meshed and heat simmered beneath her skin. How could he do that with just a look?

She shifted, the movement making her breathtakingly aware that she was still wrapped in his arms, naked, her lower body coming up against Christo's erection.

She saw his pulse throb at the contact. The simmer became a scorching blaze, running like wildfire along her veins and over her skin.

'I was thinking you're not the man I imagined you were.'

'Really?' His eyebrows rose, his body tensing.

'There's more to you than I thought,' Emma admitted. 'More to like.'

Christo's features eased and the corner of his mouth curled up. 'You certainly seemed to like me well enough last night,' he murmured in a drawl that dragged through her body like fingers ruffling velvet. She felt a tremor ripple through her belly.

One large hand traced an arabesque along her spine, slowing as it drew low towards her buttocks. Emma's breath stilled as her body thrummed into needy awareness.

'I did, didn't I?' Her voice was husky.

'And *I* like *you*.'

Emma swallowed hard. The words weren't fancy. Yet the way he said them, teamed with the way he looked at her, made them sound like something profound. Something significant.

For a second anxiety gripped her. She'd vowed not to fall for romantic fantasy again. Except this was no extravagant, gilded compliment designed to turn her head. This was plain and unvarnished...and she believed him.

There was tenderness in his touch and in his expression, as well as a good dollop of anticipation. An anticipation she shared.

Mutual attraction was simple and straightforward. She just had to remain clear-headed. Never again would she make the mistake of imagining there was love between them.

'So,' he murmured, 'If you like me and I like you...'

That roving hand palmed her bottom and tugged her flush against him. Emma's breath snagged as his rigid length slid up against that needy spot between her legs. Automatically she curved closer, seeking more.

'Then maybe,' she finished for him, 'we should spend more time together.' On the final word he nudged so close, she felt her flesh part to accommodate him.

Emma's eyes widened at how easy it was and how very, very good. She was just wrapping her fingers around his shoulder to pull even herself closer when Christo shook his head, a grimace, as if of pain, tugging at his mouth.

'Wait.'

Then he was gone, turning away for a condom, leaving her shocked to the core that she hadn't thought about protection. Giving herself to her husband was becoming the easiest thing in the world.

Emma chewed on that fact, wondering what heartache that boded for the future.

It wasn't just heat building inside her. She told herself it was arousal, hunger for the magic he'd shared with her last night. Emma blocked her mind to the possibility it might be anything more.

Then Christo was back, wrapping her close, meeting her eyes with a blazing look that banished all doubts. It was, she decided, time to quit worrying and go with the flow.

He smiled and it was like a light going on in the darkness. The radiance mesmerised her.

'Now, about spending more time together. I have a plan to bring us *very* close together.'

'You do?' Her voice was breathless. For his hand was already skimming her thigh, urging her to lift her knee higher over his waist.

The action spread her open against his groin where furnace-like heat beckoned. Emma shuffled closer and the friction of their bodies aligning sent a zap of energy to every sense receptor. He bumped his hips forward and her breath stopped.

'That feels so good.'

'We haven't even started yet.' The devil was in his eyes as he rubbed against her. Then he claimed her mouth in a slow, sultry, seductive kiss that led to a world of bliss. And from there to a whole morning spent in his arms and a haze of delicious wellbeing.

The haze lingered.

For four days they stayed in Athens, satisfying the public hunger for sightings of Greece's favourite billionaire and his new bride.

It wasn't as difficult as Emma had expected. Christo made everything easy, diverting her when she felt nervous, introducing her to people who were genuinely pleasant and interesting. Never leaving her side. She grew accustomed to the weight of his arm around her waist, or his long fingers threaded through hers, as if it were the most natural thing in the world.

As if her husband enjoyed touching her as much as she delighted in his touch.

They mingled with the rich and famous at exclusive restaurants, a gala gallery opening and a couple of parties. They had cocktails on the luxury yacht of an Italian billionaire who was interested in Christo's Athens redevelopment plan. Instead of leaving her to talk business with their host, Christo drew her in and mentioned that the property in question had been owned by her family for years. That she had a commercial interest in it. Emma had been stunned by the acknowledgement, feeling a flush of satisfaction and pride that her Papou's far-sighted purchase was now to be the centrepiece of a significant development.

She felt almost sophisticated in a daring designer outfit of white silk trousers and a vibrant red top with a deeply slashed V down the back that Christo couldn't resist. As they stood talking to their host, Christo kept running his fingers down her bare skin, making her tingle all over.

A week earlier she'd have thought he was doing it for the benefit of the paparazzi who were settled in small boats with telephoto lenses trained on the cruiser.

Now she knew better. For if Christo was attentive in public it was nothing to what he was like when they were alone. He was always touching her, always close, always finding new ways to bring her pleasure. She spent all night in his arms. They showered together, ate together, yet the urgent hunger between them grew more, not less, intense.

It was as if, that first night in Athens, they'd pulled down the barriers to reveal a need that couldn't be assuaged. Each day it increased. As if this were a proper marriage and they really were honeymooners.

When Emma let slip that despite her stop-overs in Athens she'd never visited the Acropolis, Christo arranged a special tour. One of the site's archaeological experts guided them around the ancient hilltop on their final afternoon. It was a wonderful experience. Even the throng of tourists, some of whom were as interested in her and Christo as in the marble temples, didn't detract from it.

Standing at the perimeter wall—watching the sunset wash the city apricot, gold then finally deep violet, as their guide told them tales of long ago—Christo pulled her back against his powerful frame, arms wrapped around her, his breath stroking her hair.

Emma felt such contentment, such joy, that for a moment it frightened her. Until she remembered she was taking one day at a time. That what they shared was based on desire, not love, and as such it couldn't last.

Strange that the knowledge wasn't as comforting as before.

CHAPTER TWELVE

THREE WEEKS AFTER their time together in Athens and things were excellent. Satisfaction filled Christo as he strode from the car park towards the old part of Corfu Town.

Anthea was growing into a happy kid instead of an apprehensive one. She adored Emma who, far from keeping her distance with a stranger's child, gave her all the warmth and encouragement she craved. Pleasure filled him, thinking of the pair together. He couldn't have asked for more.

The nanny's recent resignation on the grounds that life at the villa was too quiet was a relief. Her play for his attention still rankled. Now he had to secure a new carer but meanwhile Dora's niece filled the role admirably.

There'd been no more innuendo in the world's press about a runaway bride. Instead he and Emma had been dubbed the world's most besotted newlyweds.

Business proceeded on schedule with none of the expected negative fallout. Actually, there was more potential investor interest in his latest project than before, thanks to the Athens publicity. His bride had been a massive hit.

And the fireworks between him and Emma were now only of the sexual sort. No more flare-ups of indignation or accusation.

Heat smote his belly. Emma was so passionate, so eager.

The one thing that surprised him was how their intimacy wasn't confined to sex. It simmered between them, as if some invisible filament bound them together—their bodies but also their minds, their thoughts, even their amusement at the same things.

Christo slung his jacket over his shoulder and quickened his step through the late-afternoon throng. Emma wasn't expecting him and he looked forward to her welcome. Sex was phenomenal with his virgin bride, a quick learner who drove him to the brink with a mere touch. But just as alluring was the way her hazel eyes widened with delight whenever she saw him. Then they glittered more green than brown, a sign, he'd learned, that she was excited or happy.

Making Emma happy was fast becoming one of his favourite things.

He strode along the Liston, the wide, marble-paved pedestrian street edging the old town. On one side graceful colonnaded buildings lined the road, housing restaurants. On the other, the restaurants' shady outdoor seating gave onto the park with its unexpected cricket pitch, a quirk dating from the years of British rule. There was an elegance to the beautiful street, now full of promenading visitors, locals and waiters hurrying past with loaded trays. But he didn't have time to linger. He was here to find his wife.

As usual the word 'wife' stirred a zap of anticipation.

He'd left Athens a day early, arriving in Corfu on Thursday, because after four days of long hours in Athens he wanted Emma.

Once the idea of rearranging his schedule to be with a woman would have perturbed him. Now he viewed it as a perk of marriage. He had a desirable wife. Why wouldn't he spend time with her? He was CEO, after all. Careful planning, a couple of extra-long days and a little delegation meant everything was under control.

He turned left into one of the narrow lanes that snaked between tall Venetian-style buildings with their pastel colours and long shutters. Small shops did a brisk trade and he dodged souvenir hunters and families with ice-creams, delighted at the anonymity he found so hard to achieve in Athens.

Since his youth Christo's actions had been reported and scrutinised. He'd spent his life carrying the weight of expectation, first of his demanding father, then of the business world and, latterly, the public with its unending appetite for gossip about the rich and famous.

Maybe that was why he liked this island so much. With a few precautions he was generally free to do as he liked.

Right now he liked the idea of surprising his wife.

Consulting his phone, he took a turning, then another, passing a small square with a tiny church and a vibrant burst of pink bougainvillea shading patrons at a café. Another turn and...

Christo pulled up mid-stride.

His breath hissed between his teeth as a phantom fist landed a punch to his gut. He rocked back then found his balance in the wide-set stance of a man ready to defend what was his.

For there was Emma, hair high in an elegant style that left her slender, sexy neck bare. She wore one of her new outfits, cream trousers that clung to the curves of her rump and hips before falling loosely to jewelled sandals that exactly matched the amber of her sleeveless top.

She looked delicious enough to sink his teeth into. But Christo's attention zeroed in on the man with her. The man standing too close, his hand on her arm, his smiling face bent towards her.

Emma didn't mind. She smiled and nodded, listening as he leaned in to murmur in her ear.

Christo surged forward, ignoring the strange sensation, as if both his lungs and his throat constricted.

A bevy of chattering teenagers came in from a side-street, impeding his progress. By the time he reached the doorway where Emma had stood, the guy was gone and she was a glow of colour further ahead.

Impatient, he strode to catch up with her, his hand curling around her elbow.

'Christo! What are you doing here?'

Watching the excited green spark in her eyes, basking in the warmth of her smile, the fierce blaze in his belly dimmed and he found himself smiling back.

'Looking for you.' Her soft skin felt so good. Her lush honey scent was rich as nectar.

Christo's chest filled with a wild riot of feelings. He recognised pleasure and relief and refused to go further. Yet even a man committed to avoiding extreme emotion registered the depth of his relief.

Had he been *scared* Emma was more interested in the stranger than him? It didn't take a psychologist to read the scars of his mother's behaviour there.

To Emma he'd implied he hadn't known about his mother's betrayal till the end. Actually, he'd known most of his life. It was only when he'd found her with a teenager from his own high school, just two years older than himself, that Christo had finally cracked. There'd been no hiding from his father the smashed furniture or his bruised knuckles as he'd taken the other guy down. His mother had hated him for that and his father had withdrawn even further.

Christo had learned not to trust women, even when they came at a high price. Not to expect love or even companionship. He'd thought of a wife only as an asset, a commodity.

Looking into Emma's open features and the genuine smile curling her lips, Christo had a revelation.

He didn't want it to be that way.

The chains of the past were too restrictive. He wanted…

The idea of what he wanted stunned him.

'Where are we going?' Emma couldn't suppress the smile that kept breaking out. She'd missed Christo ever since he'd left for Athens on Monday morning. Here he was, back early.

For her? A shiver of excitement tugged through her belly and she strove to suppress it.

'Somewhere we can talk.' He threaded a way through the maze of alleys, emerging on the road behind the neo-classical Palace of St Michael and St George. Minutes later they descended a ramp built into the city walls to the tiny Faleraki beach.

It was one of her favourite places. Quiet and cut off from the bustle, the little bay looked across the water to the city ramparts, the towering Old Fortress, and beneath it the marina packed with yachts. Further down the beach a ramshackle pier provided a platform for local kids who were fooling around and jumping into the depths.

Christo led her to the point at the end of the small beach and the outdoor café. Unsurprisingly, a waiter emerged instantly, leading them to a shaded spot apart from other tables. It was the sort of thing that happened all the time with Christo, whether because they recognised his face or read him as a man who expected and happily paid for the best.

Instead of a table, they were installed on a comfortable couch under a wide umbrella. Their cool drinks and a platter of food arrived minutes later, set on the glass coffee table beyond which the aquamarine shallows gave way to deeper water the colour of lapis lazuli.

Emma sighed and sank back into the cushioned seat. She could get used to this.

Just as she'd grown used to the warmth of Christo's hand enfolding hers and the buzz of delight she got when he looked at her as if she were special. Those eyes...

Her heartbeat stuttered and seemed to pause before stumbling back into rhythm.

No. She wouldn't allow flights of fancy. This charge of excitement, like his heated expression, was about desire, attraction and physical pleasure. Nothing more.

'What brought you back from Athens?' He shrugged, those powerful shoulders riding high. Still he held her hand and it struck her that his expression was different, more guarded than she'd seen it in weeks. 'Is everything all right? Are you okay?'

She sensed something had changed. Something important.

His response proved her too fanciful. 'Everything's perfect. Just as it should be.' He leaned across to add ice to his ouzo, watching it cloud. 'I simply felt like taking a long weekend.'

Christo turned, lifting his glass. Automatically Emma raised her glass of tangy local ginger beer.

'Yia mas.' To us. A traditional toast, but when Christo leaned near, with that blazing look in his eyes, Emma felt...

She blanked that thought, wishing she'd ordered a shot of fiery ouzo instead of a soft drink. Something to jerk her out of useless imaginings.

'Who was that man?'

'Sorry?'

'The man you were with.' Emma caught the echo of something hard in Christo's tone, like steel hidden beneath velvet. For a moment she wondered if it could be jealousy. The possibility made something foolish within her swell.

'A local businessman.'

Christo sipped his drink then put it down and turned more fully towards her.

'And his business with you?' There it was again, a hint of sharpness.

Emma was torn between delight and disappointment. Just because Christo was possessive didn't mean anything. She was, for now, his wife. She'd seen how far he'd go to protect the public image of a happy couple.

The bubbling happiness she'd felt since the moment he'd sought her out in the old town faded.

'Emma?' Concern coloured his voice as he took her drink from her fingers then captured that hand too. 'What's wrong? What did he—?'

'Nothing! Nothing's wrong. He didn't do anything.' With a deep breath she pushed aside that silly sense of dissatisfaction and smiled. 'He runs a business decorating and catering for weddings. He interviewed me for a job.'

'A job?' She might have said she was flying to the moon, given his expression of blank surprise.

'Something to use my skills.' And earn an income. She needed funds to get her business off the ground. She didn't want to wait ten months till they went their separate ways and she received money from the Athens project.

'You're bored?'

Emma tilted her head, surveying him. 'I need to work, Christo. The villa is lovely and I have exciting plans to turn it into an exclusive resort. But that's longer term.' At least till she could get money to seed the first stages.

'This man—he offered you a job?'

Emma saw the tight angle of Christo's jaw and hesitated. 'He's consulting his partner first, but he was very positive.'

In fact, his enthusiasm had given Emma pause. The work had sounded good, despite the commuting time from the villa, but he'd been a little too friendly, his personal interest in her obvious. She hadn't really felt comfortable, had already decided...

'I don't want you working for him.'

'Sorry?'

'He's not trustworthy.'

'You know him?' Christo was a stranger to the area.

'I know his type. It wasn't business he had in mind.'

Exactly what Emma had thought. Yet Christo's assertion, implying he had the final say over her actions, stirred indignation. She tugged a hand from his and picked up her glass, taking a long swallow, then putting it down with a click on the table.

'*I* will decide whether or not to take the job.'

The glint in his eyes told her he wanted to disagree. 'You're my wife. You don't need to work.'

Emma arched her eyebrows. 'You're worried what people will think?' She could just about forgive his attempted intervention, given her own concerns about the guy who'd interviewed her. But to be told she couldn't work because of Christo's image...

Christo shook his head. 'I'm not trying to trap you at home. I have nothing against you having a job. I'll help you find one, if you like. I just don't want someone trying to take advantage of you.'

Perhaps that should sound strange coming from the man who'd traded on her besotted naivety to trap her into marriage. Instead it sounded *caring*. Not merely the result of macho possessiveness. There was a good dose of that, judging from the jut of his jaw. But there was more too.

For a second it reminded her of the old days, with her family, and particularly Papou, being over-protective. In the past Emma had found that trying, but she realised it felt good to know someone cared. She'd missed that.

'Emma.' Christo bent closer, as if trying to decipher her thoughts.

'You're not worried the press would say a billionaire's wife shouldn't work?'

A crack of laughter sounded. 'As if that's relevant!' Then, just as suddenly, he turned sombre. 'But I'm serious about that guy. The way he looked at you, he definitely wasn't thinking about work.'

Emma looked into Christo's strikingly handsome face, looking for self-interest, for some hint of manipulation. All she read was concern.

Once more that glow of warmth filled her.

She squeezed the big hand that held hers just a fraction too tight. 'Okay, I'll bear that in mind.' She'd already decided not to take the job, but she didn't want Christo thinking he could order and she'd immediately obey. He was domineering enough without further encouragement.

For long seconds he said nothing. Then he nodded and Emma released a pent-up breath. This felt like a victory. More. It felt like caring and respect.

Deep inside something tight and knotted frayed.

Christo gathered her against him, shifting so they both faced the glorious view. A shoal of fish glinted, turning in the crystalline shallows a few metres away. A yacht appeared around the promontory, its sail pristine white against the deep blue of sea and distant land.

Emma felt the comforting thud of Christo's heart and the warm weight of his arm around her. His breath feathered her hair and she inhaled his unique cedar, leather and spice scent. Elation rose.

'I'm glad to be back on Corfu, Emma.'

She smiled up at him, surprised to hear herself admit, 'I'm glad too.'

'Busy?' The deep voice came from behind Emma next morning as she sat in the courtyard loggia. Warm hands covered her shoulders and slid down her bare arms.

The pencil spilled from her hand onto the table. Her eyelids flickered as tingling heat rushed through her. She breathed deep, inhaling the familiar scent of Christo mingling with the last wisteria blooms. It was a heady mix.

Did he pull her close or did she lean back? Either way, as usual, she melted.

It was less than an hour since she'd left him and a giggling Anthea playing hide and seek in the garden. Two hours since Christo had held Emma piniioned against the wall of the shower, water sluicing over the pair of them, lips soldered together as he'd pumped into her, bringing them both to rapturous completion.

Thinking of it made her nipples peak and awareness tighten her inner muscles.

She sighed as he bent, nuzzled the hair from her neck and grazed his teeth where her neck curved into her shoulder. Emma shuddered. He knew all her sensitive spots.

'You're too distracting. I'm supposed to be working.'

Yesterday's conversation had reminded her how much she still had to do to get her business off the ground. She'd researched the market and competitors, checked local government approval processes and developed a business plan. She'd begun a website, scouted local suppliers and made plans for changes to the villa. But her non-existent cash flow meant she couldn't proceed as fast as she'd like.

Christo lifted his head and Emma bit her tongue rather than voice the protest that rose to her lips.

'On the weekend?'

She opened her mouth to say that was what he did, spent the weekends working, but it was no longer true. Last weekend there'd been a couple of calls to the Italian they'd met in Athens to discuss their joint venture. But that was all.

What had happened to the busy entrepreneur who'd initially seemed out of place at the villa?

'What are the drawings for?' Christo sat beside her at the table, pulling his chair so close his leg brushed hers and her shoulder nudged his upper arm.

She sighed and closed the papers. 'It's a long-term vision for the villa next door. But my main focus right now really needs to be on getting this place ready.'

'You're sure you want to do that?'

'Of course.' She needed the income and she had the skills to make it work. Eventually, when she and Christo divorced, this place would be hers free and clear.

Strange how the thought of being free of Christo no longer held the allure it once had. In fact, it chilled her to the bone despite the morning's warmth.

* * *

Christo had problems with the idea of outsiders here. Security would be a nightmare but, more than that, the place was their private haven. It wasn't modern like his Athens apartment but it felt like home. More than the ostentatious house where he'd grown up ever had.

'You won't mind sharing your home with strangers?'

Christo felt Emma's muscles tighten almost imperceptibly at his words. Yet she'd seemed rapt in the idea when she talked about it before.

Because she needs to support herself. Because you robbed her of the inheritance that should be hers, at least temporarily.

A decent man would give Emma back everything he'd taken.

Christo considered himself decent, if tough. He dismissed a pang of conscience.

'It's either that or move out completely. I'd rather be on hand when there are guests, to deal with their needs.'

'What about your privacy?'

'That's not a luxury I can afford.'

Christo stilled. He felt like a heel. 'Care to show me the drawings for next door?' When Emma hesitated, he reached forward. 'May I?'

She shrugged. 'Why not? Papou bought the neighbouring property, but it needed a lot of work, and he got sick not long afterwards so he never got around to doing anything with it.'

Christo surveyed the drawings. 'You have a good eye,' he murmured, lifting the top page to look at the next and the next. 'This could be something special. Even better than developing this place.'

'You think so?'

He met her stare, noting the excitement in her eyes at

odds with the press of her lips. As if she were scared to expect too much.

'I like the combination of modern and traditional. And extending the outdoor living space next to this—' he pointed '—is it a sunken garden?'

'It is, with a fabulous view over its own cove.'

'It would make a perfect venue for exclusive celebrations.'

'Weddings in particular.' She was enthusiastic now. 'I could lure a lot of people from overseas for a romantic wedding in Greece. Or anniversaries, or private holidays. One day, when I'm solvent, I'll tackle the remodelling.'

'I could help with that. My company specialises in property development.' Though on a much larger scale.

Emma spun round in her seat, her eyes huge. 'You threatened to withdraw your money from my uncle's business unless I stayed married to you. Yet you're *offering* it to me now?'

Not Christo's finest hour. He'd been desperate to convince Emma to stay with him. That need hadn't gone. It was just tempered by other things.

Feelings. It's tempered by what you feel for her. What you want her to feel for you.

Christo's pulse hammered high in his throat. Suddenly he didn't feel as invincible as usual.

'You agreed to my terms and I trust you to keep them,' he said, as if that was all he wanted, her presence for another ten months.

Christo paused, wondering if she had any notion how significant that admission was. Trust didn't come easily to him. Yet he'd discovered in Emma a woman unlike any he'd known. A woman who might disagree with him, but who, he was sure, wouldn't lie. She was sexy and passionate, gentle and emotional, practical and forthright. She cared for orphans and ageing housekeepers and maybe even for him.

Everything within him stilled as he acknowledged how much he wanted that.

'I want you to be happy and fulfilled, Emma.'

His words clearly took her by surprise, despite all they'd shared. But why shouldn't she be surprised? He'd couched their intimacy only in terms of sex. He'd let her imagine their connection was all about desire and satisfying carnal appetites. The truth, he'd discovered, ran far, far deeper.

Still she hesitated.

'Look on it as an advance against the money I owe you from the Athens property.' Not that he intended to use her funds for this. It would be his gift, but she didn't need to know that now.

Emma tilted her head to one side, as if trying to see him better. 'That would virtually dismantle the hold you have over me. You do realise that?'

Christo shrugged as if it were a small thing. As if his heart wasn't pummelling his ribs sickeningly and his neck wasn't prickling at the thought of her slipping away from him. But it wouldn't come to that.

'Until the year's up I still have ultimate say over the property.' He couldn't relinquish total control yet.

Slowly she nodded. But the reminder of that ace up his sleeve didn't dim the wonder in those hazel eyes. Her expression made him glow. As he had when he'd found her yesterday and she'd looked at him with such patent delight.

Had anyone ever looked at him as Emma did? For sure, he'd never felt this way about any other woman.

He lifted his hand to her satiny cheek, brushing it with the back of his knuckle. Something welled high in his chest and he opened his mouth to tell her...

'Emma!' A child's voice rang out and they turned to see Anthea and Dora's niece step out of the house. The new nanny released the girl's hand and predictably she flew across the courtyard to Emma's side like a bullet.

Emma gathered her up, settling her on her lap and nodding as Anthea told her how she'd helped tidy up.

Seeing the two together, the sensation in Christo's chest twisted into something powerful and barely familiar. This was how he'd imagined them, even better than he'd imagined. Yet it wasn't mere satisfaction he experienced.

Abruptly Anthea stopped chattering and turned to him, holding her arms out. 'Cwisto!' Inevitably her lisp made him smile. 'Up, pease. Up!'

It still stunned him that he'd built a rapport with Cassie's daughter. That he hadn't inadvertently hurt her because of his lack of experience. Guilt and the shadow of the past had persuaded him it wouldn't be possible. That he didn't deserve her trust.

Christo looked from Anthea to Emma and absorbed a barrage of emotions. Who'd have believed his world would be upended by two females? One tiny and demanding. The other feisty yet sweet. Both vulnerable. Both adorable.

Emma passed the little girl over to him, and he read in Emma's expression something he hadn't seen before. He wanted to freeze that moment, analyse that look, question her. But Anthea was wriggling, demanding he take her to see the baby birds in the nest they'd found in the garden.

He got up, slanting a look at Emma. But she turned away, folding the plans that riffled in the breeze.

Later, he told himself. This was too important to ignore.

CHAPTER THIRTEEN

'THE PLACE DEFINITELY has excellent potential,' Christo said as they left the empty villa and headed down the path to a private cove, smaller but no less beautiful than theirs next door. With each step their view of the jewel-toned water improved. Drifts of wildflowers, pink, white, blue and yellow, frothed up against the boles of massive olive trees and iconic tall cypresses.

Emma nodded, trying to stifle bubbling excitement that Christo was so positive about the place. All through their inspection Christo had asked tough, insightful questions. He'd closely examined the house and outbuildings which Emma hoped to turn into extra accommodation.

'It would take a lot of money to renovate,' she said. The more they inspected, the more she feared she'd underestimated costs. Emma knew events management but nothing about building. That was Christo's field.

He took her hand, weaving his fingers through hers. Emma's breath stalled then accelerated to a gallop. Ever since Athens he took every chance to touch her, to be close. The attraction between them was real, not manufactured for the press.

Was that why her heart sang when he touched her?

It might not be love but this...fling felt wonderful. As if she'd undone the shackles of grief, self-doubt and anger and had stepped free of them. She felt lighter at heart than she could ever remember.

See? She could enjoy the moment. Take pleasure like a sophisticated adult and...

Christo smiled and her thoughts frayed. He tugged her hand, leading her off the path and onto the deserted crescent of fine sand. Metres away the sun glinted off shallow water that sparkled like gems. It was a private paradise, screened at this end of the beach from open water by a tumble of rocks. There was just the shush of the sea on sand, a songbird in the trees above and Christo.

Yearning trembled through her.

'Marketed right and run well, it would be worth the investment. It can't be left. A vacant property will just degrade. And with this—' he gestured to the private beach '—you're onto a winner.'

Emma nodded, struggling to focus on the property, not on the man. 'I've tried to calculate how much it would cost but I haven't got very far.'

He turned back, his grey-blue eyes snaring hers. 'Leave that to me. I'll get someone onto it.'

'You will?' Was he serious about helping with the place?

'Of course.' He released her fingers and instead wrapped both hands around her waist. 'I'll release the resources so you can remodel. My staff will chase up the best local builders.'

Emma was so stunned it took a second to register what he was doing with his hands. Until air wafted around her torso as he urged her arms up, pulling her top over her head.

'Christo!' She darted a look around the empty beach. 'We can't.' Yet her breathlessness proved she was more excited than outraged. Especially when, with one swift movement, he hauled his shirt over his head and dumped it on the sand.

Emma's heart beat too fast as she took in his muscled body. She'd discovered one of her favourite things was to lay her head on his chest, feeling the strong thud of his heart beneath her ear and listening to it hammer as she flicked his nipple with her tongue, or slid her hand down to squeeze his shaft and tease him till he growled and rolled her beneath him.

No growling now. Christo shucked his shoes and the rest of his clothes while she stood staring. She'd thought herself accustomed to the sight of him, all taut muscle and proud virility. But she'd never seen him under the bright blue sky, stark-naked and mightily aroused.

He looked like some Greek god, perfectly proportioned, formidably sexy and utterly intent. Her body softened in anticipation. Involuntarily her inner muscles squeezed and she felt the slick wetness of arousal.

'Believe me, Emma, we can.'

In seconds he'd undone her bra and tossed it onto his clothes. The sun warmed her bare flesh but it was nothing to the blaze of heat as his gaze licked her. She thrilled at the ardour she read in his face, yet they were outdoors and...

'Don't cover yourself, sweet Emma.' She hadn't realised she'd made to cover her breasts till warm hands shackled her wrists. 'Please? I want to see you. You know we're private here. You can trust me.'

Standing there half-naked, feeling totally exposed, Emma realised she *did* trust her husband. More than she'd once believed possible.

'You want sex on the beach?' Emma felt a ripple of shock. But then, despite weeks of passionate sex, she'd been a virgin just a short time ago. This was still new.

He smiled, and her heart took up Zumba behind her ribs. 'With you, I want sex everywhere.'

Christo's gaze snared hers. Arousal beat hard and low in her pelvis. She told herself this was merely physical. Nothing else, nothing to worry about. Conveniently she silenced the part of her that said this felt like far more than sex.

'If you want,' he added. His hands hung, fisted, by his sides and Emma read tension in the line of his jaw.

He meant it. He'd leave her be if she chose. Contrarily, the realisation conquered her natural reserve. She toed off her sandals, her hands going to the zip of her skirt. Then she paused, one last doubt surfacing.

'If we have sex it's not because you've promised to help refit the villa.' She held his gaze, willing him to believe. 'I'm not like your mother. I don't do sex for money.'

Christo stood unmoving so long, she wondered if she'd said the wrong thing. But how could it be wrong when it was the truth?

Finally he unlocked frozen muscles and shook his head. 'You're nothing like her, Emma. You think I don't know that?'

She lifted her shoulders. 'I don't want any misunderstandings between us.'

'Good.' He stepped so close his erection brushed her skirt and she shivered as need corkscrewed through her lower body. 'Just honesty between us now. That's what I want. And you, sweet Emma. I want you so badly.'

Christo's words set off a chain reaction inside, making internal muscles spasm needily and her heart thrum wildly. 'In that case, I hope you have a condom.'

He did. By the time Emma was naked he was sheathed and she was on her back on the warm sand, Christo kneeling like a conquering hero between her legs. His eyes had that glazed look he got when aroused and, when he nudged her, she automatically rose to meet him, the sensation so exquisite, she stifled a cry of delight.

'Don't hold back, *glyka mou*. I like hearing you.'

With a tilt of his hips Christo slowly drove in till she felt him lodged right at her heart. Emma told herself that was impossible, but that was how it felt when he tenderly kissed her on the lips and gently rocked against her, evoking sensations that should be just physical but which felt profoundly emotional too.

Like caring, homecoming, sharing, lo…

Warning bells clamoured and Emma knew she had to

break the spell of his tenderness. It was enough to make her believe in things she shouldn't.

Holding tight to his shoulders, she lifted her head and grazed his ear with her teeth. Then, as he'd said he liked hearing her, she whispered to Christo just what she wanted him to do next.

It was like igniting gunpowder. For a millisecond there was breathless stillness, then he erupted in a surge of powerful energy, driving against her in an erotic rhythm that stole her breath as his hand moved first to her breast, then to the sensitive bud between her legs and…

'Christo!' His name was a hoarse shout over and over again that faded to a gasp as he took her to a peak, then another, shattering with her in a cataclysmic orgasm that engulfed them in rapture.

When she was back in her body, Emma felt filled to the brim, sated and spent yet emotional and needy, blinking back tears of reaction to the most astounding experience of her life. All she knew as she hugged Christo close was that she wanted to stay this way for ever.

Gradually her breathing eased and her heartbeat too. Still she clung tight, absorbing the scent of sweat and sex and maleness, feeling the slippery silk of her lover's skin against her.

Not her lover. Her husband.

Or maybe more.

Her breath tore from her throat.

'Come on, let's wash the sand away.' The deep voice murmured in her ear as Christo moved, ignoring her protest and lifting her into his arms.

The water, though not cold, was chilly enough to shock her into full alertness. He waded into the water, carrying her in his arms, and Emma clung to him as if she hadn't spent her childhood swimming several times a week. She didn't want to think about why she felt so needy.

Later, as they lay sprawled on flat rocks at the end of the beach drying in the sun, Emma found herself doing what she'd told herself she wouldn't—seeking more from Christo.

It wasn't his money she wanted and, while he made her feel like a goddess when he took her in his arms and made love to her, Emma wanted to understand him.

Because she loved him.

She'd tried to stifle the knowledge but it wouldn't be silenced any more. She'd told herself it was just sex between them, sex and a business arrangement. But she'd deluded herself. The Christo she'd discovered in Greece was the same man she'd fallen for in Australia. It was only the aberration of the loveless marriage that didn't fit the man she'd come to know and like all over again.

Except, after having heard him describe his parents, she had an inkling about how he could separate love and marriage.

Unfortunately she couldn't do that and the realisation terrified her. Was she fooling herself again, tumbling into love with this man? Did she really know him or did she only think so?

And, if she did, what did she do next?

'Tell me about Cassie.'

'Sorry?' Christo opened one eye and squinted down at the damp honey-brown hair on his chest where Emma rested her head. He enjoyed the feel of her there, her body soft against him, one thigh over his so the intimate heat between her legs was tantalisingly close.

'I wondered about your stepsister.'

Christo frowned. 'Why?'

Emma lifted her head, her palm on his chest. Her eyes were sombre. As if, while he'd been lazing on a cloud of wellbeing, she'd been in a bleaker place altogether.

'*Glyka mou!* What's wrong?' Concern rose instantly.

She shook her head. 'Nothing. I was just thinking…' She shrugged then looked at him almost defiantly. 'How much I don't know about you. You never mention Cassie. But I feel she was important to you.'

Christo stared, stunned at the woman who, once again, turned his world upside down. Any other lover would be snuggled bonelessly against him, enjoying the comedown from that amazing high they'd shared. But not his Emma.

Why was he surprised? Emma was unlike any other woman.

'You said we'd be honest with each other.'

'That doesn't mean I want you prying into ancient history.'

'I see.' She didn't pull away but her luscious body stiffened. Her eyes grew shuttered, no longer reflecting the green of the sea but turning a flat, muddy brown. She turned her head away and guilt stirred in his gullet. He should have tempered his response, not barked at her because she'd touched on what he hated to think about.

Christo's heart thumped as he waited for Emma to roll away but she simply subsided where she'd been. Though the way she held herself reminded him of an animal nursing a wound, stillness betraying pain.

He lifted a hand to stroke her, then stopped.

Christo had spent half a lifetime not thinking about this. He baulked at opening up the past. Yet this was the first time Emma had asked him for anything.

Except a divorce.

He huffed an amused breath at the memory of her breathing fire as she'd demanded he release her from their marriage. She'd been so outrageously, provocatively sexy. At that moment he'd thought he'd die if he didn't have her.

Just as suddenly Christo's amusement faded.

He had her for now. But for how long? He wanted her

permanently, and not because of Anthea or words on a legal document. He just…wanted her for himself.

He dropped his hand to her hair, feeling the suck of her indrawn breath against his chest. For some obscure reason, this mattered to her.

And since Emma mattered to him…

Christo turned his head, his gaze drifting across the blue-green sea.

'She was eleven or twelve when she came to the house. A shy little thing with freckles, plaits and the biggest brown eyes you've ever seen.' Eyes just like Anthea's.

Against his chest Emma stirred but said nothing.

'My father and his second wife had just returned from their honeymoon. Cassie had stayed with relatives in the States while they travelled.'

'How old were you?'

'Almost eighteen.' Two years older than when he'd discovered his mother with her teenage lover. At eighteen Christo had worked in the family business and studied, living up to his father's demand that he excel at both.

'You really only met her once?'

'For a weekend. She arrived on Friday and left on Sunday.' Christo swallowed, the action hurting, as if something sharp had lodged in his throat.

Emma sat up. 'Christo? What's wrong?'

He jerked his gaze round to her, biting the urge to say *he* was wrong.

Get a grip, Karides.

He levered himself up to sit, draping his arms over his knees. 'Nothing. It's okay.'

Was he reassuring himself or her? Despite the sun, his nape prickled with cold.

'She was shy, even with her own mother, and with my father…' He shook his head. 'I think I mentioned he was a tough man. He hadn't a sentimental bone in his body. As for being kind to little girls…

'She tried to avoid him as much as possible and I helped her.'

He'd felt sorry for the kid, given her mother had seemed more concerned about placating her new husband than helping her daughter acclimatise to a new country and a new family. Christo, used to being alone, had been charmed by Cassie's hesitant smiles and shy interest. For the first time in his life, he'd felt he could make a difference.

There was a terrible irony there, if only he'd known.

'I took her swimming and sailing.' Getting her out of his father's way. 'And she used to watch me draw. She found my cartoons amusing.' That, if only he'd realised, had been his worst mistake. His father was annoyed enough at him 'wasting' his time with Cassie, but to have her encourage his scribbling wasn't to be borne. The old man viewed his interest in art with suspicion, a sign of weakness in his heir, who had to be tough and ruthlessly efficient. Real men didn't draw or play games. They closed deals, kept a tight rein on business and took hard decisions.

'She must have enjoyed being with you.'

Christo nodded. 'Yes. She even laughed, when she thought my father wasn't around.' He noticed a pebble on the rock at his feet and threw it, watching it arc over the water, then disappear as if it had never been.

Just like Cassie.

'But my father noticed.' Christo found another pebble and threw it. 'He was concerned about me. Apparently, with my stepsister I was soft and lacking seriousness. He was trying to make a man of me. Not someone who frittered away his time playing games or being sentimental over a kid.'

'I don't think I'd have liked your father.'

Christo turned to see Emma sitting, arms wrapped around her legs, chin resting on her knees. Even scowling she made his pulse quicken.

'He was moulding me so I could face whatever the commercial world threw at me. He lost his own father early and didn't want me struggling as he had.'

Emma's eyes met his and something thumped deep in his chest. 'The world isn't just commerce. There's love and friendship and family.'

Not as far as his father had been concerned. 'The upshot was he decided Cassie wasn't a good influence.'

'But she was only a little girl!' Emma's gaze widened.

Christo spread his hands. 'He felt I wasn't acting like a man.'

That had cut deep, especially as Christo had spent his life living up to his father's expectations.

'There's nothing manly about making a little kid feel alone and scared.'

Christo nodded. 'I agree. But he didn't see it that way. He'd never been one for close relationships. His marriages were about possessing beautiful women who enhanced his kudos.' He paused. 'Anyway, he decided Cassie couldn't stay. She was shipped back to relatives in the States.'

Emma looked aghast. 'Just because you'd been nice to her?'

At last she understood. 'Because I had to be tough. He wouldn't allow anything else and I...' Christo sighed and looked away '...accepted that.' Which made it even worse. 'So she went to America and I never heard from her again. After a while, I forgot about her. Occasionally I'd wonder what she was doing but I never followed up.' Bitterness was sharp on his tongue. 'So I didn't know the relatives who took her in later decided they didn't want another kid to look after. She ended up in foster care, shunted from one place to another.'

'It wasn't your fault.' Emma's whisper slid through him like the serpent in Eden, so tempting.

'Because of me she was banished to live her life with people who didn't want her. Meanwhile, I got on with *my* life as if she didn't matter at all.'

Christo threw another stone out into the water with such force, he almost wrenched his shoulder. 'If I'd done the honourable thing, if I'd bothered to check up on her, things might have turned out differently. She might still be alive.' He dragged in air to fill tight lungs. 'But I'm stronger now. I didn't do right by Cassie, but you can be sure I *will* do my duty by her daughter.'

Emma curled her arms tight around her knees and stared out to sea. Beside her Christo did the same, clearly not wanting to talk further.

Who'd have thought a simple question about his step-sister would reveal so much? Combined with what he'd told her before, it painted a picture that made her heart lurch with sympathy and pain. It was even worse than she'd thought.

A cold, controlling father and a distant, self-absorbed mother. His family hadn't been a family at all. It was re-markable they'd produced a man with as much decency as Christo.

Emma had heard his self-reproach as he'd spoken of Cassie. As if he, as a teenager, could have gone against the girl's mother and stepfather to provide a home for her.

Who'd provided a home for him?

He spoke of doing the honourable thing and about duty. Was that what drove Christo? Emma recalled his words when he'd found her in Corfu. About giving her his name and his word, as if that pledge was more important than love.

Which made sense for a man who didn't know love at all.

For a man who possibly never would.

The experts said what you experienced as a child co-loured your character for life. That lack of caring in a child's life stunted their emotional growth.

Emma's abdominal muscles spasmed as the pain inten-sified. She'd convinced herself she was over Christo, that she could enjoy uncomplicated sex then move on. But she'd given her heart to him in Australia and hadn't stopped lov-ing him, despite anger and disillusionment.

Contrary to what she'd told herself, she'd secretly hoped Christo would come to love her. She'd taken his kindness, passion and ability to make her feel special as signs he'd begun to feel for her what she did for him.

Emma gritted her teeth as the pain settled into a cold, hard ache in her belly and chest.

She'd thought he was softening towards her. That they'd shared more than sex. There'd been companionship and caring, humour, a sense that they were building something together.

In a flash of blinding clarity she realised she'd seen what she wanted to see.

Christo was driven by an unshakeable sense of duty. It was there in his determination to care for his step-niece. To look to the needs of Dora, of all his staff, and Emma too.

No matter how much she admired him for the honour-able man he'd become despite the odds, duty was no re-placement for love.

She shut her eyes and pictured him with Anthea, re-membering his hesitation. True, his wariness was easing, and hopefully that relationship would blossom even more.

But Emma couldn't expect miracles. A man driven by duty, who had no experience of love, would never give her what she needed.

They'd found common ground but that was based on sex. Everything, even his desire to be here on the island, hinged on that and his need to portray the fiction of a happy family to the watching world.

Look at the way he'd snapped at her question about Cassie. Christo hated sharing anything personal. Her status as his wife didn't give her special privileges there.

Her husband was as likely to fall in love with her as snow falling in summer.

Even if theoretically it were possible, could she live with him in a one-sided relationship for the rest of the year, hoping for a miracle?

Emma had never thought of herself as greedy. Yet the idea of giving her all to the man she loved, knowing he felt only a sense of responsibility and lust for her, made her crumple inside.

What if the lust faded? What if someone else caught his eye? That was likely given the glamorous circles he moved in. Emma knew part of the reason he desired her was because she was a novelty to him. Despite the makeover in Athens, she wasn't cut out for his world.

With a hiss of indrawn air Emma shot to her feet. Seconds later she was stumbling across the sand to the scatter of discarded clothes.

'Emma? What's wrong?'

She swayed, struck by a blow of need so strong it almost felled her. The perverse, futile need to turn around and run straight back to Christo.

But what would that achieve? She needed distance. Time to think, to sort out her head and her heart.

'I've just remembered…something.' She grabbed the froth of her cotton lace skirt and stepped into it, yanking up the zip. 'I need to get back to the villa.' Her head spun uselessly as she tried to come up with an excuse. 'There's something I need to do.'

'What is it?'

He was behind her, so close his breath kissed her bare

neck and hair as she wrestled with her clothes. She forced herself to take a deep breath and drag the top on, feeling the material abrade her nipples. But she didn't have time for a bra. She had to get away.

A warm hand closed on her elbow and she jumped so violently, he let go. But now he was before her, those penetrating eyes concerned. It was a terrible temptation to think she was wrong. That maybe Christo did feel…

Emma reared back. Her lovesick heart wanted to believe in a happy ending when she *knew*, when he'd already spelled it out as clearly as he could, that he only wanted sex, and stability for his niece. She'd already fallen for wishful thinking once. She knew better now.

He stood before her, naked and powerfully built, and her longing was so great she had to avert her eyes.

'Talk to me, Emma.' His voice was warm velvet, enfolding her.

She stepped back, almost tripping over a sandal. 'Not now. I have to go—'

'I'm not letting you go anywhere when you're clearly upset.' He crossed his arms over that powerful chest, the picture of masculine obstinacy, and fear crested. Fear that if she wasn't careful she'd convince herself to stay, to settle for being a mere convenient wife rather than someone he cherished.

'It's not up to you to *let* me go anywhere.' Emma took refuge in anger, though it was only surface deep. She was too miserable to muster real outrage.

Then he did what she'd feared. Instead of blustering he turned gentle. As if he really cared about her.

'I'm worried about you, *glyka mou*. What's happened?'

Emma drew a slow breath and raised her eyes to his. 'I can't go on like this. I can't—' she waved one hand in the air '—keep up the pretence for a whole twelve months. This isn't going to work.'

From concerned, his proud features immediately turned stony. 'How can you say that? It's working beautifully.'

She shook her head, tugging her gaze away, feeling the instant ease in tension as she did. 'For you. For Anthea maybe. But not for me. I just can't do it any more.'

Emma registered a ripple of movement in his big frame, as if from a rising tide of energy. 'But you will. You gave your word.'

His voice was cooler than she'd heard in ages, each word clipped. The voice of a stranger.

'No! You forced me into a situation where I had no choice. I took your devil's bargain because that's all I could do. But it's impossible.'

Christo stepped towards her and she shrank back. Instantly he froze.

'Please.' Her voice wobbled and she had to work to get the words out. 'I need to be alone.'

Emma's breath came in laboured gasps. She swung around and fumbled for her sandals. But as she scrambled towards the path a hard hand closed around her elbow.

'Not so fast.'

CHAPTER FOURTEEN

CHRISTO REELED. HALF an hour ago they'd been wrapped in each other, lost in a blast of ecstasy so intense he was sure it had marked him for life.

Emma had marked him. Her sweet generosity. Her fiery strength. Her gentle caring.

He'd never known a woman like her. Had never expected to and had certainly never anticipated the effect she'd have on him.

Now he was entangled, caught so fast in the net of his own longing that there was no escape.

She couldn't expect him to let her go. Not now. Not when he'd glimpsed paradise with her. Christo had learned never to expect miracles. Everything in his world always came at a price.

But, despite everything, Emma had given herself to him freely, unstintingly. Not just in bed, but in so many other ways, ways that made him think the boundaries he'd known all his life could be broken. That if he made the effort perhaps there could be *more*.

He wanted that more so badly. He wanted Emma.

'Talk to me, Emma.' Nausea stirred at the thought of her so distressed. Of *him* distressing her. She trembled in his hold but didn't try to escape.

'What is it? Is it because of what I did? Because I didn't save Cassie?' Before he'd shared that, Emma had been content in his arms.

Guilt over his stepsister lay heavily, only lightening occasionally. When Anthea smiled her increasingly cheeky grin or put her hand in his. Or when Emma gave him that glowing look that made his heart stop.

'What?' Emma turned and his gut contracted when he saw that her lashes were spiked with tears.

'You despise me, don't you?' The words ground from him, revealing the depths of his fear.

Once he'd never have admitted that to anyone, even himself. He'd learned, almost before he could walk, to conceal weakness. But Emma stripped away his ability to pretend. Self-preservation should have kept his mouth shut about the past, but for once he'd wanted to share everything because it was Emma wanting to know.

Look where that had got him.

'I don't despise you.' Her words were choked and unconvincing.

Christo's pulse beat raggedly. He knew he'd guessed right. Yet still he couldn't release her. He slid his hand to her wrist, feeling the tumultuous pulse there.

'Then what? You weren't in a hurry to leave before I told you about Cassie.'

'It's not that.' Her gaze slid from his and Christo felt the lie like a blow to the back of his legs severing his tendons.

Now he found the willpower to release her and step back.

'Don't lie to me, Emma.' That was one of the things he treasured about her. She always told him the truth.

'I'm not—' He felt her gaze on him. 'Christo? Are you all right?'

He grimaced. Even now, when she knew the worst of his faults, Emma could find it in her to be concerned for him. She was too caring for her own good.

'No. I'm not.' He hefted a breath, trying to fill lungs that had seized. Looking down into drenched hazel eyes Christo realised he had no option but to tell *her* the truth. The whole truth, that he'd been grappling with for weeks now. 'I can't let you go.'

She stepped back and Christo felt as if he'd cracked right through the middle, seeing her retreat.

'You have to.' He heard her desperation and knew this was his last chance.

Pride be damned. He couldn't let her go without a fight. 'I need you, Emma. Please. I…love you.'

He'd never thought to hear, much less say, those words. They were foreign on his tongue but as soon as he said them something that felt remarkably like peace settled around him.

It was short-lived.

Emma flung up her hand as if to ward him off. 'Don't, please. That's too cruel.'

Gently Christo captured her hand and pulled it down, resisting the impulse to tug her to him and never let her go. 'Why is it cruel?'

He was the one being rejected. But seeing Emma so distraught tempered his reaction.

Sad brown eyes met his. 'You're just saying that because you know that I…' Her chin came up. 'I was in love with you when we married. You think you can make me stay if you pretend to love me now.'

Christo shook his head, ignoring the dart of pain at the fact she spoke of loving him in the past tense.

'I'm not pretending, *karthia mou*. I promised to be honest with you.' He paused, watching her eyes widen. 'I want more than a convenient marriage. I want you as my partner, my love, the one that I cherish for the rest of my days.'

Instead of the response he'd hoped for, Emma's mouth turned down at the corners. Pain clouded her expression.

'It's too late, Christo. Once I might have fallen for that, but not now.'

'I see. You don't trust me after all.' He couldn't blame her. He'd set about winning her with ruthless efficiency. Now, looking back on his determination to put his ring on Emma's finger, he understood it was because he'd been falling for her from the very first. At the time he hadn't had the emotional understanding to recognise he was falling in love, yet he'd known instinctively he needed this woman in his life.

Emma shook her head, her hair a tangle around her shoulders. Her red top was inside out, her skirt drooping on one side where the zip hadn't pulled up all the way, and her nose was pink. She was still the most beautiful woman he knew. Christo's heart gave a mighty thud, as if trying to leap free of his rib cage and throw itself on her mercy.

'I won't hold you to our agreement.' It killed him to say it but how could he keep her by force? 'Your uncle's business is safe. Your assets are too.'

He read surprise on her face and pushed harder.

'That's what I was going to tell you today. That I want this to be a real marriage. That I want more from you than just a legal agreement and a home for Anthea.'

Her chin tilted. 'And sex.'

He nodded. 'And sex.' The thought had an inevitable effect with a surge of blood to the groin. 'I want more, Emma. I'm greedy. I want *you*. The whole of you. I want to be the one you care for because I care for you. I *love* you.' The words came easier this time, despite the fact he felt stretched on a torture rack by her lack of response.

Christo stood, waiting for her to capitulate, to admit she cared for him even a little. To give him hope.

Nothing. Just that frozen look of shock.

Defeat was a boulder crushing his chest, flattening his very being. Yet he couldn't give up. His feelings for her were too vital.

Finally he dragged out the words. 'I won't stand in your way, Emma. But, wherever you go, I'll be there. Hoping you change your mind. If you go to Melbourne, I'll buy a home there. If you stay in the Corfu villa, I'll look for a place nearby.' He dragged his hand through his hair, silently admitting his desperation. 'After all, you'll want to see Anthea from time to time.' He prayed she did. It looked like being the only way he'd get to see Emma.

'But your business is based in Athens!'

Christo huffed out a terse laugh. 'You think that will stop me?' He shook his head. 'For you I'd give that up. I've got more than enough money for a lifetime.' As he said it Christo felt an unexpected sense of freedom. Never in his life had he contemplated a world without Karides Enterprises. 'There's more to life than business.'

His father would be spinning in his grave.

But this was his life. Not his father's.

Emma faltered back a step, her hand going to her throat. 'You couldn't. It's your life.'

'*Part* of my life,' he said slowly. 'A part that I enjoy, most of the time. But there are more important things in my life now. Like you.'

Emma heard his words and told herself this was a trap to keep her in a convenient marriage.

But when she saw the excitement and wonder in Christo's eyes it was hard not to believe him.

'I'm not my father, Emma. I saw his life and I didn't want it, even as I spent my time learning how to be him.'

'No,' she whispered, unable to stop herself. 'You aren't him. He sent Cassie away. You tried to help her. You're helping her daughter.'

That had to count for something. Christo was a better man than his father.

'I love you, *karthia mou*.' There were those words again. He called her 'his heart'. How was a woman supposed to resist that? 'Ah, Emma, don't cry.' He lifted a finger to her face, brushing away the single tear that had spilled down her cheek. 'I didn't mean to hurt you.'

'I just don't know what to believe.'

His hand dropped. 'If nothing else, believe I'll never intentionally hurt you again.' Christo swallowed. 'I've got a lot to learn, like how to care for a family. Maybe that's why I was so determined to win you and keep you. For my own selfish reasons and not for Anthea at all. I understood, though I couldn't admit it, that I needed you. For your beautiful, loving heart.'

To Emma's amazement he took a step away. A chill enveloped her.

'If I thought it would work I'd promise you jewels and designer clothes. There's a luxury yacht off Santorini, a ski chalet at St Moritz and a chateau in the Loire.' As she watched, his intent gaze grew cloudy. 'But I know you, Emma. You care about people more than things. There's nothing more I can say. Words alone won't convince you.'

His eyes were bleak, his sensual mouth a grim line. Every line of that strong, superb body spoke of pain.

And it struck her that she believed him. These weren't empty words. He really would change his life to win her, move to Australia to be with her.

Even in the days of their courtship Christo hadn't actively lied. She'd been the one spinning fairy tales out of his kindness and gentle wooing, building them into far more than he'd ever implied.

She stared into those smoky eyes, feeling the depth of pain he didn't bother to conceal. Christo stood there, uncaring about his nakedness, as if nothing mattered but convincing her.

'You'd really give up the business for me?'

Fire sparked in those eyes. Emma saw blue flames ignite. 'I'll do whatever it takes. Just say the word.'

Abruptly the dreadful tightness wrapping her ribs eased and she took a shuddery breath of relief. Of hope.

'I might still want those designer clothes if I'm going to look like a billionaire's woman.'

The fire in his eyes became a blaze of heat as he absorbed her words. 'Clothes don't make the woman, Emma.'

'Or the man.' She nodded at his naked body and he shrugged, a smile flickering at the corner of his mouth.

'I'm hoping you'll decide it's what's inside that counts.'

If Emma hadn't been so close she'd never have seen the shadow of self-doubt in his expression. Never have noticed the way his pulse thundered too hard at his temple. As if, despite all his experience bringing off hugely profitable deals, Christo still feared he wasn't good enough for her.

Emma stepped up to him, putting her hand to his pounding chest. 'There's something you should know.'

Christo's hand clamped hers to him. His jaw tightened, as if expecting the worst. 'Tell me.'

'I tried but I never fell out of love with you.'

It took long seconds for her words to sink in. 'You still love me?' Beneath her hand Christo's heart took up a helter-skelter rhythm that matched hers.

Emma nodded and suddenly they were both grinning. His hands framed her face. 'You love me.' This time he said it as if he believed it.

'And you love me.' Now she could see it in his face, feel it in the rippling tremor that passed through him. How wrong she'd been, imagining Christo incapable of deep emotion. For there it was, clear as day.

Then his hands were on her, not undressing her or seducing her, but lifting her high and swirling her round and round till the world spun and the only solid thing in it was Christo.

Finally he stopped, panting, and collapsed on the sand, cushioning her as she landed on him.

'My own Emma.' He wrapped his arms around her. 'You give me heart to be the man I never thought I could be.'

'And you give me courage to be more than I'd ever thought possible.' The moment felt so huge, so momentous.

'Stop talking and kiss me, wife.'

Instead of taking offence at his command, Emma gladly complied. Then she made a demand of her own, which provoked one of Christo's trademark sexy smiles and kept them on the beach for hours celebrating.

EPILOGUE

AFTER MONTHS OF detailed planning and intense work the neighbouring villa was finally open. The residence was elegant and well-appointed and the gardens a triumph. Christo's staff had provided expert assistance but it was Emma and her team of locals who'd pulled it all together.

Christo stood in the sunken garden, redolent with the velvet scent of roses, cypresses and the salt tang of the sea. The days grew shorter but, as if ordained by fate, or perhaps his wife's sheer positivity, the afternoon sun shone bright in a cloudless sky.

His gaze wandered from the draperies of sea-green gauze and silk that led from the shallow steps, past the flowering shrubs, to the pergola where he stood. The place had a festive air.

'You look like the cat who swallowed the cream.'

Christo turned to Damen, grinning beside him.

'Can you blame me?'

His friend shook his head. 'The transformation is stunning.'

Christo knew he was talking about the villa, once sad and neglected, now an inviting showpiece. But the real change, he knew, was within himself. He was a different man from the one who'd flown to Melbourne to secure a commercial property and a convenient wife.

Not for the first time he paused to wonder at old man Katsoyiannis agreeing to the deal. He'd been as sharp as a tack, nobody's fool, and so protective of his granddaughter. Had he seen what Christo hadn't? That Emma was the perfect woman for him?

'Emma's the one responsible.' Not just for the renovation, but for the change in him.

'She's a miracle worker, and not only with bricks and mortar.' Damen clapped him on the shoulder. 'I've never seen you looking so relaxed, or so happy.'

Christo shrugged, not bothering to conceal a smile. 'What can I say? Marriage agrees with me.' It wasn't just the fact that he delegated more and worked mainly from their home in Corfu. The life he shared with Emma and little Anthea was filled with joy. 'You should try it.'

Ignoring Damen's choke of shock, he turned away.

There was Dora, surrounded by relatives and friends. The familiar faces he'd come to know from Corfu. A scattering of invitees from Athens. On the other side of the garden Emma's cousin Maia chatted to Clio, both looking effortlessly chic, and both ignoring the attempts of men aged from seventeen to seventy to catch their attention.

Neither woman could hold a candle to his Emma.

'There she is.' Damen's voice made him look past the crowd.

At first all he saw was Emma's friend Steph descending the steps to the garden. Did that explain the breathless quality of Damen's voice? Christo hadn't missed the undercurrent between them.

Then he forgot all else as he caught sight of Emma.

Once again she wore the slim-fitting gown of cream that made her waist look impossibly small and she as fragile as gossamer.

Except his wife was anything but fragile. She was strong and determined, but kind and caring too. *Loving.*

His breath escaped on the thought.

Loving. That was Emma.

Her head was up, an antique lace veil framing her features. With every step the tourmaline eardrops he'd given her swung and gleamed, but they couldn't outshine the happiness on her face. As Emma's eyes met his Christo felt that familiar thump, as if their two hearts beat as one. Then she smiled and the world turned radiant.

Her uncle walked beside her, beaming. And…

'Cwisto!' Anthea barrelled into his legs, wrapping her arms around his thighs and crushing her posy of flowers.

'Here, sweetie, stand with me.' Steph, in her green bridesmaid's dress, beckoned the little girl, but Anthea shook her head.

'Can't I stay with you, Cwisto?' Big brown eyes met his. He knew he was being manipulated but did he care?

'Of course.' He took her hand in his. 'You're part of this too.'

For, in renewing their vows, Emma committed herself to both of them. As he committed himself to her.

Then Emma's uncle led her forward and Christo took his bride's hand, drawing her close. Never had he felt such profound emotion as when he saw the love in her clear gaze.

'You take my breath away, *karthia mou*.' He bent his head and gathered her to him, kissing her until he felt her turn satisfyingly boneless.

A small hand tugged his trouser leg and Anthea's piercing whisper penetrated. 'Not *now*, Cwisto. Be good. You have to wait till *after* the pwomises.'

The crowd laughed and Emma's eyes danced as she leaned back, breathless, in his embrace. 'Yes, there's plenty of time for kisses later.'

'I'll hold you to that, *agapi mou*.' Then, grinning, he lifted Anthea in his other arm and turned to the celebrant.

* * * * *

A DIAMOND DEAL
WITH THE GREEK

MAYA BLAKE

To Carly, my editor, for being the instrument that gives my words true meaning.

Thank you!

CHAPTER ONE

ARABELLA 'REBEL' DANIELS stood at the back of one of the many lifts that served the giant glass and steel masterpiece that was the Angel Building, and waited for the group of four to board. Swallowing down the lingering taste of the second double-shot macchiato she'd given in to this morning, she took a deep breath to calm herself. Although she'd needed the boost very badly at the time, the effect on her nerves now prompted a bout of regret.

Caffeine and panic did not mix well, and, after two long weeks of subsisting on both, she was more than ready to ditch them.

Her heart pounded with trepidation, but, thankfully, she couldn't hear it above the loud music playing in her ears.

Grappling with what would greet her once the lift journey ended was consuming enough, although there was also the real and present albatross of having lost her biggest sponsor three weeks ago and the resulting media frenzy, to deal with. Of course, far from the wild speculation that she was using booze and drugs to cope with her problems, the media would've been shocked and sorely disappointed to know the strongest substance she'd touched was coffee.

She stared unseeing before her, the words of the letter that had been burning a hole in her bag for the last two weeks emblazoned in her mind.

Arabella,
First of all, happy twenty-fifth birthday for Wednesday. If you're surprised at this out-of-the-blue communication, don't be. You're still my daughter and I have a duty of care to you. There's no judgement on

my part for the way you've chosen to live your life.
Nor are there any strings attached to the enclosed
funds. You need it, so put pride aside and use it. It's
what your mother would've wanted.
Your father.

Steeling her heart against the lance of hurt at the stark words, Rebel shifted her mind to the banker's receipt that had accompanied the letter.

The five hundred thousand pounds deposited into her bank account was a little less than what her sponsors would've donated had she still been on their books, but it was enough to get her to the Verbier Ski Championships.

This time she couldn't stop her insides from twisting with guilt and a touch of shame.

She should've tried harder to return the money.

Too much had been said between her father and her that couldn't be unsaid. Even after all these years, the pain and guilt were too vivid to be dismissed. And nothing in her father's letter had given her cause to think his views weren't as definitive as they'd been the last time she'd seen him.

He still laid the death of his wife, her mother, firmly at Rebel's feet.

Suppressing her pain, she tried to ignore the pointed looks from the lift's occupants. At any other time she would've turned the music down, but today was different. Today, she would be seeing her father again for the first time in five years. She needed a full suit of armour in place but the music was all she had.

When another suited businessman sent her a scathing look, she mustered a smile. His eyes widened a touch, his ire rapidly morphing to something else. Rebel looked away before her attempt to excuse her music's loudness turned into anything else. Keeping her eyes on the digital counter, she exhaled as the lift reached the fortieth floor. According to what she'd been able to glean from their very brief, very stilted conversations over the last week, her accountant father worked for Angel International Group as their CFO. He hadn't volunteered any more information when she'd asked. In fact, any further attempt to pave a reconnecting road with her father had been firmly blocked. Just as he'd firmly blocked her initial attempts to give back the money he'd given her.

The deeply wounding knowledge that her father was only doing his duty to the wife he'd loved and lost so cruelly should've driven Rebel's actions, not her manager's insistence that the money was the answer to all their prayers.

But it was her father's insistence that the money was hers no matter what that had led her to finally confessing the money's existence to Contessa Stanley. Her manager had had no qualms about Rebel using the funds. Especially since Rebel had recently lost yet another big sponsor due to the continued domino effect created by the sensational reports splashed all over the media. Even her retreat from the spotlight had been looked upon negatively, with wild speculation as to whether she was finally in rehab or nursing a broken heart.

With her chances of finding new sponsorship dwindling by the day, and the championship deadlines racing ever closer, Rebel had finally given in to Contessa's arguments.

Which left her not just in a state of confusion about why her father was now avoiding her after reaching out, at last, with his letter, but also having serious qualms about using money she hadn't wanted to touch in the first place.

'Excuse me?'

Rebel started as the man closest to her touched her arm. Plucking out one earbud, she raised an eyebrow. 'Yes?'

'Did you not want this floor?' he enquired, interest flaring in his eyes as he held the lift doors open and avidly conducted a study of her body.

Groaning inwardly, Rebel wished she hadn't let impulse drive her here until after she'd gone back home to change from her yoga pants and vest top after her morning training session. Muttering her thanks, she slid through the throng.

Hitching her yoga mat and gym bag firmly onto her shoulder, she turned the music volume down as she stepped out of the lift. Plush grey carpet, broken only by a set of massive glass doors, stretched as far as the eye could see, with complementing grey walls interspersed with wild bursts of colour in the form of huge flower arrangements. On the walls along a wide hallway, high-definition images of some of the world's most gifted athletes played on recessed screens.

The whole placed smelled and looked hallowed and expensive.

Rebel frowned, wondering whether she'd walked into the wrong place.

For as long as she'd been aware her father had worked as an accountant for a stationery company, not a slick outfit whose employees flitted past in expensive suits and wore futuristic-looking earpieces. Unable to accept that the father who'd vociferously voiced his hatred of her chosen sporting career would have anything to do with a place like this, Rebel moved towards the set of glass doors and pushed.

Nothing happened. Pushing firmer, she huffed when the door refused to budge.

'Uh, you need one of these to enter,' a voice said from behind her. 'Or a visitor's pass and an escort from downstairs.'

Turning, Rebel saw the man from the lift. His smile stretched wider as he waved a matte black card. The unwillingness to prolong the stomach-churning meeting with her father dragged another smile from her reluctant cheeks. 'Damn, I guess I was a little too impatient to get up here. I'm here to see Nathan Daniels. You couldn't help me out and let me in, could you? I'm Rebel, his daughter. We had an appointment and I'm running late…'

She stopped babbling and gritted her teeth as he took his time looking her up and down again. Fingering the sleeves of the sweater tied around her waist, Rebel waited for his gaze to meet hers again. 'Of course. Anything for Nate's daughter. Awesome name, by the way.'

Pinning the smile on her face, she waited for him to pass the card over the reader and murmured, 'Thank you,' as he held the door open for her.

'My pleasure. I'm Stan. Come with me, I'll show you to Nate's office. I haven't seen him today…' he frowned '…or this week, come to think of it. But I'm sure he's around somewhere.'

Rebel couldn't stop her heart from sinking further at Stan's news. Although now she was here, she realised she'd only *assumed* her father would be at work today. The hurt she'd tried for so long to keep at bay threatened to overtake the small amount of optimism she'd secretly harboured these past two weeks.

Pushing it back, she followed Stan along a series of hallways until they reached the first of two brushed-metal doors in a long, quieter corridor. 'Here we are.'

Stan knocked and entered. The outer office was empty, as was the inner office once Rebel followed him in. Frown deepening, he turned to her. 'Looks like he's not here, and neither is his PA…'

Sensing what was coming, she pre-empted him. 'I'm happy to wait. I'm sure he won't be long. If he's not back soon, I'll give him a call.'

Stan looked uncertain for a moment, then he nodded. 'Sure.' He held out his hand. 'I'd love to take you out for a drink some time, Rebel.'

Rebel barely stopped herself from grimacing. 'Thanks, but I can't. My social calendar is booked up for the foreseeable future.' She had no intention of dating anyone any time soon, either casually or otherwise. At this time of year, she had her hands full dealing with her harrowing guilt and grief.

The press liked to speculate why Rebel Daniels loved to

party hard in the weeks leading up to Valentine's Day. She'd deliberately tried to keep that façade of wild child in place. The last thing she wanted was for anyone to dig beneath the surface, find out the truth about what had happened in Chamonix eight years ago. Besides protecting her beloved mother's memory, the guilt she had to live with was monumental enough without having it exposed to prying eyes.

Now that her dreaded birthday was out of the way, her sole focus was the upcoming championship.

Smiling to take the sting out of the refusal, she breathed a sigh of relief when Stan gave a regretful shrug and left.

Rebel slowly turned and stared around the glass-walled office that belonged to her father. Exhaling, she allowed herself to scrutinise the expensive polished-leather chair and mahogany desk, upon which items had been laid out in the meticulous way her father employed. Insides shaking, she approached his desk, her eyes on the single personal item that stood to the right side of it.

The picture, set in a childish pink and green frame, was exactly as she remembered it when she'd given it to her father on his birthday twelve years ago. At thirteen years old, laughing as she rode a tandem bike with her mother in the picture, Rebel had had no idea her family was about to be ripped apart a few short years later. Or that the decimating of her family would be her fault.

She'd had no cares in the world, secure in the love from a father who'd adored his wife and daughter, and a mother who had encouraged Rebel to pursue her dreams, regardless of any obstacles that stood in her way.

It was that relentless pursuit of her dream that had shattered her family. She knew that. And yet, she'd never been able to walk away from her dreams of pursuing a ski-jump championship. Deep in her heart, Rebel knew walking away would be betraying her vivacious and hugely talented mother, who'd never been quite able to achieve a championship win of her own.

Her heart ached as she passed her hand over the picture. Her father had never understood her need to keep chasing her dream. He'd been harsh and critical to the point where they hadn't been able to stay under the same roof without endless vicious rows. But even then, Rebel had never imagined walking away would mean losing her father for this long. She'd never thought his condemnation and lack of forgiveness would be set in stone.

She dropped her hand. She was here now. She was about to undertake the most important challenge of her career. Before that happened, she needed to know whether there was a way to reconcile with her father.

Forcing the nerves down, she looked around, seeking clues as to his whereabouts. His computer was turned off, but his desk calendar was still set at a date two weeks ago. Unease spiked as she recalled Stan's words. Deciding not to read too much into it, she walked to the far side of the vast office, and set her yoga mat and gym bag down. Another half an hour of pacing, and her nerves were screaming that something wasn't quite right. After leaving yet another message on her father's voicemail stating that she wasn't leaving his office until he called her back, she put her phone on the coffee table along with her sweater, and rolled out the yoga mat.

The situation with her father, a bandaged but far from healed wound, had been ripped open by his letter, bringing fresh anguish. That anguish was affecting her concentration, something she could ill afford. Greg, her trainer, had commented on the fact today, hence the addition of yoga to her exercise regime.

She'd made it through the trials to secure herself a position on the championship-seeking team. She couldn't afford to take her eye off the ball now, no matter how unresolved her issues were with her father.

Dropping onto the mat, she plugged her earphones back in, stretched and closed her eyes. Legs crossed in front of her, she took several breaths to centre herself, then began to move through her positions.

The first few tingles she attributed to her body dropping into a state of relaxation. One she welcomed after the turmoil of the past few weeks. But when they persisted, growing with each breath, Rebel rolled her shoulders, mildly irritated and more than a little anxious that she would truly find no avenue of relief until she spoke to her father.

Then the scent hit her nostrils: dark, hypnotic, with traces of citrus and more than a hint of savagery. At first she believed she was dreaming its complexity. But with each breath, the scent wrapped tighter around her senses, pulling her into a vortex of sensation that increased the tingling along her spine.

Slowly lowering herself from downward dog, she lay flat on her stomach and extended her left leg behind her, hoping the taut muscle stretch would dissipate the strange feeling zinging through her body. She repeated the exercise with her right leg, welcoming the burn.

But the distraction wasn't sufficient. Her concentration slipped further.

Gritting her teeth, she sat up and stretched her legs wide, perpendicular to her body. She aligned her torso to one leg, then the other, then leaned forward on her elbows and slowly raised her pelvis off the floor.

The curse was thick and sharp enough to pierce the cocoon of her music.

Rebel's eyes flew open.

Sensation hit her like a charging bull. The air knocked clean from her lungs, Rebel gaped at the imposing man who sat with one leg hitched over the other and his arms crossed over a wide, firm chest.

Steely grey eyes pinned her in position. Not that she would've been able to move had her life depended on it. Frozen on the floor, she could only stare as the most arresting man she'd ever seen uncoiled himself from his sitting position and stood to a towering, dominating height. His navy three-piece suit was sharp and stylish, and drew attention to broad shoulders, a trim waist and strong thighs, but even without those visual aids, his sheer beauty was potent enough to command her attention.

Her muscles strained, lactic acid building in a body that screamed for relief, but Rebel couldn't heed it.

The man advanced, bringing the scent that had so thoroughly shattered her concentration even closer until it fully encompassed her. There was a vague familiarity about him, like a stranger she'd caught a glimpse of a lifetime ago. But the sensation passed as he drew closer.

Her chest tightened, her lungs struggling to work as he crouched down in front of her and jerked the earbuds from her ears. Flinging the wires to the floor, he leaned forward until every inch of her vision was crowded with him.

'You have exactly three seconds to tell me who the hell you are, and why I shouldn't call Security and have you thrown in jail for lewd conduct and trespassing.'

CHAPTER TWO

DRACO ANGELIS WASN'T a man overly prone to emotion or volatile impulses. And yet as he stared at the woman before him he wanted to curse again. Loudly and far more filthily than he had in a long time.

He told himself it was because the floor show she'd been giving his male employees for the last fifteen minutes was losing him money with each second her sinuous body undulated. More than that, she was drawing attention to a matter he wanted to keep under wraps by performing said floor show in Nathan Daniels' office. In a business often accused of being shady and underhanded, Draco had striven to keep Angel International above reproach. He'd succeeded beyond his wildest dreams by keeping all his dealings professional, above board and strictly private. None of his clients were permitted to publicise details of their relationship with his company save for a carefully prepared press release at the time of signing.

Draco kept that same stranglehold on his personal life.

But with the sudden disappearance of Nathan Daniels and the suspected reason behind it, Draco knew it was only a matter of time before the whispers grew to wild speculation and brought unwanted attention to both facets of his life.

And this…siren performing moves fit for a certain type of gentlemen's club right here on his CFO's office floor was the last thing he needed.

As to the pull he'd experienced in his body and especially in his groin as he'd watched her… Well, he could deal with the reminder that he was a full-blooded male.

What he wasn't prepared to deal with was her interrupting his—

'Lewd conduct?' A sultry laugh detonated his thoughts, slamming him back to the room and the sensual vision still frozen in position before him. 'I think that's a bit of a stretch, don't you?'

A thick bead of sweat trickled down her earlobe and over her jaw. He tracked it, unable to drag his gaze away as it rolled over her heated skin to disappear between small but lush breasts. He ruthlessly suppressed the growl that rose in his chest and clenched his jaw.

'You think it's a stretch to perform lasciviously in front of a window to the clear view of everyone in my company?'

Her back bowed as she flexed her hips, a smile curving her full lips. 'I wasn't aware what I was doing was so distracting. Do you mind stepping back?'

'Excuse me?' Irritated surprise held him rigid.

'I'm almost done. If I stop now, I'll have to start all over again. Sorry, I'm a little OCD like that. I need room for the last two positions, so if you don't mind…?'

Draco was sure it was pure shock that propelled him to his feet, not the secret need to see her complete her set. All the same, he stepped back, his jaw clenched harder as he folded his arms and stared down at the lithe body sprawled at his feet.

She balanced on her elbows, her torso straightened. Slim muscled legs slowly lifted off the floor, maintaining the perpendicular position for several seconds, before meeting in the middle in a sleek upside-down formation. Draco watched her stomach muscles delicately vibrate as she centred herself, her skin bathed in a sheen of sweat as her toned body achieved the perfect line.

As a former athlete himself, Draco appreciated the discipline it took to hone one's body into the ultimate competitive instrument. And while part of him approved of the

level of skill being displayed before him, the greater part
was eyeing the delicate, muscled perfection of her body.

And detesting himself for it.

Whoever this woman was, she had no right to be here.

About to step forward and end this nonsense, he halted
mid-step as she dropped one leg to the floor behind her.
The sexy agility in her body arrested him, drying out every
flaying word he'd meant to deliver as he stared.

Thee mou.

Anyone would think he hadn't seen a female body before. He'd dated sportswomen at the peak of their careers
and slept with more than his share of them. And yet something about this woman drew him as no other had done in
a very long time.

That thought sent another bolt of anger through him.
Rousing himself, he stepped forward, just as she lowered
her other leg and straightened.

She wasn't very tall, only coming up to his chest. But
her deep blue eyes sparked with a fire and attitude that
made her appear six feet tall. Her chin, pointed and determined, and her mouth, still curved in that sultry, albeit
slightly wary smile, made him think thoughts that had no
room in this space.

'Now, where were we?' she asked, her voice reminding
him of smoky rooms in gentlemen's clubs.

Draco dragged his mind from images of unwanted decadence to a far more appropriate ire. 'We were addressing
your unsolicited presence in my building.'

'Ah, yes, you wanted to know who I was?'

'I see you've skilfully avoided my trespass charge.'

'That's because I'm not trespassing. I have a right to be
here.'

'I seriously doubt that. Sanctioning half-naked women to
perform acrobatics for my employees as part of their busy
workday isn't part of my business model.'

'We're talking about my supposed floor show, right?'

She glanced behind her. Catching sight of the group of men staring avidly through the glass from a few offices away, she smiled and waved.

A glowering look from Draco sent his employees dispersing, although a brave buck, Stan Macallister, dared to wave back.

Deciding it was time to bring this farce to an end, Draco strode to the desk of his AWOL CFO and snatched up the phone.

'This is Mr Angelis. Send Security up to Daniels' office. I have an unwanted guest who needs to be removed from the premises. And inform my head of security that I want a report on my desk as to why this breach has happened before the day is out.'

He slammed down the phone with more force than was needed.

'Wow, was that really necessary?'

He turned to find her standing in the same position before the window, her hand on her curvy hips and her head tilted to one side. The loose knot of her silky black hair fell lopsided as she stared at him with one eyebrow raised mockingly.

'I have a client meeting in less than half an hour. I'd throw you out myself but I don't have time to take a shower before then.'

Her expression slipped at the thinly veiled insult. Draco felt childish satisfaction at scoring a direct hit. Absurdly, he'd been off balance since he'd seen her from his office next door. His need for transparency in all things had transmitted to his office layout, and with the open-plan setting and see-through glass windows across the floor he could keep an eye on most of his employees. Although he liked to believe it was unnecessary where his employees were concerned as he'd earned their loyalty, he'd learned the hard way that loyalty came at a cost.

The alternative career he'd had to choose was a cutthroat

one at best. He'd made a few hard bargains along the way to get him where he was.

What he hadn't bargained for today was seeing a decadently curvy woman on display on his CFO's floor. He'd stopped an important call mid-conversation, a move he'd never made before. Now he had an irate, egocentric client waiting for him to call back. And a snarky stranger openly mocking him.

'I hope you don't feel too silly when you find out who I am,' she said in that voice that snagged his senses, made him strain to hear her every word.

'I'm not interested in who you are. My security will furnish me with that information if I need it. What I am interested in is you being escorted off the premises—'

'Okay, this is getting ridiculous. My name is Rebel Daniels, Nathan Daniels' daughter. I'm here to have lunch with my father. I forgot to sign in downstairs so Stan let me in. My dad wasn't here. I assumed he was in a meeting or something, so I thought I'd wait for him. The yoga thing was just to relieve a little bit of stress.'

Several questions stormed through Draco's mind. Was his security so lax that someone could just *forget* to make themselves known downstairs and still make it up here? She was Daniels' daughter? Why was she stressed?

'Your parents named you *Rebel*?' Mildly disconcerted at the least relevant question that had chosen to fall from his lips, he watched a smile twitch at the corners of her mouth.

'Hardly, although my mother did wonder why she hadn't thought of that when I started using it at fifteen.'

Draco waited, wondering at the shadow that crossed her face a moment later. When she continued to stare at him, he pursed his lips. 'So your *real* name is?'

'I thought you weren't interested.' She turned and bent over to pick up her yoga mat.

He forced his gaze from her delectable behind to her bare feet, then away from her altogether when he realised he was even growing fascinated with her peach-painted toenails. 'I'm only interested in you if it helps me locate your father.'

Her head jerked up, the rolled mat held against her body as she frowned at him. 'What do you mean locate him? Isn't he here?'

'Did you have any reason to think he would be?' he countered.

'Of course I did. Why else would I have come here?'

Draco spotted two burly men rushing towards the office. His head of security looked extremely nervous. As he should be. He held up his hand when they reached the door. 'When did you last speak to your father?'

Her gaze darted from the men back to him, a tiny flash of nervousness darkening her eyes. 'Why, what does it matter?'

'Because I would very much like to speak to him too.'

Her eyes widened, again a minuscule motion that he otherwise would've missed had he not been watching her closely. 'So he's not here?' she pressed.

'I think we've established that, Miss Daniels. Now are you going to answer me, or shall I hand you over to them?' He jerked his head at the security men.

She frowned. 'What exactly is going on here? If my father's not here and you want me to leave, I will. There's no need to throw your weight about. And I certainly don't need to be escorted out.'

'But you were in here on your own for over fifteen minutes. Who knows what information you've made yourself privy to?'

'Are you accusing me of *stealing* something?' she snapped.

'Did you?'

'Of course not!'

'I'll leave them to be the judge of that. I'm sure you'll be released in a few hours once the security footage has been analysed, your belongings searched, and your alleged innocence confirmed.' Draco motioned for his men to enter.

His head of security entered, followed by his assistant. Draco ignored their contrite expressions. 'Take Miss Daniels' bag—'

'You can't be serious!'

'And the yoga mat. Make sure she's not in possession of anything that doesn't belong to her—'

'Okay, fine. I'll answer your damn questions.'

The men paused.

Draco shook his head. 'Take them. Leave her shoes. I'll let you know when I'm finished with her.'

She sent him a look filled with pure vitriol and her fingers clenched around the yoga mat as the younger guard stepped towards her. Eyes flashing blue fire, she released her hold on it, slipped her feet into her knee-high boots and propped her hands on her hips.

'Shall we get this ludicrous inquisition over with?'

Sparks virtually flew off her. In another time, Draco would've enjoyed stoking that fire just to see how high her conflagration burned. It'd been far too long since any emotion besides bitterness, guilt and the rigid control he'd put in place ruled his life. Anything beyond that was a luxury he could ill afford.

It was the same control that dictated he take hold of this situation before it blew up in his face. He'd allowed his suspicions about Nathan Daniels to go unquestioned for far too long as it was.

He straightened. 'Come with me.'

'Where are we going?' the question was snapped back immediately.

'My office.'

'Uh…sir?'

He turned to his security chief.

'We need the lady's full name in order to log her into the system.'

Draco raised an eyebrow at her.

Her mouth pursed, bringing his reluctant attention back to her plump lips.

'It's…my name is Arabella Daniels,' she muttered reluctantly.

It took less than a second for Draco to place her. Arabella Daniels had once been a promising cross-country skier until she'd abruptly changed disciplines to become a ski jumper. Although she'd remained in the top ten for the last few years, the twenty-five-year-old woman had never risen above fifth in competitions. Probably due to her off-piste antics.

His mild shock subsided into a heavy dose of distaste, but he kept his expression neutral as he dismissed his men and strode to his office.

He waited until she entered, then activated the privacy setting on his windows. Once the glass was frosted, he perched at the edge of his desk and watched her pace warily in front of him. The burn in his groin as he followed her lissom figure made him kick out a chair.

'Sit down.'

'No, thanks. I thought you had an important meeting? Or was that just a fib rolled up as an insult?'

'It wasn't a lie. But the party concerned will understand. I tend to surround myself with reasonable, rational individuals.'

She paused in her pacing, her eyes narrowing. 'Is that supposed to be some sort of dig?'

'I know who you are, Miss Daniels.'

'Well, since I told you my name, I should hope so. I wouldn't like to think you were thick or anything, seeing as you seem to be the head honcho in this glass playhouse.'

'So the rumours are true.'

'What rumours?' she asked, her expression growing more wary.

'You take pride in being deliberately offensive and exhibiting wild behaviour.'

'And you don't seem to like being told things the way

they are. In fact your actions reek of more than a touch of melodrama. Why is that? Are you overcompensating for something?' Her gaze conducted what started off as a mocking perusal. But a trace of heat flared up her cheeks when her eyes dropped below his belt.

When her gaze darted away, Draco allowed himself a stiff smile. 'I've never needed to overcompensate for anything in my life, Miss Daniels. If I had time to waste and felt so inclined, I'd give you a demonstration.'

'You assume that *I* have the time to stand around listening to your rubbish. Keep your veiled threats, ask me what you want to know and let us both get on with our lives.'

'You seem a little off balance. Is it because you feel out of your depth?' he drawled.

She jerked the hair band from her hair. Thick, silky jet waves fell over her shoulders and down her back before she started combing her fingers through the tresses.

'Why would I feel like that? Just because you're being disgustingly unreasonable—'

'Or is it because you don't find me as gullible as you do the men you like to associate with?'

'I don't know what you think you know about me, but if these absurd questions are why you brought me in here—'

'You like to dominate your men, do you not?'

She tossed her head. 'Only when they beg me to. Do you want me to dominate you? I'm fresh out of horse whips but I'm sure I can get inventive with a pair of boot laces.'

His gaze dropped to her knee-high boots. 'I'm sure you can, in the right circumstances, but I'll pass.'

She wrinkled her nose and Draco's temperature rose, along with his irritation. 'Why? Because you always wait for the right circumstances? How boring. Giving in to your impulses might just surprise you.'

Draco bared his teeth in a smile that had been described by the tabloids as his dragon smile. He knew its effect well enough to know it'd made its mark when her agitation escalated.

'I find that people like you easily confuse the reckless with the impulsive. Personally, I find the wait builds the anticipation.'

Her gaze held his for one bold heartbeat, then she glanced away. Although she engrossed herself in his office decor, Draco was certain she wasn't as bored with him as she pretended to be. The colour in her cheeks was more pronounced and the pulse beating at her throat had increased. His own blood thickened as he followed her figure. He assured himself, now he knew who she truly was, this mild fascination with her would swiftly abate.

'Well, as interesting as this all is, I'm one hundred per cent sure you know very little about me. And I have to insist you either get on with your ever-so-important questioning, or tell your guards to return my things.'

'You're attempting to compete in the Verbier Ski Championships this year. Shouldn't you be training instead of making an exhibition of yourself and taking extended lunches?'

She inhaled sharply and turned towards him, all pretence at being bored vanishing from her expression. 'You know who I am?'

'I make it my business to know people like you.'

'What do you mean, people like me?'

'Reckless athletes, who try to buy their way into the big leagues.'

She stalked to where he leaned against his desk, her whole body bristling with anger. 'How dare you? That's a ridiculous and totally unfounded allegation.'

'I know enough. The rest I don't intend to bother myself with.'

Her hands clenched. 'Just who the hell do you think you are?'

'I'm the man who intends to make sure all the sponsors

you've been chasing the last month drop you from their books. People like you paint talented and dedicated sportsmen and women in a bad light, not to mention your reckless behaviour on and off the ski slopes needs to be stopped once and for all. You have three measly sponsors left, who probably, mistakenly, think your notoriety will bring their products the attention they crave. Perhaps I'll let you keep them.'

Her eyes had been widening with each condemnation. Slowly, shock replaced her anger. And this time, when she looked around at the trophies and pictures that decorated his office, her interest was genuine.

Draco knew the moment the penny dropped.

Her lustrous hair flew as she whirled back to him. 'You're Draco, the super-agent.'

'I'm Draco Angelis, yes.'

She swallowed. 'You represent Rex Glow.'

'Your former sponsors? Yes.'

She inhaled sharply, but the next question wasn't what Draco had expected it to be. 'And my father *works* for you?'

'You're surprised by that.'

A frown clamped her brows. 'Well…yes, to be honest.'

'Why?' he fired back, his need to probe the reason behind Nathan Daniels' disappearance returning.

'Because…' She hesitated, a trace of pained bleakness flitting over her features. 'Let's just say the world of competitive sports isn't his first love.'

He folded his arms, alarm bells clanging loudly. 'Well, he was my chief financial officer up until two weeks ago, when he seemed to fall off the face of the earth.'

'And you're looking for him because…?'

'There's a small matter of a half a million pounds that seems to have evaporated from my company's accounts. I would very much like to speak to him about that,' Draco replied, his eyes narrowing at the mixture of guilt and trepidation that froze on her face.

CHAPTER THREE

REBEL KNEW SHE'D given herself away a split second before Draco straightened to his imposing six-foot-plus height and took the single step that brought him to within a whisper of where she stood. His broad shoulders and the cloak of power draped around him eclipsed her every thought and action. But even without them, the expression on his face as he stared down at her dried the words that rose to her lips.

This man was responsible for Rex Glow dropping her. While a significant part of her was enraged by the blatant admission, the greater part of her was shocked by the other information he'd imparted.

He was her father's boss. A father who, for all intents and purposes, had disappeared. Along with the uncomfortably *exact* amount of money that had landed in her bank account. The shock of it rendered her attempt to keep a neutral expression hopelessly futile.

'Tell me where your father is,' he pressed.

In that moment, Rebel understood why this man was named The Dragon. His steely grey eyes were cold and deadly enough to freeze the Sahara. And yet his nostrils flared with white-hot anger that promised volatile, annihilating fire.

'I…I don't know where he is.'

Black eyebrows clamped darker. 'You expect me to believe that?'

'You can believe what you want. It's the truth.'

'You admitted to having been in touch with him lately. And you came here to meet him, did you not?'

'We spoke briefly on the phone a couple of days ago. Lunch was mentioned, and I thought I'd surprise him today...' She trailed off, unwilling to elaborate that she'd done most of the talking, while her father had remained stonily monosyllabic. Rebel struggled to hide the hurt that lanced her heart from knowing her father would've probably rejected any firm plans had he known she'd intended to come here today.

'I urge you to come clean now, Miss Daniels, before things get worse for you and your father,' Draco Angelis threatened.

The first tendrils of fear clawed up her spine. 'If you must know, we didn't make any firm plans. It was a spur-of-the-moment decision to stop by and see if he was free for lunch. I haven't seen him in a while and I thought—'

'How long is *a while*?'

'That's between my father and me, and none of your business.'

Firm, sinfully sensual lips pursed. 'You don't think my CFO's sudden disappearance and you turning up unannounced in my building is any of my business?'

'So he's taken a brief vacation. So what?' she speculated wildly, her unease growing as suspicion mounted in Draco's eyes.

'Considering he hasn't taken one in the five years he's worked for me, you'll pardon me if I find his sudden need for one, without speaking to me first, more than a little suspect. Besides, we have a procedure for absences. My employees don't make a habit of just not turning up to work when the mood takes them.'

'Because that would guarantee them an on-the-spot sacking?'

'Perhaps not on the spot. I would demand an explanation first before the sacking ensued.'

Rebel forced an eye roll, which was far from the nonchalance she tried to project. 'So you're not just a dragon to work for, you're an ogre as well? Congratulations.'

Sharp grey eyes, surrounded by the most lush eyelashes

she'd ever seen on a man, lasered her. 'You find this subject amusing?'

Anger surged through her. 'About as amusing as discovering that you seem to have a personal vendetta against me when we've never even met before.'

His face tightened, his expression growing even more formidable. 'We didn't need to meet before I knew exactly what sort of person you are. Your antics in the last half an hour have only confirmed it.'

'Really? Would you care to share it with me or should I take a few wild guesses?'

'You've barely scraped through into ski finals for the last few years because your work ethic is average at best. You're more concerned with headlining in the tabloids with your extracurricular activities than putting in the hard work to secure yourself a position in the championships.'

She swallowed hard before her temper got the better of her. 'I'll have you know I was an under-twenty-one record holder for two years.'

'But you haven't placed higher than fifth in the last six years. Your position in the rankings has fallen in direct proportion to the rise of your notoriety. It doesn't take a maths genius to work out where your true interests lie. Which is why I wonder why you even bother.'

Anger gave way to bewildered hurt, but Rebel locked in her emotions, determined not to show him how his words affected her. 'I'm still at a loss as to how all of this or anything in my *private* life concerns you.'

'If it concerns my client, it concerns me. Besides, it's only a matter of time before your reckless actions have a direct impact on another athlete,' he retorted pithily, his gaze boring harder into her, condemnation stamped in every pore.

Draco Angelis' reaction was too strong for Rebel to believe his motivation stemmed from concern for his client alone. But she was too busy struggling not to react to the accusation of recklessness to pay it much heed.

The only thing Rebel wanted was to leave his office and his oppressive presence. She needed the head space to ponder exactly what her father was up to. And whether the money he'd sent her was indeed embezzled funds as her every instinct shrieked it was. The enormity of what that would mean struck cold dread inside her.

'I think we're done here, Mr Angelis. Rex Glow is no longer my sponsor, so I don't have to listen to you or your groundless accusations about my life. If you choose to believe whatever nonsense you read in the papers, then that's your problem, not mine.'

He made no move to stop her as she headed for the door. She knew why the moment she tried to pull it open and found it unyielding.

'Open this door now.'

Cold steel eyes pinned her in place. 'I'm not finished with you.'

'But I am with you,' she replied, a vein of panic rising in her belly. She rattled the door harder, but the reinforced glass didn't budge an inch.

'You can leave once you tell me where your father is hiding.'

She whirled at the hard demand. He was less than a foot from her, his stance even more imposing than before. His scent attacked her senses a second later, once again cutting a dangerous swathe through her thought processes.

The man wasn't just a dangerous dragon. He was a precariously beautiful creature, his face and body an alluring, breathtaking combination designed to trap helpless prey.

Not that she was one!

'Do you jump to conclusions about every single subject or are my father and I being singled out for special treatment?'

'You think I want my company exposed to the fact that my CFO has embezzled from me?'

Renewed panic gripped her insides. 'Where's your proof that he has?'

'The evidence isn't concrete yet, but what I've found so far doesn't look good. It's only a matter of time before we trace where the funds ended up. His not answering my calls or emails doesn't exactly look promising.'

'What…what would you tell him if he answered?'

Draco's narrowed eyes scoured her face. 'He's served me well for five years. I'd be prepared to listen to his explanations.'

'Before throwing the book at him?'

'You think I should let him go scot-free if he's guilty?'

Her heart lurched. 'Since we haven't established that he's done anything wrong, I think this is a moot point.'

'Sadly, your poker face isn't as flawless as you think. You know where he is. Tell me now and I'll consider not pressing full charges.'

'I don't know where he is. I swear,' Rebel answered.

Draco took the last step that separated them and grabbed her bare arm. The hand still clutching the door handle dropped as raw electricity raced across her skin. Intense tingling tightened her every cell, straining towards the point of contact with a severity that stole her breath. Her lips parted as she fought to get air into her lungs.

Above her, Draco inhaled sharply. The expression on his face reflected her bewilderment for a second before the cold façade slid back into place.

'You may not know where he is, but you know something. I suggest you come clean now.' He repeated his earlier threat.

Rebel shook her head. If her father had truly embezzled the money he'd deposited in her account from the Angel International Group, there was no way she could get it back. And right now, Rebel couldn't be sure which was worse—confessing her suspicion of her father's guilt, or informing Draco Angelis that she had used the funds to secure her place in the Verbier tournament. From Draco's censorious reaction to her as an athlete, Rebel knew he wouldn't hesitate to condemn her as an accessory to the crime and have her thrown in jail.

'Arabella, this is your last chance.'

The sound of her name on his lips sent shafts of disconcerting fire through her belly. The sensation was so powerful it weakened her knees, and the secret place between her legs was dampening with each second his hand remained on her.

God, what was wrong with her? She'd heard her girlfriends confess to growing wobbly at the knees when some hot guy glanced their way at a nightclub. She'd secretly rolled her eyes at that implausible statement, knowing she'd never be one of those women. The shocking sensation ramming through her right now filled her with horror and more than a touch of anger.

She parted her lips, but Draco shook his head, his other hand rising to clamp her other arm.

'Think carefully before you speak.'

She pulled in a deep, sustaining breath. 'No,' she stated firmly.

'Just so we're clear, to what exactly are you saying no?' he breathed softly, dangerously.

Rebel ignored the warm breath washing over her face and raised her chin. 'To answering any more of your stupid accusations. To being kept prisoner in this office. To you having your hands on me. No to everything. Now, let me go before I scream this place down.'

'Scream all you want. This room is soundproof.'

'How very convenient. Do you do this a lot, then?' she taunted.

'Do what?' he sliced at her.

'Drag women in here and hold them against their will?'

A muted curse in a language she didn't understand

spilled from his lips. 'No woman has been in here who didn't want to be.'

The images his words conjured up jarred her into squirming before she forced her muscles to lock tight. 'So you admit to seducing women in your office during the workday?'

A chilled smile parted his lips. 'You assume that I do the seducing.'

'So women not only stage floor shows in your offices, they also seduce you behind closed doors into the bargain. Your poor thing. How on earth do you get any work done?'

'You have a reckless, smart mouth, Arabella.'

Another zing went through her, but she fought it tooth and nail. 'Along with a smart brain. So if you think anything's going to happen here other than me walking out the door in the next minute, think again.'

'You set too high a premium on yourself, I think.'

'Ah, so if I were to strip right here right now, you'd turn me down?'

'You won't. You like to pretend otherwise, but I'm willing to bet, deep down, you're less Lady Chatterley and more Miss Prude.'

The droll observation brought heat to her cheeks. Dear God, he was making her blush *again*?

'Well, sadly for you, you'll never find out.'

'I will. If I wish it, you'll get your chance to strip for me in the very near future. At a time and place of my choosing when I know we won't be interrupted in any way.'

'Wow, you must tell me where you acquired your crystal balls. I'm running out of ideas for Christmas presents.'

Dear Lord. Was she truly standing in front of him, discussing his balls?

He freed one arm. Rebel was about to exhale with relief, but her breathing stuttered as he curled his long fingers over her nape and tilted her chin with his thumb. She'd never imagined the skin along her jaw was sensitive until experiencing Draco Angelis' branding touch. Now every nerve in her body screeched as her heart raced and her blood heated.

His head lowered a fraction and his gaze dropped to her lips. He was about to kiss her. And she couldn't move.

Rebel grew frantically aware of every desperate breath that passed between her lips, her own gaze unable to shift from the mouth drawing ever closer to hers.

'I don't need crystal balls. My human ones are more than adequate to deal with challenges from the opposite sex. But we're straying from the subject. Tell me what you know, Arabella.' Again that smile peeled back a layer of her skin and exposed her to sensations as alien as a distant galaxy.

'For the last time, take your hands off me. I don't know where my father—'

The buzz of an intercom from his desk froze her words. Draco tensed, the flex of his jaw exhibiting his displeasure at the interruption.

'Mr Angelis, I'm so sorry to disturb you, but I have Olivio Nardozzi on the line again. He refuses to leave a message or be put on hold. He says you promised to call him back fifteen minutes ago.'

He raised his head, but he didn't let her go. Nor did his gaze move from her lips as he answered, 'Tell Olivio I'll speak to him in two minutes. Tell him he can either hold or wait for my call.'

'Yes, Mr Angelis.'

The intercom clicked and silence once more engulfed them. Draco didn't seem in a hurry to speak, or do anything but hold her prisoner.

Rebel knew she had to move, but for the life of her she couldn't get her legs to work. So she employed her best defence. 'Another one of your angelic, perfectly reasonable, *high-maintenance* clients?' she mocked.

With a slow, deliberate movement, his thumb rose from her chin to pass lazily over her lower lip. 'There will come a time when this delectable mouth will get you into trouble you won't be able to escape from,' he drawled in a low, dark voice that resonated deep within her.

'Tick tock, Mr Angelis.'

His grip firmed, the fire branding her deeper. Then he released her with an abrupt move that spoke of barely leashed emotion. Before she could escape, he caged her in by placing his hands on the glass door either side of her.

'You have until six o'clock tonight to tell me what you know about my money. Trust me, you don't want me to come after you.'

She wanted to dare him to do his worst, but Rebel bit her tongue. Draco Angelis had already demonstrated that he had the power to strip her sponsors from her with nothing more than a hatred of her vivacity. Sure, she'd taken a few risks on the ski slope that had earned her a name in the sport. But they'd all been carefully calculated and had taken into account the injury she'd sustained when she was twenty-two. Without those risks, she'd have fallen even further down the rankings and lost all her sponsorship long before now.

As much as she wanted to tell Draco to take a running jump, if she wanted to get to the bottom of her father's actions, or have a last chance at securing the Verbier championship and laying a few ghosts to rest, she needed to retreat and regroup.

A tug on her Lycra training bottoms drew her thoughts away from her mother and her errant father. She gasped as Draco slid a business card into her waistband. The backs of his fingers brushed her skin and her muscles jumped at the contact.

Before she could form an effective comeback to his audacious action he stepped back. A moment later the frosty glass cleared and a click released the door.

'I assume I'm free to go now?'

He lifted the phone and punched in a series of numbers. 'Provided you're not held by my security, then yes, you may leave. But we both know you're guilty of something, Arabella. Make the wise choice and use my private number. I guarantee you won't like the consequences if you don't.' He sat down behind his desk. The infinitesimal twitch of his chair away from her was as definitive a dismissal as any as he spoke into the phone, 'Olivio, my apologies for keeping you waiting. I hope you're chomping at the bit to speak to me because you've given further consideration to my offer?' His voice rang with charming familiarity, not at all like the ire he'd demonstrated towards her.

Rebel could barely recall stumbling from Draco's office and summoning the lift that raced her back down to the ground floor. She assumed she was free to leave when the Angel head of security met her on the ground floor with her belongings. Thankful that she wouldn't be required to answer any more questions, Rebel took her bag and yoga mat and hurried out into the weak February sunshine.

The light breeze that whispered over her skin brought a little clarity, but her senses were too focused on the card burning against her skin, and the grave certainty that the money she'd used to secure her place in the Verbier tournament was indeed money stolen from a man who seemed to have the lowest, blackest opinion of her, to feel the cold.

Plucking the card out of her waistband, she stared at the black and gold inscription and the private number etched into it.

Rebel wanted to rip it into a dozen pieces and scatter them to the four winds. But deep in her heart she recognised the foolhardiness of doing so.

She might not understand why her father had chosen to help himself to money that didn't belong to him and then pass it on to her. Their last few rows had been awful enough for her to imagine he was done with her as long as she chose to keep competing. For him to have followed her career closely enough to know when she needed help at once lifted her heart and plunged it into despair. Not in a million years would she have wanted him to help in this way.

Jerkily, she searched for her phone and dialled as she hurried away from Draco's building. The moment the line connected, she rushed to speak. 'Contessa, have the cheques we paid out to the tournament organisers cleared?'

Her manager snorted. 'Well, hello to you too. And the answer to your question is yes, the cheques cleared this morning, so did the money we paid for your travel, accommodation and equipment. We only need an extra fifteen thousand for incidentals, but I'm sure your remaining sponsors will front you that. I was going to pop round to your flat tonight with a bottle of champagne to celebrate. I know you don't like to drink during training, but I thought a sip or two wouldn't hurt...' Her voice trailed off for a moment. 'Rebel? Is something wrong?'

Rebel exhaled shakily, her vision hazing as she fought panic. 'And there's no way we can get any of it back?'

'*Get it back?* Why would we want to do that?' her manager demanded, her voice rising.

'I...I just...it doesn't matter.'

'Obviously it does. Tell me what's happened.'

Unwilling to drag Contessa into her problems until she confirmed the depth of the trouble she was in, she forced lightness into her voice. 'Ignore me. Just last-minute nerves. You can come over, but can we give the champagne a miss, though?'

'Of course...are you sure you're okay?' the older woman pressed.

'I'm sure. Talk to you later.'

She hung up and immediately dialled her father's number, already suspecting it wouldn't go through. When the mechanical voice urged her to leave a message, Rebel cleared her throat. 'Dad, it's me...again.' She paused, a new fear chilling her heart. Draco Angelis wasn't above having her father's phone traced. Until she got answers for herself, Rebel didn't want to lead the man who made her spine tingle with dread and other unwanted emotions straight to her father. 'Call me. Please. I need to talk to you.'

Feeling helpless for the first time in a very long time, she hung up. Plugging her earphones in, she ramped up the volume and hurried to the Tube, all the while willing her focus away from the card she'd tucked back into her waist-band, hoping against hope she wouldn't be forced to use it.

CHAPTER FOUR

DRACO READ THE bullet points in the report for the second time and closed the file. He spared a thought as to why his CFO hadn't bothered to cover his tracks, then dismissed the useless thought. The *why* didn't matter.

The inescapable fact was that a crime had been committed. By Daniels and his daughter.

Draco didn't doubt for a second that she was neck deep in this theft. Her guilt had been written all over her face, despite her trying hard to hide it. Her racing pulse had condemned her just as definitely, no matter how much her smart mouth had tried to distract him.

A muscle ticced in his jaw as he remembered the velvet softness of that mouth…the smoothness of her skin. Arabella Daniels didn't use just her mouth to distract. She used her whole body. The need to remind *his* body hours later of that potent tactic irritated Draco as his car raced through the wet, lamplit streets towards the Chelsea address his investigators had supplied him with.

Another bout of irritation welled inside him.

He'd known Arabella wouldn't honour the deadline he'd given her. Six o'clock had come and gone three hours ago, and, despite the conclusive, almost cynical evidence of theft he held in his hands, the daughter of his CFO had remained silent.

Closing the electronic file, he opened a thick manila envelope that held a completely different set of problems. While Draco was satisfied that months of hard work were poised on the edge of finally reaping rewards, he couldn't believe the seemingly inescapable strings Olivio Nardozzi had attached to the contract in his hand.

But he hadn't come this far to lose.

Carla Nardozzi, champion figure skater, number one in the world, was a prize every sports agent wanted. Hard-working, charismatic, almost virginally shy, she would be the jewel in his agency's crown…if her father weren't leveraging an unthinkable condition to signing his daughter with the Angel International Group—

'Sir, we're here,' his driver interrupted his thoughts.

Draco alighted from the car and stared at the two-storey Victorian façade. While he hadn't been surprised Arabella lived in Chelsea, he'd expected her to inhabit a glitzy condominium, not a homey dwelling on a leafy suburban street. Mounting the shallow steps to the door, he pressed her intercom.

The door released half a minute later. Draco told himself he didn't care if she didn't bother about her security, but by the time he arrived in front of an open doorway on the first floor irritation had given way to anger.

Loud music pumped from what seemed like a hundred speakers, although he couldn't immediately see them as he went down a short hallway and arrived in a sizeable living room painted snow-white, and decorated with splashes of purple and pink.

He didn't have time to be offended by the jarring decor because he was once again confronted by a scantily clad Arabella Daniels, who didn't bother to look up as he walked into the room.

Draco dragged his gaze from her cross-legged figure enough to take in the fact that she was packing for a long trip. Escaping with the proceeds of her ill-gotten gains, perhaps?

He gritted his jaw and waited.

A moment later her head snapped up. Blue eyes met his, widened, before her mouth dropped open. 'You're not Contessa,' she shouted above the pumping rock music.

'No, I am not.'

Her eyes darted from him to the darkened hallway and back again. She set aside the sleek, specialist, lightweight skis that Draco knew cost several thousand pounds, and rose lithely to her feet. 'You…I wasn't expecting…what are you doing here?'

'Do you always answer your door without checking to see who you're letting in?' he bit out.

She shrugged. 'I thought you were Contessa, my manager. She's the only one who knows where—' She stopped and waved her hand. 'Let's get back to *my* question. What are *you* doing here?'

'If you insist on playing this game, I'll give you one guess, *after* you turn that racket off.'

Her pointed chin tilted and she folded her bare arms. 'No. If you don't like my taste in music, feel free to reuse the front door.'

Stopping his gaze from conducting a full scrutiny of her body, clad in vest top and hot pants, Draco stalked to the entertainment system set on top of an artsy-looking vanity unit and stabbed the off button.

'Hey, you can't do that!'

He turned and faced her, willing himself not to react to the mingled scent of peach shampoo and delicate perfume that infused his senses now his eardrums weren't being shredded.

'Did you forget the time, Arabella? I'm willing to give you the benefit of the doubt on the off-chance that my deadline escaped your notice because you don't possess a watch?'

Her frowning gaze slid from the silent music system to his face. Her arms tightened and her stare grew bolder. 'I have a watch. Several, in fact. I know exactly what the time is.'

The cold blaze of anger chilled his insides. He welcomed it far more than he welcomed the lick of fire that had flamed in his groin at the sight of her bare, shapely legs. 'I can only conclude, then, that you thought my last words to you were a joke?'

She made a humming, almost accommodating sound under her breath. 'Not quite. You don't seem the joking type. I don't imagine you'd appreciate a joke if it reared up and bit you hard.'

'So that's how you live your life? On the edge of reckless jokes?'

She shrugged. 'You know what they say…if you're not living on the edge, you're taking up too much room.'

The urge to grab her, drag her close, just as he'd done in his office, assailed him. He stabbed his hands deep into his pockets to curb the impulse. Arabella Daniels took pleasure in flaunting her risqué behaviour. Draco wasn't here to be riled. He was here to do the riling. To let her know she wouldn't be getting away with stealing from him.

'But if you insist on a definition,' she continued, 'I'd say I considered your words more of a suggestion…perhaps an invitation? As you can see, I opted to reject both.'

Draco drew in a breath, unable to accept that anyone could have so very little self-preservation. Back in his office, he'd considered her careless attitude a front, but now he wasn't so sure. But then why was he surprised? He knew first-hand the sort of person he was dealing with. Wasn't such a creature the same one responsible for reducing his sister's dreams to dust? He'd trusted his precious Maria's well-being and burgeoning talent to someone he'd thought would treasure and harness them. Instead, his sister's life had been irrevocably destroyed.

The rock of guilt and bitterness that resided in his gut pressed hard and punishing. He'd taken his eye off the ball, relentlessly pursued his own dreams, and his sister had suffered for it. Continued to suffer for it. Draco absorbed the expanding pain he'd become used to bearing. He was grateful for it, in fact. The reminder of the past was as timely as it was bracing.

He looked past her to the suitcases, clothing and equipment strewn on the living-room floor. 'Going somewhere?'

'Yes, as a matter of fact,' she replied. 'And you're interrupting my packing, so...'

Draco sauntered forward, his gaze narrowing on the two skis already wrapped in protective binding and the third one that she'd been wrapping when he walked in. 'Your equipment looks new. Expensive. Have you come into a windfall perhaps?' he enquired.

She tensed. 'It's none of your—'

He slashed his hand through the air. 'Enough. I have irrefutable evidence that every single penny your father misappropriated ended up in *your* bank account. Whatever his motives were for taking the money, he didn't seem inclined to cover his tracks. I've already given you enough time to come clean, but it looks like you prefer to wallow in lies and snarky banter. My time is valuable, Miss Daniels. I refuse to waste any more discussing your guilt. Now, are you prepared to take this seriously or shall I cut my losses and let you explain to the authorities how you came to be in possession of half a million pounds belonging to me?' He took his phone out of his pocket and gripped it, fingers poised over the buttons.

Her arms dropped from their belligerent position. As he'd spoken she'd grown paler, but there was still more than enough fight in her eyes for Draco not to be under the misconception that she'd seen the light of true contrition. 'I wasn't lying. I don't know where my father is, and I didn't have anything to do with the taking of the money.' Her brows clouded. 'Are you sure this isn't just some misunderstanding?'

He bared his teeth, cold amusement making him shake his head. 'I'm not in the habit of *misunderstanding* the whereabouts of my company's funds.'

She paled further. 'I told you, I don't know where my father is.'

'Have you tried calling him?' he fired back.

'Several times.' Her fingers spiked into her loose hair, and for the first time Draco witnessed her undiluted distress. Satisfaction lanced through him. He was finally getting through to her. Herding her into a position where she couldn't fail to see that he wouldn't be swayed from seeking restitution. 'He hasn't answered my calls.' The tiny note of bewilderment in her voice suggested she wasn't lying.

'Be that as it may, the funds ended up in your bank account.'

Her full lips firmed for several moments before she nodded. 'Yes.'

He exhaled. 'So, are you willing to answer my questions now?'

She nodded again.

'The championships don't start for several weeks. The training grounds in Verbier won't be open for another month. So where were you going?'

'I have a friend with a chalet in Chamonix. I was going to stay there while I train.'

'You mean you were fleeing the country with your ill-gotten gains?' he sneered. 'Perhaps meet up with your father and celebrate getting one over on me?'

She flinched. 'No.'

'Just…no? You're not going elaborate?'

'What more is there to say? You say you have evidence that the money ended up in my account. Will you believe me if I say I didn't know it was coming in the first place? That when it arrived I tried to return it?'

He lifted a brow before staring at the expensive items on the floor. 'Really?'

'Look, I know what you're thinking—'

'I seriously doubt that. Picking up the phone and instructing your bank to return the funds was too much effort, but spending it wasn't?'

'I didn't spend it. Not immediately.'

He placed the phone back in his pocket and stared at her until her gaze dropped. 'I'm sure you're going to explain that.'

'The money arrived after Rex Glow and the rest of my sponsors started dropping like flies, thanks to you, I'm guessing.' Her white-hot glare threatened to thaw the edges of his icy anger. 'My father must have realised what you were doing…' she paused…but it was already too late.

'So you're saying your father not only took my money, he also breached my company's confidential secrets?' He couldn't stop the growl that accompanied the question.

'No! I don't know.'

'You keep saying that, and yet all signs point to you hiding something.'

Her mouth worked for several seconds, before she blew out a breath. 'Fine, if you must know, I hadn't spoken to my father in years before I heard from him two weeks ago.'

He tensed. 'Why not?'

'*That* is definitely none of your business,' she snapped, her fingers spearing into her hair again and tossing the heavy tresses over her shoulder. 'But I did try to find out about the money the few times we spoke afterwards. He assured me there were no strings attached. That it was mine to use. And when a few more sponsors dropped me…'

'You went ahead and used it, without a single thought as to its true source?'

'You might automatically suspect everyone you meet to have nefarious motives, but the father I knew before we… lost touch was hard-working and *honest*. I don't know what you did for him to—'

'Excuse me?' Her audacity stunned him. 'Are you trying to wheedle your way into somehow blaming me for this?'

'My father isn't here to account for what's happened, is he?'

'No,' Draco muttered, a daring solution to the conundrum he'd been toying with taking root and firming in his mind. 'He's not. But you are.'

Her eyes widened. 'What's that supposed to mean?'

He stared into the clear depths, unable to pull his gaze away. 'It means the sins of the father will have to be paid for by the daughter. Especially when she's turned out to be a direct beneficiary.'

'Right. Hold that thought for a second.' She turned and walked to the sound system. She toyed with a few buttons before pressing one. About to warn her against restarting the ear-bleeding music when they weren't finished talking, Draco stopped when low, sultry, Middle Eastern fusion music flowed into the room. He stared, his gaze compelled by the sinuous movement of her body as she returned to where he stood. 'I'm afraid I'm not interested in whatever plans you've concocted, Mr Angelis.'

His fists balled harder in his pockets. 'By all means refuse if you feel you're in a position to. I'll bring myself to wait.'

Her mouth curved in a ghost of a smile. 'No need to wait. I have a plan in mind for how you can get your money back.'

Not what he'd been expecting. Or what his new plan entailed. But... 'I'm listening.'

'My manager has received a request for me to star in a reality TV show after the championships are over. I wasn't going to accept, but, since I now have no choice, I'll hand over the proceeds from the gig to you—'

'No.' The word shot out of him with a brevity that rocked him.

She blinked. 'Umm...what?'

'I said no.'

'I heard you. I just don't understand why you'd refuse, seeing as it's my life and I can do what I want with it. Also, I thought all this posturing and threatening was so you'd get your money back?'

'Not in three months' time. And not after you'd whored yourself in front of a camera to repay me.'

She inhaled sharply. 'You did not just say what I think you said.'

'Isn't that what it amounts to? You opening your life to intense scrutiny until every dirty scumbag out there knows what brand of toothpaste you use and what you wear to bed at night?'

'It isn't that type of show—'

'They are all *that type of show*. If you think otherwise, you're naive as well as stupid.'

'And you're an arrogant ass, who's under the illusion he can dictate to me. I don't doubt that you wield a lot of power in the sports world.' She laughed self-mockingly. 'You've already shown you can strip me of my sponsors, although I'm still not completely sure why, but I'm damned if I'm going to give you power over my personal life. You don't agree to my proposal, then fine, have me thrown in jail. Although how that gets you back your money is beyond me.'

Draco looked down at her, a small part of him unwillingly intrigued by her relentless fire. It spoke to a part of his nature that wasn't relevant any longer. These days he harnessed his cold passion to controlling his empire. And to ensuring Maria wanted for nothing. Any other emotion was superfluous.

The reminder of his sister brought him back to reality.

'You're bluffing. People like you love the good life too much to bravely accept a jail term, but before you deny it, tell me, are you willing to risk your father going to prison for his crimes?'

She froze, her eyes widening. 'My father? I thought you said *I* would repay the money?'

'That doesn't absolve him of wrongdoing. My company is being audited at the end of the month. Regardless of who repays the funds after that, the crime will be discovered.'

'But…I can't pay back half a million pounds by then,' she blurted.

'I know,' he replied with more than a drawl of satisfaction.

The shadow he'd glimpsed earlier settled over her face, her eyes darkening as she stared at him. 'You have the power to stop this. If you want to. That's what you've been hinting at all along, isn't it?'

'That depends on whether you're prepared to meet my demands.'

She shook her head. 'If you expect me to pull out of the championship, then the answer's no.'

'You want to compete that badly?'

She bit her bottom lip, then released it. Her mouth trembled slightly before she exhaled. 'Yes.'

Draco wasn't aware his hands had left his pockets until they cupped her shoulders. Delicate bones and soft, silky skin registered along his senses, even as he spoke. 'Are you willing to can the bravado and listen to me for five minutes?'

'If you insist.'

He drew her closer. He told himself it was because he needed her close so she didn't misunderstand what he planned to say to her. 'I insist.'

Her gaze dropped to his mouth for a moment before sliding away. 'Fine. I have training at five in the morning, so if you don't mind, can we just get on with it, Mr Angelis?'

'Draco.'

Her eyes flew back to his. 'What?'

'For what I have in mind, you'll need to start calling me by my first name. Try it.'

'Umm…no—'

He slid a finger beneath her chin to hold her steady. 'Say my name, Arabella.'

Her nose wrinkled. 'I prefer Rebel.'

'I think we've established that what you prefer is low on

my priority list. I will call you Arabella. And you will say my name, without the snark or the attitude.'

'Fine... Draco.'

His fingers tightened. 'Once more, with feeling.'

'This is *truly* absurd... *Draco*.'

The sultry decadence of his name on her lips arrowed straight through his rigid control, reminding him unequivocally that his libido was alive and well. For a hot second, Draco spied himself from the other side of the room, observing the unfolding scene with growing astonishment.

Was he really contemplating this insane course of action?

Then he reminded himself why he was doing this.

For Maria. For the sister he'd let down so severely. For the sister whose eyes filled with pain each time she looked at him, and yet was determined to rise above bitterness. To *forgive*.

Draco hadn't quite mastered that particular technique. Wasn't sure he wanted to. Bitterness and pain were his correct penance for letting his sister down, for ruining a life that had once held so much unbridled potential.

If he could get back even a shadow of joy for his sister, he would do whatever it took.

'Earth to Draco?'

The sinful drawl brought him back to himself. To the room where low decadent music thrummed to a sensual rhythm, and where a reckless siren in hot pants could well be the answer to what he needed.

He really was going crazy...

He jerked as soft fingers grazed his jaw. The touch was gone a second later, but its earthy power streaked fire across his senses.

'If I haven't turned you into a zombie, can you tell me why me calling you by your first name is necessary in this grand plan of yours?'

He stared into her flawless face. With her wide eyes and parted lips, she perfectly emulated innocence. Except he knew she was duplicitous to the core. She was wild, totally remorseless and disturbingly reckless with well-documented antics both in her professional and personal lives.

Those heinous traits would guarantee that he would remain sexually and emotionally detached—not that the latter was in doubt—from the plan he intended to carry out.

This was for Maria. And Maria alone.

'If you want to keep your father and yourself out of jail, I need you to pretend to be my fiancée for the next three months.'

CHAPTER FIVE

REBEL'S FIRST THOUGHT after the shocked laugh that erupted from her lips was, 'I'd rather skydive naked. Twice.'

She knew the words hadn't remained mere thoughts when Draco's features tightened with formidable displeasure. His mouth twisted in a cruel yet fascinating line that drew her gaze to the sensual curve she'd warned herself not to keep staring at.

'If you think that's your worst nightmare, then you haven't experienced hell.'

'I'm sorry…were you serious?'

If anything, she succeeded in angering him more. Although he barely moved, his overpowering presence filled the room with an oppressive aura that strangled the breath in her lungs. 'Did you not guess that I wasn't the joking type?'

'Yes, but…why on earth do you need a fake fiancée? And why me?' she tagged on, stunned that the absurd questions were falling from her lips.

Again his mouth twisted and he shook his head, as if he was having trouble accepting the very subject he'd initiated.

'The *why* will be explained after you accept my proposal. The *why you* is because you happen to be in the position of being in my debt, literally. And because your reputation fits what I need.'

She couldn't stop the lance of hurt that stabbed her. 'My reputation?' she asked, even though she knew she was inviting further hurt.

'You have a loose relationship with the truth, and you steal. Why not add pretence to your repertoire?'

Rebel jerked away from him. Or she tried to. Draco held on easily, taking firmer hold of her shoulders. Despite the sensations shivering through her at that contact, she forced herself to speak. 'Because not even a million pounds and a dozen acting awards could make me pull off *pretending* to like you. Let me go.'

Grey eyes gleamed dangerously. 'I'm not a man you want to cross, Arabella. So I suggest you give serious thought to giving me what I want.'

'And I suggest you give serious thought to what you're asking me to do. In what universe would anyone believe we're even remotely *attracted* to one another, let alone engaged to be married?'

He didn't answer her immediately. Instead his hold loosened until his fingers merely brushed her skin. Slowly, they left her shoulders and trailed down her arms. Light. Barely whispering. Electrifying. Rebel had thought his forceful grip was bad enough, but the light caress of Draco's fingers along her skin started fires in places that stunned and alarmed her.

The pads of his fingers grazed the inside of her wrists. Rebel couldn't have stopped the wicked shiver that raced through her any more than she could've stopped breathing. Despite telling herself to step away, to stop this disturbing assault on her senses, she remained rooted to the spot as he traced her racing pulse.

A half step closer and one scant inch separated them. This close, she could see the tiny gold flecks in his eyes that added an extra layer of dynamism to Draco Angelis she wouldn't have thought impossible. His rich scent blanketed her with dark, dangerous promise as the music she'd stupidly thought would clear her thoughts added to the thick, sensual pool she was drowning in.

He stared down at her, eyes piercingly direct, reading every emotion she desperately tried to hide. Then he lowered his head.

Her breath lodged in her lungs as, for the second time that day, the belief that Draco Angelis was about to kiss her shook her. Wild anticipation roared through her, shocking her with its intensity. Surely she couldn't want this?

The brief, superficial liaisons she'd had in the past had always left her cold. To the extent that no man had been allowed to go beyond a few kisses, despite the tabloids' wild speculations about her sexual antics. She'd been content being a virgin with no thought as to what her first sexual encounter would be like simply because it hadn't been a concern.

Now with every atom in her body screaming at the mere thought of being kissed by this man, the reality of her sexual innocence hovered like a time bomb above her head.

Would he think her some sort of freak? Would he laugh his head off?

Pull yourself together!

What on earth did it matter what Draco Angelis thought? He would never place high enough in her life to ever find out. Just as she would never allow this kiss to happen…

About to step away, Rebel found herself captive once more when he shackled her wrists. The mouth tantalisingly close to hers drifted past. His breath warmed her jaw, then the sensitive skin beneath her earlobe.

'You don't think we have chemistry?'

'N-no,' she forced out.

'Then why is your pulse jumping? Why does your breath catch every time I swipe my fingers across your skin?' he husked in her ear. 'You've been staring at my mouth for the last minute and licking yours in anticipation of my kiss. Do you want me to kiss you, Arabella?'

'No. No!' This time when she jerked out of his hold, he let her go. Striding to the other side of the room, she crossed her arms over her chest, keenly aware of the tightness in her breasts and the telltale pearls of her nipples. 'I don't know where you're going with this—'

'You doubted our ability to pull off an authentic attraction. I've just proved you wrong.'

'You've just proved that we're both half-decent actors. I'll grant you that much. It still doesn't answer my question as to why I'd ever think of indulging you in this absurd caper.'

His eyes darkened dramatically. Coupled with his glare and the stubble gracing his firm jawline, Draco's 'fallen angel' demeanour ratcheted up her already racing heartbeat. He clenched his fists at his sides, his nostrils flaring briefly before he inhaled control back into his body. The whole process was fascinating to watch and Rebel found herself following every subtle movement.

'It seems you were right. I wasted my time coming here.' With an arrogant shrug, he cast another condemning glance around the room, then strode to where she stood. 'I'll be reporting you and your father to the authorities the moment I leave here. I suggest you save yourself a few hours of unwanted attention, and don't try and make a run for it. No doubt the press will get hold of the story by morning anyway. I'll also be pursuing civil charges to recover the stolen money so make sure you hire a good lawyer.'

He was leaving. Just as she'd wanted.

He would be pressing charges against her and her father. Killing her chances of reconciliation or putting her nightmares behind her so she could finally lay her mother's ghost to rest.

Just what she didn't want.

As he walked past her and disappeared through her living-room door, Rebel knew she needed to stop Draco. But what had happened between them minutes ago had struck a vein of irrational apprehension in her heart. Whatever his ultimate plan was in seeking a fake fiancée, she was instinctively convinced she would come out the worst for it.

But the alternative…

Ice drenched her as her front door was pulled open.

The alternative for her father was unthinkable. She'd already deprived him of the love of his life. Could she sit by and watch him be deprived of his freedom as well?

'Wait!'

He froze in the doorway. The hand gripping her door handle tightened, but Draco didn't turn around. Fear climbed up her throat, the thought that he might carry on walking a live wire snaking through her.

'Can we talk about this some more?' she addressed his silent frame.

He released the door and faced her. 'No. You're under the impression that you can bargain with me. You can't. Either agree to my demands or face the charges.'

She swallowed. Leaning against the hallway wall, she speared her fingers through her hair, seeking rationality in a world gone wildly askew.

'I don't even know what I'm agreeing to exactly.'

'I've given you the broad parameters of what I want from you. The finer details will be ironed out once I have your agreement.'

She chewed on her lower lip. 'So I agree to be your pretend fiancée for three months and you call off the search for my father and drop all charges?' she verified.

His jaw flexed for a moment. 'Provided you play your part right, yes.'

'And nothing I agree to will interrupt my training programme?'

'Your training will proceed as you wish, but you have to be prepared to accommodate a travelling schedule. Considering you were attempting to relocate, that shouldn't be a problem. I assume you're doing your dry-land drills at the moment?'

She gave a surprised nod. 'Yes, I've been alternating the on-site training and dry-land training. I return to the snow next month.'

'We'll work out a different schedule when the time comes.'

'I…okay.'

They stared at each other, Rebel unable to believe what she was a hair's breadth from agreeing to. Draco's expression remained shuttered, but he stared at her with an intensity that pierced her to the soul.

'I think you'd better tell me exactly what you want from me. I can act it up with the best of them, but I'm not sure I can pull off wide-eyed innocent if that's what you require.'

Draco stepped back into the hallway and she released a breath she hadn't known she was holding. With an agile foot, he kicked the door shut. Sauntering back, he leaned one shoulder on the opposite wall. 'Since that's the type of woman I'm trying to avoid, my suggestion is that you be yourself with one or two modifications.'

'Just so we're clear, what do you think I am?'

'A reckless pleasure seeker with very little regard for anyone's feelings but her own.'

Rebel wasn't sure why her stomach dropped and rolled or why disappointment cut so deep. She had nothing to prove to Draco Angelis. His opinion of her didn't matter. All that mattered was her father was safe from whatever hellhole had been intended for him. She still had a chance at closure, might even dare to seek absolution for the wrongs she'd done.

'And the modifications you seek?' she asked past the hard lump lodged in her throat.

He straightened from the wall, his height and breath dominating the space so she was aware of nothing else but him.

'You will not see any other guy while you're with me. Any past liaisons are officially over as of tonight. As far as the public is concerned, you're mine and mine alone.'

The possessive throb in his voice rammed home his acting ability. 'Is that all?'

'For now. We'll discuss any further addenda as and when they come up.'

'How democratic of you,' she murmured under her breath. 'Who exactly are we faking all this for?' she asked curiously.

He thrust his hands in his pockets and rocked on the balls of his feet. 'Do we have an agreement?'

Rebel swallowed hard, a chasm opening up before her she couldn't see a way out of. 'Yes.'

Draco gave a single nod before he strode back into her living room. By the time she followed him in, he'd taken a seat on her small white sofa. The sight of him, dark and imposing, on her dainty sofa sent another fissure of alarm skittering through her. But there was no backing out now. She'd agreed to this.

'Sit down.'

She curbed the snarky comment that tripped on her tongue and sat down on the armchair opposite him. Draco had nearly walked out and doomed her father to criminal prosecution. While she didn't know why her father had done what he'd done, she wasn't about to risk dicing with Draco again. Instinct warned he wasn't prone to giving second chances.

'Do you know of Carla Nardozzi?'

Rebel frowned. 'The three-time champion figure skater? Of course. Everyone knows who she is.' The twenty-four-year-old was stunningly beautiful, with a talent that had seen her soar up the figure-skating rankings halfway through her seventeenth year. She was the darling of the sports world, with sponsorship deals that had made her one of the richest sports stars by the time she was twenty-one. Her talent and success, coupled with her shy and innocent demeanour, had given her an unattainable, almost royal-princess allure that only added to her appeal.

'I want her.'

An unpleasant zing jerked Rebel in her seat. Viciously unwilling to examine the feeling, she stared back at Draco. 'Then I'm at a complete loss as to why you're sitting in my lowly Chelsea flat when you should be somewhere on the Upper East Side in New York courting her. That *is* where she lives, isn't it?'

'She divides her time between there and her training facility in Switzerland. But at the moment, she's at her father's estate in Tuscany.'

'Even better. You could be reunited with her in less than two hours. I'm sure she'll eventually see past your… interesting traits to a happy ever after with you.'

A dark frown clamped his straight brows. 'Happy ever after? What the hell are you talking about?'

She shrugged. 'You just said you want her…oh, is she playing hard to get? Is that what this is about? You want to use me to make her jealous?'

His frown deepened, then he shook his head. 'You misunderstand. She's playing hard to get, but not in the way you think. I want her as a client, but her father's standing in my way.'

Rebel despised the relief that poured through her. It pointed to an interest in Draco's private life that shouldn't be piqued. In any shape or form.

She straightened her back and cleared her throat. 'Right. I'm still at a loss as to why you need a fiancée.'

Draco sat forward and planted his elbows on his knees. 'During our last few meetings, Olivio Nardozzi hinted heavily that he'll let me sign his daughter only if I brought something…more to the table.'

'More? He wants you to date his daughter in order to secure a business deal?'

A whisper of disdain crossed his rugged face. 'I suspect he has something more permanent than dating in mind.'

That unpleasant zing returned, harder than before. 'So you intend to beat him at his own game, all for a business deal?'

Disdain morphed into something darker. Bitterness edged with pain. His features cleared a second later, but the image lingered in Rebel's mind, sparking a different interest altogether.

'I have other reasons for pursuing this.'

'Such as?' she asked before she could stop herself.

His eyelids dropped. The hands dangling between his knees slowly clenched into fists and bleakness settled over his face. Rebel was certain he wasn't aware he was exhibiting such a strong and telling reaction to her question. Her breath stalled in her lungs as she watched him battle to get his emotions under control.

By the time he raised his head, his expression was once again formidably neutral. 'My other reasons are private.'

She shook her head. 'I don't like surprises. I heard you on the phone yesterday. There was familiarity between you.'

'And your point is?'

'I hardly think Papà Nardozzi would be hell-bent on pairing you with his daughter if you two hated each other's guts.'

His eyes gleamed. 'I've known Carla since she was a teenager.'

'And…?' she pressed, disconcerted by the need to probe deeper.

'And our past bears no relevance to this deal. Your role is to help me convince Nardozzi that I'm already taken.'

Pushing aside the burning need to know more about his past with Carla, she asked instead, 'Will he sign his daughter with you if you don't give him what he wants?'

'He's on the brink of achieving the biggest endorsement deal any sports personality has ever acquired, through my company,' he replied. 'Javier Santino, the sponsor, is growing tired of the unnecessary delays. Nardozzi needs to be made aware of where I stand once and for all.'

'A simple *no* to him won't suffice?'

His eyes turned hard. 'Some people don't understand the word. They believe it's their right to have what they want simply because they want it.'

The direct taunt stabbed her deep, but she managed to

keep her composure. Standing, she folded her arms. 'Okay, I get it. So we're talking a few outings with me on your arm to convince Papà that he needs to find another suitor for daughter dearest?'

'It requires a little more than that. Nardozzi is hosting a charity gala in Italy this Sunday. He's invited me to stay at his Tuscany estate the day before the gala. He's made it clear he won't be discussing the deal, which means he intends to push his personal agenda instead.'

'So I'm expected to come to Tuscany with you this weekend?' she asked, feeling a curious dredging in her abdomen at the thought of sharing her private time and space with Draco Angelis.

'Yes. We'll fly out on Saturday and return on Monday morning.'

Rebel paced the short distance to her window and settled her agitated body against the sill. 'I still don't get why you're humouring him if you don't think he'll walk away from a deal he clearly wants.'

Draco remained silent for a full minute, prompting her to think she'd misstepped without knowing. When his face tightened again, she was sure she'd hit a nerve somewhere.

'I don't just want to represent Carla for this deal. I want her to change training teams. I want to be in charge of her training.'

The sense that she was missing a key element in this scenario nagged at her. The idea that it might be far from platonic was another notion she couldn't dismiss. But Draco had made it clear he wasn't prepared to share that side of his plan with her. 'I wasn't aware agents had a say in which training teams their clients took on.'

'They don't. Not normally,' he said abruptly, before rising to his feet.

About to ask him to elaborate, she bit back her words when he swerved towards her. 'Before we leave for Tuscany, we need to ensure our relationship attracts the appropriate public attention.'

'Won't it raise suspicion for us to be suddenly engaged?' she queried.

'I'm an intensely private man. I'm not in the habit of broadcasting my liaisons. It won't be a problem to let slip that we've been dating for a while. A few might find it hard to believe that *you* haven't publicised our association, but hopefully we'll convince them that some of my good traits have rubbed off on you.'

She rolled her eyes. 'If I didn't know better I'd think you just attempted a joke.'

His grim lips twitched, but his face remained stoic. 'I'll have my PA email you a list of restaurants I prefer to dine in. If you have any objections, let her know. Please provide her with your training schedule, and I'll try and work around it.'

Rebel supposed she ought to be grateful he was accommodating her needs. But having her time monopolised so completely stuck in her craw. 'You need anything else? Like fingerprints or a sample of DNA?'

His eyes travelled with acute intensity from the top of her head to the tips of her bare toes and back again before he met her gaze with a raised brow. 'Such invasive procedures won't be necessary, but perhaps you'll make an attempt to address your wardrobe issues for the next three months?'

'What wardrobe issues? I thought you preferred me the way I am?'

One corner of his mouth lifted in a shadowed sneer. 'Consider this another minor modification. Skin-tight leather hot pants and see-through tops have their place somewhere on the fashion landscape, I'm sure. My PA will furnish you with a reputable stylist's details. Make use of it.'

'Wow. Do you make a habit of issuing orders like a drill sergeant or am I just special?'

'It seems to be the only way I can get through to you.'

'Really? I don't recall getting the honey treatment, just the rancid-vinegar one.'

He crossed the floor to stand before her. Rebel watched, heart leaping to her throat as he raised his hand. His thumb traced her lower lip as it had done in his office. Except this touch was slower. Deadlier in its intensity.

'You'll get the honey when you deserve it. In the meantime, I'll leave you to practise giving *me* the honey. We're dining out tomorrow night. Make sure you bring your A-game. Remember what's at stake here, Arabella. Fail me and all bets are off.'

She was still slumped against the windowsill when he walked out. Even the firm click of her front door didn't rouse her from the fevered daze rushing over her.

Rebel had no idea of when she finally moved, although she managed a quick call to Contessa begging off her manager's visit, and also to inform her of the change of travel plans. Then she returned her clothes and skis to their rightful place, and made herself a cup of light cocoa.

It was another treat her trainer would no doubt chastise her for, but cocoa had always helped her sleep better. And she needed to sleep.

She needed the escape of slumber to help her *not* think about Draco Angelis. She needed to *not* think about honey or sinful caresses or A-games. Or the dark hunger veiled behind his censure and bitterness.

For one thing, the danger that accompanied the man held a mesmeric quality that spelled doom for any self-preserving creature.

For another, Rebel had always been recklessly attracted to danger.

CHAPTER SIX

THE FLOWERS ARRIVED at eight a.m., just as she was donning her gym gear. Greg, her trainer, who'd arrived at her door five minutes earlier for their run to the gym, raised an eyebrow as he walked in with an armful of the most exquisite arrangement of calla lilies Rebel had ever seen.

Besides the flowers, the black sculptured vase holding the stems was equally breathtaking.

Greg whistled as he set it on her small dining table. 'Flowers from Gilla Rosa. Someone's all out to get your attention.'

Rebel, still taking in the stunning delivery from the florist who only catered to A-list celebrities, attempted a smile. 'I guess so.' Spotting a card, she plucked it, her nerves jangling alarmingly as she opened it.

Château Dessida.
Eight o'clock tonight.
Can't wait.
D

'Château Dessida, huh? I thought you weren't dating anyone?' She started as Greg moved away from where he'd been reading the card over her shoulder.

As her trainer, he was one of a few people who knew how dedicated she was to making the championships. He also knew her occasional outings to nightclubs were coping mechanisms so didn't give her grief about it.

About to confirm that she wasn't actually dating, Rebel bit her lip. There were twelve hours before she had to begin her performance as Draco Angelis' fiancée, but it seemed her acting debut was about to commence. 'I wasn't…until fairly recently.' She dropped the card on the table and propped her foot on a dining chair to finish lacing her trainers. Then she went through her stretching routine.

The six-foot ex–body builder eyed her. 'Don't mean to judge but—is it wise getting involved with anyone so close to the championships?'

Rebel tossed out a laugh that was a million miles from genuine. 'Probably not, but isn't there a cliché about not being able to help who you fall for?'

His dark blond brows spiked. 'It's that serious already?' The brotherly concern in his eyes made her feel a heel for the subterfuge, but Rebel forced herself to remember why she was doing this.

'Cliché number two—I guess when you know, you know?' She grabbed her water bottle and tucked her phone and keys into her pockets.

Greg glanced at the flowers before he followed her out of the door. 'Here are a few more—hard work is its own reward. You've worked hard to get where you are. So don't take your eye off the ball.'

Rebel rolled her eyes, but kept the smile pinned on her face. 'As if there's any chance you'll let me. Besides, you never know. True love might be the extra-special ingredient I need to win this thing.'

She set off before he could reply. Although he caught up with her easily, he refrained from speaking, for which Rebel was grateful. But cranking up her earphones to near maximum didn't stop her mind from reeling at the full assault Draco seemed to have mounted. It was obvious he was setting the scene for their fake relationship to achieve maximum publicity in minimum time, but she would've welcomed a little more time to get used to the idea before being hit over the head with it.

Sadly, the pummelling came at an even more frantic pace the moment she returned from her morning training.

She'd barely stepped out of the shower when her doorbell rang. The courier delivered a five-page document that detailed Draco's schedule for the next fortnight and boxes to tick as to her preferred sources of entertainment. Her mouth dropped open when she read the extensive list and the final bullet point that told her the courier would return in an hour to retrieve the answered document.

Irritated, she started to tick random boxes, but by the next page a cheeky smile twitched at her lips. Crossing out several lines of questions, she scrawled one answer across the page. Then proceeded to do the same on the following pages.

She answered the courier's knock with a smile, which turned into a scowl when she spotted a sleek estate car pulling up behind the courier's van.

The six outfits and matching accessories the stylist delivered fitted perfectly, and the quirky but stylish edge to the designs made them ones she would've picked out for herself, had she come across them in a boutique. With the only exception that the delivered items had featured a designer way out of her price tag.

Deciding going with the flow was better than raising unnecessary hell, she was stepping out of a sleeveless white jumpsuit when her phone buzzed.

She sprawled across her bed to get it. 'Hello?'

'I hope your intention isn't for the next three months to be a tedium of modifications to our agreement.'

Rebel tried to ignore the tingling along her spine that Draco's deep voice elicited. 'Umm, I don't do well with cryptic. What did I do wrong now?'

'Crossing out questions about your personal interests and giving one inappropriate answer isn't acceptable.'

'Oh, right. You don't like pole dancing?' she quipped, tongue firmly in her cheek.

'Or bungee jumping. Or eating blindfolded in a blacked-out room. Skydiving—with my clothes on—might be a consideration if we had the time. We don't.'

Rebel rolled over and contemplated her black polka-dot ceiling. 'Are you sure you've got the balls for skydiving? Not everyone does.'

'Is that a dare?' he growled.

'Maybe. I'll answer the rest of your boring questionnaire if you agree to skydive with me once the championships are over. If you have the stones, that is.'

'I don't need my stones to skydive. They're for a specific purpose.'

Rebel was thankful she was on the phone when her face flamed at his words.

'Yeah, whatever. Do you accept?'

'No, Arabella. I don't accept your invitation. Not everything in life needs to be attacked with adrenaline-fuelled ferocity. And I prefer to see how you fare in the coming week before I make plans for months down the road.'

The bite in his voice erased any trace of mirth left in her. Rising, she shifted to the edge of her bed and stared at the delicate tissue paper and couture boxes strewn on her bed and floor. Suddenly, the sight of the expensive clothes produced a whiff of unease inside her. Try as she might, she couldn't dismiss the insane idea that Draco Angelis was somehow marking her with an indelible stamp of possession.

'Have I rendered you speechless for once?' he drawled.

Rousing herself, she answered, 'I answered the first page of your document. I think that should get us through this first week, don't you?'

'You ticked only one activity that interests you for every posed question.'

'So I like nightclubs. What's wrong with that?'

A faint growl rumbled down the line. The muscles in her stomach quivered as an image of a rousing dragon flashed through her mind. 'We will discuss it further tonight. I'll be there at seven-thirty. Make sure you're ready.'

He hung up before she could reply. Which was just as well since the answer on the tip of her tongue would no doubt have released the fire-breathing monster on her.

Rebel chose to wear the white jumpsuit simply because her afternoon training session overran and it was the only item of clothing that didn't need careful ironing. Slipping her feet into black and gold heels, she accessorised with a long gold necklace and chunky bangles, then caught her hair up in a loose knot before completing the look with gold chandelier earrings and a white clutch.

She was waiting on the kerb by the time Draco drove up in a gleaming black sports car. Pulling the door open, she slid into the soft leather bucket seat. And immediately clocked his tight-jawed irritation.

'Are you in the habit of hanging out on street corners waiting for your dates?'

She took her time to secure her seat belt, which didn't go as smoothly as she wanted because her every cell had grown hyperaware of the powerful and arresting man behind the wheel. He'd swapped yesterday's three-piece suit for a darker set, minus the waistcoat and tie. With the light grey shirt unbuttoned at the neck, she glimpsed a few wisps of dark silky hair that had her quickly averting her gaze.

Once she got the belt's metal housing to click, she drew a breath. Then wished she hadn't when his clean, spicy aftershave attacked her senses. Draco smelling good enough to devour wasn't a thought she intended to dwell on. 'I only came down to save you time. Please don't tell me I've offended your gentlemanly sensibilities?'

His mouth pursed. 'I'd prefer our association not to begin with hints of impropriety.'

'I was standing outside my flat, Draco, not in a red-light part of town.'

He pulled up to a red light

and locked cool grey eyes on her. 'It wouldn't have been too much trouble for me to walk to your door.'

Rebel wasn't sure why his solicitous remark robbed her of breath. Competing in a high-octane sport meant lady-like sensibilities were often mocked. She'd trained herself a long time ago to be one of the boys or risk acquiring a sneering nickname. She'd thought herself immune to needing gentle consideration. And yet the thought of Draco treating her with the tiniest deference caused a lump to rise in her throat. Her father had worshipped her mother that way, bending over backwards to grant her smallest wish.

Her mother had grumbled, but she'd always done so with a teasing smile. The memory thickened the lump in her throat, even as the acute lance of pain pierced her heart.

Struggling to retain her composure under Draco's intense stare, she cleared her throat. 'Noted. I'll do better next time.'

Surprise lit his eyes, but he turned away without response as the light turned green. The rest of the short journey passed in silence.

Château Dessida, located in a side street off the King's Road, was tiny and extremely exclusive. It was renowned for its French fusion-themed dishes, the three-Michelin-starred chef who ran the kitchen rumoured to personally select which customers patronised his establishment. He also reserved the right to publicise who dined in his restaurant, with famous photos making his millions-strong social-media following green with envy.

Draco tossed his car keys to the waiting valet and guided her through the canopied doorway.

'It's show time,' he murmured in her ear.

Before she could grasp his meaning, he pulled her close and settled a hand over her hip. Despite the layers of clothing separating them, Rebel felt his touch as keenly as if he'd branded her bare skin with a hot iron. Biting back a gasp, she stumbled. Draco's other hand shot out to grasp her waist.

'Steady, *agapita*. You okay?'

Held immobile, she stared up at him, then grew dizzy all over again as his mouth stretched in a dazzling, captivating smile. Rebel knew she was gaping, but for the life of her she couldn't look away from the stunning transformation on Draco's face. Gone was the fire-breathing ogre who seemed to find fault with every word that spilled from her lips.

In his place was an Adonis who oozed charm and attentiveness as the hand on her hip rotated in a slow caress and his other hand gripped her tighter.

'Arabella? Baby, are you okay?'

Absurdly, it was the combination of her name and the endearment that tossed her out of her stupor. Sucking in a long, restorative breath, she summoned a bare-toothed dazzler of her own. Leaning closer, she tiptoed her fingers up his chest.

'Laying it on a bit thick, aren't you, *baby*?' she remarked through clenched teeth.

The hand on her waist drifted up her arm, leaving a trail of goose bumps. 'Your neat little stumble attracted the right attention. We're now the spectacle for a few dozen pairs of eyes to feast on.' With a little too much practised ease, he lifted her faux-fur wrap from her shoulders and handed it to a cloak attendant.

Irritation jerked through her. 'I didn't do it on purpose.'

'Then it's a good thing your lover is here to catch you when you're adorably clumsy, isn't it, sweetheart?' Light fingers framed her cheek, his smile continuing to blind with its fake brilliance.

Rebel was about to snap for him to ease off with the false charm, but her words dried in her throat when Draco's name was boomed from over her shoulder.

François Dessida, a short, wiry man with thick, flowing brown hair, greeted them with a short but effusive torrent of French, which Draco answered flawlessly. Introductions were made, a few Gallic shrugs thrown in the mix, then

François clicked his fingers. As if by magic, the maître d' appeared with a discreet camera.

Rebel found herself wedged between the two men, Draco's hand back on her hip as he dragged her close enough for there to be no doubt as to their intimacy. Resurrecting her smile, she held her pose through several snaps, then exhaled in relief when François clicked his fingers again.

Wishing them a pleasant evening, he disappeared back into his domain.

By the time the maître d' showed them to their table, having stopped at a few tables when Draco returned greetings, Rebel felt as brittle as glass and just as transparent.

Her smile was fracturing at the edges and with each brush of Draco's hand on her—a gesture he seemed bent on repeating often in this insane charade—her insides clenched tight.

The moment they sat down and he'd dismissed the maître d' with their wine order, he leaned forward.

'What's wrong?' he breathed smoothly, but she caught the steely edge in his voice.

'Can we dial down the touchy-feely stuff, please?' she whispered.

'The idea is to exhibit that we're utterly besotted with each other. That involves a degree of contact.'

Thankful they'd been seated at an intimate table away from the nearest guests, she replied, 'But not three thousand degrees of it. Can we not be a couple who are discreet about their PDA?'

'To all intents and purposes, I'm about to propose to you tonight. We're starting what will become one of the most memorable nights of our lives. And you expect me to keep my hands off you?'

Her mouth dropped open. 'You're about to propose?'

'That's generally how engagements happen,' he replied.

'No, I meant…you're going to do it *here*?' Her gaze darted around only to confirm they were still the subject of great interest. Anxiety clawed up her chest. Which was absurd because all this was make-believe.

'You don't seem pleased about it,' he quipped.

Struggling for composure, she threw on a mock pout. 'I guess because you've ruined the surprise. Now I have to sharpen my acting skills even more.'

He reached across the table and took her left hand. 'I'm sure you'll rise to the occasion admirably.' Raising her hand, he kissed her ring finger.

The flash of a phone camera a second later confirmed the reason for the gesture. But it didn't stop her belly from flipping over with a mixture of anxiety and dread. The moment he set her free, she drew her hand into her lap and curled it into a fist. She was fast becoming aware that she wasn't as immune to Draco Angelis' touch as she'd assured herself she was. The chemistry she'd denied so vehemently last night was alive and well, and growing with each passing second.

Draco's stellar performance continued throughout their appetiser and main courses. He tucked into his plate of braised veal and roasted vegetables soaked in red wine sauce, while she pushed her truffled chicken escalope around her plate, taking the occasional bite when he sent her a speaking look. By the time the course was over, the food had congealed in her stomach.

'Something on your mind?'

'You asked for my A-game. I don't think I can bring it. I'm not sure I can pull this off,' she blurted once their wine glasses had been refilled.

He inhaled sharply, his eyes snapping with displeasure. 'I suggest you find a way to make it happen. We've set the ball rolling on this. It's too late to change your mind now. Even if your father makes a triumphant return and you somehow find yourself with another windfall, you still have an agreement to fulfil.'

The remnants of wine she'd just swallowed turned sour

in her mouth as she twisted the wine-glass stem between her fingers.

The sensation of falling deeper into a bottomless chasm grew. She jumped when Draco leaned closer. 'He hasn't returned, has he?' he enquired.

Pursing her lips, she shook her head. 'No, he hasn't.' Despite her calling him every free moment she'd had today, her phone remained silent.

'Has he done this before? Disappeared without a trace?'

Pain dredged through her. With every fibre of her being, Rebel wished she could answer in the negative. 'Yes, he's done it before.'

Draco's gaze sharpened. 'When?'

'When…when my mother died. After her funeral, he left home. He didn't return for three months.'

He frowned. 'How old were you?'

'I was seventeen.'

'And he left you alone?' The bite was back, the charming façade he'd worn all night slipping to reveal the ruthless man beneath. Absurdly, Rebel felt a tiny bit of relief at seeing the real man, even though this version of Draco remained a formidable force that battered at the foundations of her existence.

Rebel shrugged. 'He had my aunt look in on me every once in a while, but I was pretty much independent by then.'

'And that excuses his actions?' Anger laced his every syllable.

Unable to risk him seeing her guilt, she stared down at her plate. 'He'd just lost the love of his life. He…he was grieving.'

'While he had a responsibility to you? Were you not grieving too?'

Her gaze snapped up. 'Of course I was!' Swallowing, she shook her head and continued. 'But…there's more to the story, Draco.'

His mouth twisted in a cynical grimace. 'Isn't there always? Sadly, more often than not, *more* is just an excuse for shirking responsibility or seeking blanket absolution.'

'We all deal with our issues in different ways.'

'Yes. And your father's way seems to be doing a runner and leaving you with the smoking gun,' he drawled pithily.

'Don't—!'

'More wine, *mademoiselle*? *Monsieur*?'

They both started. Draco recovered first, reaching out to take the bottle from the waiter and dismissing him. When she shook her head, he set the bottle down without refilling his own. Silence cloaked them for several minutes, with Rebel trying hard to stem the tremors charging through her body.

She couldn't believe she'd spilled her guts to Draco, given him further ammunition against her and her father.

'You gave me your word. You will not back out of this,' he stated with unmistakable gravity.

For myriad reasons, she wanted to take back her promise. But each and every reason that tumbled through her head was a selfish one. And they all centred around how Draco Angelis made her *feel*. Unbalanced. Apprehensive. An all-encompassing excitement each time he touched her. A craving for more of that touch.

But her feelings didn't matter here. Winning the championship in order to keep her mother's memory alive and ensuring she found a way back to her father were the two most important reasons to stick with this. She couldn't do either from a prison cell.

After a brave sip of wine, she set her glass down. 'I won't back out. From this moment, I'm all in.'

CHAPTER SEVEN

DRACO EXHALED THE BREATH locked in his chest and nodded. He refused to acknowledge the anxiety that slowly seeped out of him as he stared at Arabella. 'And I have your assurance that this is the last time I'll have to deal with a change of heart?'

A shrug lifted her smooth, bare shoulder. 'I'll try not to make a habit of it, but I reserve the right to throw a mini wobbly if this charade gets a little too much. I'm human after all, not a robot.'

Had she been a robot, she would've earned the title of sexiest robot created. Her gold accessories highlighted her perfect, vibrant skin, drawing his gaze to her slim neck, delicate collarbones and the delectable shadows between her breasts. The spark that had started in his groin when he'd pulled her close at the door surged into a flame. He shifted in his seat, his trousers growing uncomfortably tight as she lifted her water glass and drank from it.

Setting it down, she sent him a furtive glance.

'This is really important to you, isn't it?' she probed.

Draco guessed that this was her attempt to steer the conversation away from her father. And while residual fury burned in his blood at the realisation that the man whose integrity and hard work he'd relied on for the past five years had turned out to be untrustworthy to the extent of abandoning his own family when he'd been needed most, Draco was content to let the matter rest. For now.

He took his time to answer, relaying their coffee orders to the waiter before he responded, 'Yes, it's important.'

She continued to toy with the crystal goblet. 'Why? And

before you say so, I think I can accurately guess it's not about the money.'

He tensed, debated for a moment how much to divulge. Maria's privacy was of the utmost importance to him. As long as he had breath in his body, his sister wouldn't know the slightest pang of further suffering. He hadn't been able to protect her when it counted. But he intended to do everything he could to ease her tiniest worry.

'No, it's not about the money, although, as a businessman, it's in my interest to protect my and my clients' assets.'

'Of course, but there's more.' It wasn't a question. It was a statement of unwavering certainty.

Normally, prying from his date was a turn-off. But he found himself answering her, while reminding himself that this wasn't a proper date. This was a charade to get him what he wanted. What Maria wanted.

'Carla Nardozzi and her father are thinking of renewing her contract with Tyson Blackwell for another three years. I intend to make sure that doesn't happen.'

Surprise sparked her blue eyes. 'But Tyson is one of the most highly sought-after trainers out there. I worked with him in a group programme myself a few years ago.'

Renewed fury flamed through him, but he banked it down. He was supposed to play the part of a besotted lover, not an angry one, exhibiting bewildering signs of jealousy. 'I'm aware of that. Why did you part company?'

She shrugged. 'I think he had his eye on bigger fish. Carla Nardozzi, I expect.'

'Consider yourself lucky. He's known to push his trainees beyond their limits.'

She smiled at the waiter who delivered her coffee, before she met his gaze once more. 'And that's a bad thing?'

Regret and bitterness locked a vice around his chest. 'It is when they eventually break.'

Her eyes shadowed with sympathy, an emotion Draco wouldn't have associated with the flighty, self-obsessed creature he knew her to be. 'This happened to someone you know?'

The vice tightened. 'Yes.' He forced the word out.

She nodded, then picked up her coffee and blew gently on it. A different sort of tightening took hold of Draco. He wasn't sure whether to be resentful of the reminder that his libido was alive and kicking or welcome the distraction from trying to grapple with the diverging personalities of the woman sitting across from him. A sympathetic listener and narcissistic thief. Was there such a thing?

'I'm sorry that happened to them. Were you close to this person?' she pressed.

Draco decided that he preferred to tackle the subject of his libido. Discussing matters that ploughed through rough and disturbing memories wasn't what he'd intended for this dinner. And yet the box that resided in his jacket pocket remained there as he lifted and tossed back his double espresso.

'Did you take care of the matter of your other liaisons as you promised?'

Mocking laughter spilled from her lips. 'First of all, I made no such promise. Secondly, where on earth did you get the idea that I had *liaisons*, plural?'

His teeth ground until pain lanced his jaw. 'There have been several photographs of you cavorting with a certain rock band for the last few weeks.'

An emotion flicked through her eyes, one that resembled hurt. 'And that automatically means I'm dating all of them?'

Tension gripped him. 'Are you?'

'No. Cole, the lead singer, used to be into snowboarding when we were younger. I met him again at an event a few weeks ago, and we just hung out for a bit.'

'In the pictures you seem to be hanging out in his lap.' The words emerged in a rumble that thoroughly irritated him.

Arabella shook her head. 'I swear, if I didn't know better, I'd think you were jealous.'

His tension increased, along with the irksome need to probe this subject. 'This is nothing more than due diligence to ensure there are no surprises down the road.'

She held his gaze, hers bold and clear. 'There won't be.'

For the second time in under an hour, tension eased out of Draco. For whatever reason his instinct was to believe her. Or perhaps on a subconscious level he knew this was a minor problem, easily resolved once the world knew she belonged to him. His gaze dropped to her bare fingers, a sudden need sparking through him.

Confirming she'd finished her coffee, he stood and held out his hand.

After a tiny hesitation, she slipped her hand in his and stood. The few diners remaining glanced their way. One or two acquaintances tried to catch his eye, but he avoided them. He'd achieved what he came here for. He wasn't sure why he'd decided to take the next step away from prying eyes but he was tired of being on show.

The maître d' materialised with Arabella's wrap. Draco draped it over her shoulders and caught her faint shiver as his fingers brushed her skin.

He'd effectively debunked her denial of their chemistry at her flat last night. But little had he known that he would be caught in the tangle of chemical reaction so strong that he'd spent the night fighting lurid dreams.

She murmured her thanks and walked beside him, her hand once more clasped in his. He stared down at her profile, forcing himself to stay removed from the ever-growing tendrils of attraction grabbing at him.

A cold, rational part of him insisted that the attraction would make their fake relationship more believable. While the part of his anatomy that refused to remained unstirred urged him to change the parameters of their agreement. To make certain sections of it real.

He suppressed that urge and led Arabella to his car.

Even if he were on the market for a brief dalliance, Arabella Daniels wouldn't be his choice of partner. Her wild, brash approach to life would never gel with his, even for the weeks-long period his affairs usually lasted. Besides, she'd all but admitted to being as unscrupulous and lacking in integrity as her father.

There was no way he could risk exposing such a person to Maria.

Satisfied with his decision, he saw her into the car and slipped behind the wheel. The return journey back to her flat went much faster. When she went to open the door, Draco growled, 'Stay.'

As before, she seemed surprised by his gesture as he rounded the bonnet and opened her door.

'Thank you.'

Taking her by the elbow, he walked her to the front door and waited as she dug through her clutch for her keys.

Another furtive glance at him prompted a twitch of a smile. She was nervous.

'Invite me up.'

Nerves turned to surprise. Then suspicion. 'Why?'

'Because there's one more thing to address before we end the evening.'

Her eyes rounded before she caught his meaning. 'Oh, the engagement ring. I thought you wanted to do that in front of an audience?'

He shrugged. 'We lost our audience while we were discussing…other matters. And I don't intend to place my ring on your finger on the steps of your flat. Invite me up.'

The breath she inhaled was a shaky one. 'Umm…okay.'

She opened her front door and he held it wide for her, then followed her up the flight of stairs to her flat. In her living room, Draco waited as she turned on lamps and straightened cushions. Then watched, bemused, as she twisted her fingers and eyed the entertainment centre.

'You seem nervous.'

She laughed and shrugged. 'Not sure why I am. I guess I've never been genuinely fake-proposed to before.'

The idea that she'd been proposed to at all sent a thin vein of tension through him. He dismissed it and reached into his pocket. As his fingers closed over the velvet box, tension mutated to something else. Something Draco faintly recognised as trepidation for this moment. The kind that ran parallel with monumental tasks he didn't want to fail at. Frowning, he pulled the box from his pocket. There'd been no words to practise because this wasn't a prelude to a love union. They were each playing a finite role with a clear endgame in mind. The moment shouldn't contain as much gravity as was moving through him.

'If you want dramatic music to draw out the suspense, just say the word. I have tons,' Arabella quipped, one perfectly shaped eyebrow raised.

He fisted the box for a brief moment. 'That won't be necessary.'

Striding to where she stood, he held it up and pried it open.

She gasped, then frowned. 'It's real. I mean, I'm not a gem expert, but that looks…real!' Blue eyes met his, alarm swimming in the depths.

His teeth gritted. 'You thought I would supply you with a fake ring?'

'Well…yes. To go with the fake engagement? I don't know why you look so offended, but that would make sense, wouldn't it?'

'It would also announce our engagement as a sham to the whole world.'

Her gaze dropped down to the box. 'But this is probably worth more than I owe you. You're sure you trust me with it?' she murmured. 'What if I lose it?'

'It's insured against loss. And theft.' Draco wasn't sure why he added that. When she raised her gaze and he spotted the hurt she tried to hide, a tiny spark of remorse burst through him. Which was absurd because this situation had come about because of her collusion with her father's duplicity. Brushing aside the feeling, he growled, 'Give me your hand.'

She hesitated for one moment. Then two. At the back of his mind, Draco faintly wondered if this was what the average man felt like when he got down on one knee. If so, then he pitied them. Her unnecessary hesitation was irritating in the extreme. And he wasn't even on one knee. Nor did he intend to be.

'Arabella. Your hand.'

Rebel slowly held out her left hand, nerves eating her alive. 'Damn,' she muttered under her breath.

Draco's gaze rose from where he held the ring poised. 'What's wrong?'

She shrugged. 'If I'd known I'd be sporting a rock like this, I'd have made more of an effort with my nails.' She kept them trimmed short for training, but a little gloss wouldn't have gone amiss. She swallowed as she caught his frown. 'Sorry, I didn't mean to ruin the moment.' Realising she was babbling, she pressed her lips together.

'There isn't a moment to ruin,' he rasped. Rebel felt the cold tug of platinum over her knuckle. Then the ring slid into place. 'And your nails are fine.'

The rectangular-cut diamond was flanked by baguette diamonds, which connected to the platinum band. In the low lights of her flat, the ring glinted and flashed as her fingers trembled. It was a perfect fit. Just how he'd achieved that was a mystery, but Rebel couldn't take her eyes off the ring's sheer perfection. Nor could she divorce her mind from wandering down a senseless road of how she would've felt if this moment were real.

Not that the man she'd have chosen would've been Draco Angelis. He was far too arrogant and domineering for her to even consider him as—

'Is it my turn to ask whether we need melodramatic music? Or do you not like the ring?' Draco drawled with a slight edge in his tone.

'It's…' *beautiful.* Wondering why the word stuck in her throat, why so many different emotions darted through her, Rebel dragged her gaze from the stunning ring. 'It's fine. It'll probably get the job of convincing Nardozzi to back off done all on its own.'

His mouth twisted. 'I think you need to put in more personal effort than that.'

Before she could answer, his phone buzzed. Slipping it from his pocket, he stared at the screen for a moment, a hint of satisfaction flitting over his features. 'Dessida has done what I requested of him.'

Why was she surprised that Draco could get men with bloated egos like François Dessida to bend to his will? 'Great,' she responded, even though an added ball of uncertainty churned in her stomach. 'We're all set, then.'

'Not quite.' He stared down at his screen for a few more seconds before his steely gaze pierced hers. 'Your body language needs a little work.'

'Excuse me?'

He turned the phone towards her. The chef had posted a picture of them on his social-media site. 'This doesn't quite do the trick.'

She flicked a glance at the picture, suddenly unwilling to look closely at it. 'Our picture has already had over half a million views. I fail to see what the problem is.'

'The problem is we're supposed to be lovers. Your posture indicates otherwise.'

Rebel forced herself to look past Draco's firm, proprietary hand on her hip. Or the fact that it sparked a fizz of unwanted sensation through her. Clinically, she perused her slightly stiff posture and the neutral expression she'd forced her features into in reaction to Draco's touch. Her gaze slid to the dominating presence beside her.

'You could've done with cracking a smile too, don't you think?' she countered.

He slid the phone back into his pocket. 'The next time we're seen together in public you'll be my fiancée. Your performance needs to be stellar.'

'Fine. I promise to fawn all over you.'

He shook his head. 'No, I'm not risking you going overboard either.'

She threw up her hands. 'What, then? You should know, I'm not the here's-a-cute-selfie-of-us-cuddling-while-walking-our-dog type.'

'Neither am I. But we need to achieve the right balance.'

'And how do you suggest we do that? Take a compatibility test?'

'Of sorts.'

He stepped forward and gripped her waist. The unexpected move, and the blistering heat from his touch, made her whole body clench tight. 'What are you doing?' Her voice rose several octaves higher than it'd been a moment ago.

'You just tensed up. If you do that every time I touch you, we might as well declare this thing a failure.'

'You surprised me, that's all,' she replied, her voice still unlike her own.

He dragged her closer and her tension mounted. 'Arabella, relax,' he rasped, his voice deep and frighteningly hypnotic.

'Said the snake charmer to the snake.'

One corner of his mouth lifted in a shadow of a smile. Then the pads of his thumbs pressed into her hip bones.

Electric sensation blasted through her. The secret place between her legs tingled wildly before singeing her with a fiery need that robbed her of breath. Draco stared at her as his thumbs continued to play over her covered skin, the direct gaze adding a potent layer of awareness to the one already blanketing her.

Just when she thought she couldn't stand it any more, his gaze dropped to her mouth. A rough sound rumbled from his chest, but she was too caught up in what was happening to her body to pay it much heed.

But she heeded the unrelenting descent of his head, and the mouth that took hers a second later.

Every single atom in her body strained to that point of contact, to the pressure that teased at first, then turned into a deeper, more breath-stealing exploration.

Rebel had been kissed before, but the expertise Draco brought to his kiss, even mere seconds into the act, melted her senses. Warm, firm lips bruised hers, the feeling of being devoured drenching her before she succumbed to it.

His hand strayed from her hip to the small of her back, compelled her closer still. Her arms moved, almost of their own accord, twined around his neck. Silky hair teased the back of her hands and Rebel gave in to the temptation to slide her fingers through his hair.

His tongue breached her mouth, the bold swipe as he shamelessly tasted her knocking the strength from her knees. Desire blistered her, tightening over her skin until her breasts ached and her nipples were needy little buds straining against her bra. Needing to relieve the ache, she rubbed herself against him.

A groan erupted from him. Lost in sensation, Rebel barely acknowledged being lifted off her feet. Or laid down on the sofa. Every frantic heartbeat begged for more of what she was experiencing. The kiss. The man. The potent smell of him that filled her nostrils and the hands moulding her body. She wanted it all with a desperation that defied logic.

When he gripped her leg and angled it over his hip, she twisted to accommodate him, the move settling him snugly between her thighs.

The unmistakable power of his erection brushed her clothed core. Lightning zapped at the contact, electrifying and so strong, they both froze. She opened her eyes to find grey eyes, dark with volatile hunger, staring into hers.

Hunger that had no place whatsoever inside the parameters of what she'd agreed to.

With a shocked, garbled cry, Rebel wrenched her mouth from his. Disengaging the fists locked in his hair, she slammed them on his shoulders and pushed.

'Get off me. Now.' Her voice was a shaky mess, light years from confident, and nowhere near rational.

Draco lifted his imposing body off hers, his control back in place as if that wild hunger she'd seen in his eyes had been a figment of her imagination. 'Calm down, Arabella.'

She jumped up and fled to the other side of the room. One shaky hand sliced through her hair as she noted she'd lost her shoes along the way to insanity. 'God, I can't believe that just happened,' she muttered under her breath.

He took his time to straighten his cuffs, then shrugged. 'We needed to be familiar with each other. Now I know what you taste like, and you won't jump whenever I touch you in public.'

'Not if you're going to paw me like you did a moment ago.'

He raised a mocking brow. 'You reciprocated in kind, *glikia mou*. I'm sure I can locate a claw mark or two on my person should I feel inclined to do so.'

Heat rushed up her face at the reminder of her wanton behaviour. Folding her arms to still her body's betraying tremble, she glared at him. 'Are we quite finished? Only I'd like to get some sleep. I have an early start in the morning.'

He sauntered past her and paused at the door. 'We are for now. Don't forget we do this again tomorrow night. With added public scrutiny thrown in.'

Her heart tripped over itself as unpleasant images of being in a goldfish bowl tore through her mind. 'Are you sure all this is just to save Carla? From where I stand, she seems to be doing just fine.' Rebel hated herself for probing, but all day she hadn't quite been able to shake the feeling that there was more to his motives where Carla was concerned than Draco was letting on. And she hated herself even more that the prime emotion when she thought about the two of them felt alarmingly like jealousy.

Draco's face hardened into a steel mask. 'I've learned to look beneath the surface, Arabella. If you bother to do the same, you'll see that things aren't always as they *seem*. Goodnight.'

She stayed rooted to the spot as he left her flat. Although his words echoed through her mind, it was the depth of feeling in his voice and wave of vivid pain that had crossed his face that stayed with her.

CHAPTER EIGHT

'YOU'RE DATING DRACO ANGELIS?'

Shock lined every inch of Contessa's face as she stood in Rebel's doorway. Her mop of red hair and electric-blue dress should've clashed horribly, but somehow the ensemble worked. Probably because her unapologetic, no-nonsense attitude dared anyone to criticise her wardrobe style.

Not that Rebel would've done so as her manager brushed past her and headed for the kitchen. She plunked the bottle of champagne in her hand on the breakfast counter and turned to her.

'Your email was a little vague as to why you weren't going to Chamonix any longer, but I'm guessing this new development has something to do with it? Tell me it's not true—' She gasped as her gaze fell on the rock adorning Rebel's finger. Rushing forward, she caught up Rebel's hand. 'What's this?'

'Umm…want to take a wild guess?'

'An engagement ring? You're *engaged*? To Draco?'

Rebel bit her lip and gave a sheepish nod.

A deeper bewilderment etched Contessa's face. 'When? And why? Damn it, what's going on, Rebel? I had no idea you'd even met the guy, never mind were dating him!'

'It sort of just happened.'

'A serious rock like this doesn't *just happen*. You've been evasive these past few weeks.' She dropped Rebel's hand, her green eyes wary and hurt. 'I thought you trusted me?'

'You know I do.'

Contessa's gaze dropped to the ring, then back up. 'Then why won't you tell me what's going on?'

Rebel didn't know Draco well enough to speak with certainty as to how he'd react to her divulging details of their agreement. And she had too much to lose to risk it. 'Because I can't. I'm sorry.'

Contessa's eyes narrowed shrewdly. 'It's something to do with your father, isn't it? And the money he gave you?' She snapped her fingers. 'You wanted me to get it all back but you never said why. Does this Draco thing have something to do with it?'

Shame and anxiety engulfed her. 'Please, I can't really talk about it. And I'm sorry to have to cut this short but Draco will be here in a minute.'

On cue, her door intercom buzzed.

'Why? Doesn't he want you to have friends?' Contessa snapped. 'Or are you suddenly ashamed of me?'

'Don't be absurd. Of course I'm not ashamed of you. I… we're going out, that's all.'

The older woman's gaze drifted over the moss-green beaded dress and platform heels Rebel wore. 'I can see that.' She hitched her stylish tote handbag higher on her shoulder, then sighed. 'Be careful, Rebel. You're more than a client to me. And I'd hate myself if you got hurt. You know he represents Rex Glow now? Have you stopped to think he may have had something to do with them dropping you?'

'Yes, I—'

Contessa shook her head. 'This engagement…well, all I'm saying is, a man like Draco can give you a lot. But he'll take more than you'll want to give.'

Rebel frowned. 'I know exactly what he wants from me. I don't intend to give him more than that.'

'The sport agents' business is a small world. He's discreet, I'll grant him that, but I know a few of the women he's been involved with in the past. They always believe they're incapable of being hurt by him, but things always end the same way. With the women emotionally and professionally shattered, and Angelis walking away without a backward glance.'

'It's a good thing that you're in charge of my career, then, isn't it?' Rebel said with a forced smile.

'What about your heart?'

'I'm fully in control of it. I know you're worried, but please trust that I know what I'm doing,' she replied, choosing not to recall the sleepless night she'd spent thinking about Draco, the kiss they'd shared, and the unfurling heat in her belly each time she relived it. Assuring herself it was a simple chemical reaction and therefore didn't warrant further thought had lost its credibility somewhere between dawn and sunrise. As had telling herself she didn't really want to know the reason behind Draco's anguished look when she'd asked about Carla in the moments before he'd walked out.

Both subjects had stayed with her all day and, the closer the time came for her date with Draco, the more uneasy she'd grown.

The intercom buzzed again, ending with a snap of impatience.

Schooling her features, she smiled at Contessa. She knew her friend and manager wasn't buying her assurances when Contessa stalked past her to the door she'd walked through minutes ago. Collecting her black purse from her bedroom, Rebel rushed after her, cursing as she stopped to lock her front door.

She caught up with Contessa as she was pulling the main door open.

Contessa and a just-arrived, smartly dressed Draco eyed each other. Despite her warning, Rebel watched her friend's eyes widen a little as she took in the full impact of the man before her. A second later, Draco glanced past her to capture Rebel's gaze.

'Good evening, Arabella.'

The sensual curl of her name from his lips sparked a higher charge in her belly. Doing her best to ignore it, she came down the last few steps and stood next to Contessa.

'Are you going to introduce me to your friend, *glikia mou*?' he asked, his voice deep and low.

The endearment reminded Rebel of Draco's Greek origin, reminded her that she knew next to nothing about him besides the circumstances surrounding the situation they found themselves in. And even then, Draco was hiding far more than he'd divulged.

Making a note to do something about it, she summoned a smile. 'This is my manager, Contessa Stanley. Contessa, meet Draco Angelis.'

Draco held out his hand. 'A pleasure to meet you.'

'Good to meet you,' Contessa replied, then her sharp looked morphed into glazed astonishment when Draco smiled. Witnessing the transformation from a few feet back, Rebel couldn't stop herself from staring at the dazzling effect of his smile. It took several moments for Contessa to regain her composure. 'I believe congratulations are in order.'

'Thank you,' he drawled. 'I'm a very lucky man.' The heated, adoring look he sent Rebel could've knocked her off her feet, had she not known it was an act.

Contessa stared at him for another long second, before she cleared her throat and turned to Rebel. 'I'll call you tomorrow. Have a good evening.'

Without another glance at Draco, she headed to the white hybrid parked in front of Draco's sports car.

Draco watched her depart with a faintly amused expression. 'Any reason why she doesn't like me?'

Rebel shut the front door and fell into step beside him, cautioning herself against walking too close. 'She's a sport manager. She suspects you were involved with my sponsors walking. She also believes the women you get involved with end up on the used and discarded heap, both professionally and emotionally.'

Any semblance of amusement vanished from Draco's face. He caught her wrist and glared down at her. 'You didn't tell her about our agreement, did you?'

'Of course not.' She pulled her hand away. 'Although I trust her implicitly,' she added.

'Be that as it may, I'd prefer it if this thing remained between only you and me,' he commanded.

'I'm not stupid, Draco. I don't want this to get out any more than you do.'

He observed her for a moment, grey eyes narrow and intense. 'Good.'

Striding to his car, he held the door open for her, his movements tense as he rounded the bonnet and slid behind the wheel.

After several minutes of silence, she glanced at him, unable to smother the question that had been bubbling at the back of her mind. 'Why *did* you talk Rex Glow into dropping me?'

She'd told herself she didn't care. That she was better off without the demanding apparel and footwear sponsor. But she held her breath as she waited for Draco to answer.

His jaw flexed for a moment. 'I didn't. They'd already made the decision to drop several athletes by the time I joined their board. Yours was just a name on the list.'

Rebel knew it was true because Contessa had informed her of others who'd been dropped. 'And you did nothing to stop it?'

Draco shrugged. 'I didn't know you. And you weren't exactly trying very hard to convince them of your dedication to your sport. You switched disciplines from cross-country to ski jumping after almost five years. Since then you haven't risen above fifth in the rankings.'

'I know you think I'm whimsical about my career, but I'm not. It wasn't an easy decision, especially with the intense training involved.'

He switched lanes suddenly, and her eyes were drawn to his powerful thighs. Recalling them cradled between hers, she turned her heating face to the window.

'Did you grow up skiing?' he asked after a few minutes.

She answered only because talking took her mind off the lurid images unreeling through her head. And perhaps because she wanted him to know that she was more than the superficial pleasure seeker he thought her to be?

'Yes. My mother was a ski jumper. She never made it past the juniors but she excelled in amateur tournaments. She taught me how to jump when I was ten. I loved it but I was stronger in cross-country skiing so it was a natural choice to do that professionally.'

'That makes sense. Less so is why you changed disciplines.'

'I stopped loving cross-country.'

'I'm guessing the reason behind is more emotional than professional?'

She wanted to hate him for the cynical edge to his observation, but how could she when it was the truth? Pain slammed through her as she glanced at his profile and replied, 'Does my mother passing away count?'

He exhaled, a look of regret lining his features. 'It counts. Unfortunately death and tragedy arrive before clarity lights our paths,' he murmured, then seemed to slip into deep thought. Expertly handling the powerful vehicle, he didn't speak until they were a few streets from the restaurant. 'But you didn't change disciplines until a few years after you lost your mother. And yet you won more cross-country competitions in that time.' The statement held a ton of questions. Questions that, should she answer, would expose the state of her hidden anguish to a man whose ruthlessness she was very much privy to.

But not answering would risk leaving him with the belief that she was shallow. Wondering why that mattered so much to her, Rebel decided on a not too revealing answer. 'I was trying to prove a point.'

'To who?'

'To myself. To my father.'

His mouth compressed, disapproval back in full force.

'You disapprove? No matter what everyone else thinks, an athlete needs a better support system than just agents and trainers. I thought I could function without one, and, yes, I was at the top of my game during that time, but in the long run it didn't work for me. So I chose to do something different. It probably doesn't mean anything to you, but I found more fulfilment in jumping.'

Draco parked the car on a quiet lamplit street in Fulham amid several late-model sports cars and SUVs. The restaurant he'd chosen tonight was another exclusive one, frequented by the crème de la crème of celebrities. A discreet security presence ensured the patrons could dine without intrusive media presence, although somehow information usually leaked out.

He helped her out, but held onto her as he shut the door. After clicking the lock, he stood in front of her, effectively pinning her against the car.

Tensing, Rebel tilted her face to look at him, expecting more of the disapproval that had bristled from him. Instead, she read a jagged understanding in his eyes. He looked almost uncomfortable as he stared down at her.

'I understand the need to find fulfilment in what you do. But I believe that it should go hand in hand with attempting to be the best you can be. You have the potential to be number one again, but you've let your emotions and superficial things get in the way of that goal for far too long.'

Draco's view of her might have altered slightly, but he still believed she wasn't committed enough to what she'd dedicated the past five years of her life to. The pang that accompanied the observation triggered alarm. How could the view of a man she hadn't known three days matter so much?

'You should really stop thinking you know all there is to know about me,' she replied.

His eyes dropped from hers, his gaze roving her face before locking on her lips. 'Everything you've told me so far has only confirmed my opinion of you.'

She swallowed, wishing the hurt in her chest and the sudden tingling of her mouth away. Forcing lightness to her voice, she said, 'Whereas I know next to nothing about the man who I'm supposed to be madly in love with. Perhaps we should rectify that before I slip up and commit a faux pas?'

'We will do that over dinner,' he replied. Then his gaze dropped past her shoulders to the unsteady rise and fall of her chest. Pushing back from the car, he completed a full scrutiny before he trapped her hand again. Lifting her ring finger to his mouth, he kissed the knuckle above the stone. 'You look incredible, by the way.'

Her breath caught, her heart tripping over itself before slamming hard against her ribs. 'Thank you. You don't look so bad yourself.' She made a show of perusing him from head to foot, secretly revelling in the freedom to look her fill of the lean masculinity that inhabited the dark suit and black silk shirt. Having experienced the power of that body up close, she found her breathing was decidedly unsteady by the time her gaze rose to meet his.

His smile wasn't as show-stopping as it'd been when he'd unleashed his charms on Contessa. But it had more genuine depth, making it even more dangerous to her equilibrium as she found herself smiling back, her senses singing as his eyes warmed and his thumb rubbed over her knuckles.

'Now that we've established our appreciation of each other's dress sense, let's go eat.'

He linked his fingers through hers and walked her into the modern decor of the Italian restaurant. Unlike before, there wasn't a chef to fawn over them or pose for pictures, for which she was glad. Although their presence wasn't brazenly acknowledged, Rebel caught a few discreet glances as they ate their first course.

But even that small disturbance disappeared as Draco furnished her with his history. His flawless English had made her think he'd been brought up in England despite his Greek name. Finding out he'd only relocated from Athens to England five years ago came as a surprise. But not as much a surprise as discovering he, like her, had lost his mother during his teens. And that he'd been a champion cross-country skier.

Rebel frowned. 'I know the name of every skier who's won a major competition for the last fifty years.'

One sleek eyebrow rose, giving him a rakish look that she strenuously resisted gawping at. 'Are you accusing me of lying?'

Lowering her gaze to the less interesting subject of her water glass, she shrugged. 'I know what I know.' And she definitely would've remembered him.

'I competed under my mother's maiden name of Christou.'

Her head snapped up. 'The only Christou I remember—you're Drakos Christou! Five-time world champion?' Rebel wasn't aware she'd grabbed his hand until he traced his thumb over hers. She started to pull away but he held her tight. And because she liked it, she stayed.

'Yes.' A lopsided smile accompanied the acknowledgement.

Knowing she was risking fan-girling over him, she reined herself in. 'Wow. You look…different.' He'd sported longer hair and a full beard during his competitions years, and although his build had been leaner, more streamlined, it had suited the sport he'd excelled in. No wonder she hadn't recognised him, despite the faint feeling of familiarity she'd experienced in his office when they'd first met. 'Why the change of name?'

The air thickened, sucking dry the easy banter that had eased their preceding courses. 'My father disapproved of my chosen career. He would've preferred it if I'd joined the family real-estate business and succeeded him. He made it clear I wasn't his son until I came to my senses and gave up skiing.'

'But you didn't give it up.'

His features tightened. 'Not until I was forced to anyway.'

With the realisation of just who Draco Angelis was, the worldwide sensation that had surrounded his departure from cross-country skiing came flooding back. 'You trained yourself for the last competition, but your knee blew out before you could win your sixth trophy.'

The hand now curled around hers tightened. 'Discovering that my trainer had been pushing me past my limits just so he could gamble on my winning the tournament left me no choice.'

A soft gasp left her lips. 'No way. What happened to him?'

His nostrils flared as he dragged in a breath vibrating with quiet fury. 'He faced game throwing and other charges, but by the time the case went to trial and the extent of the gambling ring was discovered, it was too late.'

Sympathy welled through her. 'Your knee injury ended your career.'

His lashes swept down to their joined hands. Slowly his grip loosened and he withdrew from her. Rebel missed the contact with an acuteness that stunned her. Drawing her hand from the table, she lowered it to her lap and balled it.

'Amongst other things. But the most important lesson I learned was to always look beneath the surface. I knew things weren't right, but I chose to ignore them because I was determined to win that final championship.' His words held raw self-condemnation that struck a vulnerable place inside her.

Self-condemnation was an emotion she'd lived with and knew well. But Draco's case was different. He hadn't rushed recklessly into a situation through selfishness. He'd been deceived by someone he'd believed he could trust.

The urge to comfort him snowballed through her, but the rigid control once more clamping his features dissuaded her.

The rest of the meal passed in near silence, and Rebel was thankful when Draco asked for the bill.

She was sliding back into his car when her phone started pinging. Digging it out, she read the congratulatory emails flooding her inbox, almost all of them from people she barely knew.

It wasn't until she clicked an attachment that she saw the first headline.

Super-Agent and Sports Star Engaged!

Rebel didn't bother to read the article, knowing this time round the carefully crafted story within was from source. About to click off her phone, she stopped as another picture from a social-media account lit up her screen, along with the history of how many times it'd been viewed.

She gasped.

'Is something wrong?' Draco asked, his gaze spearing her as he paused in the act of securing his seat belt.

She showed him the picture taken of them earlier, as he'd kissed her hand outside the restaurant. The quality of the photo was much too good to have been taken with a discreet phone camera. 'Did you know the paparazzo was there?'

Shrugging, he pressed the ignition and the car roared to life. 'Of course. That was the whole point of the act, wasn't it?'

For a moment, Rebel couldn't speak. Her hand trembled as she tucked her phone back in her bag. She called herself a thousand kinds of fool for each dart of hurt that lanced her. She'd dropped her guard for a handful of moments. So what?

If the figures were to be believed, the public were lapping up the image of a loved-up 'Drabella'.

'Yes, I guess it was,' she replied quietly.

'Then we'll chalk up the night as a success. Put on your seat belt, Arabella.'

Woodenly she complied, then lapsed into silence. After all, what else was there to be said?

Draco left her at her door with instructions to be ready for his chauffeur on Saturday. The announcement that they would be travelling via his private jet to Tuscany was carelessly thrown over his shoulder as he returned to his car. He seemed in a hurry to get away, so Rebel nodded through it all, then hurried inside.

Keeping a tight leash on the ball of emotions that had lodged in her chest, she climbed the stairs to her flat. Her feet froze on the last step as she saw the figure standing in her doorway.

Time and age had taken their toll on the man whose profile was visible in the hallway light, but Rebel would've recognised him anywhere. 'Dad?'

He jerked upright from his slumped position. The eyes her mother had insisted were the exact shade of her own widened a touch before dimming with wariness.

'Arabella.'

Her avid gaze sprinted over him, took in the pertinent details of weight loss pronounced by his baggy clothes, his thinning hair and unshaven face, before meeting his shadowed eyes.

'What…what are you doing here?' Considering she'd been frantically calling him every day for the past two weeks, the question was absurd, but the shock of seeing him again after so many years battered her thought processes.

'I came because of this.' He held up a copy of the latest edition of the evening newspaper. The picture on her phone was blown up on the broadsheet. Rebel's gaze darted away from the picture of her face as Draco bent over her hand, and took a step closer, her insides clenching with hurt as she stared at her father.

'I call you every day for weeks and you don't answer, but you turn up because of a picture in the paper?'

'It's not just any picture, though, is it?' he replied, that trace of condemnation she'd prayed never to hear again underlining his words. 'You need to end whatever this is, Arabella. Now.'

Shakily, she approached him and indicated the door. When he moved away, she inserted the key, opened it and thrust it wide.

She went inside, then didn't breathe until she heard his footsteps behind her.

Looking over her shoulder, she asked, 'Would you like a cup of tea?'

'Arabella—'

'I'm going to boil the kettle. You're already here. You might as well stay for tea.'

She hurried to the kitchen, kicked off her shoes and turned on the kettle. Her father walked in a few seconds later. After giving the room a once-over, he dropped the newspaper on the counter, pulled out a stool at the breakfast bar and sat down.

Struggling to contain her anxiety, Rebel got busy fetching mugs. Once the kettle boiled, she made the tea and slid a cup to him. 'Can I get you anything with it? Biscuits? A sandwich?'

He cradled his cup but made no move to drink it. 'You can tell me what this is about.' He indicated the paper.

'Can we forget about that for a minute, please?' Before he could respond, she rushed on. 'Where have you been? *How* have you been?'

'Away. Fine.' He continued to avoid her gaze, and with each second that ticked by Rebel's heart broke all over again.

'I'm sorry, Dad,' she whispered. 'I don't know how many more times I can say it.'

His breath shuddered on a deep exhale. 'The apology doesn't matter, Arabella. It never did. You're my child. Forgiving you was never a problem.' He pointed to the picture.

'But this is a problem. We spoke a few days ago, then over-night you go and do this?'

Her fingers clenched around her mug. 'You make it sound as if we have long talks on a regular basis. You may have known where I was and what I was doing, but I had no idea where you were. Until two weeks ago, I hadn't heard from you in *years*! And when I did try to talk to you after that, you barely said a handful of words to me. So, no, it hasn't been overnight for me, Dad, but years. Years during which you've watched over me, apparently. How else would you have known I'd been dropped by my sponsors?'

His fingers clenched around the mug. 'I had to.'

Pain clawed deeper. 'Because it was your *duty*? That's what you said in your letter, wasn't it? Was it your duty to deposit stolen money in my account?'

His head jerked up. 'You know?'

'Of course I know. According to Draco you didn't do a great job of hiding your tracks.'

He pushed away the tea and stood. 'Is he threatening you? Is that what this *engagement* is about?' He lurched towards the door. 'I'll turn myself in.'

Slamming her own cup down, she launched herself in the doorway. 'You can't!'

He frowned at her. 'Why not?'

'Because…it's too late. I've used the money and Draco knows it. If you go down, so do I.'

'But you didn't know it was stolen.'

'That doesn't matter. If Draco decides to press charges, I'll automatically become an accessory.'

Her father's throat worked as he swallowed. His head bent forward, and she glimpsed weariness in each move-ment.

Hesitantly, she placed a hand on his arm. 'Why did you take the money, Dad?' she asked, because deep down she knew he hadn't really changed from the upright, hard-working man she'd grown up admiring. 'Surely you must have known you wouldn't get away with it? That I'd be in the frame too if you were caught?'

He veered away from her, heading back to the stool. His rejection cut deeper but she stood her ground.

'I wasn't…' He stopped and shook his head. 'I wasn't thinking straight. I thought I could sell our old house and replace the money before he found out.'

'Why? Why was this so important to you?' she demanded, desperate for some indication that this hadn't been just duty for him.

'I promised your mother I'd look after you. It was one of the last things I said to her before…' He stopped again.

Rebel swallowed the sob that stemmed from her soul. 'She's gone, Dad. But I'm still here.'

Her father's head slowly rose from its heavy slump, then he speared her with haunted eyes. 'You took her from me. Then you began to turn into an exact copy of her.'

Her heart shrank. 'You hate me for that, don't you?'

He shook his head, his blue eyes swimming with sorrow, sharp and ocean-deep, even after all these years. 'I don't hate you. I could never hate you. But…I can't stand to look at you. Not when you were twenty and we fought constantly until you left home. And not now.'

The stark declaration wrenched a sob free as a part of her died.

'Where do we go from here, Dad?'

'I don't know. You've always known how I feel about your skiing. I always knew it wouldn't end well. And it didn't, did it?'

'Dad—'

'You don't need to talk me round. I know you'll do as you please, like always. But I know this thing you're doing with Angelis isn't the answer. The man is a predator.'

She wanted to refute the allegation. But really, what evidence had she apart from one evening's conversation where a small part of his life's story had tugged at her heartstrings? Draco had reverted to type soon enough.

Besides, she had even less of a choice now. After seeing her father still locked in grief after all this time there was no way she could stand by while he suffered for something he'd felt compelled to do because of her.

Heart in her throat, she shook her head. 'I can't, Dad. Like I said, it's too late.'

A full minute passed before he stood. He paused beside her by the kitchen door, but made no move to touch or even look at her. 'Goodbye, Arabella.'

Her tears came thick and fast long before he shut the door. And it was only through sheer exhaustion that sleep finally overtook her in the early hours.

CHAPTER NINE

THEY LANDED AT Pisa Airport mid-morning, before being flown by helicopter to Olivio Nardozzi's estate in northern Tuscany.

Draco alighted first before helping Rebel down. Guiding her beneath the rotating blades, he draped his arm around her waist and steered her to the path that led up to the sprawling mid-twentieth-century villa.

Although her mint-green sundress and matching sweater did nothing to alleviate the deep sizzling sensation his touch sent through her body, Rebel was too numb to do more than stay at his side as they approached the wide terrace that overlooked an aqua-tiled Olympic-sized pool.

She'd woken up raw and aching, unable to relive the conversation with her father without experiencing a hopeless, consuming pain at the thought that there could be no easy reconciliation. Not if her father couldn't look at her without—

'Whatever is wrong with you, Arabella, I suggest you get it under control right now,' Draco slashed in a fierce undertone. 'Now is *not* the time to drift into a trance.'

Rebel dragged herself back from the edge of the abyss, thankful that the unseasonably warm weather provided her with the perfect cover of her sunglasses as she blinked back rising tears.

'Not even a love trance with you in the starring role?'

He sent her a glance filled with combative censure, and a touch of disappointment. Reaching down, he plucked the sunglasses from her face and tucked them into his tailored trousers.

'We both know I've been far from your mind since you

boarded my plane in London this morning. I don't expect to be the subject of your thoughts night and day, but I expect you to be both physically and *mentally* present for this to work.' His voice was a low, hard throb so they wouldn't be overheard, but each word held unmistakable warning.

'Cool your jets, Draco. I haven't suddenly taken leave of my senses,' she whispered. Then in a pseudo Marilyn Monroe voice, she added, 'I'm still besotted with love for you and can't wait to tell our hosts what a lucky woman I am to have captured your elusive heart.'

They rounded another sun-dappled terrace and came face-to-face with Carla Nardozzi. Dressed in a pale yellow, clinging sundress, she stood next to an older man Rebel guessed to be her father, Olivio. Judging from their frozen expressions, it was clear her last words had carried. Before embarrassment could kick her hard, Draco strode to the middle of the terrace, where their hosts waited.

'Olivio, good to see you again.' He clasped the older man's hand in a firm greeting, then turned to his daughter. 'Carla, a pleasure, as always.' Draco's smile was warm as he leaned down and kissed the stunning, model-thin figure skater on both cheeks.

Rebel fought the acid-tipped spears that attacked her insides as she watched the scene.

Carla Nardozzi's limpid green eyes stayed on Draco for a second longer than Rebel thought was necessary before both father and daughter turned to her.

Returning to her side, Draco caught her hand in his. 'Allow me to introduce Arabella Daniels.'

Olivio was the first to greet her, eyes a shade lighter than espresso measuring her shrewdly. 'Welcome to my home, Miss Daniels. I look forward to making your further acquaintance,' he said in a thick accent.

'Thanks. And I'm sorry if you overheard me just then.'

'Nonsense. A woman should shout her love for her man from the rooftops. If it is genuine, that is,' Olivio declared.

His eyes dropped to her engagement ring, his scrutiny long and intense before he smiled at her.

Rebel forced her own smile wider. 'Oh, I'm glad you think so. Not everyone approves of public displays of affection.'

Carla came forward, her hand outstretched. Her caramel-streaked, chocolate-brown hair was pulled up into a severe chignon, the effect showing off the sleek lines of her jaw and neck. 'A pleasure to meet you.'

Rebel shook her cool hand, but before she could reply, Carla continued, 'So, it's true, then, what the papers are saying? You two are really engaged?' Her eyes drifted briefly over Rebel before they returned to Draco. Seeing the almost imploring look in the other woman's gaze, a boulder wedged in Rebel's midriff.

'Yes, it's true. I've finally succumbed to my heart's desire.' Molten grey eyes met Rebel's in a look designed to fool the most hardened heart.

Feeling him about to lift their linked hands and kiss hers as he had on Wednesday night, Rebel tensed her arm. Moving closer, she draped her hand on his chest and rose to kiss his cheek. His muted exhalation was the only exhibition of surprise at her move.

'But...didn't you two meet only recently?' Carla pressed, her eyes darting searchingly between them.

Rebel laughed and shook her head. 'We only chose not to make our relationship public before now since Draco is a *monster* when it comes to his privacy.'

Carla's smile was a little stiff. '*Sì*, I haven't forgotten.'

The boulder in Rebel's chest grew. 'Anyway, it's all out in the open now. Which is just as well because from the moment I met Draco, I knew my life would never be the same again. Fortunately, he felt the same and now doesn't mind shouting it to the world. In fact, he wouldn't leave my flat earlier this week until I'd accepted his ring and everyone knew I belonged to him. Isn't that right, darling?' She let her gaze drift over his face, stopping to linger at his mouth before meeting his eyes.

His eyes gleamed without a trace of mockery as his head angled towards hers. 'Only because my heart insisted you were mine, and I wasn't about to let you get away.'

A delicate throat-clearing fractured the moment. And yet Rebel couldn't look away from Draco, despite the astonishing evidence of his superb acting skills.

He broke the connection first. Rebel slowly sucked in a restorative breath before facing their hosts.

'Apologies for being sceptical. We wanted to be sure the media wasn't playing tricks on us,' Olivio stated. 'But now that you have confirmed this news, we must celebrate.' He snapped his fingers and a member of his staff rolled forward a serving trolley. At Olivio's nod, the server plucked a bottle of vintage Pol Roger champagne from a silver ice bucket and popped the cork.

'Not for me, thank you,' Carla said when she was offered a glass. 'I have another training session in an hour.'

'Ah, *sì*.' Olivio smiled indulgently. 'My daughter, she's the ultimate perfectionist. Never resting until the gold crown is on her head. And then she gets to work again the very next day.'

Carla paled slightly, a trace of anxiety passing over her face before she regained her composure.

Beside her, Draco tensed and a momentary trace of anger pursed his lips. But he lifted his glass at Olivio's prompt.

'To your future union. May it last for as long as there are stars in the sky.'

Carla excused herself as soon as the toasts were done, walking away with a painfully erect posture. As soon as he'd finished his drink, Olivio summoned another member of staff.

'This is Stefano, your personal butler. He will show you to your rooms and give you a tour of the grounds and facilities when you're ready. I have a few more guests arriving today, but tonight we're doing things a little informally. Food and drinks will be ready whenever you are out here on the terrace. There's nothing more special than dining al fresco on a cool Tuscan night.' Although he smiled, the warmth didn't quite reach his eyes.

The men shook hands, and Draco steered her out of the room.

The interior of the villa was opulence personified, with marble the dominant feature gleaming on the floors and walls. Followed a close second by Carla. Her pictures and trophies were displayed proudly on every surface. On the walls, several portraits and pictures with world leaders and dignitaries documented her from childhood to womanhood. It was clear Olivio regarded his daughter as his prized possession.

Rebel batted away the desperate envy she felt towards the other woman as the memory of the scene with her own father threatened to cut her off at the knees. Locking it away at the back of her mind once more, Rebel focused instead on the endless stream of Carla-mania, experiencing a touch of unease as she realised how extensive the displays were.

She was forcing herself not to think about the more disturbing interaction between Draco and Carla when she entered their designated suite and stumbled to a halt. Peripherally, she heard Draco dismiss Stefano and shut the door behind him, but she couldn't look away from the bed.

It was huge. Set on a pedestal made for lovers. With no other bed or divan in sight.

'Staring in horror at the bed won't let it magically dissolve into twin beds, *glikia mou*,' Draco drawled as he walked past her, pulling his shirt from his trousers as he crossed to what she assumed was a dressing room.

She stared, dry-mouthed, as he unbuttoned his shirt and shrugged it off. Discarding it on the centre island, he toed off his shoes as he went to a shelf and selected a white polo shirt. Barefooted, he strutted back into the room, then paused, one eyebrow raised at her.

'Are you staring at me in horror now because you want *me* to disappear?'

Rebel knew she was gaping at his contoured chest. The expanse of golden, vibrant skin made her tingle from head to toe. Which was bad. Really, really bad.

'I...we didn't discuss sleeping arrangements,' she blurted.

'Because it was inevitable that we would have to share a room with one bed in it for obvious reasons.'

The fever that had gripped her spiked. 'Well, you should've told me so I was better prepared, seeing as I'm not as well-versed in fake engagements as you seem to be.'

'Keep your voice down,' he warned as he sauntered towards her.

'Oh, please. You don't really think Olivio's skulking outside, eavesdropping on us, do you?'

He stopped in front of her. Still shirtless. More devastating to her senses. 'You tell me. Do you think our performance convinced him?'

'I don't think anything convinces Olivio that he can't hold physically in his hand.'

Grey eyes narrowed at her. 'What makes you say that?'

'Most people keep their trophies in a cabinet in a special room. He keeps Carla's trophies and pictures within easy view and reach, as if he needs a visual reminder of his and her success. I bet he's framed every endorsement he's negotiated on her behalf too. So I guess you were right about this.' She wriggled her ring finger. 'If nothing else, the fat diamond should work for us. Can you put your shirt on?' she snapped, forcing her knees to lock so she didn't retreat from the sinful temptation that was his bare torso. Or worse, lunge at him!

Both his eyebrows arched and a wolfish grin curved his lips. 'Why, Arabella, you'd think you'd never seen a half-naked man before.'

'Whether I have or not isn't the question here. It is whether the visual…situation is my choice, or whether it's imposed on me.'

'I see you've regained your smart mouth. If nothing else, I suppose it's better than your sullen mood this morning.'

Draco watched her eyes dim as if a switch had been turned off. For the first time in his life, he wanted to curse himself for stating a truth when discretion would've been the better part of valour. Truth be told, he hadn't enjoyed sharing space with a silent Arabella. He hadn't on Wednesday night either on the drive back from dinner. But *then*, he'd been reflecting on their dinner conversation, a part of him wondering whether he'd taken leave of his senses somewhere between the first and second courses. No other explanation made sense as to why he'd divulged intimate details known only to his closest family. Even the trial he'd mentioned had been held behind closed doors to protect Maria.

He'd eventually reasoned his behaviour away as a necessary evil in the task he'd undertaken. In the grand scheme of things, what did it matter if Arabella knew a few more details about him than he was comfortable with? He seriously doubted that she would step out of line with the threat of criminal charges hanging over her head.

He'd expected things to resume as planned, only to be met with a woman who, while he'd felt a modicum of satisfaction that she wasn't jumping at his touch any more, didn't seem inclined to engage with him on any level whatsoever.

And that had been before he'd seen the heavy traces of anguish shadowing her eyes this morning. He'd spotted the evidence of tears beneath her cleverly applied make-up the moment she'd stepped on the plane that not even the sunglasses had been able to disguise. Her mournful posture when she didn't think she was being observed had added to the mounting evidence that something had happened between Wednesday night and this morning.

'Arabella? Is something wrong?' he prompted when she remained silent.

A burst of laughter tripped from her lips but her gaze refused to meet his. 'Right at this moment, nothing that a quick chat about our sleeping arrangements won't fix.'

She was being evasive, but, short of shaking the truth out of her, Draco had no choice but to bite down on his frustration. 'You're that concerned about sharing?' He glanced at the bed. 'The bed is big enough for two. Or are you afraid you'll attack me in the middle of the night?'

She shrugged. 'I already have a few black marks against me. I'd rather leave grievous bodily harm off my list of sins.' Her tone was light but held a brittle edge that sliced at him. He searched her expression, his fingers itching to catch her chin and make her look at him so he could see beneath the snarky surface.

Draco wasn't entirely sure why he didn't. Perhaps he was wary of exposing a different set of problems. Where Arabella was afraid of close contact with him, was he craving it with her? More than that, was he craving more of the closeness he'd felt when he'd opened up to her about his past?

He stepped back abruptly. The questions were absurd in and of themselves. They were both playing a part. Closeness was a given. But not to be mistaken for anything he needed, never mind craved.

'If you're that worried about it, you take the bed. There's a living room through there with a comfortable enough sofa.'

He tugged his polo shirt over his head and returned to the dressing room to don his loafers.

'Do you want a tour of the training facilities?'

Her nod held relief. 'If you hang on a sec, I'll change into my trainers.'

When she joined him a few minutes later, she'd tied her hair into a ponytail. Stefano showed them where several golf buggies were parked in a neat row after Draco refused a personal escort.

He took the path that curved west of the villa, then aimed the buggy towards the domed building that sat atop a small hill. 'You seem to know your way around.' Her tone was neutral, as if she didn't care whether he answered or not.

When he glanced her way, her face was angled away from him.

His jaw clenched for a tight second. 'Yes. I've been here a few times. I advised Olivio during the training-facility build five years ago.'

She frowned. 'That implies a friendship. But you don't react to each other as friends do.'

'Probably because over the years we haven't seen eye to eye on a few issues.'

Her gaze flitted to him, speculated, then drifted away. 'But he still wants you to marry his daughter.'

Draco shrugged. 'Purely for dynastic reasons.'

Her mouth firmed and minutes ticked by as they crawled up the hill.

Bringing the buggy to a halt before large studio doors, he stopped her as she went to get out. 'I don't like it when you're quiet. If there's something on your mind, spit it out.'

Dull blue eyes met his. 'I thought you didn't like it when I used my smart mouth?'

His gaze dropped to the plump lips in question and heat dredged through him. 'I'm finding that I prefer it to your silence.'

She froze. They stared at each other for several charged seconds, the atmosphere growing thick and sultry, until she broke the connection and jumped from the buggy. 'Be careful what you wish for or I may never shut up again,' she said over her shoulder.

Deciding that it wasn't a scenario he was completely dissatisfied with, Draco followed her into the facility. The main feature was the enormous ice rink, around which several specialist gyms and sports-health centres had been installed. He found Arabella in the weights room, inspecting the state-of-the-art equipment.

She looked up as he entered. 'I'm in charge of my own training this weekend so the bench press is out of the question.'

'What are you swapping it with?'

'Free weights.'

He shook his head. 'You can't switch this far into the training.'

'It's only for this weekend. I talked it over with my trainer.'

'A small change can go a long way to hurt you. If you don't need to change it, don't. I'll spot you.'

Her eyes widened. 'Don't you have other stuff to attend to?'

'They will be dealt with. But not at the risk of neglecting your training.'

She blinked at him, her mouth dropping open to form responses that never emerged. Again he felt the gravity of unspoken words.

When minutes ticked by, he gritted his teeth. 'Are you happy with that?'

A shrug lifted her shoulders. 'Sure. If you want.'

As they left the gym the sound of blades cutting across ice filled the hall below. They both paused and watched as Carla, dressed in a white leotard, glided across the frozen surface.

She moved with effortless grace, years of practice making her fearless as she executed jumps and pirouettes that had seen her rise to the top of her game.

As he watched her, the wretched pain that came with wondering what Maria could've been slammed into him. Gripping the railing, he stared at the figure below and saw the image of his sister, her wide, infectious smile lighting her face as she did the only thing she'd ever dreamt of doing.

'She's breathtaking.'

He heard the voice from afar, lost as he was in torment-ing memories. 'Yes, she is,' he breathed, still unable to take his eyes off the figure. Draco wasn't sure how long he stood there, wishing he could change the past. Know-ing he couldn't.

When he resurfaced, Arabella had moved a short dis-tance away, facing away from the railing with her arms folded. Her face was averted, but he caught the pain etched deep into her profile.

About to call her name, demand that she tell him what was wrong once and for all, he froze as a dark tingling seized his nape. A door slammed shut at the far side of the rink and he watched a figure glide to where Carla had stopped in the middle of the ice.

Every nerve in Draco's body tightened as he recognised the man.

'Draco?' Rebel's voice came from a tunnel of darkness.

'Hmm?'

'Are you okay?'

'No,' he bit out.

'What's going on?'

'That man Carla's talking to. That's Tyson Blackwell.'

Arabella turned around, glanced down at the ice. 'Did you know he was going to be here?'

'No. Olivio chose not to inform me of that fact.' His grip tightened around the smooth railing, the urge to rip it from its moorings clawing at him.

'Right. As devious as that sounds, unless you intend to stare Tyson to death, can we get out of here, please?' Her voice trembled, her features pinched in misery.

Without waiting for an answer, she vaulted out of the door and rushed down the stairs.

He emerged into sunlight, fury still burning in his chest. Draco had never felt inclined to cause bodily harm. Not when his trainer had sent him down a path that had ruined his dream. Not even when he'd surfaced from his nightmares to find his sister's life equally ruined.

But seeing Blackwell here, preparing to sink his teeth into yet another victim, Draco had to fight hard to resist the urge to march back in and rip the man to pieces.

Instead, he forced one foot in front of the other. Reaching the buggy, he slammed on the ignition, wishing he had an engine far more powerful than a battery-packed one.

Beside him, Arabella sat in silence once again, her hands folded in her lap, her features remote. The volatile emotions churned harder inside him. A roar mounted in his head.

With no outlet, hopelessness closed over him, dark and devastating. In that moment, Draco knew his only choice was to drive. So he let the silence reign.

CHAPTER TEN

'COME THIS WAY. I know a back way to the suite,' Draco said, his voice a gruff command.

From the moment she'd seen his face as he watched Carla skate, Rebel's world had turned dark and her misery had bloomed. Like toxic smoke, it'd sped through her veins, insidious and inescapable, until her body was steeped in it.

Up until that moment, she hadn't realised she'd been using Draco as a balm against the gaping wound of her father's rejection since she'd stepped on his plane this morning. It didn't matter that the man was often times cold and ruthless, or cutting and dismissive. It didn't even matter that, when it came right down to it, she was an unwitting criminal, who dangled between jail and freedom at the sole discretion of the man she was relying on to drag her from her nightmares.

All she'd cared about was that she was with him, and not at her flat, reliving each word her father had said. She'd been sure it was why the thought of a history between Draco and Carla chafed as much as it did.

Draco's face as he'd watched Carla glide over the ice had hammered home a different truth—her reasons for relying on Draco weren't wholly for the sake of avoiding thinking about her father.

The level of her misery had forced her to acknowledge another truth. Draco obviously cared for Carla beyond platonic or business interests.

'The sight of Carla with that man upsets you that much?' she forced herself to ask, because she couldn't *not* know.

'Yes, it does,' he grated as they mounted stairs that ended in two wraparound terraces.

Her heart dipped, along with her ability to think straight. She followed almost robot-like as he took the left wrap-around terrace, which brought them to a set of French doors. He thrust it open and they entered the hallway that led to their suite.

She stepped in front of him as he was about to head to the living room.

'Carla means more to you than just getting her away from Tyson Blackwell, doesn't she?' she challenged, absently wondering why she couldn't stop herself from probing a point that seemed to lance her with arrows of bewildering pain.

Draco frowned. 'Of course. You think I'd go through all this for someone I didn't care about?'

Rebel's hand shook as she lifted it to her temple. 'Sorry, I'm confused. You care enough about her to want to save her from Tyson, but it's just the marrying her that you're against?'

'I'm against being manipulated, period,' he snarled. 'Somewhere along the line, Olivio has obviously concluded he can leverage my private life to suit him. That's not going to happen. Now if you're done with your questions, I'd appreciate not being interrogated further about this. You know your role. Just play it and we'll be fine.'

He went to the drinks cabinet. Grabbing a bottle of single-malt whisky, he pulled the cork and poured two fingers into a crystal tumbler.

He knocked it back in one clean swallow. Then he slammed the glass down and clenched both hands in his hair.

Several Greek curses fell from his lips as he paced the floor.

Chest tight with emotions she refused to name, she eyed him. 'You do realise that if you insist on continuing this façade and you don't do anything about the state you're in, you're going to blow this charade wide open, don't you?'

He paused mid-stride. 'Why do you think I'm in here knocking back drinks instead of out there, punching Blackwell's face in?' he growled.

Rebel flinched. She needed to walk away, leave him alone to handle this on his own. She wasn't equipped to deal with anyone's emotional fallout; not when she was actively hiding from her own. But she'd also never seen anyone care this deeply...not since witnessing the unstinting adoration between her parents. She'd deeply missed the overflow of warmth from that special bond. So even though a physical ache lodged in her chest as she watched Draco try to wrestle his emotions under control, she remained rooted to the floor beside the armchair.

'Are you going to talk to Carla about this?'

'I'll have to. I can't let this go any further. Olivio might not listen, but I hope she will.'

He dropped his hands from the back of his neck and then stared at his trembling fingers. He seemed fascinated with his body's reaction. Then slowly he clenched his fists and exhaled. Although his body calmed, the Draco who walked past her with a curt, 'I need a shower,' possessed eyes so bleak they were almost black.

She instinctively reached out and grasped his arm. He jerked to a stop, his gaze going to where she held him, then back to her face.

'Arabella, I'm not thinking very rationally right now,' he rasped. Residual fury vibrated off him, emotional aftershocks that threatened to bury her the longer she stayed this close.

'I know, and I'll be quick. I just wanted to say, if you can help it, don't let this eat you up too much.'

'As long as that bastard is sniffing around her, it'll eat me up.'

'But—'

His hand shot out to grip her arm, the other coming up to hover over her mouth. His thumb slid across her mouth.

'Enough, *glikia mou*. I don't want to think about Black-well any more. So enough. Okay?' Bleak eyes searched hers, pleading.

At her nod, he dropped his hand. And replaced it with his mouth. Shock held her still long enough for him to delve between her lips. Then pure, unadulterated sensation took over. Her moan rose up from her soul, excavating every yearning she'd tried to suppress since Wednesday night. Her hands gripped his bare arms, the fierce joy of touching him somewhere else besides his nape and face piercing her. She strained up, plastering her needy, super-charged body against his, and earning herself an answering groan in return. One hand trailed the length of her back to her be-hind, then splayed open to drag her even closer. She ground against his erection, her nerves tingling, the secret place between her legs dampening, readying itself for this man…

This man who didn't belong to her.

He nipped at the corner of her bottom lip just as she jerked away from him. They parted and she was left with a coppery taste in her mouth. Draco's eyes zeroed in on the spot, a hiss issuing from his lips. 'Arabella *mou*…your lip.' He reached out. She danced out of his way.

'It's okay, I'm fine.' She licked at the spot again, and he groaned.

'Sweetheart, let me—'

'No. You can't do this, Draco.'

He stared at her for a frozen second, his breath shudder-ing in and out. With another curse, he threw his head back and closed his eyes for a brief moment. Exhaling one last time, he stared straight at her. 'No. I guess not. But next time, tell me which body part you want me to cry on before I go thinking everything is available to me.'

'How about we agree right now that *none* of it is avail-able to you?'

His gaze dropped to her mouth. 'So I get your *words* and nothing else?'

'Wasn't that what you wanted?' she replied.

A stiff smile twitched one corner of his mouth. 'Thanks for the reminder.'

He strode out of the room with long, angry strides. Rebel waited till she heard the faint sound of running water before she hurried to the dressing room. She swapped her trainers for heels that would elevate her attire back to smart casual. Combing out her hair, she sprayed perfume on her wrists before grabbing her bag and slipping out onto the terrace. She reclined on the shaded lounger, willing her racing pulse to subside as she plucked her phone and earphones from her bag. Cranking up the music, she tucked up her legs to her chest.

Much as she'd have liked to escape the suite totally, she didn't want to risk running into Olivio or any of his guests without Draco in case the agitation bubbling beneath her skin showed. If Draco wanted to stay, he would need his acting skills to get them *both* through tonight and tomorrow.

Rebel grew drowsy as her pulse finally calmed and her thundering heartbeat stopped roaring in time to the music.

The feeling of a soft blanket being draped over her roused her from sleep. Draco sat on the twin lounger, his eyes a lot less volatile than they'd been. In fact, he looked downright solemn and perhaps even a touch contrite.

'How long have I been asleep?' she asked around a dry mouth.

He handed her a cool drink, which she accepted and sipped gratefully. 'Long enough for your cycle of crazy music to play three times.'

So just over two hours. 'It's not crazy music. It calms me down.' She bit her lip as she said it, wondering if she would unwittingly set him off.

But he remained seated, his gaze steady on her. 'I owe you an apology. You were trying to help and I...took advantage.'

A knot she hadn't acknowledged unravelled inside her.

'You warned me you weren't thinking rationally. I should've let you go, not insisted on saying my piece.'

His mouth twisted. 'Your piece, brief as it was, was very welcome. It saved the shower wall from getting a pounding.'

'Yikes. Not sure you'd have come off without serious battle scars, what with *all* that marble.'

He grinned, then sobered after a few seconds. 'While you were asleep, I spoke to Olivio. He won't discuss his business with Blackwell, but it turns out he's not staying at the villa. I guess Olivio wasn't prepared to risk one of us walking out.'

'Did you get a chance to talk to Carla?' she asked.

He shook his head. 'She was resting after her training.'

Rebel twirled the straw through her drink. 'So what now?'

'We can go down to dinner. Or we can stay here and have dinner brought up to us. We are newly engaged, after all.'

The thought of not having to put on a show in front of strangers was hugely appealing. She'd fallen asleep before she'd worked things through and now the events of the afternoon came flooding back.

Setting her half-empty glass down, she braced her elbows on her knees and massaged her temples.

He frowned. 'Are you all right?'

'I'm trying to wrap my mind around all this.'

Draco sighed, a wave of cold misery rushing over his face before he schooled his features. Then he released a breath. 'Perhaps a further explanation would help?'

'Please,' she murmured.

For almost a minute, his jaw clenched tight. 'After my knee blew out and my career ended, I shut everyone out. I was angry with myself for not seeing what Larson and his team were up to. I just gave my statement to the police and let them handle it. What I didn't know was that they'd missed one crucial member of the team. Larson's nephew.'

Her heart leapt into her throat as she made the connection. 'Tyson Blackwell?'

Draco nodded grimly. 'He was in charge of my sister's training.'

'Your *sister*?'

'Yes.' He blew out a ragged breath. 'Maria was a figure skater. She and Carla are best friends. They don't see each other as regularly any more, but she idolises Carla. Watching Carla's videos was the only thing that pulled her from the brink after the accident.'

'What happened to Maria?'

'What always happens when Blackwell's in charge. He pushed her past her limit. She was doing a quadruple rotation she was woefully unprepared for when she fell and hit her head on the ice. She fractured her third vertebrae and lost the use of her arms and legs.'

A sob strangled Rebel's chest. 'No!'

'By the time I got my head on straight after my own accident, Blackwell had covered his tracks. He stood trial but he only got an eighteen-month ban for two of his trainees missing doping tests. He got off scot-free for what he did to Maria.' Bitterness and anger twisted his face.

The same expressions he'd exhibited this afternoon as he'd watched Carla skating…

Had she got it wrong? Had she attributed a different spin on Draco's feelings for Carla? The pressure eased in her chest. Surely he wouldn't have gone to the trouble of engineering a fake engagement to put off a woman he could have had if he felt so inclined? From the first, it'd been Olivio's manipulation and Tyson Blackwell's presence in Carla's life that had enraged Draco.

Relief punched through her, startling a laugh from her throat.

'What?' Draco demanded.

'I…nothing.' She sobered and reached out, curling her hand around his jaw before the action fully registered. 'I know it's hard to believe, but what happened to your sister wasn't your fault.'

He shook his head. 'It was. Larson didn't broadcast it but I knew he had a nephew. I was so focused on my career, I didn't pay attention to the team my father had hired for Maria. If I'd been around more, I would've noticed that things weren't right.'

'Sorry to break it to you, but if you couldn't see it in your own team, how would you have noticed it in your sister's team?'

Raw anguish propelled him to his feet. 'I was her older brother. I was supposed to look after her!'

The weight of her own guilt crushed down on her. 'Blind spots when it comes to our family are dangerously common.'

He stopped and stared down at her. 'Your father?'

She shrugged, her chest clamped in a steel vice. 'Me. My mother. We all have our faults. Some are a little more unforgivable than others.'

Exhaling sharply, Draco strode to the terrace railing a few feet away and gripped it hard. The muscles in his back bunched as tension gripped him harder. 'I had you investigated—I'm sure you understand why. Your mother died in a skiing accident. You weren't responsible for her death.'

The blood drained from her face, and her lungs closed up. Dropping her head forward, she desperately tried to get her blood pumping again.

Sound faded in and out as she tried to breathe.

'Arabella!'

A moment later, Draco swung her into his arms and strode back into the suite. The sofa was the closest comfortable surface. He placed her there and drew the blanket over her and crouched before her. 'I shouldn't have left you in the sun for so long.'

'I'm fine.'

'You're not. You didn't eat on the plane and you haven't

eaten since we got here,' he huffed. Rising, he headed for the door. Rebel heard him issuing instructions to Stefano before he returned to the living room.

Despite the guilt eating her alive, she couldn't look away from him as he sat on the coffee table and leaned towards her. Brushing her hair from her face, he tucked a strand behind her ear. The side of his finger smoothed over her cheek to her jaw before repeating the caress.

The gesture was so sweet, she wanted to relive it over and over. 'Are you going soft on me, Draco?' she murmured.

'Only until you're back on your feet,' he murmured back. 'Then it'll be all-out war again.'

She sighed. 'War is exhausting.'

'Who have you been fighting, *glikia mou*? Besides me, that is?' he asked, his voice a gentle rumble that lulled her from the secret place she'd inhabited for far too long.

'My father.'

'You've seen him?'

Her gaze clashed with his. 'Will you hate me if I say yes?'

He stilled, his finger dangerously close to her pulse. 'Family is complicated, I get that. Besides, I gave my word that if you fulfilled your part of the agreement, I'd forgive the debt.'

Relief flooded her. 'All right, then. He was waiting for me when I got in on Wednesday night.'

Draco frowned. 'At your flat?'

'Yes. He'd seen the news of our engagement in the paper.'

One brow rose. 'Let me guess—he came to warn you off me?'

She nodded. 'He's not a fan of yours.'

His mouth twisted. 'I don't have many of those these days who aren't contracted to me in some fashion or other.'

Her eyelids felt heavy again, but she fought them open. 'I was your fan way before you turned into Draco the Dragon.'

'*Efkharisto*, Arabella.'

'I love the way that sounds.'

'What?'

'The Greek…and my name.'

She stared up at him, her breath catching all over again at the sheer dynamic beauty of his face. Then she shut her eyes when his image swam. 'Why am I drowsy again?'

'Probably because you haven't slept well recently.'

'Hmm. You're bad for my health.'

His mouth twitched. 'You were telling me about your father.'

'Yes. He offered to turn himself in so I wouldn't be engaged to you any longer. I refused.'

She wasn't sure whether the sharp exhalation came from him or her, but she pressed on. 'I told him it was too late. I'd given you my word. Besides, I don't think prison dungarees would suit me, do you?'

'You'd look good in anything, but perhaps prison gear shouldn't be on anyone's wish list.'

'I agree. Anyway, he accepted that there was nothing he could do so…' She tried to shrug, but couldn't quite pull it off. Sorrow clawed at her, her father's words still fresh, and deep, and anchored into her heart. Tears brimmed and rolled down her temples.

This time Draco's hiss was audible. 'What did he say to you?'

'I asked when I'd see him again. He said he…he couldn't look at me without seeing my mother…and that it hurt too much that she's no longer alive, so he intends to stay away.'

He surged to his feet. '*Thee mou.* What sort of man is he?' he raged.

Rebel struggled up. When he tried to stay her, she grabbed his hand. 'You don't understand, Draco. He loved my mother. I mean *really* loved her. It shattered him completely when she died.' Another tear rolled down her face. She swiped at it with her free hand.

'It still doesn't excuse his treatment of you.'

Her heart ached that she couldn't tell Draco the last piece

of her life's puzzle. But after hearing him condemn himself and anyone who'd been responsible for his sister's injuries, Rebel knew he would never forgive her for causing her mother's death. 'Does it hurt? Sure. But I don't want him to be in pain because of me. If he can find some peace away from me, then...'

Draco made a rough sound at the back of his throat. Raising her head, she met his laser-sharp gaze. 'You'd sacrifice that? A lifetime's relationship just so he could be happy?'

Her tiredness was receding. But with more clarity came harrowing pain. 'As opposed to him being miserable with me? Yes, I would.'

'You're...extraordinary,' he husked out.

She raised one eyebrow. 'You seem surprised.'

The knock on the suite door stopped their conversation. Draco stared down at her for several heartbeats before he called out for Stefano to enter.

The trolley was heaving with meats and sausages from the barbecue going on by the poolside, Stefano informed them. Warm focaccia bread, with olive oil and garlic sauces, and an assortment of salads were unearthed from beneath domed dishes.

Dismissing Stefano, Draco heaped a plate with food and set her tray down on her lap. After seeing to his own, he sat down next to her. They ate in companionable silence, for once at ease with each other's company.

Her insides clenched momentarily at the thought of the tight secret lodged inside her. She'd thrown caution to the wind and told him as much as she could about her relationship with her father. Despite Draco's harsh views, she knew he wouldn't go after her father as long as she kept up her end of the bargain.

She was used to flying through the air without a safety harness or a net to break her fall. Ski jumping was one of the riskiest sports out there, and yet she'd thrown herself into it without a backward glance.

She glanced at Draco and found his gaze, direct and intense, on her.

Perhaps it was time to take a different, equally exhilarating, risk.

CHAPTER ELEVEN

THE SOUND OF the door shutting woke Rebel in the early hours. She'd said goodnight to Draco shortly after their meal last night with an arrangement to head out to the gym at five a.m.

Turning over in bed, she stretched her limbs, groaning with relief at the most restful sleep she'd had since her father's letter had brought her nightmares about losing her mother surging back. She hadn't even needed her earphones to drown out the demons.

Glancing at the clock, she noticed it was only four-fifteen. Had Draco headed out to get his own training in before he trained with her? Pushing aside the covers, she sprang out of bed. On the off-chance she was mistaken, she peeked into the living room. The sofa bed had been tucked away and the sheets folded up.

Deciding to join him, Rebel changed into her exercise gear, caught up her phone and earphones, and left the suite. Knowing she would get lost if she tried the shortcut, she went through the villa, unease striking all over again at the gratuitous display of Carla Nardozzi's pictures and trophies.

She stepped out into the crisp air, thankful that the whole estate was well lit. After stretching her arms and legs, she placed her earphones in and struck out in the direction of the facility.

The studio door stood ajar when she reached it. She slipped in and muted her music.

The cry from the direction of the ice rink froze her steps.

Changing direction, she entered the room to witness the tail end of an argument between Carla and Tyson Blackwell.

He had her gripped by the arms, Carla's whimper echoing across the room.

'You want to win another glitzy trophy? Then do what I tell you to do!'

'A triple axel into a death spiral sounds insane!'

'Damn it, maybe I am wasting my time with you. All your competitors are doing it. Fail to master it and you can kiss your career goodbye.'

He flung her away from him. Carla tried to catch herself but went sprawling onto the ice.

Rebel stepped into the light. 'Hey, you can't talk to her like that!'

Tyson whirled from his fallen victim. 'Who the hell are you?'

'Someone who can see that you're pushing her way too hard.'

He shooed her away. 'The way I run my training programme is none of your business. Now, I suggest you clear off.'

'I'm not going anywhere. Unless Mr Nardozzi decides to throw me out, of course.' From the corner of her eye, she saw Carla drag herself up and totter on her blades.

Turning, shock slammed through Rebel at the full blast of the younger girl's glare before Carla carefully schooled her features.

'She's my father's guest. She's here with Draco Angelis.'

Even from several dozen feet away, Rebel saw malicious interest spark in his eyes. Leaving Carla's side, he slid across the ice to her.

'So you're Angelis' little piece on the side I've heard so much about this past week.' His head tilted. 'You look familiar. Do I know you?' A suggestive leer draped his face.

'Yeah, in your dreams.'

The leer evaporated. 'This is a training session, not a spectator event. Please leave.'

Rebel looked past him to where Carla stood, a forlorn

figure in the centre of the ice rink. About to call out to her, she spun at the sound of thundering footsteps.

'Arabella!'

The urgency in Draco's deep voice sent a delicious spark down her spine. 'In here,' she called out.

He surged into the room a second later, his eyes narrowing as they zeroed in on her. 'You were supposed to wait for me—' He froze as he spotted Tyson Blackwell. Then he looked past him to where Carla was poised.

When Draco's eyes clashed with Rebel's, his rage had quadrupled. 'What the hell's going on here?'

'I'm conducting a training session. Have you been out of the game so long you've forgotten even the basics, Angelis?' Tyson sneered.

Draco ignored him. Striding to the edge of the ring, he called out, 'Carla. Come here.'

'Hey, what the hell—? Stay where you are, girl,' Tyson countered.

After a moment's hesitation, Carla skated to Draco. This close, the finger marks where Tyson had gripped her were visible against her pearly skin.

Fury flared through Draco's nostrils. 'Did he do this to you?' he grated out.

Hesitantly, Carla nodded. Draco pointed a finger at Tyson. 'You're finished. If you know what's good for you, find a deep dark hole and disappear inside. If I see you around one more skater, the only place you'll be heading to is jail to join your bastard uncle.'

'You have no authority here, Angelis. I have Olivio's full support. If you think you're going to change that, forget it,' he snarled. Glancing at Carla, he added, 'We'll pick this up later.' Tyson rolled back to the other end of the ice rink, kicked off his blades and stormed out via another entrance.

Holding out his hand, Draco helped Carla down. 'Take off your blades. I'll take you back to the villa.'

With a dazzling smile at Draco, Carla replaced her blades with heeled boots and tucked her hand through his arm.

Despite choosing to believe that there was nothing romantic between Draco and Carla, Rebel's stomach still contracted with irrational envy as she watched them disappear through the door.

'Right. Guess I'll see you when I see you,' she muttered, unprepared for the renewed misery snaking through her. Just as she was unprepared for Draco to suddenly reappear as she mounted the stairs to the weight room.

'What do you think you're doing?' he snapped.

She paused on the second step. 'Umm…going training?'

'Not without me, you're not.' Taking her arm, he walked her out and sat her on the remaining unoccupied passenger seat of the buggy, which happened to be behind a less-than-happy-looking Carla.

Draco walked Carla to the villa door once they arrived, his low murmuring voice eliciting several nods from her before she went in and shut the door behind her.

His demeanour changed as he strode back to the buggy. Sliding behind the wheel, he flicked her a glance. 'Get in the front.'

She complied, simply because she wanted to be closer to him. She was barely seated when the buggy surged forward. The five-minute journey felt like hours, the easy silence they'd shared last night a smoky figment of her imagination.

As they crested the hill she cleared her throat. 'Are you upset with me?'

His jaw clenched hard before he spoke. 'Damn right. You were supposed to wait for me. Instead I returned to find you gone.'

'I woke up early and thought you were here, at the facility.'

'I'd just gone to get a drink of coffee. We agreed to come here together. At five. Instead I found you here, in the cross hairs of a man I wouldn't trust with my goldfish.'

'Then we should be thankful I'm more substantial than a goldfish, shouldn't we? And for the record, I pack a hell of a punch when threatened.'

His eyes narrowed. 'Is that jibe aimed at me?'

'Unless you plan to attack me, no.'

His hand slashed through the air. 'I don't like this. In case you've forgotten we're still playing a role. One Olivio is keeping a close eye on.'

'Being engaged doesn't mean we're joined at the hip. You were worried about overcooking things. You not letting me out of your sight runs the risk of doing just that. You can frown all you want, but it's the truth.'

'I hardly think not wanting to be parted from you sends that message. Certainly not at four o'clock in the morning when you should be in bed with me.'

Rebel sighed. 'You found me, Draco. I'm okay. Let's chalk it up to a win because my getting here early stopped Tyson from manhandling Carla more than he did.'

Fury detonated. The vibrations from him threatened to flatten her. 'What if you'd been on your own with him?' he seethed.

'I wasn't,' she stated simply.

He fisted his hair for a charged second before he jerked out of the buggy. 'You wanted to train so badly? Let's get to it, then.'

Rebel followed him in, her senses surging higher as she followed his ruggedly lean body up the stairs to the weights room.

Over the next hour, he set a blistering place, his commands bullet fast and relentless.

'Faster!' he shouted over the sound of the treadmill.

'Lower!' he boomed from behind her as she sank into another excruciating squat.

'Damn it, lock your elbows.'

'Damn it, they *are* locked!'

He leaned over the weight bar vibrating with the tension in her triceps. 'Are you being smart with me?' he snarled.

'I don't have a single smart left in me, Drill Sergeant,' she ground out.

Their eyes met. Battled. Then his stormy grey eyes moved over her sweat-drenched body as she lowered the bar and pressed it back up.

'Ten,' he rasped, without taking his eyes off her bare midriff. 'Nine,' he supplied helpfully after another shredding lift.

'Draco…'

'Eight.'

'Stop,' she gasped.

'Seven. Stop counting?'

'Stop…staring.'

'No.' His gaze moved to her breasts and his breathing altered. 'Six.'

'Grrruuuugh!'

'Is that even English? Five.'

'I hate you!'

'I hate you back. Four.' He squatted and brushed back the wet tendrils at her temple. 'Three.'

'You're…touching me, Draco. You want me to fail,' she panted.

'Never. Almost there, *glikia mou*. Two.'

Pain rippled through her body as lactic acid surged through her system. 'One!' she shouted.

He stood over her and took the weight from her trembling grip.

Rebel stood and shook her hands, relief pouring through her wrists and biceps as her pumping heart settled. 'Piece of cake.'

Draco came up behind her, and held a bottle of water to her lips. She drank thirstily, then, just because she could, she relaxed against him, rubbed her back against his front.

His breath hissed in her ear. 'Why do you drive me crazy like this?'

'Umm…you make it too damn easy?'

Dropping the bottle, he flipped her round. '*Thee mou*, your mouth!'

'Is all the workout you need?'

With a pained grunt he smashed his mouth on hers. Strong arms banded her waist and she linked her arms around his neck as he picked her up and walked forward to the martial arts area. Her body hit the mat none too gently, but Rebel didn't care. Draco was kissing her and her senses were on fire. This time when he parted her legs, she welcomed him, holding her breath until he rolled his hips against her.

'Oh!' She thrilled to the shudder that rolled through her.

'Damn, you're so responsive,' he groaned against her mouth.

'Complaint?'

'Compliment.'

'Okay. Proceed.'

He consumed her, each lick, bite and pinch twisting them higher, until they broke apart, desperate for the sweet sustenance of oxygen. Weaving her fingers through his hair, Rebel just gloried in the weight of him and the hand sliding up and down her calf.

'Arabella?'

'Drill Sergeant?'

His mouth stretched against her cheek. Her heart flipped over at the thought that she'd made him smile. Turning her head, she stole a kiss. He groaned again. 'We can't do this here.'

'In this room, this villa, or this country?'

'Definitely not in this room. I'd prefer a different bed and a different villa to one owned by Olivio Nardozzi. How would you feel about leaving a day early and switching to a different country?'

'What about Olivio?'

A hard smile curved his lips. 'My wanting to be alone with you away from this place should serve as a further convincer.'

Her breath shuddered. 'And do you?'

He fused his mouth to hers in a hard kiss. 'Enough to put my pilot on standby to leave immediately after the gala tonight.'

'So…where would you take me?'

His nostrils flared as his eyes darkened. 'I have homes in most of the major sports-orientated cities around the world. But wherever you want to go, I can make it happen.' He leaned down and brushed his growing stubble against her cheek before placing an open-mouthed kiss on the racing pulse at her throat.

'Do all your homes have what I need to train?'

'Of course,' he murmured.

'What about Greg?'

His head jerked up, blazing eyes piercing hers. 'Who's Greg?'

'My trainer.'

He relaxed a touch. 'Get him to send me your training schedule. I'll take care of you until your dry-land drills are over. He can take over again when we get to Verbier.'

Her heart leapt. 'You're coming to the championships?'

'You're my fiancée. How would it look if I'm not there by your side?'

Rebel told herself the lurching of her heart was a good reminder that all of this wasn't real. That what they were doing had a coldly calculated purpose and a finite conclusion, no matter that she'd decided to risk making it a little bit more than the platonic undertaking they'd agreed.

Mentally shaking off the voice that probed the wisdom of changing the parameters of their agreement, she grimaced at him. 'I'm not sure I want you as my trainer if every training session is going to be like this.'

'It's not going to be like this,' he returned. 'It's going to be worse.'

Her eyebrow shot up. 'Worse?'

'I've seen what you're capable of. You protest at every drill, yet you can easily achieve so much more.' A frown locked between his eyebrows. 'It's almost as if you don't want to achieve your full potential.'

Her gaze dropped from his probing look.

He caught her chin in his hand. 'Arabella?'

'I…it's not that. I want to win this championship. More than anything.'

'But?'

'But I'm afraid after that there'll be nothing else. Nothing to strive for. My father is gone, Draco. I don't know if I'll ever see him again. Once the championships are over, I'll have nothing.'

His frown dissolved, but his jaw clenched. 'Why were you doing it in the first place?'

'Mostly for my mother. I want to honour her memory.'

'But not with a win? How is coming fifth when you can be champion truly honouring her?'

'It wasn't so much the winning, as just participating in the sport she loved.'

He shook his head. 'I don't buy that. And I don't think you do either. This still has to do with your father, doesn't it? What is it?'

She swallowed the rock that lodged in her throat. 'He didn't want me to become a professional skier. Like your father, he wanted me to do something else. My mother and I talked him around with…with a promise that I'd give up once I won a major championship.'

Fury roared through his eyes. 'So you've been deliberately holding yourself back because of a promise you made when you were…how old?'

'I was fifteen.'

'You were a child!'

'But old enough to understand what promises meant.'

A scalding curse ripped through the room. He levered himself off her and stood glaring down at her.

'So that's what you're going to do for the rest of your life, always achieving a little less than your potential because of a father who doesn't have a problem betraying you?'

Pain bit deeper. 'Draco…'

'What would your mother have wanted for you?'

She closed her eyes, her insides a churning river of sorrow. 'For me to compete. And win.'

He crouched down and lifted her to her feet. 'And what do *you* want, Arabella?'

Sharp tears prickled the backs of her eyes. 'I want everything. To keep my promise to my father. To honour my mother. And to win multiple championships.'

He shook his head, a tinge of bleakness in his eyes. 'You're realistic enough to know that we never get everything we want. And by fruitlessly hanging onto one dream, you're jeopardising everything else.' He let go of her and took several steps back.

Rebel wasn't sure why that deliberate withdrawal sent a wave of panic through her. 'Draco?' She reached for him, but he stepped farther away.

'Choose, Arabella. Either you're in this all the way or you're not.'

Her hand balled into a fist, the vein of shame she'd always felt when she'd held back instead of going all in during competitions thickening uncomfortably. 'Why? What is it to you?'

'I'm not asking you to choose for me. I'm asking you to choose for yourself.' He paced in front of her but still kept out of reach. 'Imagine yourself thirty years down the line. Is this the legacy you'd want to leave? That you deliberately fell short of reaching for your goals?'

'No.' The word charged out of her, fired from a place she'd deliberately closed off because the desires that resided there were too painful to dream about. Being forced to confront them sent a wave of sadness through her. Because in order to achieve what she truly yearned for, she would be throwing away any chances of reconciliation with her father. But then what were the guarantees that they would reconcile when he'd stated plainly that the very sight of her wrecked him? Was she in danger of throwing out one dream to follow another that might never come true?

The memory of her mother pierced her thoughts, of her beautiful smile and ecstatic cheering when Rebel had won her first junior championship. All the way home Susie Daniels had babbled her pride and hopes for her daughter's future to anyone who would listen. That day had been one of the happiest days of Rebel's life. She wanted to relive that day again. And again. She wanted that memory of her mother to never fade. Never cease to inspire her. With a shaky breath, she looked at Draco. 'No, I don't want that.'

He breached the gap between them and caught her face in his hands. His eyes glowed with a fire she wanted to believe was pride. But then he angled his head and kissed her, and her every sense coalesced into pleasure. He didn't let up until the need to breathe drove them apart.

This time the look in his eyes when their gazes met was one of pure predatory hunger. Sliding his hand down her arm, he laced their fingers and tugged her to the door.

'Come. Let's go and get this day over with so I can begin kicking your ass into gear,' he drawled with unabashed relish.

'Just remember, I kick back.'

He laughed. 'How soon you forget yourself. Insubordination of any kind will only make things worse for you.'

'How did I know you'll try to get your way with threats?'

'Those aren't threats, *glikia mou*. They're golden promises.'

CHAPTER TWELVE

REBEL WAS STILL hiding a smile that threatened to split her face when they returned to their suite. The look in Draco's eyes as she walked away to take her shower could've buckled steel.

All through the day as they mingled with guests whose names she forgot almost as soon as Olivio made introductions, she felt the weight of Draco's hungry stare. Not that he left her side for more than a few minutes at a time. By the time they returned to their suite to get ready for the gala, Rebel was sure she would spontaneously combust if he glanced at her one more time.

But he did more than glance at her when she emerged from the dressing room at a few minutes to eight.

'I'm good to go,' she addressed a tuxedoed Draco, who was nursing a small whisky as he gazed out into the Tuscan night.

He turned. He froze. His scrutiny was thorough, taking in every inch of her white Greek-style gown, cinched in at the waist and collared at the throat with gold metal. At her wrists her favourite gold bangles clinked as she moved nervously beneath his intense…increasingly frowning gaze.

'Draco…?'

'*Thee mou*, you look breathtaking,' he rasped.

'Maybe next time, lead with that, instead of the frown?' she suggested with a nervous but pleased laugh.

He discarded his drink on a nearby surface and came towards her, the frown still in place. 'I've seen the guest list. More than half of them are male sports stars with overblown egos and the impression that they can have anything, or anyone, they want.' He captured her hand, his grip tight. 'Just remember, you're my fiancée. I'll kill anyone who dares to make a pass at you.'

Rebel had ceased trying to fight the insane chemical thrill that his touch and his words brought. She was firmly immersed in whatever was happening between them. So what if a part of her had taken more than a moment or two during the day to wonder what it would be like to be truly engaged to Draco? *That* was the part of her she needed to control.

Now that she'd decided to fight all out for her dreams, she couldn't afford to get emotionally tangled with Draco. Walking away from this charade without emotional loss was imperative. The physical side, the potent chemistry that wrapped them in its own formidable force field, she could handle. And as she'd seen with so many of her friends and acquaintances, the chemistry didn't last for anyone, once explored.

'Well, I hope you'll keep the bloodletting at a distance. I don't want my gown ruined,' she replied.

Exhaling, he muttered something under his breath about her mouth, then tugged her after him to the door.

The ballroom holding the gala was themed like the rest of the villa—an exhibition of marble and Carla Nardozzi. The event, purportedly to raise money for children's sports in Third World countries, was in danger of being overshadowed by the Olivio and Carla Nardozzi Show.

The woman in question, dressed in a white and silver gown that moulded every inch of her skin from throat to feet, her face impeccably made up and her hair caught up in her signature chignon, glided forward on her father's arm to greet them. Compliments were exchanged, but Rebel noticed Carla's gaze barely stayed on her before it returned to Draco. And this time there was no disguising the keen interest in the younger woman's eyes. An unpleasant sensation coiled inside Rebel.

'Carla told me what you did this morning,' Olivio said,

his gaze on Draco. 'She was lucky to have you there to intervene for what I'm sure was just a misunderstanding with Tyson. But I owe you my thanks nevertheless.'

Draco's gaze hardened. 'It wasn't a misunderstanding. And Arabella was there too. In fact, she stopped the situation from escalating.'

Carla laughed. 'Hardly. I had things under control.'

Shock froze Rebel for a second. 'He was manhandling you, and trying to force you to do a dangerous move you weren't ready for!'

Carla's mouth pursed. 'You were there for only a few minutes, Miss Daniels. I only meant I wasn't prepared to do that move at that time of the morning when I'd barely warmed up.'

'A dangerous move is a dangerous move, no matter the time of day it's performed,' Draco inserted with unmistakable gravity. Although his bleak expression cleared a moment later, Rebel's heart squeezed at the naked pain and guilt he carried for what had happened to his sister.

'Then you'll be pleased to know I succeeded in my attempt this afternoon,' Carla said.

Olivio smiled with smug satisfaction. 'Now that we've cleared that up, perhaps we can get on with the evening? Draco, Carla has a few people she's dying for you to meet. I promise to take care of your beloved while you're away.'

Short of offending their host—a move she didn't doubt Olivio would hold against Draco—she had no choice but to slide her hand through Olivio's proffered arm.

Draco's gaze dropped to the point of contact, his nostrils flaring slightly. Olivio's laughter held a touch of edgy mockery. 'She's only going across the room, not to the ends of the earth.'

When Draco's eyes gleamed dangerously, Rebel smiled, thinking it wise to defuse the situation.

'He told me before we left our suite that he'll kill any man who strays too close to me tonight. Perhaps I ought to level the playing field by stating that I'll gut any woman who looks at him the wrong way. Does that help, darling?'

Draco's gaze caught hers, the promise of retribution echoing clearly, before dropping to her mouth. 'It helps.'

'Such passion,' Olivio drawled.

Rebel placed her tongue firmly in her cheek. 'You don't know the half of it.'

Carla slipped *both* her hands through Draco's bent arm, her gaze daring as it met Rebel's. 'Come on. It's almost time for us to take our seats and I may not have time later.'

Rebel walked away, the smile pinned on her face hopefully disguising the fact that her insides were still knotted with an unhealthy mix of anger and jealousy. Draco might not have romantic intentions towards Carla, but the younger woman clearly had other ideas.

'So when is the big day?' Olivio enquired in between playing the attentive host to his mingling guests.

Rebel frowned, dragging her eyes from where Carla was plastered to Draco's side as they chatted with a basketball star and his wife across the room. 'Big day?'

'The wedding. Surely that's what every woman thinks about the moment she's proposed to?' His brown eyes drilled into hers, as if hoping to catch her in a lie.

'A wedding takes time to plan. Besides, I have a championship to think of before we get round to setting wedding dates.'

'Ah, yes. I understand you dabble in cross-country. Or is it jumping?' His teeth were bared in a semblance of a smile, but his eyes were slowly hardening, a hint of a sneer in the espresso depths.

Rebel tossed her head. 'I'm sorry, is there an insult in there somewhere? Only I despise insinuation.'

Another guest approached. Olivio slipped into charming host mode, chatting and smiling until they were once again alone. Then he turned so his back was to the room.

'My Carla needs a man like Draco in her camp to keep her at the top of the game.'

'Isn't she already at the top? And isn't Draco's offer of representation going to achieve what you want?'

'The sort of contract he's offering is one that can be broken at any time. What I need from him is a firmer commitment.'

Rebel arranged her features into fake astonishment. 'What are you saying? That you want me to give up the man I love to your daughter?' Her voice caught, her whole body clenching hard with a stormy sensation that had nothing to do with the role she'd agreed to play.

'I'm in a position to make sure it's worth your while.'

Struggling with the sudden pounding of her heart, she lifted her hand to her throat in a dramatic pose. 'And how much is ripping out one's own heart and throwing it under a bus worth these days?'

Olivio assessed her shrewdly. 'Will a million euros do it?'

Over his shoulder she spotted Draco and Carla, now standing alone. His head was bent towards her shorter form as she murmured in his ear. Rebel couldn't dismiss the evidence that they made a striking couple.

Looking away from them, she stared at Olivio. 'Sadly, I don't think you've thought this through properly. You want me to walk away from a dynamic, wildly successful man, whose net worth I'm guessing eclipses yours many times over, and who I also happen to be in love with, for a mere million euros?' She injected as much sarcasm into her voice as possible. 'And even if I was crazy enough to consider your offer, you forget, there's nothing between Carla and Draco.'

Olivio made a dismissive gesture. 'Romance just needs the right circumstances to be rekindled.'

Rebel's breath locked in her lungs. *'Rekindled?'*

His superior smile widened. 'I see he chose not to tell you.'

'Perhaps he didn't think it important enough,' she replied, although her voice lacked the conviction she'd been able to project thus far.

'Or perhaps his male pride still smarts from the fact that I put a stop to their dating three years ago because my Carla was too young for that kind of intensity and didn't need the distraction. I don't apologise for looking out for her best interests. But Draco should be made to see he's letting his bruised ego get in the way of a perfect union.'

The poisoned knife that seemed to have impaled her sternum wasn't easing up, no matter how much she tried to breathe through it. In fact, with every second that passed, numbness spread through her body. 'Again, I don't see how any of this interests me. Draco put his ring on my finger. I need a little more than a second-hand tale of infatuation to discard it.'

The soft background music that had accompanied the pre-dinner drinks faded and the lights blinked, indicating it was time to take their seats. Rebel saw Draco and Carla head their way.

'You don't want to make an enemy of me, Arabella,' Olivio warned.

'Oh, I don't know if that'll make a difference, Olivio. This one seems to take pride in collecting enemies,' an intruding voice suggested.

She tensed as Tyson Blackwell stopped beside them, a glass of champagne in his hand. From across the room, Draco's face contorted with barely contained fury as he swiftly headed back towards her.

'What can I say? Meek and mild have never been friends of mine. And I find it hard to bite my tongue at the best of times when someone is being mistreated right in front of my eyes.'

'Maybe you should learn,' Tyson ground out.

'Where's the fun in that?' she fired back.

'Everything okay here?' Draco's icy voice joined the

conversation. In the light of what Olivio had just imparted, Rebel found she couldn't look at him. Not without betraying herself. And now more than ever, knowing how much she wanted to win the championship—ironically thanks to Draco helping her admit the truth she'd been hiding from—she couldn't afford to let her mask slip.

Tyson smiled indulgently at Carla before he shrugged. 'Your girl seems to need convincing about what she saw this morning. As I explained to Olivio, I get passionate every now and then in my quest for excellence. Carla knows she has nothing to fear from me, don't you, *bella*?'

The look that passed between them made Rebel wonder if they were sleeping together, but the younger woman's gaze immediately returned to Draco. With the knowledge of their full history, she could no longer stop the arrows that pierced her heart as she watched them. With a heavy buzzing in her head, she took in Draco's almost protective shielding of the figure skater from her trainer, and Carla's proprietorial hold on his arm.

Pain lanced sharper her as the lights blinked again.

'We need to take our seats,' Carla said without answering Tyson's allegation.

The trainer's face hardened. Glancing away, Rebel caught Draco's enquiring gaze. Unable to deal with it, and not wanting to, she turned away, and followed the usher who stood ready to guide them to their table.

Her breath caught painfully as Draco took over pulling out her chair. 'Arabella?'

'Everything's fine,' she said lightly, flashing an empty smile before reaching for her water glass. Expecting him to take the seat next to her, she glanced up to find him walking away.

Discovering she'd been placed as far away as possible from him with Carla and Olivio on either side of him shouldn't have come as a surprise. Inhaling shakily, she summoned a smile for the tennis star and his expectant wife to her left and introduced herself to the soccer star on her right. Beyond him, Tyson Blackwell smirked at her as he took his seat.

As the courses were served and practised speeches given, Rebel picked at her meal and tried to make conversation, even as a part of her was staggered at how drastically different the evening had turned out from how she'd imagined when they'd left their suite. Just from the simple disclosing of one small fact she hadn't been privy to.

A fact Draco had deliberately neglected to mention.

As if compelled, her gaze lifted from her plate. Across the table, steel-sharp eyes met hers, and, despite the charming smile gracing his lips as he nodded at something Carla was saying, Rebel saw the unyielding questions lurking and the grim warning wrapped around each of them.

Tyson Blackwell laughed loudly at a joke and Draco's jaw tightened. Rebel didn't doubt that Draco's motivation for wanting Tyson Blackwell banned from training was genuine. The man was dangerous. For that reason alone, she had to keep this up. As to why Draco had kept his prior relationship with Carla from her…

She vowed to ask him the moment they were alone.

Looking up, she caught his gaze again, the deeper warning in his eyes tensing her spine.

He didn't need to remind her they were playing a role. Letting go of her glass, she tucked her hand beneath her chin. Allowing her gaze to grow languid, she puckered her lips and blew him a kiss.

His smile evaporated. His fist tightened around his poised knife until his knuckles gleamed white.

Beside her, the tennis star's wife laughed. 'That certainly caught his attention.'

Rebel forced a giggle. 'You think so? A girl has to use whatever weapons she has in her arsenal these days.'

The pregnant woman leaned in closer and nodded. 'I hear ya. Especially when there are shameless predators around who feel they have more rights to your man than you do,' she whispered conspiratorially.

Rebel swallowed, wincing inwardly as the words struck bone. Humming in agreement, she battled her way through further conversation, making sure not to glance Draco's way again.

At the stroke of midnight, the gala ended with a closing speech from father and daughter.

Rebel was saying goodbye to the tennis couple when Draco arrived at her side. 'Arabella, we need to—'

'Draco? You said you wanted to talk to me after the gala?' Carla joined them, expertly insinuating herself between them. 'I've done my bit for the night, so I'm all yours.'

'Carla, I'll come and find you in a while—' He stopped as she shook her head.

'It's been a long day and I want to get to bed soon,' she said softly, her eyes wide and limpid. 'And since you insist on leaving right away, I hope you don't mind if we talk now or I risk falling asleep mid-sentence.' Her smile was wide and perfect.

Draco responded to her smile with one of his own, but Rebel saw the tension that gripped his shoulders when he turned to her.

She pre-empted him with a fake smile and a hand on his chest. His muscles contracted and she dropped her hand. 'It's fine, darling. I'll go and take a shower, and warm your side of the bed. I know how much you love that.'

The look Carla sent her could've shattered granite. Rebel walked away before her smile slipped, holding her head high and avoiding eye contact with the guests drifting out of the ballroom.

She made it to the suite with only Stefano approaching to ask if she needed anything. Thanking and dismissing him, she shut the door behind her, relief mingled with a heavy dose of raw trepidation welling inside her.

Rebel didn't think she'd lost sight of what she was doing

at any point in the shockingly brief time since she'd crashed into Draco's world. So how had she arrived here, deeply unsettled by emotions she could barely explain?

She was in lust with him, that she couldn't deny. But why did her heart ache this much at the thought of Draco having dated Carla? Putting it down to anger over the deliberate trap Draco had let her walk into with Olivio earlier, she lurched from the door, tugging off her shoes as she entered the dressing room. Their cases had been packed and stood neatly by the centre island.

Realising she couldn't shower without having to repack, she left her shoes by the cases and went into the living room. The urge to pour herself a drink and numb the disquieting emotions surging beneath her skin was strong. But stepping up her training meant no alcohol, even for emotional-crutch purposes.

Snorting beneath her breath, she plunked down on the sofa, only to jump up again as Draco's scent curled around her. Heart leaping in her throat, she crossed the living room and sank into the armchair. Grabbing the remote, she turned on the TV.

She was channel-surfing, ignoring the antique fireplace clock that announced that Draco had been gone for an hour, when the door opened.

'Arabella.' Her name was a curt demand.

She muted the TV and stood, cursing the renewed anxiety swirling in her stomach. 'In here.'

He entered the room. Every cell in her body felt as if it'd been zapped with liquid nitrogen when she took in his dishevelled state.

'Wow. You know you can't forcibly save her if she doesn't think she needs saving, don't you?'

A muscle in his jaw flexed. 'What are you talking about?'

She walked to him, caught the betraying scent oozing from him and her heart dropped further.

Keep walking.

She went to the dressing room. Tugging on the handle of her case, she dragged it behind her, only to stop short when he filled the doorway.

'What are you doing?'

'I assume this charade is over, since you stink of her perfume, your hair's all over the place and your jaw is covered in peach lipstick—seriously, though, that "lipstick on the collar" thing is so last-century soap opera. Anyway, I'm guessing either your talk was wildly successful or she refused to take you up on your role as saviour. Judging from your scowl I'm guessing it was the latter.'

'Arabella—'

'By the way, thanks for making me look like a fool tonight. You told me you were trying to get her father to drop his matchmaking. You never said anything about the daughter being head over heels in love with you.'

His scowl deepened. 'Carla has had a crush on me since she was a teenager. It's nothing.'

'Oh, believe me, it's something. A very big something. Especially since you two *dated*.'

He looked momentarily disconcerted, then he shrugged. 'I took her out a few times when she lived in London a few years ago. So what?'

She laughed. 'Only a man like you would ask that ridiculous question.'

'What's that supposed to mean?'

She sighed. 'Never mind, Draco.' She moved forward, expecting him to get out of her way. He didn't. 'Oh, right. I guess you want this back.' Letting go of her case, she tugged the ring off and held it out to him.

'What the hell do you think you're doing?' he growled, his voice jagged ice chips.

'Come on, you can't surely want to prolong this farce! You're wearing another woman's lipstick on your skin, for heaven's sake. Stay. Leave. Do whatever you want. But here's where I step off this crazy train.'

She stepped forward, intending to shove the ring in his pocket. He caught her wrist, trapping it against his chest in a tight grip. Underneath her fist, his heart slammed hard and fierce.

'Put the ring back on,' he sliced at her.

She jerked at her hand. He held on tight.

'God, what do you want, Draco?' she railed, knowing she was inches away from losing control.

'You, Arabella. I want you.'

CHAPTER THIRTEEN

'EVER SINCE I walked in on you performing that ridiculous yoga pose, I've thought of little else but having you beneath me in my bed. Did I not make that perfectly clear this morning?'

Rebel clawed at the strands of sanity blissfully fleeing her mind. 'Again. The lipstick on your face tells a *very* different story.'

With a thick curse, Draco released her, but kicked the door shut. 'Stay here. If you walk out that door I'll make you regret it.'

'Oh…charming.'

He stalked to his case and flung it open. Extracting a fresh pair of trousers and a clean shirt, he slammed it shut.

Rebel stared in disbelief as he jerked his tuxedo jacket off, followed by the dress shirt and trousers. Her mouth dropped open at the sight of him in his black briefs, a picture of ripped, bristling, male perfection, using the shirt balled in his fist to swipe at the lipstick on his face. Stunning was a woefully inadequate description of Draco Angelis' male stature, his perfectly proportioned body overlaid with smooth dark olive skin that just begged to be touched. Worshipped.

From somewhere she regained the use of her vocal cords. 'Umm… Draco—'

He flung the shirt away. 'Shut your mouth and listen for once in your life. I didn't kiss Carla. She kissed me.'

Rebel let her rolling eyes speak for her.

'And before you call it a convenient excuse, no, I didn't see it coming.'

'So you spent the last hour fighting her off?'

He glared pure fire at her. 'I spent the last hour *talking* to her. This—' he flicked impatient fingers at his face '—happened as I was leaving her.'

'Okay, if you say so.'

He glared harder. 'I do say so,' he ground out.

Her stomach quivered. 'And?'

He pulled his clean clothes on, then spiked his fingers through his hair. The silky strands settled, but not by much. He still wore a tumbled-out-of-bed look that was at once heart-throbbingly perfect and deliciously indecent. Snapping up the suitcase, he crossed to her and took her bag. 'She knows what she stands to lose if she carries on using Tyson Blackwell as her trainer. The ball is now in her court. I just hope she doesn't take too long to make her stand.'

A harrowing bleakness threaded the edge in his voice. Her hand on the door, Rebel glanced back at him. 'You tried. Isn't that enough?'

His eyes were a raw, turbulent gunmetal; the skin around his mouth was pinched. 'No, it isn't. Should Maria see on the news one day soon that a tragedy has happened to Carla and I hadn't done everything I could to stop it, it'll finish her. And with Blackwell in charge, it's not a case of if but when. I can't let that happen to either of them.'

Rebel let out a shaky breath. 'So...this engagement *is* really about helping Carla through forcing her father's hand, and not a male-pride thing to get back at Olivio because he stopped you from dating her three years ago?'

Already dark brows clenched in a thunderous frown. 'I see Olivio has filled your head with nonsense. Open the door, Arabella. We're leaving. I can't stand to stay in this place another minute. The moment we're on my plane, you'll tell me what else that bastard filled your head with. I didn't think it was possible, but you've grown even more insufferable since the damned gala.'

Purely for self-preservation purposes, she opened the door and walked out of the suite. Stefano waited in the hallway and took charge of their bags. The walk to the helipad was swift and they were lifting off within minutes.

They boarded Draco's plane and took off with Rebel having no clue where they were going since Draco had disappeared to take a shower. On his return, he clamped the phone to his ear, and conducted several conversations in rapid-fire Greek. A solid hour after take-off he finally hung up and flung his phone on the table between them.

He dragged his hands down his face, but she thought the look he levelled at her was a little less incandescent.

'Is it safe to ask where we're going now?'

He blinked at her, then his gaze dropped to the ring, which had somehow found its way back onto her finger. 'I was going to take you to my water villa in the Maldives. It's secluded and beautiful and rainbow-coloured fish swim up to you to say hello. But after the stunt you pulled tonight—'

'Which stunt are we talking about?'

Narrowed eyes sizzled at her. 'The getting-your-head-filled-with-lies part, followed by the part where you tried to dump me.'

'Oh. Right.'

'Yes. Right. You don't deserve the Maldives. And I don't want to be stuck on a plane for half a day with a woman who drives me insane, and yet who I want to make love to more than I want to breathe.'

Rebel was glad she was seated. His powerful, enthralling words buffeted her like a freak storm, raising her heart rate and melting her insides. 'I guess that's completely rational. So do I get a destination?'

'No. You'll find out when we get there. Tell me what else Olivio told you,' he commanded.

She told him, leaving nothing out. Draco shook his head once and uttered a curse. She grimaced. 'Sorry. But on a positive note, now he thinks I'm not going to step aside easily or be bought off, he might rethink his plans?'

'I doubt it. Men like Olivio rarely change their ways. But

I have to try something. Maria will never forgive me if I don't,' he said grimly.

'Surely you understand that you don't have total control over this?'

He didn't reply and several minutes passed before she asked, 'So, what now?'

His gaze rested on her, scrutinising her from face to midriff and back again. 'I have my investigators digging deeper for anything they can find on Blackwell. Come here.'

Temperature spiking from an infusion of wicked excitement, she rose and rounded the table.

He drew back and patted his lap. 'Sit.'

She hitched her gown up and swung one leg over his thighs. His breath hitched as she lowered herself and settled onto him. Shaking his head, he gave a low, deep laugh. 'I should've known better than to expect you to sit side-saddle with your legs daintily crossed,' he teased.

Face flaming with embarrassment, Rebel drew back. 'Sorry, I'm fresh out of dainty,' she quipped. Bracing her hand on the table, she started to rise.

He clamped his hand on her hips. 'Stay. How is it that your relentless mouth hasn't seen you thrown into an institution long before now?'

Heat rose higher, but this time from the blatant presence of his arousal between her legs. 'Umm…I'm nice to little old ladies and I don't walk under ladders?'

His hands slowly travelled up to shackle her waist. Leaning forward, he stopped a hair's breadth from her lips. 'I want you like crazy, Arabella Daniels.' His voice was a warm, whispered rumble over her lips. 'Nothing has changed since this morning. So tell me you want me too.'

'I want you too,' she delivered, although she couldn't accept that nothing had changed. Tonight's events had unleashed emotions she didn't want to brave uncovering just yet. Hell, she might leave that box sealed for ever.

He stared at her for endless seconds. One hand came up

and teased the hoop that formed the neckline of her dress. When it reached her pulse, he traced it, a light, delicate touch that lit a flame on every nerve ending and concentrated it at her core.

His touch, still light, still tormenting, drifted up to her eyebrows, her cheek, then over her lips. A pained groan ripped from his throat.

'I want to kiss you. *Thee mou*, I want to kiss you so badly.'

'And you're holding back because…?'

His hand dropped back to her waist and his head jerked back to the headrest. 'We're landing in three minutes.'

Cutting disappointment warred with the need to know where they were. Knowing she could do nothing about one and maybe something about the other, she looked out of the window onto a black, inky landscape with only a set of runway lights breaking the vastness.

'You've brought me to the middle of nowhere?'

'Indeed. No one can reach us unless I want them to, or they're prepared to swim a hundred miles in every direction.'

'We're in the middle of the ocean?'

'On my island in the Aegean.'

'How long are we staying?'

'That depends entirely on you. Play nice and I won't fly us north and dump you in a Gulag.'

He rose with her in his arms and walked them to the sofa. Setting her down, he secured her seat belt, then settled down away from her. Glancing at him, she witnessed the strain in his features and bit her lip against a smart quip as his fists bunched on his thighs.

The second they touched down he released his belt and hers, then stood with her.

'Arabella?'

'Yes, Drill Sergeant?' she responded, trying her utmost to stem the anxiety flooding her.

'I'm going to have you. The moment we're alone again, I intend to make you mine. Speak up now if that isn't what you want because you won't be using that smart mouth for talking later.'

Every sharp retort evaporated from her head as erotic images flooded her. 'I want it. I want you.'

His breath shuddered out and he nodded once before moving to the door. An SUV stood a short distance away and he guided her to it before sliding behind the wheel. More lights than she'd seen from above lit their path, but all she could see was vegetation and a profusion of flowers.

'You'll get the grand tour tomorrow after your training,' he rasped, his gaze not moving from the road ahead.

Two long roads and corners later, Rebel sat forward in her seat, her widening gaze on the villa ahead. It was built into the side of the hill, with multi-layers she stopped counting after five. In the dark, welcoming golden lights lit up the vast property, pitching it against the night sky like a wonderful masterpiece.

'Draco, it's stunning.' She craned her neck to see more of it as they neared.

'It's not the Maldives, but it's one of my favourite homes.'

'Water villas and brightly coloured fish are overrated.'

He drove past a pillared entrance with double doors, and through a giant, arched trellis. He stopped before a square wooden gate and entered a code. The gate glided back on a smooth rail and they drove along a narrower drive that led to another pillared entrance. It wasn't until Draco parked and she alighted that her gaze was drawn upward. 'That's a pool. A see-through pool,' she blurted, blown clean away.

His mouth curved. 'You get to have your water villa after all.' He walked round to her, swung her up in his arms and whispered in her ear, 'You can swim naked in there if you want to. In fact, I insist on it.'

He was striding forward as she fought her way through a blush. Codes were entered along the way, a lift accessed that shot them up and spat them out on an upper level. Then they were in Draco's bedroom. He slid her down his body, slowly, torturously, not bothering to hide the thick evidence of his arousal. It nudged her belly as he tugged her even closer. The hands that had shackled her on the plane were twice as hard, twice as demanding, as Draco finally unleashed the ferocious hunger that screamed for satisfaction. He devoured her mouth, muttering words in Greek she didn't understand in between long, ardent kisses. Their groans mingled as each kiss fed the hunger and need for a greater assuaging.

He fisted her hair, his fingers holding her tight as he trailed his tongue over her jaw to the pulse racing at her throat. He lapped at it, his moan deep and primeval. '*Thee mou*, you taste like paradise. And sin. And every forbidden thing in between.'

Her hands, frantically exploring his covered back, bit into his flesh as he nipped at her collarbone. Never having imagined that area to be an erogenous zone, she felt her knees threaten to buckle as Draco explored her. Her eyes grew heavy, drawing half closed as sensation arrowed south and pooled between her thighs. Desperate to discover as much of him as she could before her faculties melted beneath the fierce onslaught of desire, Rebel pulled his shirt up and dragged her nails over his heated skin.

The hiss that heated her cleavage was followed by another savage curse. He dragged his head upward. 'You mean to torment me, don't you?' he rasped thickly.

Slightly shocked by the allegation, she blurted, 'I'm only touching you. You want me to stop?'

His laugh was darkly amused. 'Not even on pain of death would I wish that.'

Stepping back, he yanked his shirt over his head. The chest she'd glimpsed from across the dressing room was now within reach. Rebel's ability to breathe became severely compromised as she glided her hand over his pectoral muscles. As she felt them quiver lightly under her touch a bold, feminine power filled her. She explored south, hesitated, then went lower and grasped him.

Her mouth parted on a silent gasp as the full thickness of him registered.

'Arabella.'

She heard her name from afar, her senses completely overcome by the power and heat of him.

'Arabella.' His voice was more strained, almost guttural as he captured her hand in his.

A sound erupted from her throat that sounded very much like a whimper. 'Draco...'

He spun her round and trapped her with one hand on her abdomen. The other slowly gathered up her gown, the slide of hot silk against her skin delicious, decadent torture. 'Play with me all you want later. But I need to take you...be inside you, right now, before I lose my head.'

She shuddered at the inflamed words. Then shuddered some more, when his clever fingers brushed her naked hip and skated along the edge of her panties. Her legs sagged and parted, the hunger between her thighs desperate for satiation.

A cry ripped from her throat when his fingers finally found her. Pulling aside the wet lace, he caressed her, muttering earthy words that drew her deeper into a sensual stupor.

He toyed with for her several minutes, then one finger slipped inside her, testing her, tormenting her. 'So wet, *glikia mou*. And mine,' he growled.

The hand on her belly tugged open her belt before reaching up to tackle the neck fastening. When it came open, Draco pulled away and spun her around. Rebel gasped at the sheer magnificence of the passion stamped across his face.

Keeping his gaze locked on hers, he pulled the dress off her shoulders. It pooled at her feet, leaving her exposed in her strapless bra and panties. Still trapping her gaze, he reached round and unclipped her bra.

Cool air hit her breasts, puckering the tight tips to harder points. Rebel wanted to cover herself, gain back a little of the control that had long fled.

At the same time she wanted Draco to look at her, drown in her as she was drowning in him. So she kept her hands down.

His eyes dropped. He made a sound that could've been her name or a curse. She didn't care because he reached out and touched her. Specifically her panties, which were torn from her body between one breath and the next. Then the world blurred as he lifted her and tossed her on the bed. The primitiveness behind the act had her shuddering wildly. She was struggling for breath when he fully undressed and prowled closer.

Anxieties she'd pushed to the back of her mind flooded forth. She'd never viewed her virginity with the sacred awe some women did, but Rebel couldn't dismiss the profundity that gripped her as she stared at the magnificent man who would be her first lover. Nor could she ignore the physical evidence of his manhood.

He was impressive. Almost a little too impressive. Apprehension clawed higher. She bit her lip to keep it down as he reached into the bedside drawer and extracted a condom.

Stretching out beside her, he glided his hand from her neck to her midriff. She arched into his touch, forcing her mind away from the power between his legs.

'I didn't desire smart talk, but I admit to being disconcerted by your complete silence.'

She bit her lip harder. 'Hmm.'

He raised his head. 'Was that English?'

Her breath burst from her lungs. 'Draco...please?'

'Begging, Arabella?' His head dipped, and his mouth grazed one nipple. He rotated the bud between his lips before flicking his tongue against it. 'Whatever next?'

When she didn't answer, he raised his head.

She blew out a shaky breath. 'Okay…fine… I'm worried. You're big…I think?'

'You think? I guess there's only one way to find out.'

She gasped as he performed the same decadent torture on her twin nipple. Unable to stand it any longer, she tugged her fingers through his hair. He continued to suckle on her even as she faintly registered the rip of foil.

Pressing her back against the bed, he levered himself over her and took her mouth with his. The thrust of his tongue was a precursor to the thick head that breached her core. She gripped his neck as he probed deeper, then withdrew. Strong arms stretched her legs wider and Draco raised his head.

Grey eyes locked on hers, he thrust inside her.

The deep flash of pain ripped a cry from her lips and drove her nails into his flesh. With her shaky gaze on his, Rebel first witnessed puzzlement, then shock, before fury glazed his eyes. 'You think…' he seethed as understanding dawned. *'You think?'*

'I…know?' she supplied on a gasp, her flesh struggling to contain his thick girth as new, delicious sensations flowed through her.

He moved, perhaps to withdraw. The drugging sensation heightened. She moaned, her fingers digging in deeper.

'Thee mou. Arabella—' he muttered as she rotated her hips, chasing more of the feeling. She tried it again. With a thick curse, he slid one arm behind her back, grabbed her waist and held her still. 'Why…?' He stopped to breathe. 'You didn't tell me you were a virgin. Why?'

'Because it was no big deal. Until it literally was.' Her hips twitched, the need to move consuming her. 'Please, Draco, if you still want me, then take me.'

'If I—' He exhaled in disbelief, his eyes squeezing shut for a long tense moment. Then he released her waist. He let her experiment for a scant minute before he took over.

Eyes pinned on her face, gauging her every reaction, he set a steady rhythm, the tension slowly draining out of him as helpless moans spilled from her lips.

Pleasure as she'd never known exploded through her as Draco filled her, stretched her to her limit, over and over. Her back arched with each thrust, an alien storm raging deep inside.

The earthy scent of their union rose to mingle with all the different, wondrous sensations. Lost in delirium, Rebel didn't know whether she was dying or being reborn.

'Arabella, look at me.'

The rough, fierce command fused her back to him, to see the look in his eyes raw and unashamedly carnal. He let her see how she affected him, let her hear each hoarse gasp and guttural groan as he took her higher until she was consumed by the need to jump off the edge of the precipice.

'Oh, God... Draco!'

'Now, Arabella. Let go.'

Rebel soared as she'd never done before, her world unfurling in a white-hot blaze that wrapped her soul in pure joy. Time stood still, granting her the gift of basking in the breathtaking experience. But eventually, her senses returned to her, albeit on a soft haziness that could only absorb the sound of the man whose thickness still registered deep inside her.

Draco watched her eyelashes lift, an indescribable feeling striking him as he traced the flush of pleasure staining her skin. The fervent need for release gnawed at him, but he held it back. He wanted to stretch out this moment for a while longer. Why, he wasn't exactly sure.

His gaze roved over Arabella's face once more. She was breathtaking.

And she'd been a virgin.

The feeling he'd been holding at bay rushed over him again. Stronger. Heavier.

She'd been a virgin. And she'd chosen him to be her first.

Was he that primitive that it turned him on more than he'd ever thought possible?

He felt himself thicken even further inside her in answer. Her eyes widened as he stretched her. Unable to deny himself any longer, he pushed deeper inside her. Her slick channel welcomed him in a tight embrace. Her back arched, presenting her perfect breasts for him to feast on. He gave himself over to sensation, the new and mind-numbing bliss sweeter than anything he'd ever experienced.

Soft, feminine arms slid around him, holding him through the buffeting storm he never wanted to subside. Inevitably it did.

Burying his face in her neck, he inhaled her sweet scent, then rolled them over. Her hand splayed on his chest.

'How long do I have before the Gulag train gets here?'

The sound of her voice sent another unfamiliar thrill through him. Draco lay there, unable to believe he was perfectly content to engage in post-sex banter. Normally, he would be dressed and out of the door before the hint of familiarity approached anywhere near contempt.

But he wasn't even thinking of drawing away now as his arms tightened around her.

'They can wait. I haven't had my fill of you yet.'

'Ah, reprieve.'

He reversed their positions, tucking her beneath him once more. 'No, not total reprieve. You didn't tell me about Olivio's attempts to bribe you until I demanded it, and you neglected to mention your virginity. Don't hold back anything that important from me again. Are we clear?'

Her eyelids dropped and she swallowed.

Unease trickled down his spine.

A moment later, she blinked. Then smiled. 'Yes, Drill Sergeant.'

Her familiar snark was lacking its signature bite. Draco tried to push away the disquieting sensation that she was hiding something else, but it lingered, cautioning him not to revel in this moment too long. Nirvana could become addictive.

Dropping his guard was foolish. This was just sex, a side bargain struck with his libido as the sole benefactor.

He would move on once his goal was attained.

CHAPTER FOURTEEN

REBEL FELT AS if she'd been asleep for only minutes before being woken up. Probably because she had. They hadn't made love again after the first time last night, but dawn light had already been tingeing the skies as they'd gone to sleep.

'Move it, Arabella. You don't want the sun to get any hotter before your run.'

She dragged her head from the pillow. Draco stood beside the bed, a tray in one hand and her gym gear in the other. He was dressed in running shorts and a body-hugging T-shirt. The sight of his body—the body she'd had the freedom to touch at will last night—sent a pulse of heat through her. Dry-mouthed, she tried to divert her gaze elsewhere as she sat up and accepted the tray. She needed to get her thoughts to coalesce so she could say something that didn't sound completely embarrassing.

But her gaze climbed his frame, lovingly exploring it until she reached his face. And the arrogant smile that graced it.

'You ogling me so hungrily isn't going to get you out of training. In fact for every minute you stay in bed, you get to do another vertical jump.'

Since vertical jumps were her favourite of the exercises, Rebel contemplated staying put. One look at his face told her it was the wrong move.

He set the bowl of muesli in her lap. 'Eat your breakfast. I'll be back in ten minutes.'

He was back in five, just as she was about to get out of bed. She froze. 'Can you…turn around, please?'

'No.' He shook out her training gear. 'You get to wear

this while you train. The rest of the time clothes won't be necessary. You might as well get used to it now.'

She bit her lip and frowned. 'If I'd known your island doubled as a nudist colony, I'd have taken my chances with the Gulag.'

He grinned, then dropped the clothes next to her. 'You'll wish you hadn't said that by the time I'm finished with you. Up.'

She'd made love with him—was still not quite sure how she'd survived that transcendental experience—and yet the thought of him seeing her naked made her whole body flame with self-awareness.

Gritting her teeth, she flung the sheets back and stood. About to reach for her shorts, she gasped when he caught her wrist and yanked her close.

His grin had disappeared, his face a taut mask of hunger and desire as his sizzling gaze burned down her body. 'First, you need to greet me properly,' he commanded.

Rebel told herself it was unwise to give in so easily, to reach so greedily for what she wanted. But she was already surging close, curling her arms around his neck and raising herself on tiptoe to reach his mouth. His slanted across hers the moment they touched, his ravenous possession of her mouth making her senses sing. He fisted her hair, angled her head for a deeper exploration, while his other hand moulded her bottom.

They were both groaning, their breathing harsh, when they parted. Rebel licked her lower lip, already mourning the loss of his kiss. 'Good morning, Drill Sergeant,' she husked out.

'Good morning, Arabella *mou*,' he replied, his face an unsmiling mask reflecting all her cravings. 'Now you can get dressed.'

A full-body tremble raking her, she turned, picked up the shorts and stepped into them. She was sliding them up when she felt his gentle touch on her lower back, just above her right buttock.

Rebel froze. She'd forgotten about her scar.

'What happened here?' he murmured.

She kept her face averted. 'An accident,' she replied, injecting as much lightness into her voice as possible.

'During training?' She heard the frown in his voice. She knew why. The scar wasn't extensive, but the wound had been deep, the scar tissue pronounced. But far deeper was the secret scar she carried on her heart. The one she couldn't tell him about because he would hate her, condemn her as no better than someone like Tyson Blackwell.

'No, it was a long time ago.' Hurriedly she snapped the waistband into place and reached for the top. Yanking it on, she schooled her features and turned. 'I'm ready. You can do your worst now.'

The eyes that met hers held lingering questions. Rebel's breath caught in her lungs; she was hoping against hope he'd let it go. She wasn't ready for the sheer magic she'd discovered last night with him to be over. And it would be if he forced the secret out of her.

After another contemplative look, one corner of his mouth lifted. 'That invitation is way too hard to ignore.' Grabbing her hand, he marched her into the lift, and pressed the button for Level Three.

Rebel read the buttons on the panel. 'There are seven levels?'

He nodded, then pushed her back against the lift wall, his hand bracketing her. 'Guess what's on the seventh level?' he murmured, his lips brushing her temple.

It felt like the most natural thing in the world to slide her hands around his tight, trim waist. 'Umm… Draco the Dragon's lair?'

His mouth twitched. 'Close. I look forward to showing you.'

The lift stopped and they stepped out onto a wraparound

terrace wide enough to fit her Chelsea flat four times over. Her breath caught as she saw the view for the first time. The Aegean glistened like a moving jewelled tapestry, meeting a sky of unmarred blue. Perfectly framing it was the white beach below and the red cliffs that formed the foundations of Draco's villa.

'It's so beautiful.'

He smiled and nodded as he guided her across the vast terrace to stone steps that meandered out of view. 'This is where I come to get away from the world. I had it built seven years ago.'

'Before your accident?'

He trotted down the stairs and she followed. 'Yes. I wanted a private place to train when I didn't need to be on the sports sites. This was the perfect place. When I became an agent, this part of the property became a good place to decompress. The other side of the villa is where I entertain.'

'How big is the island?'

He reached the bottom of the stairs and stretched. While he waited for her to do the same, he adjusted the timer on his watch. 'Four kilometres across. Which you will run twice with three minutes shaved off your usual average. Go.'

He set off through an archway of trellised bougainvillea, disappearing out of sight before she'd taken the first step. She caught up and managed to keep up by the skin of her teeth. Sweat poured off her body by the time they finished the second course, the sun hot on her face as she rehydrated. Her gaze caught Draco's as she swallowed the last drop, and she almost choked at the heat that blazed from his eyes.

'Let's get you inside,' was all he said as he took the bottle from her and disposed of it.

The seventh level was just as she'd suspected. A vast area, twice the size of a basketball court, held gleaming exercise machines in all shapes and sizes. There was even a boxing ring tucked into one corner.

Rebel turned a full circle. 'I was wrong. This is more like Dante's seventh circle of hell.'

He smiled and led her to an exercise mat. 'Hell is good. It helps you appreciate heaven more.'

She found out just how much he relished putting her through hell over the next three hours. He upped her regime by thirty per cent, then grunted with satisfaction each time she achieved her target.

Pride burned in her chest as she pushed her body to the limit. And just for the hell of it, when he called time, she did another ten vertical jumps more than he'd instructed her to.

'Fine, you've made your point. Don't get cocky,' he growled.

She laughed and swiped at the sweat pouring off her temples. 'Yes, Drill Sergeant.'

Turning, she braced her foot against the wall and stretched her arches. She was about to step back when she sensed him behind her. All through training she'd seen the banked hunger in his eyes. Even without looking at him now, Rebel knew he'd finally released the tight grip on his restraint.

'Keep your hands on the wall.' His voice was a deep, primitive rumble that took complete control of every nerve in her body. She shook just from the power of it.

She felt him drop into a squat behind her. A moment later, he grasped one ankle and took her trainer and sock off, then did the same to the other. Standing, he slipped his hands into the waistband of her shorts and peeled them down her legs.

'Draco,' she murmured hesitantly as he widened her stance.

'Yes?'

She shut her eyes with a tiny grimace. 'I'm sweaty.'

'Yes, you are,' he agreed with a decadent relish that tightened her skin and increased the tempo beating at her core.

His hands slid up to her breasts and he lowered the

front zip of her top. Leaving it hanging open, he cupped her breasts on a deep groan.

She shuddered as he tweaked her nipples, her whole body a receptive vessel eagerly absorbing the expert attention being lavished on it. Several mindless minutes later, she felt him drop low again.

Rebel wasn't prepared for the sensation that blazed through her next.

'Draco!' Her eyes flew open and she glanced down to see the source of her pleasure. Molten eyes met hers as his tongue lapped at her nether lips. The view alone was enough to send her into orbit. He grounded her with a firm hand on one thigh, then parted her flesh with his other hand to reach the bundle of nerves that ripped a scream from her the moment he flicked his tongue against it.

He might have caressed her for seconds. Or hours. Time ceased to exist or matter. All she could process was the encroaching tide of bliss that rushed over her and pulled her under.

She resurfaced to find herself still upright but caught in his arms.

'You're exquisite, Arabella *mou*. Truly exquisite,' he rasped against her ear. 'And all mine. Why did you let me believe all those things said about you in the media?' he added gruffly, his tone holding a touch of contrition.

Senses still swimming, she tried to find the right words to reply. 'Umm…you seemed blissfully wedded to the idea that I was a wild, wicked siren. But it was just the…white noise I needed to…to forget.' She bit her lip, wondering if she'd gone too far. Rushing on, she added, 'I told you, you didn't know everything about me.'

He grunted, his hand cupping her core in a shockingly possessive hold. 'From now on *I* will be your white noise. You get to be the wild, wicked siren only with me. And no more hiding important stuff from me. You'll be straight with me on everything. Understood?'

Her heart lurched. 'Draco...I...'

His hand moved between her thighs, melting away the apprehension and budding guilt, and leaving nothing but fevered anticipation behind.

When he picked her up, and walked over to the weight bench, Rebel gave up trying to formulate a single thought.

He arranged her over the bench. The rasp of the condom being ripped open barely registered against her buzzing senses before he was once more in control of her, his hands on her waist, his power at her throbbing centre. He took her higher than he had last night, almost rough in his possession as he drew every ounce of pleasure from her. His guttural shout as he followed her into bliss echoed in her ears as she lost her mind to sensation once more.

For the next three weeks they fell into a rigid routine. Intense training twice a day, six days a week. In between training, they made love, picnicked at various spots on the island, or ate their meals on whichever breathtaking level of Dante's villa took their fancy. On her first rest day, he took her out on a launch to his yacht moored on the other side of the villa. Rebel had seen the impressive vessel on their morning runs, but nothing had prepared her for the beauty of the *Angelis*.

Draco had smiled indulgently as she rhapsodised over the vessel, then let her take the wheel as they sailed around the island.

By some unspoken agreement, their conversation didn't stray into too personal territories, as if they were both emotionally wary, having bared their innermost cores to each other in the first week of meeting.

Of course, Draco didn't know of the last layer, the one she feared would be uncovered each time his gaze lingered on her scar and she pretended not to notice. Or when he kissed it during lovemaking and she felt the question on her skin.

Although, more and more, an equally insidious fear

trickled through her each time her gaze caught her engagement ring. The craving for everything happening between them to be real had taken permanent root in her heart. She couldn't shake it off, and with each day that passed it embedded itself deeper into her heart.

It was there, silently clamouring for attention, when she woke from an afternoon nap on their last week on the island and went in search of Draco. His expansive office was located on Level Two. It was the only place in the private villa besides the gym that she went into with clothes on, having refused point-blank to risk entering a room while Draco was on one of his many videoconferences.

She heard his dark, smoky voice now as the lift doors parted, and heard his deep laugh before she saw him, the sound so beautiful her footsteps slowed. In contrast her heart leapt, then filled with a powerful emotion that threatened to knock her to her knees.

She stepped into the sunlight as he threw back his head and laughed again. The clear joy in his face caught her breath as a certain knowledge pounded through her.

She had no time to process it because Draco turned his head and saw her. She expected him to wave her to the sofa at the far end of the room where she usually waited for him to finish; her eyes widened as he held out his arm to her.

Warily, she stepped forward, then gasped when he jerked her into his lap. Face flaming, she glanced at the wide screen.

The woman bore a striking resemblance to Draco, her dramatically beautiful face and the headrest of what could only be wheelchair announcing who she was.

'Maria?'

She smiled. 'So I finally get to meet my brother's fake fiancée.'

Rebel's gaze flew to Draco's. He shrugged. 'Maria and I don't have secrets. Not any more.' A hint of regret washed over his face, but it was gone a moment later when his sister replied.

'Enough of that, brother. So we had to learn our lesson the hard way. We got through it,' she admonished gently. Then her gaze swung to Rebel. 'But he still didn't tell me about you until the story hit the papers.'

Draco's hand curled over Rebel's hip as he peered at his sister. 'I was trying to protect you.'

Maria rolled her eyes. 'I live in an ivory tower, Draco, guarded twenty-four-seven by security and private physicians. A scandal or two wouldn't hurt to get the blood pumping.'

Rebel laughed. 'I tell him that all the time.'

'And let me guess, he does the "dragon breathing fire" thing—yep, there it is.'

They both turned to see the deep scowl marring Draco's face, and dissolved into laughter.

He reached up and tucked a strand of hair behind Rebel's ear before cupping her nape in a possessive hold. 'Very funny.'

'He makes it so easy, doesn't he?' Rebel chuckled.

Maria sighed. 'Almost too easy.'

'Enough from you two.' He pointed at his sister. 'I'll see you next week.'

Her grey eyes softened. 'I can't wait. And I know you're doing your best with Carla, but please remember that not everyone who needs help necessarily wants it. I love you no matter what.'

Beneath her, Draco tensed for a second. Then a weight seemed to lift off his shoulders. The smile he sent Maria positively glowed. 'You stay out of trouble.'

Maria rolled her eyes again before her gaze swung to Rebel. 'It was nice to meet the reason for my brother's bigger smile. I hope we meet in person one day.'

She signed off and the screen went blank. Draco turned his monitor off and an awkward silence descended.

Unable to stand it, Rebel cleared her throat. 'I'm the reason for your bigger smile? Does that mean I get an extra half hour's sleep tomorrow morning?' she teased, praying her heart's wild leaps wouldn't show on her face.

Draco snorted. 'In your dreams. Maria's a hopeless romantic who sees hearts and happy ever after in every cloud.' His grip tightened. 'You want an extra half hour's sleep? You *earn* it.'

She managed to keep her expression composed, despite the hollow that caved in her stomach. 'And how do I go about earning my sleep? Scrubbing all seven levels of your villa?'

'The only manual labour I require from you besides your training is on my person,' he replied.

Like a flame on gasoline, the air erupted with desire. The hand around her nape caressed with rough insistence. Then he pushed her off him. 'Take off that dress,' he growled.

She took it off, but before he could grab her she dropped to her knees. Draco froze, giving her the precious time she needed. Before her nerves could get the better of her, she reached for his waistband and lowered his zipper. A hiss erupted from his lips but he raised himself up to help her ease off his shorts and briefs.

She grasped him, emitting a soft gasp as the power and steel of him sent a thrill through her. She caressed him from root to tip and back, lazily, worshipping him. Then she took him in her mouth. Quickly learning what pleased him most, she teased and sucked with just the right amount of pressure for the vocal sounds of his pleasure to fill the room.

At some point his fingers fisted her hair. For an alarming second, she feared he'd pull her away. Her gaze raced up to find his locked on her, his face a tortured mask of brutal hunger. Whatever he read in her face made him nod. Absorbing every expression on his face, feminine power roaring through her, she revelled in owning him as he succumbed greedily to her ministrations.

Afterwards, he caught her beneath her arms and tucked

her up into his lap. Depositing an almost reverent kiss on her temple, he said gruffly, 'For that, *glikia mou*, you can have a whole extra hour in bed tomorrow.'

Draco watched Arabella sleep the next morning, thankful for the reprieve of not having to keep his guard up. He wasn't even sure what he was guarding. The emotions crowding through him had snuck up on him, slipped in and taken up residence while he'd been busy making love to Arabella. Or had it been when she'd met and exceeded his expectations each time he'd set her a physical challenge? Or the times when he'd found himself living for her fearless, smart mouth to draw laughter from him?

However it'd happened didn't even matter.

Maria's observation about his obvious contentment had rocked him, planted the evidence firmly in his lap, before she'd signed off, blissfully unaware of the wreck she'd left him with. But it was a wreck shrouded in fog on a black night of lies. He knew in his gut Arabella was hiding something big from him. She tensed and evaded him far too often for that not to be the case.

He despised himself for not confronting it head-on, for giving himself leave for one more day with the excuse that the investigative report he'd done on her had provided him with enough pertinent details about her. Everything else she'd revealed so far had been harmless.

She couldn't hurt Maria, and that had been enough.

But she could hurt you. His chest tightened, and he pushed the thought away. He could only be hurt if he let this thing spin out longer than their agreed time.

So far his investigators had found nothing on Tyson he could use and Olivio remained intransigent. Draco hated to rely on no news being good news, but more and more he was accepting that the choice might not be his as to whether Carla remained out of danger. She might have been partly responsible for his sister turning a corner during the bleak years after her accident, but Maria was much stronger than he'd ever given her credit for.

He would protect Carla as much as he could, but Draco was beginning to realise that some things were indeed out of his hands.

Arabella rolled over in her sleep, straight into his arms. He was pulling her close even before caution kicked in. She opened her stunning blue eyes and smiled, and he kicked caution to the kerb.

Sliding her arms around his neck, she stretched against him. 'Thank you for my extra hour. It was *heavenly.*'

'You're welcome. Now let's see if this is equally heavenly.'

He lowered his head, took what was his and silenced the clamouring of his instincts.

CHAPTER FIFTEEN

THE PACE CHANGED drastically over the next three weeks. Although she was fully installed in Draco's chalet in Verbier, Rebel barely saw him. Her training had stepped up another gear with Greg and a team Draco had hired now in charge of her on-site drills.

She hadn't realised how much she'd missed the snow until she stood at the top of the ramp on the first day. Breathing in the frigid air, she felt peace settle over her as her mother's smiling face wove into her mind. She suffered a moment's regret for the years she'd wasted being less than she could've been. How could she have ever believed she could go through life like that?

'Ready?' Greg's voice piped from behind her.

'Ready.' She adjusted her goggles a final time and planted her skis, the sheer joy of being here, doing what she loved, firing through her.

Greg counted down and sounded the klaxon. She grimaced as she pushed off a millisecond later than she'd intended.

She could already imagine the conversation with Draco later that night in her head.

Blocking it out, she poised her body for the lift-off. Exhilaration burst through her as her feet left the ramp. The elation her mother had felt and passed down to her wrapped around her as she soared.

Her mother had loved her beyond her own life. Rebel knew that had she survived the accident that had claimed her life, she would've forgiven Rebel's part in it.

It was time to forgive herself. Time to come clean to

Draco. If for nothing else, for the chance to take the risk of baring her heart to see if there was a future for them.

Although things had remained the same on the surface, Rebel had felt a shift in Draco the day after she'd met Maria via video link. He hadn't smiled as widely at her jokes, nor lingered in bed with her when they'd both had a little time on their hands. By the time they'd left the island, the only time she'd felt fully connected to him was when they'd made love.

She couldn't let it carry on. He'd helped her achieve life-changing clarity, the least she could do was give him the complete truth about herself in return. What he chose to do with it was up to him.

Her heart squeezed as the ground rushed up to her. Bending her knees, she executed a perfect landing and skied to the bottom of the hill.

'You know you're going to hear about that take-off, don't you?' Greg said via the mic in her ear.

She grimaced and made a face at the camera that was recording all her jumps for Draco to review later.

'I'm not scared of the dragon,' she quipped, lying through her teeth.

Greg laughed. 'You're in the minority, then.'

Grinning, she skied to the edge of the enclosure, toed off her skis and got back on the escalator for another test jump. She had three days before the championships began, and Draco had found less and less to criticise her about as she'd perfected her jump.

She didn't doubt that he would chew her out for the millisecond delay. But he would be doing so while in the same room with her. And after four days without him, she didn't care if he berated her for half the night. As long as she got to spend the other half in his arms.

She was showered and in bed, anticipating Draco's arrival, when her phone rang. She saw his number, and her heart sank.

'Unless you're calling me from the living room, consider your entire accumulation of brownie points docked.'

'I'm calling you from the emergency room,' Draco replied, tersely.

She jerked upright, her heart slamming hard against her ribs. 'Are you okay?'

'I'm fine, Arabella. Unfortunately, Carla isn't. She's in intensive care as we speak.'

'No! What happened?'

'She fell, hit her head. She hasn't suffered any spinal injuries, but the doctors aren't taking chances. The air ambulance brought her to Rome from Tuscany this morning.'

Rebel's hand tightened around the phone. 'How is Maria taking it?'

'She's being exceptionally strong,' he responded, his voice reflecting a quiet pride. 'I flew her down this afternoon.'

'I'm glad she's there with Carla.'

'Yes. Arabella, I don't know when I'll be able to come to Verbier.'

Her stomach hollowed, bringing with it a tinge of shame for her selfishness. 'It's fine,' she mustered with as much grace as she could. Then, remembering her vow this morning, she added, 'When you do get here, though, we need to talk.'

Tense silence greeted her. Wondering whether the line had dropped, she glanced at her phone. She was still connected. 'Draco?'

'I'm here. We will talk as you wish.' Voices murmured in the background. 'I have to go.'

'Umm…okay—'

He hung up before she could stumble through telling him she'd missed him. Or, even more, that she loved him.

Because she did.

She'd agreed to stage a flawless performance of make-believe love. Instead she'd fallen in love for real.

The irony didn't escape her as the phone dropped from her numb fingers into her lap. Looking down, she caught sight of her engagement ring. Her heart cracked open at the real possibility that she might have to take it off in the very near future. After all, even if Draco saw past her role in her mother's death and forgave her, she had no guarantee that he would want to be with her, never mind on a permanent basis.

Her heart shuddered at the phantom loss even as it contemplated the real one. Desperate to flee the bleakness snaking through her, she grabbed the remote and flicked on the TV.

Every channel carried the news of Carla Nardozzi's accident, with the blame laid firmly at Tyson Blackwell's feet. Footage of the moments before the accident had been leaked to the media, and the trainer had been arrested.

Relief for Draco and Maria for the delayed justice and closure surged through her. Turning the TV off, she lay back in bed, sending up a silent prayer that she and Draco would be granted a chance for a fresh start.

Carla Nardozzi was put into a medical coma the day before the opening ceremony of the Verbier Ski Championships.

Draco called with another terse apology—one that was becoming a common occurrence. And one that Rebel brushed off with a light tone and a heavy heart.

Her first competition took place that afternoon. With Greg and Contessa and the rest of her team in her camp, Rebel should've been ecstatic when she placed second by the end of the first day. Instead she kept her phone on her lap all through dinner with the team, her heart jumping each time she felt a ring that turned out to be her imagination. Tuesday and Wednesday were even better days. By Thursday she was leading the women's ski-jump category, with her name suddenly on every sports commentator's lips. Contessa excitedly booked interviews and negotiated with new sponsors who wanted to be associated with the new and improved Rebel Daniels. Rebel nodded and smiled through it all, but inside she was dead with complete misery.

She was getting ready for her final afternoon session on Friday when Greg walked into the recreation room. 'I've just had a note that there's someone wanting to see you in the VIP hospitality box.' His dark frown spelled his displeasure. 'They won't tell me who it is and I can't bring them back here. I'm going to have to come with you.'

Her heart leapt into her throat, her whole body revving into invigorating life as she jumped up. Draco had arrived!

'It's fine. I have my personal official here with me.' Rebel waved at Greta, the woman who'd been assigned to her.

Greg's lips pursed as he handed over the note. 'Are you sure?'

'I'm sure,' she insisted, rushing towards the door.

Rebel asked Greta to point her in the direction of VIP box number sixteen. The older woman struggled to keep up as Rebel sprinted ahead. The box was at the far end of the luxurious championship course, directly overlooking the ski-jump platform. Slightly out of breath, she entered the semi-lit room, leaving Greta in the hallway. Spotting the figure looking out to the course, she hurried towards him.

'Drac—Dad!' she amended as her father faced her.

'Hello, Arabella.'

'What are you doing here?' The question emerged like an accusation.

She was happy to see him, of course she was, but the scything disappointment of not finding Draco here raked her raw without the numbness to protect her.

'I'm sorry for the cloak-and-dagger stuff. But I wasn't sure you'd want to see me. Not after the way we parted.'

Pain she'd thought she'd grappled under control fired through her. 'You were the one who didn't want to see me any more, remember?'

He sighed. 'I should never have said that.'

'Why not, if you meant it?'

'I didn't *mean* it. It was wrong, but that was just my grief talking.'

Weariness weighted her shoulders. 'It's okay, Dad. I get it now.'

His light blue eyes widened. 'You do?'

'Yes, I do.'

We need to talk.

Draco had lost count of the number of ways he'd dissected those four words, hoping to disembowel every worst-case scenario they might represent. Each time, a new one had reared up stronger, more venomous than before.

What good thing had ever come from those words? Hell, weren't those same words his own lead-in to a break-up with a girlfriend who suddenly grew too clingy? Or an underperforming employee who needed to be kicked into touch or kicked out? He'd never been at the receiving end of them, of course.

Until now.

He read the box numbers as they flashed past, the location Greg had given him stuck in his brain. He wanted to reach his destination yet he dreaded what would happen when he got there. That dread was partly why he'd stayed away. Sure, Olivio Nardozzi had finally wised up to the fact that the daughter he'd viewed as little more than an asset he'd kept too tight a grip on was in danger of slipping away from him and had begged for Draco's help. But everything he'd done for them could've been done from his Verbier chalet, within touching distance of Arabella.

Except he hadn't been sure Arabella would wish to be at his side.

The *not* knowing had finally got to him. He needed to know where he stood, whether her request to talk was a precursor to her walking away from him.

He neared box sixteen and flashed his Access All Areas card at the stout woman guarding the hallway. A few steps away from the door he froze at the sound of Arabella's voice.

'You lost the love of your life because of me.'

'Arabella, don't—'

'No. Don't try to mince your words. If I hadn't disobeyed you both and gone out skiing on my own, she'd still be alive today. She'd be here with you and we'd still be a family.'

Horror clawed up Draco's spine.

'We tell everyone it was an accident, but it wasn't, Dad, and we both know it. I rebelled against my parents. You warned me not to go skiing when there was a blizzard warning. I waited until you'd gone to the village to do the grocery shopping, then snuck out. I wanted what I wanted and it ended up killing her.'

A ragged breath echoed out into the hallway. 'You'll never know what coming back to see the note that she'd gone after you did to me. To have never got the chance to say goodbye…'

'Because of me. I know, Dad. You'll never know how much I wish I hadn't—'

Draco didn't realise his feet had moved until he was standing in the room. Twin pairs of blue eyes swung his way, one narrowing in wary dislike, and the other rounding with the same horror spiralling through him.

'You had a direct hand in your mother's accident?' he rasped, blinding rage eclipsing everything else.

She swallowed, her eyes pools of dark horror. 'Draco… I…'

'After agreeing we'd be up front with each other, you didn't think to tell me you selfishly and irresponsibly put your own mother's life in danger?'

'Draco—'

He waved her silent, her voice a bleak implication he didn't want ringing in his ears. Shaking his head, he laughed. 'But then you didn't exactly agree to the *up-front* part, did you? I was too caught up in…other things to recognise that you avoided that particular stipulation.'

She stepped towards him. 'I wanted to tell you. Draco, please believe me—'

He silenced her with a slash of his hand. 'I let you into Maria's life. She already thinks you're the most incredible woman to walk the earth. And you've turned out to be no better than the man who put her in the wheelchair.'

She gasped.

Nathan Daniels stepped forward. 'Now hang on there, Angelis—'

'Save it. I have no time for either of you. If I never see either one of you again in this lifetime, it'll be too soon.'

Rebel watched Draco walk out, her ashen world turning a soulless, all-encompassing black. From far away, she heard her father call her name. She probably responded, because the worried look in his eyes receded.

'I know this probably wasn't the best timing, but I didn't want to do it after the fact.'

Struggling to think past the pain slashing at her heart, she frowned. 'Do what?'

'Tell you that your mother would be proud of you and what you've achieved. Whether you win today or not, we're *both* proud of you. And I sold our old house. I'm sure you'll agree we need to make new memories?'

Her breath shuddered. 'Yes.'

'I'm seeing a grief counsellor. And I also intend to pay back the money, Arabella. I don't care how long it takes, I'll make things right.'

Tears welled in her eyes. 'Dad—'

'Miss Daniels, it's time to go,' Greta said from the doorway.

She glanced at her father. He nodded. 'We have a lot to talk about, I know. But you need to go and see all your hard work pay off.'

She blinked the tears away. 'Will…will you come and watch me?'

He swallowed hard before he nodded. 'Yes, I will.'

She walked back with Greta, picked up her skis and made her way to the waiting area. She was the first to jump, which helped because once again blocking everything and keeping her mind blank were imperative.

This time it wasn't just her mother's face that spurred her on. Her father's solemn eyes and quiet pride flashed too. Her timing was laser-perfect, and she soared higher than she ever had. But as the snow-white ground rushed up to meet her, a piercing realisation lanced through her.

It's not enough. I want love too.

Unbidden, Draco's words from weeks ago when he'd made her realise she was holding herself back from winning popped into her mind.

We never get everything we want.

Her feet crashed to the ground and she cartwheeled into the barrier. A collective gasp rushed through the frigid air. Officials nearby rushed to her aid, but Rebel was already struggling to her feet.

Draco might believe they never got what they wanted, but she had proved otherwise.

She wanted him. She loved him. She'd never got the chance to tell him. No way was she willing to accept what had happened in the VIP room as her fate until she'd stared him in the eye and said her piece.

She was toeing off her skis when an excited Greg and Contessa rushed towards her. 'Did you see?' Contessa screeched. 'You jumped two *metres* farther than the world-record holder!'

'My God, Rebel, what happened up there?'

I got my heart smashed into a million pieces.

She smiled and shrugged. They waited in the pen for the remaining competitors to jump. With each one that didn't make it as far, Greg and Contessa squealed. If they noticed she wasn't as excited, they refrained from commenting.

Then her name erupted in lights as the winner. Tears welled and her whole body shuddered as she imagined the spirit of her mother wrapped around her in a warm, comforting glow.

Half an hour later, Rebel stood on the podium and waved to the crowd, an even harder determination burning in her chest. Returning to the dressing room, she entrusted her trophy to Contessa and her skis to Greg, then hurried into the shower, with a promise to meet up later.

Slipping on jeans and a long-sleeved top and layering it with a hoodie and beanie to finish off her disguise, she left the grounds and walked to a taxi stand. Whether Draco had left Switzerland or not she still had to collect her belongings from his chalet. But she prayed he would be there. She pulled her phone from her bag and brought up the text app.

When I said we needed to talk I actually meant that I would talk and you would listen. So you owe me another 'We need to talk' minus the fire-breathing antics. Where are you?

She pressed *'send'* with her heart in her throat, and waited.

An answer pinged a second later.

Behind you.

Rebel whirled, her foot slipping on the ice before she righted herself. A black limo crept towards her, its back window slowly winding down as it neared.

Draco's molten grey eyes pierced hers as the car drew to a stop. He alighted and held the door open for her.

She stayed on the pavement. 'You were creeping behind me on the off-chance that I would text you?'

'No, Arabella. My hopes have dropped to nil where you're concerned.'

Her heart stumbled, but she'd come this far. She needed to see this through. 'I need to get my things from your place.'

His eyes shadowed, but he nodded. 'I'll take you. You can talk on the way.'

She slid into the plush interior and retreated to the far side. He regained his seat and slammed the door, sealing them in semi-dark silence.

They travelled a mile with Rebel trying to find her nerve. 'You missed my victory dance on the podium.'

'No, I didn't.'

Her breath caught. 'You were there.'

'I couldn't leave.'

'Too many potential clients to schmooze?'

'The farthest thing from my mind.'

She bit her lip and looked out of the window. When she saw how close they were to Draco's chalet, she cleared her throat. 'Everything you heard me say to my father I'd planned to tell you. Yes, I should've told you when you asked me about my scar, or afterwards. But I'm not perfect. I made a mistake.'

He exhaled. 'Arabella—'

'No, I'm not quite finished. What I did in my past doesn't give you the right to act like an ass. I made a horrible mistake when I was only seventeen that tortured me and which I was still paying for when I met you. But you know what? I've learned to forgive myself, ironically, thanks to you.' She pointed a finger at him. 'But you decided to heap on me anyway—why, because you think I haven't suffered enough?'

A wave of regret washed over his face. 'No. You've suffered more than enough.'

She sagged back in her seat, bewilderment and pain eating at her. 'Then why?'

'I knew what you were keeping from me was big. I just didn't realise how I would feel to know you had a secret like that you couldn't trust me with. I despise secrets and knowing something this monumental had happened in your life and you were hiding it from me... I lashed out without thinking.' He turned suddenly and lunged for her hand. 'Everything I said in that room was inexcusable. I'd braced myself for something else—'

'What?'

'You, breaking up with me. And not the fake engagement either. You said we needed to talk—'

'And you immediately slid into complete-bastard mode?'

'I'd had too much time to dwell on a few worst-case scenarios.'

She didn't want to get her hopes up, not when his words still stung so deeply. 'And the worst was me breaking up with you?'

He slashed a hand through his hair, his breathing ragged. 'I'm in love with you, Arabella. Deeply. Completely. The past few weeks have been hell when each time I wanted to say it, I knew you were keeping something from me. Something that might mean the end of us. Going along with the charade just to keep you close felt like the safest option, but I hated it, and so I overreacted when I finally heard the truth.'

With supreme effort, Rebel regained her power of speech. 'You're...in love with me.' Parts of her were coming alive that she wanted to send back to sleep. Until she was completely certain she wasn't dreaming this.

'You forgot the deeply, completely part.'

She shook her head. 'I still don't understand why you were so mean to me. As for my father...what he did was inexcusable, I know, but he intends to make amends. He did what he did because he loves me. He lost his way for a while, but I think he deserves a chance to make reparations.'

Draco nodded. 'He does, and I intend to give him one. We've already agreed a payment plan for the money he took.'

Her eyes widened. '*What?* When?'

'I went back to the VIP room to beg you to let me take back my words. He was still there. We talked. Then we watched you win together.'

Her hand flew to her mouth as she choked back a sob. 'That does not touch me in any way.'

A hint of an arrogant smile curved his mouth. Then his face turned solemn again. 'I will do better, if you give me a chance. Please, Arabella.'

'You really love me?' The words shook out of her.

He cupped her face, his gaze contrite and direct, and filled with an emotion that caught at her hard. 'Deeply. Completely. You challenge me, you make me feel alive. I give you hell and you laugh in my face. I want that every day for the rest of my life.'

Rebel leaned into him, unable to be this close and not want more of the man she loved more than life itself.

'I hope you realise I'm going to live off this grovelling for the next sixty years?'

He tensed but replied, 'And I will fall at your feet every time and beg forgiveness.'

'Wow. Okay, that sounds like a plan.'

'Does that mean what I think it means?'

'You're in love with me. I'm in love with every infuriating inch of you. I hate you for breaking my heart and making me sad on the day I won my major trophy, but I love you for agreeing to be mine for the rest of our lives.'

He squeezed his eyes shut and dropped his forehead to hers. '*Thee mou.* You wreck me, Arabella. I love you.'

When they reached the chalet, he dragged her inside, then sealed his lips to hers in a fervent reminder of what had brought them together and what was in store for them.

Finally letting go of the fear and letting joy in, she closed the gap between them and slid her arms around his neck. 'I love you, too. Oh, and don't bother getting yourself fixed. I plan on wrecking you every day for as long as we both live.'

* * * * *

LET'S TALK

Romance

For exclusive extracts, competitions and special offers, find us online:

- facebook.com/millsandboon
- @MillsandBoon
- @MillsandBoonUK

Get in touch on 01413 063232

For all the latest titles coming soon, visit
millsandboon.co.uk/nextmonth